MURTY CLASSICAL
LIBRARY OF INDIA

Sheldon Pollock, General Editor

KOUHALA
LILAVAI

MCLI 29

KOUHALA

कोऊहल

LILAVAI

Edited and Translated by
ANDREW OLLETT

MURTY CLASSICAL LIBRARY OF INDIA
HARVARD UNIVERSITY PRESS
Cambridge, Massachusetts
London, England
2021

SERIES DESIGN BY M9DESIGN

Library of Congress Cataloging-in-Publication Data

Names: Koūhala, author. | Ollett, Andrew, 1986– editor, translator. |
Container of (expression): Koūhala. Līlāvaī. |
Container of (expression): Koūhala. Līlāvaī. English.
Title: Līlāvaī / Kouhala ; edited and translated by Andrew Ollett.
Other titles: Murty classical library of India ; 29.
Description: Cambridge, Massachusetts :
Harvard University Press, 2021. |
Series: Murty classical library of India ; 29 |
In English and Prakrit; Devanagari script.
Includes bibliographical references and index.
Identifiers: LCCN 2020015930 |
ISBN 9780674247598 (cloth)
Subjects: LCSH: Love poetry, Prakrit. |
Jaina literature, Prakrit. |
Classification: LCC PK5013.K8 L513 2021 |
DDC 891/.3--dc23
LC record available at https://lccn.loc.gov/2020015930

CONTENTS

INTRODUCTION

The Historical Context

The author of *Līlāvaī* gives a very brief account of his family at the beginning of the story (vv. 18–22), describing his father and grandfather as ritually observant Brahmans. One commentator has taken *koūhaleṇa* in v. 22 as the name of its author, and most modern scholars have, accordingly, attributed *Līlāvaī* to a poet named Kouhala.[1] None of the traditional scholars who cite or refer to *Līlāvaī* mentions the author's name. I refer to him here as "Kouhala," without insisting that this really was his name.

Regarding the date of the story, there is little to add to the evidence A. N. Upadhye, the first modern editor of *Līlāvaī*, discusses in his introduction. The earliest author to refer to *Līlāvaī* appears to be Anandavardhana, who, in his *Light on Resonance* (*Dhvanyāloka*, mid-ninth century), speaks of an episode in which King Satavahana journeys to the nether-world. Anandavardhana justifies the episode by referring to the threefold classification of stories into divine, human, and divine-human. Since this classification appears at the begin-ning of *Līlāvaī* (v. 35), it seems likely that this story is the one Anandavardhana had in mind. Upadhye notes that *Līlāvaī* accords closely with the description of the "story" (*kathā*) genre in Rudrata's *Ornament of Literature* (*Kāvyālaṅkāra*, also ninth century).[2]

Kouhala never refers to any of his predecessors by name, but it appears that he borrows several ideas and phrases from

Haribhadra's *Story of Samaraiccha,* which was probably composed early in the eighth century. He briefly mentions the Rashtrakutas and Solankis in v. 1068. The Rashtrakutas were a powerful dynasty in the Deccan during the latter half of the first millennium, and the Solankis, better known as the Chalukyas, were their principal opponents in this region. Based on these considerations, Upadhye assigned *Līlāvaī* to around 800 C.E., and I see no reason to revise his estimate.[3]

Much of the story takes place in a holy site called Sattagodavari Bhima, where the Godavari River splits into seven streams before it flows into the Bay of Bengal. In *Līlāvaī*, this place features a Shiva temple and a monastery. Unlike some of the other places in the story, I know of no references to Sattagodavari Bhima in literature prior to *Līlāvaī*. Hence it seems likely that Kouhala had a personal connection to it. Upadhye identifies this place with modern-day Daksharama, or Draksharama, in coastal Andhra Pradesh.[4]

The Prakrit Romance

Līlāvaī is, according to its author, a "story" (*kahā*). And to repurpose a cliché, there are two sides to every story. The story appears, on the one hand, as a *telling*: one person tells a story to others, on a specific occasion, and with a specific purpose. Thus, Kouhala, in explaining how he first came to tell the story of *Līlāvaī,* says that his wife asked him for "a bit of pleasant entertainment" (v. 33) on a clear autumn evening. Insofar as it is a telling, a story might be told in simple and straightforward language, to allow listeners to follow it easily, and it might be organized around the principle of suspense, to maintain the listener's interest.[5]

On the other hand, stories like *Līlāvaī* are also literary products. Thus at the end of *Līlāvaī* (v. 1331) Kouhala asks the public to accept the story, just as he had told it to his wife, as a work of literature. Insofar as stories are works of literature, they do not belong merely to the moment of their telling but also to traditions of storytelling, each with an evolving set of themes, conventions, and poetics. Indian literary theorists recognized the story as a genre, and provided a number of characteristics by which it could be differentiated from other literary genres.[6] Yet no synthetic account of the poetics of storytelling as such in classical India is available. Story literature itself, however, often reflects on its own sources and narrative strategies, as we will see in the case of *Līlāvaī*.[7]

To what specific traditions of storytelling does *Līlāvaī* belong? It is, first of all, in the Prakrit language. The author himself identifies its language as Prakrit (v. 41) and also as "the local language of Maharashtra" (v. 1330). Prakrit was one of the main literary languages of premodern India, with a literary tradition extending back to the first or second century C.E. It is often figured as an alternative, indeed as an opposite, to Sanskrit, but the two languages are quite close in linguistic terms, and for many centuries serious students of literature were expected to be familiar with both.[8] The author appears to give voice to the conceit that Prakrit is more appropriate to a female audience (v. 41). Second, it is almost entirely in verse, and its metrical form of choice is a meter called the *gāhā*, which was typical of Prakrit literature. Third, although stories can in principle be about anything,

Līlāvaī is about winning the hand of a young woman, Lilavai, in marriage.

We can group *Līlāvaī* with a number of other stories that share these three features and call them "Prakrit verse romances." Besides Kouhala's *Līlāvaī*, which is Shaiva in orientation, all of the other stories were written by Jain authors.[9] If we look beyond Prakrit verse, we find a number of stories that had been composed in Prakrit prose before *Līlāvaī*. Here, too, all of the surviving examples were written by Jain authors. One of them, Haribhadra's *Story of Samaraiccha* (eighth century), seems to have influenced Kouhala. Another, Uddyotana's *Kuvalayamālā* (779 C.E.), is, like *Līlāvaī*, named for a principal female character, and hence scholars have grouped it with *Līlāvaī* in the category of "heroine novels."[10]

Turning now to stories in Sanskrit prose, it seems likely that Bana's *Kādambarī* (seventh century), with its multiple levels of narration and its elements of fantasy, inspired the wave of literary storytelling that crested in the eighth and ninth centuries, when *Līlāvaī* was probably composed. For later authors, such as the eleventh-century theorist Bhoja, *Līlāvaī* and *Kādambarī* illustrate the formal diversity of the story as a genre: the one in Prakrit verse, the other in Sanskrit prose.[11] Hence we may hypothesize that *Kādambarī* inspired Kouhala to reimagine the traditional theme of star-crossed lovers for Prakrit. Such a reimagining involved not only telling the story of Lilavai in Prakrit verse, but also synthesizing "story" as a genre within the Prakrit literary tradition. And Kouhala, in turn, inspired a number of other authors to compose romances in Prakrit verse. They likely considered him a fellow traveler, with Jain luminaries such as Palitta, Haribhadra, and Uddyotana, on the path of Prakrit storytelling.

Kouhala describes the story as divine-human (v. 41). This designation also appears at the beginning of Haribhadra's *Story of Samaraiccha,* likely Kouhala's source.[12] In calling his story divine-human, Kouhala had in mind fantastic elements that are common to other storytelling traditions, above all those associated with the legendary *Great Story.*[13] The world of the story is populated by all manner of semidivine beings: *vidyādharas* (sometimes translated as "sorcerers"), *siddhas* (associated with magical and alchemical techniques), *yakṣas* (associated with inexhaustible wealth), *gandharvas* (flying musicians), *rākṣasas* (man-eating monsters), and *apsarases* (celestial nymphs). Even the human characters are granted magical powers and good luck, or karma, beyond what we might expect.

In contrast to many other stories, rebirth plays a very marginal role in *Līlāvaī.* All of the threads of the story are spun out, and brought together, within the lifetime of the main characters. Several characters say that reunion in the next life is uncertain, if not impossible (vv. 713, 1013).

The Story in Overview

The story centers on three young women: Lilavai, Mahanumai, and Kuvalaavali. Lilavai is a princess of Sinhala, the island that we call Sri Lanka. When she was born, a disembodied voice proclaimed that whoever married her would rule the entire earth. Her father, the human king

Silameha, had married Saraasiri, a *vidyādhara* princess who had been cursed to live among men. Mahanumai is a princess of Alaka, the mythical city near Mount Himalaya; she was born to Nalakubara, a *yakṣa* prince, and Vasantasiri. Vasantasiri is Saraasiri's sister, who had been married off to Nalakubara after Saraasiri's curse. Thus Mahanumai and Lilavai are cousins.

Kuvalaavali was born to a human sage, Viulasaa, and the *apsaras* Rambha, who had successfully tempted him away from his austerities. One day a Gandharva prince, Chittangaa, visited the grove where the young Kuvalaavali was playing and convinced her to marry him on the spot. When discovered by her father, the lovers flee. Later Kuvalaavali, abandoned by her husband as well as her father, attempts suicide, but her mother, Rambha, appears from heaven and has her adopted by Nalakubara and Vasantasiri. Kuvalaavali is therefore Mahanumai's adopted sister.

One day Mahanumai, Kuvalaavali, and their friends go to Mount Malaya, in the far south, to play on a swing. There Mahanumai meets and falls in love with Mahavanila, a *siddha* prince. He gives her a ring that repels poisonous serpents, and she gives him a pearl necklace. Mahanumai and Kuvalaavali return home to Alaka, where Mahanumai suffers in separation from Mahavanila. Mahavilaa, a companion of Mahavanila, arrives bearing a letter and a message from the prince. Kuvalaavali sends a message back on Mahanumai's behalf, but Mahanumai wants to go back to Mount Malaya at once and offer herself to Mahavanila, even without the consent of their parents. Kuvalaavali attempts to dissuade her by telling her own story. As a compromise, Kuvalaavali goes to Mount Malaya herself, while Mahanumai waits impatiently in Alaka.

Kuvalaavali returns with terrible news: Mahavanila had been captured by enemies and could not be freed. In despair, Mahanumai and Kuvalaavali decide to spend the rest of their lives as ascetics at an ashram near a holy place called Sattagodavari Bhima.

In the meantime, Lilavai's father turns his thoughts to her marriage. He sets up portraits of various kings in her bedroom, and Lilavai falls in love with one of them: King Hala, also called Salahana or Salavahana, who rules from the city of Pratishthana on the Godavari River. Lilavai's father accordingly sends her from Sinhala to Pratishthana. When her retinue sets up their camp near Sattagodavari Bhima along the way, Mahanumai and Kuvalaavali come to know of their cousin's presence, and upon meeting her, tell her their story. At this point Lilavai makes a fateful vow: she will not be married until Mahanumai is reunited with Mahavanila, and Kuvalaavali with Chittangaa.

This is all background to the principal story. King Hala sends his general, Vijaananda, on a mission to subdue King Silameha, Lilavai's father. After taking counsel with Pottisa, one of Hala's ministers, Vijaananda decides instead to pursue a diplomatic course, and travels to Sinhala by boat. He is shipwrecked but eventually makes his way to Sattagodavari Bhima, near the coast. There he meets a Pashupata ascetic, the sole resident of a monastery, who tells him that a man-eating monster called Bhisananana prowls the area after dark, and therefore asks him to repair to the nearby ashram of Mahanumai and Kuvalaavali.

There Vijaananda hears everything from Kuvalaavali. On learning that Lilavai was on her way to meet Hala, he reveals that he is in fact Hala's minister. He is taken to Lilavai's camp and meets the princess, and then hastens back to Pratishthana to tell Hala everything that he has seen and heard.

When Hala hears Vijaananda's story, he sends him back to Lilavai with a gift: a pearl necklace that had come into his treasury after a military campaign. Lilavai receives the gift respectfully, but Mahanumai and Kuvalaavali immediately recognize it as the necklace they had earlier sent to Mahavanila as a gift. They surmise that Mahavanila is no more. Mahanumai tries in vain to get Lilavai to proceed to Pratishthana and marry Hala. She then sends Vijaananda back with a gift for Hala: the ring that she had once received from Mahavanila.

On Vijaananda's return, Hala loses all hope of marrying Lilavai and sinks into a depression. His adviser, the monk Naajjuna, suggests that they journey to the underworld, where they can at least enjoy pleasure and magical powers. Hala agrees, and descends to the underworld with the monk. At the last gate, they encounter a young man held fast by serpents; because Hala has the serpent-killing ring, they disperse on his approach. The young man turns out to be Mahavanila, who returns to Mount Malaya, while Hala returns to his city. At dawn Hala marches out toward Sattagodavari Bhima with his army. When he arrives, he meets the Pashupata ascetic and receives a mantra from him to use against Bhisananana. Hala's army joins battle with Bhisananana's forces, and Hala employs the mantra and decapitates the monster.

Bhisananana turns out to be Chittangaa, who was cursed by Kuvalaavali's father to take on that monstrous form. The three grooms—Hala, Mahavanila, and Chittangaa—now gather at Sattagodavari Bhima, where their three brides—Lilavai, Mahanumai, and Kuvalaavali—are waiting, having been apprised of recent developments by Vijaananda. First the marriage of Mahanumai and Mahavanila is celebrated at Alaka, and then the marriage of Lilavai and Hala in Sinhala, where Hala receives still more magical powers from the *siddhas, vidyādharas,* and *yakṣas.* Finally Hala and Lilavai return to Pratishthana.

Inspiration and Sources

The principal male character in *Līlāvaī* is a king who is variously called Hala, Salavahana, or Salahana in the story (in Sanskrit sources the names Hala and Satavahana are used). King Hala of Pratishthana features in many legends and stories.[14] It is unclear what specifically connects this figure to the historical Satavahana dynasty, which ruled over much of the Deccan between the first century B.C.E. and the early third century C.E.[15] It is difficult to say which parts of the Hala legend in *Līlāvaī* have been borrowed from earlier stories and which have been invented by Kouhala. Bana, in his *Story of Harsha,* relates a legend about King Satavahana: he received a single strand of jewels from his friend Nagarjuna, who had recovered it from the underworld after being brought there by serpents. The idea that Salahana and Naajjuna, to use the Prakrit spellings, were friends, and that the latter had made several visits to the underworld, is taken up in *Līlāvaī*, and appears in several other sources.[16] Kouhala himself seems to acknowledge the wide circulation of such legends when he has Vijaananda, Mahanumai, and Kuvalaavali pass an entire night telling stories about Hala (v. 898).

There is, however, something curious about the cast of characters in *Līlāvaī*. Tradition knows Hala not only as a legendary king but also as an author. *Seven Centuries* (*Sattasaī*), an anthology of seven hundred single-verse poems, is one of the oldest and most highly prized works of Prakrit literature, and in its third verse Hala is named as its compiler. Several premodern commentaries on *Seven Centuries* agree in attributing more poems to Hala, or Satavahana, than any other author.[17] Some of the legends about Hala depict him as an inspired poet; others represent him as a liberal patron of literature; others, as someone who miraculously brings out the literary potential in others. Here is one story from a collection compiled by a Jain monk in 1349 C.E.:

> Once King Satavahana asked the Goddess of Speech
> for a favor. He wanted his entire city to become poets
> for just a single morning. The goddess assented,
> and on that day one hundred million verses were
> produced. They made up the text that is called
> *Sātavāhanakam.*[18]

Kouhala appears to acknowledge Hala's reputation as a patron of literature in verse 72, and often depicts him in the company of poets (vv. 104, 131, 940, 1020). But Hala is not the only character in *Līlāvaī* associated with *Seven Centuries*.

Pottisa, Hala's shrewd minister in *Līlāvaī*, is also identified as the author of several verses in *Seven Centuries*. So, too, is Kumarila, another one of Hala's ministers in *Līlāvaī*.[19] It therefore seems as if Kouhala's imagining of Hala's court was based on stories told about *Seven Centuries,* or perhaps commentaries on the anthology that are now lost.

Kouhala's decision to make Hala the hero of his story seems to be connected to his decision to compose the story in Prakrit. *Līlāvaī* engages with the Prakrit literary tradition, and if Hala is not the founder of that tradition—the "first poet of Prakrit," as one seventeenth-century author called him—he is nevertheless one of its best-known figures.[20] Besides casting Hala and some of his fellow Prakrit poets as characters in his story, Kouhala uses a number of ideas and motifs to evoke and associate himself with an earlier dispensation of Prakrit literature that is symbolized by Hala, his capital Pratishthana, and the Godavari River. These symbols are brought together in an early Prakrit anthology, *Vajjālagga:*[21]

It's a husband's virtue that makes
a devoted wife, not the woman's lineage.
When Hala went to heaven, the Godavari River
did not leave her master's place, the city of Pratishthana.

The Godavari is to Prakrit what the Sarasvati is to Sanskrit. Ever since providing the setting to many of the poems in *Seven Centuries,* it has been associated with the Prakrit literary tradition. It therefore seems significant that much of *Līlāvaī* takes place along the Godavari River, and, more particularly, at Sattagodavari Bhima, which is "down-stream" from Hala's city of Pratishthana, in the same way that Kouhala's *Līlāvaī* is "downstream," in historical terms, from Hala's *Seven Centuries*. Kouhala's *Līlāvaī* features scenes of women bathing in the Godavari, just as in *Seven Centuries*, and not just near Pratishthana (v. 61) but also near Sattagodavari Bhima (v. 750). Kouhala seems to be not merely drawing from the Prakrit literary tradition for his narrative but situating his story as a novel development within the same tradition.[22]

One figure who is traditionally associated with Hala is Palitta, a Jain monk who wrote *Taraṅgavaī*, the earliest Prakrit romance. He is generally said to have been one of Hala's court poets, and many verses in *Seven Centuries* are attributed to him. Kouhala was probably familiar, either directly or indirectly, with *Taraṅgavaī*.[23] Perhaps he deliberately excluded Palitta because he did not want his *Līlāvaī* to be associated with a specifically Jain tradition of storytelling. Hala, the editor of *Seven Centuries*, began his anthology with a salutation to Shiva, but the religious world of *Līlāvaī* is more insistently Shaiva: all of the temples described in the text are either temples to Shiva or to his wife, the goddess usually called Bhavani here, and the nameless ascetic at Sattagodavari Bhima is identified as a Pashupata, a follower of a particular tradition of Shaiva thought and ritual.[24] What, if any, consequences this Shaiva orientation has for the story or its themes remains unclear, but it does mark Prakrit literature of this period as distinct from that of earlier periods.[25]

Themes

Līlāvaī is a love story, and unsurprisingly there is a great deal of reflection on the experience of love. Mahavilaa gives a slightly tongue-in-cheek lecture on the subject that references many of the traditional ideas about love (vv. 537–549). It is stipulated in Indian literary theory that a romantic story requires that the main characters belong to the higher classes, and *Līlāvaī* is no exception.[26] The reason for this stipulation, at least in the case of *Līlāvaī*, is that the higher classes are held to a higher standard of conduct. This is especially true for women: the reputation of their families, and indeed much of the social order, depends upon their having the "right" sexual relationships, which is to say, relationships to which their parents have given their approval. Thus the manner in which the characters in *Līlāvaī* pursue their relationships has a strong normative element. Unsanctioned sex must be avoided at all costs.

A. K. Warder has observed that *Līlāvaī*, in contrast to *Kādambarī*, for example, does not achieve great depth of characterization but instead relies on graded character types.[27] This is most evident in how each of the three women relate to unsanctioned sex. Kuvalaavali gives in to the temptation, and suffers for it almost immediately. Mahanumai is tempted, but is effectively restrained by Kuvalaavali. Lilavai, by contrast, is hardly tempted at all, although it is suggested several times that she would be if she were to see Hala in person and not merely in a portrait. Thus, one way of reading *Līlāvaī* is to see it as a study of contrasts in the regulation and domestication of female desire.

Another important theme of *Līlāvaī* is the role of fate and

karma in human affairs. What are we to do when the course
of events seems determined by circumstances beyond our
control? In some cases the characters adopt an attitude
of resignation (vv. 223, 311). In others they recognize that
circumstances may indeed change (v. 1000). When faced
with hopelessness, the characters are persuaded not to
succumb to depression and suicide, which would foreclose
the possibility of their hopes ever being realized. Instead,
they are advised to follow nobler forms of world renuncia-
tion: Kuvalaavali and Mahanumai withdraw to an ashram in
the forest, and Hala withdraws to the underworld.

Vijaananda suggests, perhaps by way of consolation, that
despite the tragedies Mahanumai and Kuvalaavali have
encountered, the goddess Bhavani has nevertheless shown
them favor by leading them to live a holy life in a pleasant
ashram (v. 728). Kuvalaavali responds that if Bhavani had
shown them any favor, then the situation would not really
have been so hopeless (v. 887). As it would turn out, these
seemingly hopeless problems are all resolved, with the
goddess somehow responsible. Nevertheless, there is no
explicit acknowledgment of divine intervention, and the
gods themselves never appear as characters in the story.

Style and Construction

A very common feature of story literature in South Asia is
that the story itself is told, in part or in whole, by its charac-
ters. This is a metaliterary device that enables storytellers
to discuss storytelling. Hence we encounter statements in
Līlāvaī about the effects of listening to stories (v. 998) or

the occasions for telling them (v. 579). It is also a way for the author to add interest to his story. The stories related by characters rarely unfold in linear time. Moreover, because the characters are not omniscient, their stories have gaps and loose ends. These gaps will be filled in, and the loose ends tied up, as the larger story proceeds toward its conclusion. The device of "emboxed narration"—a story within a story—can be employed repeatedly, resulting in multiple levels of narration. We may contrast emboxed narration with direct narration, in which the author relates the story in his or her own voice.

The story of *Līlāvaī* is told in a unique blend of emboxed and direct narration. The story begins with direct narration —we are asked to imagine ourselves as listening in on a story that the author tells his wife one autumn night—but quickly shifts to emboxed narration when Vijaananda arrives in Hala's court and tells his story; it returns to direct narration two-thirds of the way through the text. Further levels are added, up to about four, throughout the emboxed narrative section. The narrative edifice seems more complex than it actually is. In fact, there is little confusion about who is the "surface-level" narrator in any given section. In part that is because the listener is addressed throughout the story with epithets that remind us who the listener is, and therefore who is speaking, such as when Kuvalaavali addresses Vijaananda as "brother."

If we consider only the surface-level narrator, it turns out that almost half of the story is narrated by women. Kuvalaavali is the speaker of about 486 verses in her own voice; by contrast, Vijaananda speaks in about 206. One might ask why it is that Kuvalaavali is the primary narrator in the story, especially when Mahanumai would have done equally well from the point of view of plot construction; Kuvalaavali, in contrast to the other women in the story, has actually had experience—albeit traumatic—of sexual love and this emotional experience positions her as a sensitive and trustworthy narrator.

The content of *Līlāvaī*, like many other specimens of story literature in South Asia, can be divided up into narrative and descriptive.[28] In *Līlāvaī*, the narrative is quite fast paced: "Its words are few, but its meaning great" (v. 968). The descriptive passages stop the clock, as it were, and elaborate on a given subject, such as the sunset (vv. 436–457 and vv. 516–528), the city of Pratishthana (vv. 1323–1326), Mount Meru (vv. 273–280), and the temple of Bhavani (vv. 235–242). These descriptions are among the most beautiful passages in *Līlāvaī*, and they are more poetically ambitious than the surrounding narrative. They are also often more syntactically complex, with a single sentence spanning multiple verses (otherwise, most verses form complete sentences). Some of *Līlāvaī's* most distinctive poetic features appear in these descriptive passages.

The vast majority of *Līlāvaī* is composed in the *gāhā* meter, characteristic of Prakrit literature.[29] There are a handful of verses in other meters, including one (v. 607) in a meter as yet unidentified. Kouhala has also included a brief section in rhythmic prose, between verses 49 and 50.

The Afterlife of Līlāvaī

Līlāvaī, "the most famous of novels in Prakrit," was read and admired by many of the great literary theorists of premodern India.[30] Subsequent authors tended to give Bana's *Kādambarī,* in Sanskrit, as the example of a story in prose and Kouhala's *Līlāvaī,* in Prakrit, as a story in verse. It is mentioned as such by Ratnashrijnana in the tenth century, Bhoja in the eleventh, Hemachandra in the twelfth, and Vagbhata in the fourteenth.[31]

While *Līlāvaī* was certainly not as popular as some other Prakrit works, such as *Seven Centuries* and *Building the Bridge* (*Setubandha*), it stacks up fairly evenly against other Prakrit classics, such as *The Slaying of the Gauda King* (*Gauḍavaha*), and fared much better than a few others, such as *Taraṅgavaī.* We owe the survival of *Līlāvaī* principally to Jain scholars, as three of the four manuscripts were produced by Jain scribes and held in Jain collections. These scholars "adopted" the *Līlāvaī,* no doubt because it represented a high literary achievement in a language, Prakrit, that the Jains prided themselves on cultivating.

Besides serving as an example of the story genre (*kathā*), *Līlāvaī* is sometimes quoted in works of poetics to exemplify particular figures of speech or character types. It is cited most often by Bhoja, the eleventh-century king of Dhar, known for his high regard for Prakrit literature.[32]

Some verses found in *Līlāvaī* also appear in other stories and collections. Verses 545, 546, and 575, for example, appear in an anthology titled *Collection of Eloquent Prakrit Verses* (*Subhāsiyagāhāsaṃgaho*), and we can assume their source is the *Līlāvaī.* In several other cases, it is doubtful

whether the verse in question is original to *Līlāvaī:* verse
1091 appears in Dhaneśvara's *Surasundarī,* composed in
1038, but it is also quoted in a metrical handbook of the ninth
century, where it is assigned to a poet named Vamautta. Two
verses (74a and 1308a) seem to have been borrowed by later
scribes from *Vajjālagga.*

Kouhala is likely responsible, at least in part, for reviving
interest in Jain circles in composing Prakrit romances, an
interest that lasted until the twelfth century. Yet the precise
nature of *Līlāvaī's* influence on later specimens of the genre,
all composed by Jain authors (*Bhuaṇasundarī, Surasundarī,
Nammayāsundarī*), awaits further research. So too does
Līlāvaī's influence on romances in other languages, such as
Apabhramsha, Kannada, and Avadhi.

Acknowledgments

I first began reading *Līlāvaī* with Diwakar Acharya
and Csaba Dezső as a student at Oxford in 2009. Csaba
had found a Nepalese manuscript of the text, and when
I told him about my wish to edit and translate it, he
kindly made images of this manuscript available to me.
I am grateful to a number of people for valuable comments
and suggestions they made on this translation over the years,
including at several workshops and invited talks. Special
thanks are due to Stefan Baums, Christoph Emmrich,
Thibaut d'Hubert, Bob Goldman, Sally Sutherland Gold-
man, Abhishek Kaicker, James McHugh, Srilata Raman,
Martha Ann Selby, David Shulman, Sarah Pierce Taylor,
Gary Tubb, Anand Venkatkrishnan, the students in my

Prakrit seminar at the University of Chicago in 2018, and, of course, Irene SanPietro. Sheldon Pollock, who suggested that I translate this text for the series, has been a remarkably supportive, unflagging, and meticulous editor.

NOTES

1   See Upadhye 1966: 18–20. Upadhye allowed that *koūhaleṇa* might retain its literal meaning of "eagerness" in v. 22, as indeed it must in v. 146, and in very similar contexts in other stories.

2   See Ingalls, Masson, and Patwardhan 1990: 429–430 (Ānanda-vardhana 1940: 330; Abhinavagupta, commenting on this text in the late tenth century, seems to have no specific knowledge of the story to which Anandavardhana refers); Rudrata's *Ornament of Literature* 16.20–23; Upadhye 1966: 38.

3   Upadhye 1966: 64–69. Upadhye, however, keeps in view the possibility that the similarities between Kouhala's *Līlāvaī* and Haribhadra's *Story of Samaraiccha* (Haribhadra 1935) could be explained by independent borrowings from a common source.

4   Daksharama, or Draksharama, a few miles from the Godavari River, is one of five major Shaiva centers (*ārāmas*) in coastal Andhra Pradesh. It has a temple to Shiva, locally known as Bhimeshvara, evidently built under the Eastern Chalukya kings in the eleventh century, as well as a tank called Saptagodavaram. See Upadhye 1966: 54–60.

5   See Kansara 1975 for "suspense" as a characteristic feature of Indian storytelling.

6   Dandin's *Mirror of Literature* (*Kāvyādarśa*) 1.38 and Bhamaha's *Ornament of Literature* (*Kāvyālaṅkāra*) 1.28 indicate that stories could be composed in all of the major literary languages.

7   Relevant to the poetics of storytelling is the theory of plot development, based on chapter 19 of the *Treatise on Theater,* discussed in Gerow 1979–1980 and Kane 1983. I know of no detailed discussion of the categorizations of stories introduced in Jain literature, for which Bhadrabahu's *niryuktis* on the *Daśavaikālika Sūtra* (189–216) provide the starting point.

8   See Ollett 2017.

9   The other stories are Palitta's *Taraṅgavaī* (c. second century

C.E., surviving only in later abridgments: see *Taraṅgalolā* and Ollett 2018), Vijayasimha's *Bhuaṇasundarī* (918 C.E.), Jineshvara's *Nirvāṇalīlāvaī* (1035 C.E., surviving only in a Sanskrit retelling), Dhaneshvara's *Surasundarī* (1038 C.E.), and Mahendra's *Nammayāsundarī* (1129 C.E.). For details about these stories, see Chojnacki 2016, who groups them together as "heroine novels." Sadharana's *Vilāsavaī* of 1066 C.E. might also be included, although it is evidently in Apabhramsha rather than in Prakrit.

10   Chojnacki 2016.

11   See Warder 1983: 498–499 (§2614), referring to Raghavan 1963: 818–819.

12   See Haribhadra 1935: 2.

13   Upadhye summarizes the elements common to the *Great Story* tradition in Upadhye 1966: 61.

14   Upadhye 1966: 42–54. See Jacobi 1876 for a detailed account of the *Hero Story* (*Vīracarita*), a long story in Sanskrit about the deeds of Satavahana. Anandavardhana also testifies to the currency of legends about the king's "great deeds" (*apadāna*); see Ānandavardhana 1940: 330. Very little work of a systematic nature has been done on the legends of Hala/Satavahana.

15   See Ollett 2017: 26–49, with references to earlier literature.

16   See Sohoni 1999.

17   See the commentaries of Bhuvanapala and Pitambara on *Seven Centuries* (Hāla 1942, 1980). Scholars have debated the reliability of these attributions, starting with Albrecht Weber's discussion in Weber 1883.

18   Rājaśekhara 1932: 147–148.

19   The manuscript of a *Śātavāhanagāthāvṛtti* at the L. D. Institute, Ahmedabad (no. 909), has a marginal note on verse 4 identifying its author as Pottisa, and seemingly citing a dictionary to identify Pottisa as Hala's minister (*hālamantrī tu poṭṭisaḥ*). Kumarila is identified as the author of verse 8 of the anthology.

20   The author is Lakshminatha Bhatta, in his commentary on *Prākṛtapiṅgala;* see Ollett 2017: 54.

21   Jayavallabha 1969: 468. The word *paiṭṭhāṇaṃ* can mean both the city of Pratishthana and "the place of one's master."

22   Some traditions also connect Hala with the *Great Story*, the lost text that seems to have been a profound influence on story literature in South Asia and beyond (namely, the two Sanskrit versions

produced in Kashmir in the eleventh century: see Tsuchida 2002).
It is possible, but in my view unlikely, that Kouhala had such a
connection in mind when composing *Līlāvaī*. For the motifs and
characters that *Līlāvaī* shares with the *Great Story*, see Upadhye
1966: 60–62.

23 See Bhayani (1993a), who notes a number of echoes in *Līlāvaī*
of passages preserved in the later abridgments of *Tarangavaī*
(see the references in note 2). There are early references to other
now-lost works that likewise appear to have been romances (such
as *Malayavatī*), and these may have also provided models for
Kouhala.

24 Strangely for a Shaiva text, however, *Līlāvaī* begins by saluting
various forms of Vishnu. Ferstl 2020 examines literary represent-
ations of Pashupata ascetics, of which *Līlāvaī* provides a relatively
early example.

25 Another Prakrit poem, *The Slaying of the Gauda King* (*Gaüḍ-
avaha*, Vākpatirāja 1975), composed around the beginning of
the eighth century and thus quite close to *Līlāvaī*, also displays
a Shaiva orientation, and includes a long hymn to the goddess
(vv. 285–337).

26 See Pollock 2016: 52.

27 Warder 1983: 488–489 (§§2599–2600).

28 See Chojnacki 2008 for a detailed study of these different aspects
in Uddyotana's *Kuvalayamālā*.

29 For the *gāhā* and its varieties see Ollett 2013.

30 Warder 1983: 477 (§2567).

31 Warder 1983: 496–497 (§2614). Ratnashrijnana refers to *Līlāvaī*
on p. 20 of his commentary on Dandin's *Mirror of Literature*.
Bhoja refers to the two stories on p. 673 of his *Illumination of the
Erotic* (*Śṛṅgāraprakāśa*). His examples were probably taken over
by Hemachandra, and Hemachandra's, by Vagbhata.

32 He cites verses 25, 62, 80, 323, 423, 489, 499, 567, 569, 1256
(partially), and 1258 in his *Illumination of the Erotic,* and 25
and parts of 1091 in his *Necklace of Sarasvatī* (*Sarasvatī-
kaṇṭhābharaṇa*). Bhoja additionally names Kuvalaavali as a "friend
since childhood" of Mahanumai, in *Illumination of the Erotic,*
p. 1238. Other authors to cite from *Līlāvaī* are Jayaratha (v. 84),
Shobhakaramitra (v. 25), the author of *Literary Investigations*
(*Sāhityamīmāṃsā;* also v. 25), and Vagbhata (v. 24).

NOTE ON THE TEXT
AND TRANSLATION

On the Text

At the beginning of the twentieth century, *Līlāvaī* was all but forgotten. C. B. Dalal had noticed a manuscript of the story in one of the collections in Patan, in Gujarat, and noted it in a report of 1914.[1] M. Ramakrishna Kavi, well-known for his discovery of manuscripts of many Sanskrit and Telugu texts, also found a manuscript, although he did not disclose where. He summarized the story, with a few quotations, in a Telugu article of 1926.[2] In 1940, the learned Prakrit scholar A. N. Upadhye expressed an interest in preparing an edition to Jinavijaya Muni, then the editor of the *Singhi Jain Series,* and within three years he had sufficient manuscript material to complete his edition. The Second World War, and "communal disturbances" in Bombay, delayed its publication until 1949. Upadhye produced a second edition in 1966. The text remained largely unchanged; in the introduction and notes he incorporated the suggestions of a number of other scholars, including V. Raghavan. Upadhye's edition of *Līlāvaī* has, until now, been the only edition available. Like his many other editions of Prakrit texts, it is a model of careful textual scholarship.

The text included here is a new edition, based upon Upadhye's edition and the readings of one additional palm-leaf manuscript ("N") from Nepal. I have maintained Upadhye's numbering throughout, for two reasons: first, all references to *Līlāvaī* in scholarship have used

Upadhye's numbering; second, any renumbering of the verses would presumably be based on a solution to the problem of "additional verses," discussed below, and such a solution seems out of reach for the moment. Readers will observe that the present text looks very different from Upadhye's, but that is primarily because I have chosen to present *Līlāvaī* in a different orthography than Upadhye did, for reasons discussed below. As far as the meaning of the text is concerned, this edition agrees largely with Upadhye's. Indeed my collation of manuscript N confirms a great many of Upadhye's readings, both those that he selected from among his three sources (e.g., vv. 580, 859), and those that he proposed as conjectures (see Notes to the Translation on vv. 512, 530, 736, 793, etc.).

This edition does not include a complete critical apparatus. The endnotes to the text are generally limited to cases where (a) there are variant readings that amount to a difference in *meaning* (thus, orthographic variation, or variation between effectively synonymous words such as *to* and *tā*, is ignored), and (b) these variant readings are *possible* from a critical point of view (thus obvious mistakes, even if they change the meaning, are ignored, especially if they result in a metrically impossible reading). I have, however, attempted to report mistakes that appear to be "associative errors," that is, errors inherited by two or more manuscripts from a common source. I have endeavored to report all of the cases in which my edition differs substantively from Upadhye's. A complete critical apparatus will be presented separately.

Although riddled with errors, the new manuscript collated

for this edition, N, is important for two reasons. First, it presents *Līlāvaī* in a different orthography than the three witnesses available to Upadhye. Those three witnesses—P, J, and B, for "Pattan," "Jaisalmer," and "Bikaner"—all seem to have been copied by Jain authors, and P and J are still held in Jain collections. They use an orthography that has come to be associated particularly with Jain texts in Prakrit: the use of *n* instead of or in addition to *ṇ* (although P has *ṇ* almost everywhere), and the use of the consonant *y* as a glide (called *yaśruti*) between vowels. Upadhye recognized that such orthographic features might not have been original to *Līlāvaī*, whose author was not a Jain, but at the same time he was reluctant to go against the manuscript evidence on this point. Thus, he decided to reproduce, more or less, the orthography of P, while at the same time noting that "[t]he possibility of getting the Mss. of the Līlāvatī in which *ya-śruti* is less frequent is not in any way ruled out."[3] But K, the manuscript that Ramakrishna Kavi consulted, was evidently written in the orthography we would expect of non-Jain Prakrit. N is written in the same orthography: it uses *ṇ* almost everywhere, and very rarely uses *yaśruti*. A scribe's orthographic choices, in my opinion, have very little text-critical value, since scribes recopy texts according to the orthographic norms of their region or community. Nevertheless, the availability of manuscript support for the "standard orthography"— standard, at least, among the manuscripts of non-Jain works—has led me to present the text in the orthography exhibited by N and K.

N is also important because of the support it lends to

certain readings. Upadhye's policy was to prefer the read-
ings of J, then P, then B.[4] On the one hand, N and B appear
to be quite closely related, sharing a number of readings that
are either clearly errors (vv. 372, 1174) or possibly errors (v.
997), besides a large number of common readings. N also is
missing some of the same verses as B (v. 227) and orders some
verses in the same way as B (vv. 98–99). We can therefore
group N and B together. On the other hand, N contains none
of the verses distinctive to B and seems to share at least one
associative error with J (v. 674). It also seems to support the
otherwise isolated reading of P in one case where that read-
ing seems original to me (v. 857). Upadhye noticed that the
scribe of P reported variant readings from another manu-
script, and that the readings sometimes correspond with
those of J (v. 669). In fact, more often those readings agree
with N against J (vv. 683, 614). This suggests that the second-
ary exemplar of P—not the one the scribe copied directly,
but the one he took down variants from—was more closely
related to N. I am thus persuaded to take the readings of N
and B seriously, even when they diverge from P and J (and
hence from Upadhye's constituted text), for example at vv.
387, 497.

Several other differences between this edition and Upa-
dhye's call for comment. Upadhye adopted two relatively
nonstandard orthographic devices of his own in his edition.
One concerns word-final nasalization, which is optional in
certain grammatical contexts in Prakrit. Where the meter
requires the preceding syllable to be heavy, Upadhye wrote
an *anusvāra*. Otherwise, Upadhye wrote a *candrabindu*,
provided that either P or J wrote the syllable as nasalized,

or wrote it without any marker of nasalization if neither P nor J wrote it as nasalized. Thus a *candrabindu* in Upadhye's edition represents a nasal that is written, as *anusvāra,* in at least one manuscript but is not metrically required. The *candrabindu* sign itself is not used in any manuscript. I have retained Upadhye's usage on this point, since the *candrabindu* is an established marker of nasalization and is not likely to cause confusion.

The second concerns the vowels *e* and *o,* which are always long in Sanskrit but are often short in Prakrit, especially at the end of a word. The Devanagari script had no separate letters for short *e* and *o* until recently, and hence sometimes the vowels *i* and *u* were used to represent those sounds. In his edition, Upadhye used *three* signs each for *e* and *o:* the standard Devanagari sign, which he used for a long vowel; a specialized sign for a short vowel that some witnesses wrote as *e/o* and others wrote as *i/u;* and another specialized sign for a short vowel that was written by all available witnesses as *e/o.* Since neither of these specialized signs is in common use, I have replaced all of them with the standard Devanagari letters for *e* and *o.* This means that the long and short versions of these sounds are not distinguished in this edition.

Finally, each of the three manuscripts used by Upadhye includes a number of verses that are not present in the others. Upadhye discussed these "additional verses" at length in his introduction but came to no definitive conclusion about them: some must surely be interpolations, but some are likely to have been original and omitted from one or another manuscript by mistake.[5] The readings of N have not cast very much light on this situation: N has reduced the number of common verses still further, since it is missing quite a few found in the others, but in general it does not include verses that are found in only one other manuscript. Those verses that were found in two or three of Upadhye's manuscripts, he numbered continuously from the beginning; those verses, by contrast, that were included in only a single manuscript, he starred and numbered as, e.g., 5*1, 16*1, and so on. I have preserved Upadhye's numbering scheme for the reasons discussed above, but the verses that Upadhye starred are marked in this edition with क, ख, etc. in the Prakrit text and a, b, etc. in the translation. Because Upadhye's criterion for starring verses was mechanical, and does not necessarily reflect a judgment regarding their authenticity, I have retained all starred verses in the text and translation. In cases where there are strong reasons to believe the verse is interpolated or otherwise intrusive, I have said so in the notes.

The manuscripts also differ regarding the story's ending. B presents a short version, and P and J present a longer version. I have taken the liberty of rearranging the verses in Upadhye's edition to reflect the two groups of manuscripts in this respect. I have also refrained from selecting one ending as "original." Upadhye hypothesized that they represent different authorial versions.[6] Without new documentary evidence such as might have been provided by N—which unfortunately stops just short of the ending—it is difficult to evaluate his hypothesis.

On the Translation

The only complete translation of *Līlāvaī* was prepared by S. T. Nimkar in 1988, "mainly for ... students of post-graduate classes" at the University of Bombay.[7] Rajaram Jain and Vidyavati Jain prepared a Hindi translation of the first 312 verses in 1990.

Līlāvaī is a single, continuous story, not divided up into books or sections. But for the convenience of the reader—and also to avoid the multiplication of quotation marks that would otherwise become necessary—I have separated the story into smaller sections based on what is happening in the story and who is speaking. The sections begin with the name of the narrator (Vijaananda, Kuvalaavali, Mahavilaa, and the poet), with the exception of the invocation, intro-duction, and conclusions. The conclusion in manuscript B is shorter than the conclusion in manuscripts J and P. Upadhye guessed they might represent different authorial versions. I have included and translated both in this volume.

I have retained the Prakrit spelling for the names of char-acters in the story. For all other names, including those of places, gods, and goddesses, I transliterate the Sanskrit terms, which are more widely known. All proper names can be found in the glossary at the end of this volume.

NOTES

1   Upadhye 1966: xvii.
2   Ramakrishna Kavi 1926.
3   Upadhye 1966: 11.
4   Upadhye 1966: 7. On the same page he cautions, however, that "a categorical judgement" regarding the text-critical value of B "has

       to be withheld till some more MSS. of the B group are available."

5   Upadhye 1966: 14–18. He notes there that 1,310 verses are common to all three of the manuscripts (assuming that the 300 verses read by P or J between 501 and 806 were also read in B, which is missing about twenty folios), but that the final calculation of the length of the text requires a number closer to around 1,350.

6   Upadhye 1966: 17.

7   Nimkar 1988: 10.

LILAVAI

१ णमह सरोससुअरिसणसच्छविअं कररुहावलीजुअलं ।
हिरणक्कसविअडोरत्थलट्ठिदलगब्भिणं हरिणो ॥

२ तं णमह जस्स तइआ तइअवअं तिहुअणं तुलंतस्स ।
साआरमणाआरे अप्पणमप्पे च्चिअ णिसण्णं ॥

३ तस्सेव पुणो पणमह णिहुअं हलिणा हसिज्जमाणस्स ।
अपहुत्तदेहलीलंघणद्धवहसंठिअं चलणं ॥

४ सो जअउ जस्स पत्तो कंठे रिट्ठासुरस्स घणकसणो ।
उप्पाअपवड्ढिअकालवासकरणी भुअप्फलिहो ॥

५ रक्खंतु वो महोवहिसअणे सेसस्स फणमणिपईवा ।
हरिणो सिरिसिहिणोत्थअकोत्थुहकंदंकुराआरा ॥१

५क महुमहवलणुप्पीडिअसेसभुअंगेण मुक्कफुक्कारा ।
पवणाऊरिअजलअरसुत्तविबुद्धो हरी जअउ ॥२

2

INVOCATION

Reverence to Hari's two claw-studded paws, which
    Sudarshana glared at with anger, flecked as they were
    with chips of bone from Hiranyakashipu's terrifying
    chest.[1]
      1

Reverence to him whose body, when measuring out the
    three worlds, came to rest, on his third step, in his
    unembodied self.[2]
      2

Reverence once more to his foot, which Balarama
    ridiculed under his breath for being unable to get
    more than halfway over the threshold.[3]
      3

Victory to him whose huge arm fell, dark as a cloud, on the
    throat of the demon Arishta, like the noose of death
    stretched out at the hour of doom.[4]
      4

May those rays of light protect you that stream from the
    jewels on Shesha's hoods, where Hari sleeps on the
    cosmic ocean. They look like shoots of the *kaustubha*
    gem pushing through the covering of Lakshmi's
    breasts.[5]
      5

The slayer of Madhu* tossing in his sleep crushed the
    serpent Shesha under him, who let out a hiss, which
    sounded the conch that woke up Hari—victory to him.
      5a

—————

* Krishna.

६ हरिणो जमलज्जुणरिट्टकेसिकंसासुरिंदसेलाण ।
   भंजणवलणविआरणकड्ढणधरणे भुए णमह ॥

७ कक्कसभुअकोप्परपूरिआणणो कढिणकरकआवेसो ।
   केसिकिसोरकअत्थणकउज्जमो जअउ महुमहणो ॥

८ सो जअउ जेण तेलोक्ककवलणारंभगब्भिअमुहेण ।
   ओसावणि व्व पीआ सत्त वि चुलुअट्ठिआ उवही ॥

९ गोरीए गुरुभरक्कंतमहिससीसट्ठिभंजणुद्धरिअं ।
   णमह णमंतसुरासुरसिरमसिणिअणेउरं चलणं ॥

१० चंडीए कढिणकोवंडकड्ढणाअससेअसलिलुल्लो ।
    णिंतकुसुंभुप्पीलो रक्खउ वो कंचुओ णिच्चं ॥

११ ससहरकरसंवलिआ तुम्हं सुरणिण्णआए णासंतु ।
    पावं फुरंतरुद्दट्टहासधवला जलुप्पीला ॥

4

Reverence to the arms of Hari, which uprooted the two   6
    arjuna trees, strangled the demon Arishta, tore apart
    Keshin, dragged King Kamsa, and lifted up Mount
    Govardhana.[6]

Victory to the slayer of Madhu, who plunged his steely   7
    arm elbow-deep into the maw of the colt-demon
    Keshin, then, with his hand far inside him, lifted him
    up to torture him.

Victory to him who devours the three worlds* after   8
    drinking the seven oceans held in his cupped palms
    like water before a meal.

Reverence to the foot of Gauri, with anklets polished by   9
    the bowed heads of gods and demons, as it rises up to
    smash the skull of the buffalo-demon, pinned under
    her weight.

Soaked with sweat from the exertion of drawing her stiff   10
    bow, its safflower dye trickling down, may the bodice
    of Chandi protect you always.

Mixed with moonbeams and sparkling like the frenzied   11
    laughter of Rudra, may the rushing waters of the
    divine river wash away your sin.[7]

———

* Shiva.

१२ जअंति ते सज्जणभाणुणो सआ
विआरिणो जाण सुवण्णसंचआ ।
अइट्टदोसा विअसंति संगमे
कहाणुबंधा कमलाअरा इव ॥३

१३ सो जअउ जेण सुअणा वि दुज्जणा इह विणिम्मिआ भुवणे ।
ण तमेण विणा पावंति चंदकिरणा वि परिहावं ॥

१४ दुज्जणसुअणाण णमो णिच्चुं परकज्जवावडमणाण ।
एक्के भसणसहावा परदोसपरम्मुहा अण्णे ॥४

१५ अहवा ण को वि दोसो दीसइ सअलंमि जीवलोअम्मि ।
सव्वो च्चिअ सुअणयणो जं भणिमो तं णिसामेह ॥५

१६ सज्जणसंगेण वि दुज्जणस्स ण हु कलुसिमा समोसरइ ।
ससिमंडलमज्झपरिट्ठिओ वि कसणो च्चिअ कुरंगो ॥

१६क दुज्जणसंगेण वि सज्जणस्स णासं ण होइ सीलस्स ।
तीए सलोणे वि मुहे तह वि हु अहरो महुं सवइ ॥६

१७ अलमवरेणासंबद्धालावपरिग्गहाणुबंधेण ।
बालजणविलसिएण व णिरत्थवाआवसंगेण ॥

Victory to thoughtful good people. They are like suns that 12
 blaze in the sky: in their presence stories, beautifully
 composed and free from fault, blossom like day lilies,
 lush with leaves and shunning dark night.[8]

Victory to him who created good people in this world and 13
 bad people as well. Without darkness, there would be
 nothing for the moon's rays to overcome.

Reverence forever to good people and bad. Their minds 14
 are always set on what others do: the ones are given
 to searching out their flaws, the others to looking
 past them.

Some may claim that no one in the whole world is ever at 15
 fault, that absolutely everyone is good. But hear what
 I have to say about that.[9] Even if they associate with 16
 the good, bad people will never lose their stain. The
 moon's spot will always stay black, despite being in the
 very middle of the moon.

The good man's conduct, however, is never ruined, even if 16a
 he associates with bad people. A woman's talk may be
 salty but her lips still flow with nectar.[10]

But enough. There's no point in getting caught up in 17
 nonsense like this, babbling like a baby.

१८ आसि तिवेअतिहोमग्गिसंगसंजणिअतिअसपरिओसो ।
संपत्ततिवग्गफलो बहुलाइच्छो त्ति णामेण ॥

१९ अज्ज वि महग्गिपसरिअधूमसिहाकलुसिअं व वच्छअलं ।
उव्वहइ मिअकलंकच्छलेण मिअलंछणो जस्स ॥

२० तस्स अ गुणरअणमहोवहीए एक्को सुओ समुप्पण्णो ।
भूसणभट्टो णामेण णिअअकुलणहअलमिअंको ॥

२१ जस्स पिअंबंधवेहि व चउवअणविणिग्गएहि वेएहि ।
एक्कवअणारविंददिट्ठिएहिँ बहुमण्णिओ अप्पा ॥

२२ तस्स तणएण एअं असारमइणा वि विरइअं सुणह ।
कोऊहलेण लीलावइ त्ति णामं कहारअणं ॥

२३ तं जह मिअंककेसरिकरपहरणदलिअतिमिरकरिकुंभे ।
विक्खित्तरिक्खमुत्ताहलुज्जले सरअरअणीए ॥

पओससमए धवलभवणुत्तमंगसअणसुहासीणाए भणिअं ।
पिअअम पेच्छ पेच्छ ।

२४ जोण्हाऊरिअकोसकंतिधवले सव्वंगगंधुक्कडे
णिव्विग्घं घरदीहिआए सुरसं वेवंतओ मासलं ।
आसाएइ सुमंजुगुंजिअरवो तिंगिच्छिपाणासवं
उम्मिल्लंतदलावलीपरिओ चंदुज्जुए छप्पओ ॥७

INTRODUCTION

There once lived a man who delighted the gods through   18
his devotion to the three holy Vedas and the three
sacred fires, and thus achieved the three goals of life.
His name was Bahulaiccha.[11] The wafting plumes of   19
smoke from his sacrificial fires left a sooty mark on
the surface of the moon—the deer-shaped spot that it
bears to this day. This man, an ocean full of jewels that   20
were virtues, had one son, named Bhusanabhatta, and
he was the moon in his family's sky. The Vedas, which   21
first came from Brahma's four mouths, took their
place in his single lotus mouth, and honored him like a
kinsman. Listen to this jewel of a story, called *Līlāvaī,*   22
that his dim-witted son Kouhala composed.[12]

It goes like this. In the twilight of an autumn night,   23
when the moon with its rays split the star-strewn
darkness—a lion with its paws splitting the pearl-
strewn cheeks of an elephant—my beloved was
relaxing on the terrace of our house. She said to me:[13]

"Look, my dear, at the night lotus in our backyard pond   24
and how the moonlight is filling its calyx:
it's dazzling white, its fragrance
heady. Bumbling around inside is a bee,
buzzing loudly as it sips unhindered
the delicious and potent liquor of its nectar,
surrounded by unfolding petals.[14]

9

२५ इमिणा सरएण ससी ससिणा वि णिसा णिसाए कुमुअवणं ।
कुमुअवणेण व पुलिणं पुलिणेण व सहइ हंसउलं ॥

२६ णवविसकसाअसंसुद्धकंठकलमणोहरो णिसामेसु ।
सरअसिरिचलणणेउरराओ इव हंससंलावो ॥

२७ संचरइ सीअलाअंतसलिलकल्लोलसंगणिव्विओ ।
दरदलिअमालईमुद्धमउलगंधुद्धुरो पवणो ॥

२८ एसा वि दसदिसावहुवअणिविसेसावलि व्व सरसलिले ।
विंभलतरंगदोलंतपाअवा सहइ वणराई ॥८

२९ एआइँ दियससंभावणेक्कहिअआइँ पेच्छह घडंति ।
आमुक्कविरहवेअणाइँ चक्कवायाइँ वावीसु ॥

३० एअं उअ विअसिअसत्तवत्तपरिमलविलोहविज्जंतं ।
अविहाविअकुसुमासाअविमुहिअं भमइ भमरउलं ॥

३१ चंदुज्जुआवअंसं पविअंभिअसुरहिकुवलआमोअं ।
णिम्मलताराआलोअं पिअइ व रयणीमुहं चंदो ॥

"The autumn makes the moon all the more beautiful, the   25
    moon the night, the night this bed of lotuses, this bed
    of lotuses the bank, and the bank these geese.[15]

"Can you hear the calls of the geese, their captivating   26
    honking made clear by the astringent stalks of fresh
    lotuses they ate, now sounding like the anklets of the
    goddess of autumn?[16]

"A breeze is blowing past, carrying mist from waves   27
    of cool water and thick with the fragrance of fresh
    jasmine buds half-opened.

"And there on the riverbank is an arcade of trees swaying   28
    in restless waves—henna decorations, as it were, on
    the cheeks of the women of the ten directions.[17]

"Do you see these *cakravāka* birds? Usually it is only the   29
    day that can ease their heartache, but here they are,
    leaving behind the pain of separation and uniting with
    each other in the ponds.[18]

"Look at how these bees are captivated by the smell of the   30
    blossoming *saptaparṇa* tree and wander off without
    even a thought for the fragrance of other flowers.

"It's as if the moon were kissing the night: water lilies   31
    adorning her ears, their fragrance her perfume, the
    bright stars her eyes.

ता किं बहुणा पअंपिएण ।

३२ अइरमणीआ रअणी सरओ विमलो तुमं च साहीणो ।
अणुकूलपरिअणाए मण्णे तं णत्थि जं णत्थि ॥

३३ ता किं पि पओसविणोअमेत्तसुहअं म्ह मणहरुल्लावं ।
साहेह अउव्वकहं सुरसं महिलाअणमणोज्जं ॥

३४ तं मुद्धमुहंबुरुहाहि वअणअं णिसुणिऊण णे भणिअं ।
कुवलअदलच्छि एत्थं कईहिं तिविहा कहा भणिआ ॥

३५ तं जह दिव्वा तह दिव्वमाणुसी माणुसी तह च्चेअ ।
तत्थ वि पढमेहिँ कअं कईहिँ किर लक्खणं किं पि ॥

३६ अण्णं सक्कअपाअअसंकिण्णविहा सुवण्णरइआओ ।
सुव्वंति महाकइपुंगवेहि विविहाउ सुकहाओ ॥

३७ ताणं मज्झे अम्हारिसेहिँ अबुहेहिँ जाउ सीसंति ।
ताउ कहाओ ण लोए मिअच्छि पावंति परिहावं ॥

३८ ता किं मं उवहासेसि सुअणु असुएण सद्दसत्थेण ।
उल्लविउं पि ण तीरइ किं पुण विअडो कहाबंधो ॥

"What more is there to say? The night is beautiful beyond
measure, there is not a cloud in the autumn sky, you   32
are at leisure, and with servants attending to us,
I would say there is nothing missing. So let's have a   33
bit of pleasant entertainment for the evening. Tell me
a story in your charming voice, one I haven't heard
before, full of *rasa* and pleasing to women like me."[19]

Hearing those words from her lovely lotus mouth, I said: 34
"My love with lily-petal eyes, on this score poets have
distinguished three kinds of stories: 'divine,' 'divine-   35
human,' and simply 'human.'[20] Earlier poets have
apparently laid down some rules for each of them.[21]
And there are all kinds of stories composed in the   36
beautiful sounds of Sanskrit, Prakrit, or a mixture of
the two that famous poets have recited. Compared   37
with them I am no scholar. The stories I could tell, my
dear, would hardly meet with anyone's approval. So,   38
then, are you trying to humiliate me, my love, for not
learning the arts of language? I find it hard enough
just to speak. Do you think I could tell a story that
goes on and on?"

३९ भणिअं च पिअअमाए पियअम किं तेण सद्दसत्थेण ।
जेण सुहासिअमग्गो भग्गो अम्हारिसजणस्स ॥

४० उवलब्भइ जेण फुडं अत्थो अकअत्थिएण हिअएण ।
सो च्चेअ परो सद्दो णिच्छो किं लक्खणेण म्ह ॥

४१ एमेअ मुद्धजुअईमणोहरं पाअआए भासाए ।
पविरलदेसिसिसुलक्खं कहसु कहं दिव्वमाणुसिअं ॥

४२ तं तह सोऊण पुणो भणिअं उब्बिंबबालहरिणच्छि ।
जइ एवं ता सुव्वउ सुसंधिबंधं कहावत्थुं ॥

"My love," my beloved said, "who needs the 'arts of   39
language'? All they do is block the path to enjoyment
for people like me. In the end, language is just what   40
reveals a meaning clearly, without troubling the heart.
What need do I have of rules? That's why you should   41
tell a story in the Prakrit language, one that can hold
a simple girl's interest. A story of the 'divine-human'
type, with only a few regional words thrown in."[22]

To this I replied: "If you insist, my fawn-eyed love. Listen   42
to this story. It has all the right elements."[23]

अत्थि

४३ चउजलहिवलअरसणाणिबद्धविअडोवरोहसोहाए ।
सेसंकसुप्परिरिट्ठिअसव्वंगुव्वूढभुवणाए ॥

४४ पलअवराहसमुद्धरणसोक्खसंपत्तिगरुअभावाए ।
णाणाविहरअणालंकिआए भअवइए पुहईए ॥

४५ णीसेससरस्ससंपत्तिपमुइआसेसपामरजणोहो ।
सुव्वसिअगामगोहणरंभारवमुहलिअदिअंतो ॥९

४६ अइसुहिअपाणआवाणचच्चरीरवरमाउलारामो ।
णीसेससुहणिवासो आसअविसओ त्ति विक्खाओ ॥

४७ जो सो अविउत्तो कअजुअस्स धम्मस्स संणिवेसो व्व ।
सिक्खवट्टाणं व पआवइस्स सुकआण आवासो ॥

४८ सासणमिव पुण्णाणं जम्मुप्पत्ति व्व सुहसमूहाणं ।
आअरिसो आआराण सइ सुछेत्तं पिव गुणाणं ॥

THE POET:
SCENE AT PRATISHTHANA

Once upon a time there was a famous region called
    Ashmaka on the blessed earth—her beautiful hips   43
    encircled by the belt of the four oceans, her realms
    resting securely on the coils of the serpent Shesha,
    her grandeur derived from the joy of being raised   44
    from the ocean's depths by the Boar at the end of
    time, and being adorned with all manner of gems.[24]
    There farmers rejoiced together in their rich harvests;   45
    the lowing of cows in pleasant villages carried to
    the horizons; joyful people would gather to drink   46
    and dance to Prakrit songs that echoed through the
    gardens. It was the dwelling place of every pleasure.[25]

It was a place where the golden age still reigned, like   47
    dharma in physical form, or the creator's very
    template, where good deeds were at home.[26]   48
    It was like a lesson in religious merit, the birthplace
    of endless pleasure, a mirror for good conduct,
    an ever-fertile field for the seeds of virtue.

अवि अ।

४९ सुसणिद्धघाससंतुट्टगोहणालोअमुइअगोआलो।
गेआरवभरिअदिसो वरवलइवेणुणिवहेसु ॥१०

सुहावगाहणिम्मलजलसओ। तरुणतरुज्जाणरिद्धिरमणीओ।
कमलसरसंडमंडिआसामुहो। सुस्साअफलभरोणमिअ-
वच्छअलावासिअपहिअजणसमाउलो। सव्वोवसग्ग-
भअरहिओ। चाउवण्णसमाउत्तो। णिच्चुसववड्ढिआआणंदो।
विविहकाणणोवसोहिअभूमिभाओ। विविहकुसुमामोअ-
वासिअदिअंतरालो। अणवइण्णकलिकालो। अइट्टपावो।
अपरिचत्तधम्मो। अणुवलक्खिअपआवो अपणट्टसोहो।
अणुवजाअचोरराअभओ। अपरिमिअगुणगणणिवासो
त्ति।

जहिं च। कामवरिसी भअवं पज्जण्णो। कामदुहाओ
सुरहीओ। सइफलाओ वणप्फईओ। अवंझाओ जुअईओ
त्ति।

What's more, it was a place where cowherds rejoiced to see 49
   their cattle feeding on soft grass; where the sky was
   filled with the sound of singing mingled with the notes
   of lutes and pipes.[27]

A place with clear ponds pleasant to bathe in; where
   young trees grew dense in beautiful gardens; where
   every line of sight would fall upon a lotus pond; where
   travelers slept at the foot of trees bent down with
   luscious fruit; where even a hint of trouble never
   arose; where the four social orders were maintained;[28]
   where joy overflowed in constant celebration; where
   groves adorned every plot of land, and the fragrance
   of all kinds of flowers perfumed the whole sky; where
   the present dark age had yet to set in and no sin could
   be found, people never shirked their responsibilities
   or had any sight of enemy forces;[29] where beauty was
   undiminished; where fear of thieves—and kings—
   never arose, and where limitless virtue resided.

It was a place where the cloud-god rained whenever it
   was needed, where cows gave milk whenever it was
   wanted, where trees always bore fruit, and women
   were never barren.

जहिं च ।

५० दूरुण्णअगरुअपओहराओ कोमलमुणालवाहीओ ।
सइ महुरवाणिआओ जुअईओ णिण्णआउ व्व ॥

५१ अच्छउ ता णिअच्छेत्तं सेसाइ वि जत्थ पामरवहूहिं ।
रक्खिज्जंति मणोहरगेआरवहरिअहरिणाहिं ॥

५२ इअ एरिसस्स सुंदरि मज्झम्मि सुजणवअस्स रमणीअं ।
णीसेससुहणिवासं णअरं णामं पइट्ठाणं ॥

५३ तं च पिए वरणअरं वण्णिज्जइ जा विहाइ ता रअणी ।
उद्देसो संखेवेण किं पि वोच्छामि णिसुणेसु ॥

५४ जत्थ वरकामिणीचलणणेउरारावमणुसरंतेहिं ।
पडिराविज्जइ मुहमुक्ककिसलअं राअहंसेहिं ॥

५५ जण्णग्गिधूमसामालिअणहअललोअणेक्करसिएहिं ।
णच्छिज्जइ ससहरमणिसिलाअले घरमऊरेहिं ॥

५६ ण तरिज्जइ घरमणिकिरणजालपडिरुद्धतिमिरिणिअरम्मि ।
अहिसारिआहिँ आमुक्कमंडणाहिं पि संचरिउं ॥११

५७ साणूरथूहिआधअणिरंतरंतरिअतरणिकरणिअरे ।
परिसेसिआअवत्तं गम्मइ संगीअविलआहिं ॥

५८ सरसावराहपरिकुविअकामिणीमाणमोहलंपिक्कं ।
कलअंठिउलं चिअ कुणइ जत्थ दोच्चं पिआण सआ ॥१२

५९ णिद्धअरअरहसकिलंतकामिणीसेअजललवुप्फुसणा ।
पिज्जंति जत्थ णासंजलीहि उज्जाणगंधवहा ॥

६० घरसिरपसुत्तकामिणिकवोलसंकंतससिअलावलअं ।
हंसेहि अहिलसिज्जइ मुणालसद्धालुएहि जहिं ॥१३

२०

There the rivers—deep and coursing strong, flowing   50
    over the soft lotus stalks, their waters always sweet—
    resembled women, their breasts large and heavy, their
    arms soft as lotus stalks, their voices always sweet.[30]
    Not only their own fields but those of their neighbors   51
    as well were protected by the captivating songs of the
    farmers' wives, entrancing even the deer.

In this wonderful country, my love, lay a beautiful city,   52
    abode of all pleasures, named Pratishthana. It would   53
    take all night just to describe it, so listen, and I will
    give you just a summary.

It was a place where royal geese would drop lotus stalks   54
    from their mouths to call out in imitation of the
    anklets of beautiful women, where pet peacocks   55
    would dance on terraces paved with moonstones
    when they saw the sky blackened by sacrificial fires;[31]
    where women with midnight trysts would take   56
    off their shining jewelry only to find their cover of
    darkness shrinking from the bright rays of jeweled
    lamps;[32] where a dense canopy of flags atop temples   57
    would block the sun's rays and make the singing girls'
    parasols redundant; where cuckoos would constantly   58
    play the messenger for couples by soothing the
    brooding anger of women at every new offense of
    their lovers; where the nose could drink in fragrances   59
    wafting from gardens dense with the sweat of women
    exhausted by merciless lovemaking; where geese   60
    craving lotus fibers would be drawn to the image of

६१ मरहट्टिआ पओहरहलिद्दपरिरिपिंजरंबुवाहीए ।
धुव्वंति जत्थ गोलाणईए तद्दिअसिअं पावं ॥

६२ अह णवर तत्थ दोसो जं गिम्हपओसमल्लिआमोओ ।
अणुणअसुहाइँ माणंसिणीण भोत्तुं चिअ ण देइ ॥

६२क अह णवर तत्थ दोसो जं फलिहसिलायलम्मि तरुणीण ।
मयणवियारा दीसंति बाहिरठिएहि वि जणेहिं ॥१४

६३ अह णवर तत्थ दोसो जं विअसिअकुसुमरेणुपडलेण ।
मइलिज्जंति समीरणवसेण घरचित्तभित्तीओ ॥

६४ तत्थेरिसम्मि णअरे णीसेसगुणावगूहिअसरीरो ।
भुवणपवित्थरिअजसो राआ सालाहणो णाम ॥

the moon's sliver reflected on the cheeks of women
    asleep on rooftops; where the women of Maharashtra   61
    would wash away the day's impurities in the Godavari
    River, dyeing its waters orange with the turmeric on
    their breasts.[33]

There was nothing wrong with that place—except,   62
    perhaps, that the fragrance of jasmine on a summer
    day would deny women the pleasure of their lovers'
    apologies.[34] Or except, perhaps, that the crystal walls   62a
    of houses let people outside see all the effects of love
    on the women inside. Or except, perhaps, that wind   63
    would blow the pollen of blossoming flowers onto the
    houses' painted walls.

In that city there lived a king who perfectly embodied   64
    every virtue, and whose fame had spread across the
    earth. His name was Salahana.[35]

६५ जो सो अविग्गहो वि हु सव्वंगावअवसुंदरो सुहओ ।
दुद्दंसणो वि लोआणँ लोअणाणंदसंजणणो ॥१५

६६ कुवई वि वल्लहो पणइआण तह णअवरो वि साहसिओ ।
परलोअभीरुओ वि हु वीरेक्करसो तह च्चेअ ॥१६

६७ सूरो वि ण सत्तासो सोमो वि कलंकवज्जिओ णिच्चं ।
भोई वि ण दोजीहो तुंगो वि समीवदिण्णफलो ॥

६८ बहुलंतदिणेसु ससि व्व जेण वोच्छिण्णमंडलणिवेसो ।
ठविओ तणुअत्तणदुक्खलक्खिओ रिउअणो सव्वो ॥

६९ णिअतेअपसाहिअमंडलस्स ससिणो व्व जस्स लोएण ।
अक्कंतजअस्स जए पट्टी ण परेण सच्चविआ ॥

७० ओसहिसिहापिसंगाण वोलिआ गिरिगुहासु रअणीओ ।
जस्स पयावाणलकंतिकवलिआणं पिव रिऊणं ॥

७१ आलिहिअइ जो वम्महणिभेण णिअवासभवणभित्तीसु ।
लडहविलआहिँ णहमणिकिरणारुणिअग्गहत्थेहिँ ॥

७२ हिअए च्चेअ विलाअंति सुइरपरिचिंतिआ वि सुकईण ।
जेण विणा दुहिआण व मणोरहा कव्वविणिवेसा ॥

He was handsome, beautiful in every last detail, although   65
    "formless"—or rather, conflict-less. He brought joy to
    the people's eyes, although "terrible to behold"—or
    rather, too brilliant to behold.[36] He was the favorite   66
    of his wives, although "a bad husband"—or rather,
    lord of the earth. He was bold in battle, although his
    enemies had submitted—or rather, he was devoted
    to strategy. He delighted in acts of heroism, although
    "he feared the world beyond"—or rather, his enemies
    were terrified of him. He was "the sun without his   67
    seven horses"—a fearless man of courage; the "moon
    without his spot"—a gentle man without flaws; "a
    serpent without split tongue"—a straight-talking man
    of leisure; "a tall tree with low-hanging fruit"—a noble
    man kind to those around him.

As the moon grows thinner in its waning phase, its full disc   68
    eventually enveloped in darkness, so the king made
    all his enemies weak, cut off from their allies. Like the   69
    moon, its orb lit up with light, and never passed by the
    earth, no one on earth had ever seen his back: he had
    conquered the whole world, and his own realms were
    illuminated by his power.[37] His enemies retreated to   70
    caves, where they spent their nights in the red glow of
    mountain plants, as if consumed by the fiery brilliance
    of his might.[38] It was he, in the guise of the love god,   71
    that beautiful women painted on their bedroom walls,
    with fingers reddened by rays of light from their
    fingernails. Without him, the works of even the best   72
    poets, thoughtfully composed over time, would have

७३ इअ तस्स महापुहईसरस्स इच्छापहुत्तविहवस्स ।
कुसुमसराउहदूओ व्व आगओ सुअणु महुमासो ॥

७४ पत्थाणं पढमागअमलआणिलपिसुणिअं वसंतस्स ।
बहुलच्छलंतकोइलरवेण साहंति व वणाइं ॥

७४क गहिऊण चूयमंजरि कीरो परिभमइ पत्तलाहत्थो ।
ओसरसु सिसिरणरवइ पुहई लद्धा वसंतेण ॥१७

७५ मउलंतमउलिएसुं विअसिअविअसंतकुसुमणिवहेसु ।
सरिसं चिअ ठवइ पअं वणेसु लच्छी वसंतस्स ॥

७६ बहुएहि मि किं परिवड्ढिएहिँ बाणेहिँ कुसुमचावस्स ।
एक्केण चिअ चूअंकुरेण कज्जं ण पज्जत्तं ॥

७७ घिप्पइ कणअमअं पिव पसाहणं जणिअतिलअसोहेण ।
अब्भहिअजणिअसोहं कणिआरवणं वसंतेण ॥

७८ विअसंतविविहवणराइकुसुमसिरिपरिगआ महातरुणो ।
किं पुण विअंभमाणो जं ण कुणइ मल्लिआमोओ ॥

७९ पढमं चिअ कामिअणस्स कुणइ मउआइँ पाडलामोओ ।
हिअआइँ सुहं पच्छा विसंति सेसा वि कुसुमसरा ॥

८० पज्जत्तविआसुव्वेल्लगुंदिपब्भारणूमिअदलाइं ।
पहिआण दुरालोआइँ होंति माअंदगहणाइं ॥

८१ अपहुत्तविआसुड्ढीणभमरविच्छाअदलउडुब्भेअं ।
कुंदलइयाए विअलइ हिमविरहाआसिअं कुसुमं ॥

wasted away in their hearts like the desires of the poor.[39]

When this man, lord of earth, was at the height of his 73
power, springtime arrived like a messenger of the
god of love. The forests seemed to herald the march 74
of spring, already hinted at by the first wafts of the
southern breeze, with the loud sound of cuckoos
on the wing. With a cluster of mango blossoms, the 74a
wandering parrot seemed like a herald: "Retreat,
King Winter, for Spring now holds the earth."[40] In a 75
single step, spring's beauty came to all the flowers of
the forest—those just budding and those that already
had, those just blossoming and those that already
had. The god of love, with his bow made of flowers, 76
has so many arrows, but what for? Won't a single
mango sprout do the job?[41] Spring took the *karṇikāra* 77
fields and seemed to wear them as a golden forehead
decoration, making his own *tilaka,* and the sesame
fields, more beautiful.[42] If the wafting scent of jasmine 78
could make the tall trees of the arcades burst into
bloom, is there anything it can't do? First, the *pāṭala* 79
flowers softened lovers' hearts with their fragrance,
then the love god's other flower-arrows entered with
ease.[43] Clusters of fragrant blossoming mango flowers 80
covered the trees so completely that travelers could
hardly spot the leaves behind them.[44] The bees forced 81
themselves on the petals of the jasmine flowers before
their season, and they fell, pale, from their tendrils,
succumbing to the grief of separation from winter.

८२ आबज्झंतफलुप्पंकथोअविहडंतसंधिबंधेहिं ।
मंदपवणाहएहिँ वि परिगलिअं सिंदुवारेहिं ॥

८३ थोऊससंतपंकअमुहीए णिव्वणिए वसंतम्मि ।
वोलीणतुहिणभरसुत्थियाए हसिअं व णलिणीए ॥

८४ मलअसमीरसमागमसंतोसपणाच्छिराहिँ सव्वत्तो ।
वाहिप्पइ णवकिसलअकराहिं साहाहिं महुलच्छी ॥

८५ दीसइ पलासवणवीहियासु पप्फुलकुसुमणिवहेण ।
रत्तंबरणेवच्छो णववरइत्तो व महुमासो ॥

८६ परिवड्ढइ चूअवणेसु विसइ णवमाहवीविआणेसु ।
लुलइ व कंकेल्लिदलावलीसु मुइओ व्व महुमासो ॥

८७ अण्णण्णवणलआगहिअपरिमलेणाणिलेण छिप्पंती ।
कुसुमंसुएहिं रुअइ व परम्मुही तरुणचूअलआ ॥

८८ विअसिअणीसेसवणंतरालपरिसंठिएण कामेण ।
विवसिज्जइ कुसुमसरेहिं लद्धप्पसरेहिं कामिअणो ॥

८९ इअ वम्महबाणवसीकअम्मि सअलम्मि जीवलोअम्मि ।
महुसिरिसमागमत्थाणमंडवं उवगओ राआ ॥

९० सेवागअसअसामंतमउडमाणिक्ककिरणविच्छुरिए ।
सीहासणम्मि बंदिणजअसद्दसमं समासीणो ॥

९१ परिअरिओ वारविलासिणीहि सुरसुंदरीहिँ व सुरेसो ।
कणआअलो व्व आसावहूहिँ सइ विअसिअमुहीहिं ॥१८

28

As tiny clusters of berries formed and its calyx started 82
to weaken, the *sinduvāra's* flowers fell away in the
gentle breeze. When spring came into view and the 83
layer of frost had melted away, the lotus seemed to
smile, its mouth opening slightly. The branches, with 84
new shoots for hands, danced with delight on the
arrival of the southern breeze, and seemed to beckon
the beauty of spring.[45] In the rows of *palāśa* trees, the 85
full-blossomed flowers seemed to clothe spring in red
garments like a groom on his wedding day.[46] After 86
gaining strength in the mango groves, entering bowers
of new *mādhavī* shoots, and then lounging upon *aśoka*
tree leaves, spring seemed truly delighted. The breeze, 87
carrying the fragrance of many other plants, touched
the delicate shoot of the mango tree. She then turned
away, shedding her petals as if they were tears.[47] The 88
forest was in full bloom, and in its midst stood the god
of love, bringing lovers under his power by raining
flower-arrows down on them.

When the love god's arrows had thus conquered the 89
whole world of living beings, the king came to the
pavilion where spring's beauty had assembled. To the 90
accompaniment of the bards' victory songs, he seated
himself on the lion throne, ablaze with light beams
from the crown jewels of the hundreds of vassals in his
service. He was surrounded by courtesans, their faces 91
blossoming with smiles, like Indra surrounded by
celestial women or golden Mount Meru by the women
of the directions.[48]

९२ अह सो एक्काए समं णरणाहो चंदलेहणामाए ।
सप्परिहासं सुमणोहरं च सुहअं समुल्लवइ ॥

९३ अइ चंदलेहे ण णिअसि मलआणिलकुसुमरेणुपडहत्थं ।
कामेण वासभवणं व विरइअं दसदिसाअकं ॥१९

९४ ता कीस तुमं केणावि मअणसरबंधुणा मिअंकमुहि ।
चिंचिल्लिआ सि सव्वाअरेण सव्वंगिअं अज्ज ॥

९५ णवचंपअकुसुमणिवेसिआआणणो केण तुह णिडालअले ।
सज्जीवो विव लिहिओ महुपाणपरव्वसो महुओ ॥

९६ केण व महग्घमअणाहिपंकजोएण तुह कवोलेसु ।
लिहिआओ पत्तलेहाओ मअणसरवत्तणीओ व्व ॥

९७ केण व कइआ सहआरमंजरी तुह कवोलपेरंते ।
करफंसविहाविअकुसुमसंचआ सुअणु णिम्मविआ ॥

९८ केणज्ज तुज्झ तवणिज्जपुंजपीए पओहरुच्छंगे ।
पत्तत्तं पत्तं पत्तलच्छि पत्तं लिहंतेण ॥

९९ एक्केक्कमवअणमुणालदाणवलिअद्धकंधराबंधं ।
चलणकमलेसु लिहिअं केणेयं हंसमिहुणजुअं ॥२०

१०० इअ केण णिअअविण्णाणपअडणुप्पण्णहिअअभावेण ।
अविहाविअगुणदोसेण पाइआ सप्पिणी छीरं ॥

१०१ तं तह सोऊण णराहिवाहि विअसंतलोअणमुहीए ।
दरलज्जोणअवअणाए पभणिअं चंदलेहाए ॥

Then the king started to joke flirtatiously with one of   92
     them, named Chandaleha.[49]

"Here, Chandaleha, don't you see? The sky is all filled   93
     with pollen carried by the southern breeze, as if the
     god of love had turned it into his bedroom.[50] Now   94
     what is this, moon-faced girl? Was it some kinsman of
     the love god's arrows that decorated you so carefully
     from head to toe?[51] Who painted on your face this   95
     lifelike bee, which seems to press its own face into a
     fresh champak flower, eager to drink its nectar? Who   96
     used costly musk paste to paint these designs on your
     cheeks, which seem like fletchings of the love-god's
     arrows? Who produced, and when, this cluster of   97
     mango buds at the edge of your cheek, which seems
     to bring forth flowers at the touch of your hand? Who   98
     is it, petal-eyed girl, who has reached such heights of
     skill today in drawing this floral design on the slope
     of your breasts, lustrous as solid gold?[52] Who drew   99
     on your feet these two pairs of geese, craning their
     necks to place lotus stalks in each other's beaks? Who   100
     was it? Surely someone intending only to show off his
     own skill, without considering whether it is right or
     wrong—the kind of person who would try to feed a
     snake milk."[53]

When she heard what the king said, Chandaleha's eyes lit   101
     up. Lowering her face with a twinge of bashfulness,
     she replied:

१०२ सो देव विद्धकुसलो चित्तअरो जेण तुम्ह दारम्मि ।
अवलंबिऊण पत्तं तइआ लिहिओ तुमं चेअ ॥

१०३ सो च्चेअ पुणो संपइ सिंघलदीवाहि आगओ एत्थ ।
तेणेअं मअणमहूसवम्मि सव्वं समालिहिअं ॥

१०४ अह एवं सप्परिहासगोट्ठिसुहसंठिअस्स णरवइणो ।
लद्धावसरं एक्केण मंतिउत्तेण उल्लविअं ॥

१०५ सो देव चारपुरिसो सिंघलवइणा णिरूविओ मण्णे ।
इमिणा विण्णाणगुणेण चंदलेहाघरे वसइ ॥

१०६ एवविहा एवविहं अच्छंति णरेसराण जे कडए ।
ते चरपुरिसा लोएहि जक्खणामा भणिज्जंति ॥

१०६क ता भणियं णरवइणा तस्सोवरि सुयणु सिंहलेसस्स ।
पेहिओ विजयाणंदो पोट्टिसवरमंतिणा सहिओ ॥२१

१०६ख तस्स कडयाउ अज्ज वि णागच्छइ कोइ कहइउं सच्चं ।
किं भणइ सिंहलेसो किं वा सेणाहिवो अम्हं ॥२२

१०७ अज्जं चिअ सिट्टुं हेरिएहिँ उवहीतडम्मि संपत्तो ।
विजआणंदो सह पोट्टिसेण परिवड्ढिअपआवो ॥

१०८ तह सो वि सिंघलेसो तद्दिअसणिरालसो सअं चेअ ।
जवसेंधणसंपुण्णाइ कुणइ दुग्गाइ अविसण्णो ॥

१०९ विसमीकरेइ उवहीतडाइँ जोएइ जुज्झभूमीओ ।
विजआणंदेण समं महाहवं महइ णिक्कंपो ॥

"My lord, there is a painter, a specialist in the realist style, who once drew your likeness on a leaf while standing at the gate of your palace.[54] He recently returned from the island of Sinhala, and he painted all of this during the spring festival." 102 103

The king was then enjoying himself at one of his literary salons when the son of one of his ministers found an opportunity to say to him:[55] 104

"My lord, I suspect that man is a spy sent by the king of Sinhala. He has managed to stay in Chandaleha's house thanks to his artistic skills. These kinds of spies, who reside in royal courts under such pretexts, are popularly known by the name of *yakṣas*."[56] 105 106

Then, my dear, the king replied: "Vijaananda has already been dispatched to the lord of Sinhala, together with the chief minister Pottisa.[57] As of today, however, nobody has come back from his camp to tell me truly what either the lord of Sinhala or his general has to say." 106a 106b

"Just today," said the minister's son, "our scouts report that Vijaananda and Pottisa have reached the ocean's shore with a large army.[58] Meanwhile the lord of Sinhala, too, has begun war preparations. In high spirits he has filled his forts with grain and fuel. He has created obstacles on the seashore and sought out locations for fighting. He is fearless and eager for a great battle with Vijaananda." 107 108 109

११० भणिअं च राइणा पिअवअंस सो च्चेअ तत्थ पत्तट्ठो ।
विजआणंदो णिअसंधिविग्गहे किं इमेणम्ह ॥

१११ जेणण्णे वि महामंडलाहिवा णिब्भआ वि भेसविआ ।
सो किं विजआणंदो वंचिज्जइ सिंहलेसेण ॥

११२ अणवेलं साहिज्जसु एअं तुह हेरिएण जं सिट्ठं ।
एसा रमणीआ मअणचच्चुरी ताव वोलेउ ॥२३

११३ एवं भणिऊण णराहिवेण सव्वाण वारविलआण ।
दिण्णाइँ महूसविआइँ बंदिणाणं च बहुआइं ॥

११४ तह संमाणिअणीसेसपणइसंतोसवसपसण्णमुहो ।
विण्णत्तो सुअणु पुरोहिएण उवसप्पिऊण पहू ॥

११५ देव सुमज्झणसमओ सज्जं चिअ मज्जणं विसूरेइ ।
दिअवरसत्थो दारे तुह णिच्चणिवेसिएक्कमणो ॥

११६ अह सो विसज्जिआसेसपणइपडिवण्णमज्जणारंभो ।
संचलिओ बंदिणसअसमूहकअजअजआसद्दो ॥

34

"My friend," said the king, "military operations are in the   110
  competent hands of Vijaananda alone. What concern
  are they of mine? He has struck fear into the hearts   111
  of other supposedly fearless kings, the heads of large
  alliances. Is this lord of Sinhala going to make him
  tremble? Find another time to tell me the news from   112
  our spies. Right now, let's enjoy this breathtaking
  dance for the love god while we can."[59]

With this, the king turned to bestow gifts on his   113
  courtesans and singers for the spring festival. Once   114
  the king's face showed he had honored all suppliants
  to his satisfaction, his household priest quietly
  approached and informed him:

"My lord, it is now midday. Your bath is already prepared   115
  for you, and there is a crowd of hungry Brahmans at
  your door, waiting for their daily allowance."

The king thereupon dismissed the remaining suppliants   116
  and agreed to begin his bath. He proceeded to
  the bathing area, greeted by cries of victory from
  hundreds of singers.

११७ ताव अ संचलिअमहाणरेंदवरवाररमणिसंवलिओ ।
भडभंडभोअमीसो जाओ अत्थाणसंखोहो ॥

११८ सहसुट्ठिअणरसंमद्दणोल्लणुम्मत्थिआणणो पडिओ ।
पोक्करइ थेरभट्टो अहो विणट्टो विणट्टो हं ॥

११९ तो सो सेवावाएण विणडिओ कह वि केहिँ वि वराओ ।
उक्खित्तो पंकगओ व जरगओ राअपुरिसेहिं ॥

एत्थंतरम्मि ।

१२० अण्णोण्णमउडसंघट्टखुडिअमाणिक्कप्रअरपक्खलिओ ।
सुहरेण सरइ एक्केक्कमंगणत्थंभिओ लोओ ॥

१२१ काहि वि वरवारविलासिणीहिँ वेसा वि संठिआ पुरओ ।
पेलिज्जंति सुवल्लहजणजोगेहिं पिहुथणेहिं ॥२४

१२२ कीए वि महासंमद्दसेअतण्णाअणीविबंधाए ।
दुव्वोज्झो उज्झिअमेहलो वि जाओ णिअंबभरो ॥

१२३ णिव्विच्चालिंगणलालसाए हिअइच्छिए समावडिए ।
बहु मण्णिज्जइ कीए वि तुडिओ थूलामलो हारो ॥

१२४ कीए वि मअमआमोअमिलिअमुहलालिमउलिअच्छीए ।
लद्धावसरो वि चिरेण कह वि वोलिज्जइ पएसो ॥

१२५ इअ सण्णावाहिप्पंतपरिअणो कह वि राअभवणाहि ।
पवणासासिअहिअओ णिअआवासं गओ लोओ ॥

And in that moment there formed a crowd made up of   117
guards, jesters, and officers, with the king's beautiful
courtesans moving about on the margins.[60] The   118
sudden crush of people pushed up against an old
guard, who pitched forward on his face and started
shouting, "Help! I'm done for!" With difficulty, some   119
of the king's servants fanned him and lifted him up,
like an old bull stuck in the mud.

Elsewhere, people moved very slowly, halting in the crush   120
of each other's bodies, and tripping over the jewels
that their constant jostling had knocked from their
headbands. The large breasts of beautiful courtesans,   121
which only their lovers were allowed to enjoy, pressed
up against total strangers standing next to them. One   122
woman, glistening with sweat in the crush of people,
struggled to hold up the belt that came untied and
slipped from her wide hips. Another woman broke her   123
large pearl necklace, but was actually glad, because
the tight embrace that snapped it was what her heart
had wanted all along. Another had plenty of room   124
but still took a while to find a place in the crowd: she
closed her eyes against the bees that buzzed around
her face, drawn by the musk perfume.

Thus the servants gossiped as people returned to their   125
homes from the royal palace and the breeze lightened
their hearts.[61]

१२६ राआ वि पवज्जंतेहिँ विविहमंगलणिहोसमुहलेहिँ ।
तूरेहिँ पढंतेहिँ अ बंदिणदिअवरसमूहेहिँ ॥

१२७ सव्वाहिँ चिअ सव्वोसहीहिँ लीलाए मज्जिऊण चिरं ।
सअलसमाणिअदेवाइतप्पणो भवणमल्लीणो ॥

१२८ तत्थ वि गोभूमिसुवण्णवत्थतिलमीसिआइँ दाऊण ।
दाणाइँ दिअवराणं भोअणसालं समल्लीणो ॥

१२९ तद्देसआलिएहिँ पणईहिँ समं पसण्णमणभावो ।
भुत्तं विविहाहारं सुरसं कालाणुरूअं च ॥२५

१३० भोत्तुं तक्कालेइअपरिअणपरिआलिओ समल्लीणो ।
अंतोअत्थाणहरं विरइअअवररअणपलंकं ॥

१३१ तत्थासीणो सहिएहिँ सुकइछंदाणुवत्तिएहिँ च ।
समुअं सुहसंतुट्टो णरणाहो एक्कसरिआए ॥२६

१३२ वामकरोवग्गिअवेत्तदंडदाहिणकरोत्थअमुहेण ।
पहुहिअअभावकुसलेण दारवालेण विण्णत्तो ॥

१३३ देव दिसाविजआओ सेणाहिवई केणावि कज्जेण ।
जरकप्पडणेणवच्छो विजआणंदो दुवारम्मि ॥२७

१३४ तो तं सहस त्ति णिसामिऊण सविसाअविम्हिअमणेण ।
भणिअं अमच्चमुहपेसिअच्छिणा पुहइणाहेण ॥

For his part, the king enjoyed a long bath with all kinds   126
   of herbs, while bugles blared auspicious songs and
   groups of singers and Brahmans sang their songs.
   Once he had finished his offerings to all the gods, he   127
   returned to his palace.

There he gave gifts to the Brahmans, including cows,   128
   land, gold, vestments, and sesame. From there he
   proceeded to the dining hall. He was in good spirits   129
   as he enjoyed delicious foods of various kinds, each
   appropriate to the season, with those of his friends
   who happened to be there at the time. After eating,   130
   another group of servants accompanied him to his
   private chamber, where there was a couch fashioned
   of choice jewels.

The king was sitting there with his courtiers, poets, and   131
   servants, happy and content, when at that moment
   his doorkeeper, who knew his master's heart well,   132
   came with his staff in his left hand and his right hand
   covering his eyes, and said to him:[62]

"My lord, for some reason your general Vijaananda has   133
   returned from the campaign and is waiting at your
   door, clothed in tattered rags."

As soon as he heard this, the lord of the earth felt a shock   134
   of disappointment. He fixed his gaze on his minister's
   face, and said to him:

१३५ हंहो भट्टकुमारिल णिसुअं जं वेत्तिएण संलत्तं ।
ता किं विजआणंदो एआवत्थंतरं पत्तो ॥

१३६ णीसेसणीइसत्थत्थवत्थुवित्थारवित्थअमई वि ।
असहाओ ववगअवाहणो अ कहमागओ एत्थ ॥२८

१३६क न य भिच्चा नेह करी न य तुरया नेय पोट्टिसो मंती ।
विजयाणंदस्स कहं कह जाया एरिसावत्था ॥२९

१३७ भणिअं भट्टकुमारेण देव विसमा जअम्मि कज्जगई ।
मण्णे तहावि एसो केण वि कज्जेण संपत्तो ॥३०

किं जहा ।

१३८ परिवड्ढिअपहुसंभावणाण एवंविहे महाकज्जे ।
असमत्तपेसणाणं मरणं चिअ सहइ पुरिसाण ॥

१३९ ता जइ कहावि एसो सिंहलराआहि परिहवं पत्तो ।
ता एत्थ तुम्ह दारे णूणं णलिअइ जीअंतो ॥

१४० अह सो च्चिअ जोइक्खो णिअकज्जगईए किं विआरेण ।
आणेह मा विलंबह दीसउ ता से मुहच्छाआ ॥

१४१ तो तक्खणराआणत्तदारवालाणुमग्गसंलग्गो ।
सच्चविओ कुघडंतुत्तमंगकमलो णरिंदेण ॥

१४२ समइच्छिऊण सुंदरि आणत्तं से सुहासणं पहुणा ।
उवविट्टो भट्टकुमारिलस्स पअवेसिअच्छिजुओ ॥

१४३ अह तत्थ सुहासणकअपरिग्गहो णिज्जणं विहेऊण ।
खणमेत्तसमासत्थो सच्छरिअं पुच्छिओ पहुणा ॥

40

"Bhatta Kumarila![63] Did you hear what the doorkeeper   135
   said? Why is Vijaananda in such a state? He holds   136
   in his mind the vast expanse of all of the principles
   of statecraft. So how could it be he has come back
   here alone and on foot? He has no servants with him,   136a
   no elephants or horses. And where is the minister
   Pottisa? How in the world could Vijaananda have been
   reduced to such a state?"

"My lord," said Bhatta Kumarila, "sometimes events take   137
   a turn for the worse. If you were to ask me, however,
   there must be a good reason why he has come back.
   Why do I say so? Men whose masters have honored   138
   them by entrusting them with such monumental tasks
   prefer death to failure. So, if in fact he met defeat at   139
   the hands of the king of Sinhala, he would certainly
   not show up at your door alive."

"Well," said the king, "there is no point speculating. He   140
   himself can throw some light on what happened.
   Bring him in without delay, so I can see his face."

The king then gave the doorkeeper the sign, and he   141
   returned with Vijaananda behind him. As the king
   looked upon him, he bowed his head to the ground.
   The king embraced him, my dear, and bade him make   142
   himself comfortable. When he sat down, his eyes did
   not stray from Bhatta Kumarila's feet.[64] Once the king   143
   had gotten him to sit down and told everyone else to
   leave, he comforted Vijaananda for a moment and
   asked him earnestly:

१४४ हंहो तुह विजआणंद एत्थ एवंविहं समागमणं ।
   णीसेसजुत्तिरहिअं अहिअं हिअअं म्ह दूमेइ ॥

१४५ तो अणुअंपाणुगअं वअणं णिअसामिणो सुणेऊण ।
   परिओसवसविसट्टंतलोअणं तेण विण्णत्तं ॥

१४६ देव महंती खु कहा एसा सुमणोरहाण संभूई ।
   कोऊहलेण सीसइ अवहिअहिअआ णिसामेह ॥

"Vijaananda, seeing you come here like this breaks   144
     my heart, especially because you came with no
     explanation."

When he heard these words of sympathy from his master,   145
     his eyes opened wide with delight, and he responded:

"My lord, it is really a long story, full of wishes that remain   146
     unfulfilled. I will be glad to tell you, and you should
     give it your full attention."[65]

१४७ मलआअलाहिवे वसिकअम्मि समिअम्मि पंडिराअम्मि ।
पारद्धे रअणाअरपरपारुत्तारपरिअम्मे ॥

१४८ भणिअं अमञ्चुसिरिपोट्टिसेण मा ता करेह परिअम्मं ।
सहस त्ति दंडसज्झो ण होइ अम्हं सिलामेहो ॥

१४९ सामण्णो वि ण तीरइ दुग्गत्थो जोहिउं परभडेहिं ।
सो उण विहिसंपुण्णो सूरो चाई सुभिच्चो अ ॥

१५० जुत्तिण्णुओ सहम्मो अहिएहिं अलंघिओ महामाणी ।
मंतुच्छाहपहाणो दुक्खं जोहिज्जइ परेहिं ॥

१५१ णअविक्कमोवहोज्जा सव्वाण वि पत्थिवाण एस मही ।
ण उणेक्कविक्कमरसा हवंति सिरिभाइणो पुरिसा ॥

१५२ ता सामणए संते संते पुरिसाण भेअविण्णाणे ।
दाणे वि संपडंते को दंडे आअरं कुणइ ॥

१५३ जं जह कमेण भणिअं पुव्वाअरिएहिं अत्थसत्थेहिं ।
तं तह पडिवज्जंता सिरीए पुरिसा वरिज्जंति ॥

१५४ ता पेसिज्जउ दूओ सामेक्कालावमुहलपत्तट्ठो ।
परहिअअभावकुसलो दच्छो कालण्णुओ धीरो ॥

VIJAANANDA:
THE SHIPWRECK

Once I had brought the king of Malaya under my 147
    power, and conquered the Pandya king, I began my
    preparations for reaching the other shore of the
    ocean.[66]

The minister Pottisa then said: "Stop these preparations 148
    at once! It will not be as easy as you may think for
    us to overcome Silameha by force. Even an ordinary 149
    enemy, if he is well fortified, is hard to defeat in battle.
    But Silameha is no common enemy. He is favored by
    fortune, brave, and generous, with loyal servants.
    He is strategic and principled. His great confidence 150
    is well earned: Many are those who have failed
    to overcome him. He values good counsel and
    determination above all. It would be difficult for his
    enemies to conquer such a man. All rulers must use 151
    both policy and valor if they aim to conquer the world.
    Those concerned only with valor never enjoy true
    success. But if one can practice conciliation, knows 152
    how to sow dissent, and has resources for bribery,
    he has no need even to consider force. Success 153
    chooses as her own those men who act according
    to the principles laid down by earlier teachers in the
    texts on statecraft.[67] So send a messenger, a skilled 154
    speaker whose every word aims at conciliation, who
    has an acute sense of the enemy's designs, who is
    adept, resolute, and ready to seize the moment.

१५५ जइ सो तेणं चिअ उअणमेइ ता साह किं पआसेण ।
वाआए जो विवज्जइ विसेण किं तस्स दिण्णेण ॥

१५६ णिसुअं च मए जह तस्स सअलजिअलोअसारसंभूआ ।
लीलावइ त्ति णामेण पिअसुआ जीविअब्भहिआ ॥

१५७ तिस्सा सुजम्मदिअहे केण वि असरीरिआए वाआए ।
देवेण समाइट्ठं सिट्ठं देवण्णुएहिं पि ॥

१५८ जह जो इमीए वरबालिआए होही वरो त्ति वरसमए ।
सो सअलपुहइणाहो लिहिही दिव्वाउ सिद्धीओ ॥३१

१५९ ता जइ कहावि सो अम्ह सामिणो तं कुमारिआरअणं ।
उवणेइ ता ण सिद्धं किं वा एत्थ म्ह पुहवीए ॥

१६० अण्णं च एत्थ एवंविहाण रअणाण भाअणोम्ह पहू ।
इअ जाणिऊण सामं तेण समं बहुमअं अम्ह ॥

१६१ तं तह सोऊण मए अमच्चसिरिपोट्टिसाहि णीसेसं ।
भणिअं अलं म्ह दूएण ता सअं चेअ वच्चामो ॥

१६२ सो जेण मज्झ दंसणसिणेहसंभावणापरिग्गहिओ ।
देइ च्चिअ मह पहुणो तं णिअअकुमारिआरअणं ॥

१६३ भणिअं पुणो वि सिरिपोट्टिसेण एवंविहम्मि कज्जम्मि ।
ण विरुज्झइ तुह गमणं सिंघलदीवाहिवाहुत्तं ॥

If he can win him over, then tell me, why expend your   155
efforts on this operation? Why waste poison on a man
who can be undone by words?

"On top of that, I have heard he has a daughter, dearer to   156
him than life, the essence of the whole world of living
beings. Her name is Lilavai. On the day of her birth,   157
a god foretold in a disembodied voice, interpreted
by the soothsayers, that whoever this beautiful girl   158
chooses as her husband will, when the time comes,
rule the whole earth and gain supernatural powers.   159
So if the messenger can somehow win over this jewel
of a princess for our master, there will be nothing
on earth we will not have achieved. What is more,   160
the king already thinks our master would be a fitting
recipient for a jewel of this kind, so a policy of
conciliation toward him seems best."

When I heard everything the minister Pottisa had to say,   161
I replied: "There is no need for us to send a messenger.
I shall go myself. If I can gain an audience with him   162
and win him over with affection and respect, he will
hand over that jewel of a princess to my master on
the spot."

"With something so important as this at stake," Pottisa   163
replied, "I will not stand in the way of your going to
the king of Sinhala yourself."

१६४ अह एवं बहुसो मंतिऊण गोसम्मि णिअअकडआओ ।
संचलिओ परमेसर परिमिअपरिवारपरिअरिओ ॥

१६५ तो तं सिरिकुलभवणं महुमहवासं दिसावहूणिलअं ।
भुवणपरिहाणिबद्धं व साअरं झत्ति संपत्तो ॥

१६६ पडिच्छंदं पिव गअणंगणस्स वसुहावरोहसिचअं व ।
रिद्धिं व महापलअस्स जम्मभूमिं व भुवणाण ॥

१६७ दट्ठुं तमंबुरासिं णरवइ परिचिंतिअंम्हि हिअएण ।
दुक्खुत्तारो एसो जह भणिओ पोट्टिसेण म्ह ॥

१६८ दीसइ पडुपवणुग्गअपडिरवपडिपुण्णदसदिसाअक्को ।
हलंतुव्वेल्लमहल्ललहरिमालाउलोल्लोलो ॥

१६९ णिंतच्छरो वि रामाणुलंघिओ णिव्विसो वि विसमइओ ।
करितुरअवज्जिओ वि हु पडिरक्खिवअमिहिहरुग्घाओ ॥

१७० असुरो वि सआ मत्तो मत्तो वि अमुक्कणिअअमज्जाओ ।
मज्जाअसंठिओ वि हु विरसो वि सवाणिओ च्चेअ ॥

Thus, Your Majesty, I took counsel with him for a   164
    while, and then I departed from our camp at dawn,
    accompanied by a select group of men.

It was not long before I reached the ocean, ancestral home   165
    of Lakshmi, abode of Vishnu, where the women of the
    directions retire, like a moat built around the world,
    or a mirror image of the sky's expanse, or a skirt over   166
    the earth's hips, or the darkness stored up for the final
    annihilation, or the birthplace of the worlds.[68]

When I saw the ocean, my lord, I thought to myself:[69]   167
    "It is nearly impossible to cross, just as Pottisa told
    me. It seems to fill the farthest reaches of the sky   168
    with the howling of its fierce winds, and it heaves
    constantly with the gathering and breaking of its
    immense waves. Although the *apsarases* have left it,   169
    it is still crowded with beautiful women—or rather,
    Rama has crossed it. Although it is free of the cosmic
    poison, it is still made of poison—or rather, made
    of water. Although its elephant and horse, Airavata
    and Ucchaihshravas, left it long ago, it still protects
    the great king, Indra—or rather, it gave aid to the
    mountain, Mainaka.[70] Although it no longer has any   170
    liquor, it is always drunk. And though drunk, it never
    transgresses its limits. And though it stays within its
    limits, it engages in trade—or rather, although it has
    no taste, it is full of water.[71]

१७१ साहेइ जम्मि अज्ज वि पअडो पवअवइसाहसुप्फालो ।
महिमंडलग्गहत्थो व्व रामचरिआइँ सेउवहो ॥

१७२ दीसंति सिरिसुवासहररइअकुसुमोवआरसारिच्छा ।
वेलावणवीइविइण्णरअणघडिआ तडुच्छंगा ॥३२

१७४ अज्ज वि तडिविअसिअसुरहिकुसुमसंदोहवासिआसेहिँ ।
वारुणिविणिग्गमो केसरेहिँ साहिज्जए जम्मि ॥

१७४ लक्खिज्जइ अज्ज वि गुंजिरालिउलवलअवाउललएहिं ।
महणुत्तिण्णेरावणमग्गो सत्तच्छअतरूहिं ॥

१७५ सेविज्जइ सरसोहंसकणइभवणेसु सिद्धमिहुणेहिं ।
जम्मि लवंगेलावणपरिमलपरिवासिओ पवणो ॥

१७६ तत्थ सुरासुरसिरमउडकोडिपरिहट्टपाअवीढंकं ।
रामेसरं णमेऊण जाणवत्तं समारूढो ॥

१७७ अकुलीणे वि सुअम्मे चलणविहूणे वि दच्छपअगमणे ।
बहुगुणमए वि लहुए णीरप्पणए वि बहुसंगे ॥

"To this day, there is an enormous causeway that tells the 171
   story of Rama, as if it were the hand of the southern
   mountain range, pointing out the determination of
   the monkey king.[72] Its sloping shores are scattered 172
   with gems that were tossed up by waves into the
   brush, as if they were flowers strewn on the ground to
   decorate the bedroom of Lakshmi.[73] To this day, the 173
   kesara plants that blossom along the shore and fill the
   air with the fragrance of their flower clusters tell the
   story of how liquor first emerged from the ocean.[74]
   To this day, the *saptaparṇa* trees, their branches 174
   weighed down with thick bands of buzzing bees,
   mark out the path of Indra's mount, the elephant
   Airavata, produced by the churning of the ocean.[75]
   There, in huts made from tender sandalwood saplings, 175
   the *siddha* couples enjoy the wind, suffused with
   fragrances from groves of clove and cardamom."[76]

With these thoughts in mind I bowed to Rameshvara, 176
   where the pedestal below his feet had been worn down
   by the crowned heads of the myriad gods and demons
   who had bowed before him, and boarded my vessel.[77]

What can be well-born in a bad family? What moves 177
   legless on nimble feet? What is rich in virtue but
   poorly thought of? What has many affairs but no
   affection? That ship: for it was not bound to the land,
   it was well covered, it had no legs, it moved adroitly
   over the water, it had many ropes, it was swift, it led us
   through the sea, and it was crowded with men.[78]

१७८ तो परिमिअपरिवारो आरूढो एरिसम्मि बोहित्थे ।
जा लंघिमो ण उअहिं ता णरवइ एक्कसरिआए ॥

१७९ उम्मूलंतो थलतरुवणाइँ आसामुहाइँ पूरंतो ।
संखोहंतो दीवंतराइँ उद्धाइओ पवणो ॥

१८० तो सो तुंगअराणिलसंखोहिअजलपणुल्लणुल्लसिओ ।
पुव्वोवहि संपत्तो गोलासरिसंगमं पोओ ॥३३

१८१ तत्थ वि विसमसिलाअडसंचुण्णिअसंधिबंधणो सहसा ।
सअखंडविसंघडिओ असमंजसकज्जबंधो व्व ॥

१८२ भिण्णम्मि तम्मि पोए सव्वेहिँ वि जाणवत्तिएहिँ अहं ।
एक्कफलए णिसण्णो गोलामुहदारमुवणीओ ॥

१८३ तत्थ लवणंबुणिब्भरसोत्तुव्वत्तंतविम्हलंगेण ।
ते जाणवत्तिआ पुच्छिअ म्हि साहेह को कत्थ ॥

१८४ सिट्टुं च तेहिँ णरवइ अहोमुहत्थं विसण्णवअणेहिँ ।
तं तुम्ह परिअणं भट्टउत्त कालेण परिगिलिअं ॥

१८५ किं कीरइ हअदेव्वाहि जेण तुम्हंविहा वि सप्पुरिसा ।
पावंति अहम्मजणोइआइं वसणाइँ संसारे ॥

१८६ ता वच्च सरीरधणाण होंति सुलहा पुणो वि सव्विहवा ।
तं जह झीणो वि ससी पावइ तं चेअ चिररिद्धिं ॥

१८७ एवं णरणाह णिसामिऊण तडिवडणदूसहं वअणं ।
कहकह वि मए मच्चुमुहाहि विणिअत्तिओ अप्पा ॥

Such was the ship I boarded with just a few companions. 178
    But before we had crossed the ocean, Your Majesty,
    all of a sudden a storm broke out, uprooting trees on 179
    the shore, filling the sky as far as the eye could see,
    and washing out the eastern islands. Our ship was 180
    driven on the wind-whipped waves all the way to the
    Godavari River delta in the eastern sea. There the 181
    ship's hull was smashed on the shore's rugged rocks,
    and it broke into hundreds of pieces, like a poorly laid
    plan come to ruin.

When the ship was destroyed, I clung to a single plank 182
    with all the members of my crew, and I drifted to the
    mouth of the Godavari River. The surges of the briny 183
    sea tossed my limp body ashore, and I asked the crew
    who had survived. They lowered their heads, Your 184
    Majesty, and with despair on their faces, they said to
    me:

"Death has swallowed up those companions of yours, good 185
    sir. What can be done? For it is due to cruel fate that,
    in samsara, disasters that ought to befall the wicked
    afflict men as noble as yourself. You must go on. Those 186
    who emerge from disaster alive can easily regain their
    former eminence, just as the moon, however thin it
    gets, always regains its former splendor."

The words I heard from them, Your Majesty, were more 187
    unbearable than a lightning bolt. Only with great
    difficulty could I turn myself back from the jaws of
    death.

१८८ परिचिंतिअंम्हि णो ते सहाइणो णेअ ईहिअं कज्जं ।
ण अ सो णिअवक्खेवो ण सामिसंभावणा ण जसो ॥

१८९ ण तहा पहाणपरिअणविणासदुक्खं पि दूमए हिअअं ।
जह हिअअसमीहिअकज्जणिफ्फलो मह समारंभो ॥

१९० पहुपेसणपत्तदृढा पारद्धणिरालसेक्कणिव्वहणा ।
परितुलिउव्वूढभरा अण्णे च्चिअ के वि ते पुरिसा ॥३४

१९१ अम्हारिसेहिं कत्तो णअपोरिसबुद्धिदेव्वरहिएहिं ।
सिज्झंति महीवइणो एद्दहमेत्ताइँ कज्जाइं ॥

१९२ परिभाविऊण तह वि हु संसारसुहासुहाइँ णिअहिअए ।
बहु मण्णिअंम्हि बोहित्थिएहिं जं तं समुल्लविअं ॥

१९३ कुग्गामकाहिलाहिँ वि उवएसो आवईसु को लहइ ।
बुडुंताण तणाइँ वि हत्थवलंबत्तणमुवेंति ॥

१९४ ता गंतूण सकडअं पुणो वि अण्णेहिं णिअसहाएहिं ।
पारद्धकज्जणिव्वहणणिच्छए सज्जिमो अप्पा ॥

१९५ एवं विच्छूढविसाअणिच्चलं णिअमिऊण णिअहिअअं ।
संचलिओ बोहित्थिअवअणुवइट्टेण मग्गेण ॥

"My companions are gone," I thought to myself, "and my   188
    task has come to ruin. Nor can my master's approval,
    or my own reputation, bring me consolation. Even the   189
    pain of losing my closest friends does not torment my
    heart as much as failing at the task I had undertaken,
    and which I earnestly hoped to accomplish. Rare   190
    indeed are those who receive a charge from their
    master with skill, who carry through what they have
    started with energy, who test the burden's weight and
    then lift it high. But how is someone like me—with   191
    no plan, no courage, no intelligence, and no fortune—
    supposed to carry out the king's ambitious designs?"

Nevertheless, as I kept revolving in my mind the   192
    vicissitudes of samsara, I eventually came around to
    what those sailors said to me. Why did I, one might   193
    ask, in a moment of crisis, take the advice of some
    fishermen from the middle of nowhere? If you're
    drowning in a well, you'll grab onto a clod of grass
    if you have to.

"I need to go back to my camp immediately," I thought,   194
    "and then the rest of my companions and I will ready
    ourselves to finish the task we started."

Thus I pulled myself together, casting off my heart's   195
    despair, and I set off on the road pointed out by the
    crew.

१९६ एलावणलवलिलवंगपरिमलालिद्धपाअवणिउंजं ।
परिलंचिऊण जलणिहिकूलासण्णं वणुद्देसं ॥

१९७ संपत्तो सरलतमालतालपीआलसालसंछण्णं ।
पुण्णाअणाअकेसरजंबुकअंबंबणिउरुंबं ॥

१९८ तं सत्तमुहविहत्तंबुणिवहणिद्धोअकलिमलुप्पंकं ।
कहकह वि देव सुइरेण सत्तगोदावरीभीमं ॥

१९९ सत्तासासाइअसाअराए गोलाए अवहिओ खेओ ।
गरुए वि महावसणे सहवाससमागआ सुहआ ॥

२०० जच्छंदमज्जणुज्झिअपरिस्समो तं पिणाइणो भवणं ।
भवभूअभआवहरं अल्हीणो तक्खणं चेअ ॥

२०१ सच्चविओ सअलसुरासुरेंदंसिरमउडपडिअचलणजुओ ।
तिउरंधअगअमअणंगणासणो गिरिसुआदइओ ॥३५

२०२ तं तिउणतिवेअतिमंततइमअं तिअसवंदिअंघिजुअं ।
थोऊण जोअसत्थत्थुईहि भावेण सूलहरं ॥

VIJAANANDA:
AT SATTAGODAVARI BHIMA

I passed a thicket of trees, draped by the thick fragrance   196
      of cardamom, *lavalī,* and cloves, and at long last I
      reached a patch of forest right next to the seashore.
      Pine, *tamāla,* palm, *priyāla,* and *sāla* trees offered   197
      shade from above, and below there were clusters of
      puṃnāga, nāgakesara, jambū, kadamba, and mango
      flowers. That, my lord, was Sattagodavari Bhima,   198
      where the dirt that is the impurity of the dark age is
      washed away by the river's stream as it split into seven
      mouths.[79]

My pain was washed away by the Godavari River where it   199
      reaches the ocean with its seven mouths. Friends will
      come to keep you company even in the most grievous
      calamity.

I bathed in its waters to my heart's content, and with   200
      my strength restored, I proceeded to the temple of
      bow-bearing Shiva, which allays the fears of all the
      world's beings. The next instant, I beheld Parvati's   201
      husband, the diadems of all gods and demons piled
      at his feet, the destroyer of Tripura, Andhaka, the
      elephant demon, and the body of the love god.[80]
      With hymns of praise from the sacred texts of yoga,   202
      I praised him sincerely, the one who embodies the
      three cosmic qualities, the three holy Vedas, the three
      sacred formulas, and the Triad, whose feet are praised
      by the gods, who bears the trident.[81]

२०३ अल्हीणो एक्कं एक्कदेससुहसंठिएक्कपासुवअं ।
परलोअपहणिवेसं व मणहरं वरमढाअअण्णं ॥

२०४ ता तत्थ सिअजडाहारविणअवेवंतकंधराबंधो ।
वअपरिणामोहामिअलाअण्णविओइआवअवो ॥

२०५ सुब्भब्भधवलभूईपसाहिओ अक्खमालिआहरणो ।
दिट्ठो भद्दासणकअपरिग्गहो णग्गपासुवओ ॥

२०६ तो तेण कअपणामस्स मज्झ वेत्तासणं समाइट्ठं ।
अह तत्थ सुहासणकअपरिग्गहो पुच्छिओ कुसलं ॥

२०७ कत्तोहिंतो तुम्हे समागआ कत्थ चिंतिअं गमणं ।
भणिअं च मए भअवं सुतित्थजत्तापसंगेण ॥

२०८ ता तेण समं बहुसो जाओ सत्थत्थसंकहालावो ।
चिरपरिचिओ व्व सो मे सणेहभावं समोइण्णो ॥

२०९ ताव अ णहंगणद्दुवहसंठिए देव दिअसणाहम्मि ।
भणिओ हं तेण महामहेसिणा साअरं बहुसो ॥

२१० एत्थम्हेहि महामइ फलमूलाहारिणो दुपव्वइआ ।
ण उणेत्थ तुम्ह जोग्गो आहारो कह वि संपडइ ॥३६

२११ तह वि हु मुहुत्तमेक्कं उवरुज्झह जा इमाओ भमिऊण ।
आणेमि किं पि विसहह साहीणं भोअणं जं म्ह ॥३७

I came upon an unusual but charming monastery that 203
could have been the entrance to the next world. In
one of its corners I saw a naked Pashupata ascetic
seated on a throne.[82] His neck was bent down and 204
quivering under the burden of his gray locks of
matted hair. Decrepitude had overtaken his limbs,
driving out the beauty of youth. His body was covered 205
with cloud-white ash, and he wore a string of *rudrākṣa*
beads.[83]

I greeted him, and he invited me to sit down on a wicker 206
stool. Once I had made myself comfortable, he asked
after my health.

"Where have you come from? What made you decide 207
to come here?" "Your holiness," I replied, "I just
happened to be making a pilgrimage to this holy
place."

Soon I found myself discussing religious and philosophical 208
topics with him at length. He showed me such
kindness as I would have expected from an old friend.
We talked, my lord, until the lord of the day had 209
traveled halfway through the expanse of the sky. Then
the great sage very politely said to me:

"I am a poor renunciant, wise one. I live on roots and 210
fruits. I am afraid you will not find the kind of food
you are used to here. Still, if you just wait a moment, 211
I will go and bring you some of the food that is
available. Please excuse me."

२१२ एवं वोत्तूण गओ अञ्झासण्णेसु पाअवतलेसु ।
तत्थ मए सच्चविअं अइट्ठउव्वं महच्छरिअं ॥

२१३ अद्दंसणाए णरवइ फलेहिं विविहेहिं वणसईए सअं ।
भरिअं भिच्छावत्तं ण तवाहि दुसंपदं किं पि ॥

२१४ अह तेणाहं णरवइ कअकरणीएण ताइँ सरसाइं ।
पाअवफलाइँ सव्वाअरेण भुंजाविओ तत्थ ॥

२१५ अह णहअलट्टभाअट्ठिअम्मि सहस त्ति दिअसणाहम्मि ।
सविसाअं तेण महामहेसिणा णे पुणो भणिओ ॥

२१६ इह भट्टउत्त णिवसइ रअणिअरो भीसणाणणो णाम ।
सो मं एक्कं मोत्तुं ण देइ अण्णस्स ओवासं ॥

२१७ ता किं पुण्णेहिं विणा एक्कं पि णिसं सुहेण ओवासो ।
लब्भइ तुम्हेहिं समं जहिच्छिअं इह भवाअअणो ॥

२१८ एसो वि सअलभुवणंतरालकम्मेक्कसक्खिणो भाणु ।
अइतोरविअतुरंगो पेच्छत्थइरिं समल्लिअइ ॥

२१९ मूलपरिमिलिअरविअरसमोसरंती उ परिचअंति व्व ।
जणिणिप्परिहोज्झं संपइ त्ति तरुणो णिअच्छाअं ॥

२२० गिरिणो दिणपरिणइसमअपिंजराअवपसंगपिंगंगा ।
पेरंततरुवणंतरिअकणअरूअ व्व दीसंति ॥

२२१ दिअसावसाणिसिसिरत्तणेण चिरवूढसरसगुरुपंका ।
आमुक्कमज्जणा संचरंति वणसेरिहसमूहा ॥

With these words, he went around to the bases of nearby 212
    trees. And there, to my amazement, I saw something
    I'd never seen before. An unseen forest goddess, Your 213
    Majesty, personally filled up his begging bowl with all
    kinds of fruits. There's nothing that austerities can't
    achieve. Then, Your Majesty, he fulfilled his duties 214
    of hospitality by very courteously offering me those
    delicious fruits to eat.

Suddenly the lord of the day was in the eighth part of the 215
    sky, and the great sage addressed me again, this time
    with foreboding:

"A night-stalking demon named Bhisananana lives in 216
    these parts, good sir. He suffers no one to stay here,
    apart from me. So, as much as I would like to have 217
    you stay here with me in Shiva's temple, even a single
    night's rest will be impossible without good karma.

"Look how the sun, who alone sees everything that 218
    happens in all the worlds and the sky, is driving
    his horses toward the western mountain. As his 219
    rays fall on the tree trunks, the trees seem eager
    to leave their retreating shadows behind, knowing
    there will be no one to enjoy them at night. As the 220
    evening's reddish glow falls upon the mountains
    and tints them, they seem to shine with gold
    between the patches of forest surrounding them.
    The evening chill drives the buffalo herds from the 221
    water, after spending the day covered in thick mud.

२२२ एक्कं चिअ सलहिज्जइ दिणेसदिअहाण णेहणिव्वहणं ।
आ जम्म एक्कमेक्केहिँ जेहिँ विरहो च्चिअ ण दिट्ठो ॥३८

२२३ अहवा किं बहुणा झूरिएण हिअइच्छिआइँ लोअम्मि ।
पुण्णेहिँ विणा ण हु संपडंति सइ सज्जणाणं पि ॥

२२४ इअ तेण भणामि तुमं जाव इमो दिअससेसगइसूरो ।
ताव सुवसइं दंसेमि जत्थ वसिओ सुहं जासि ॥

२२५ भणिअं च मए भअवं किं काही सो णिसाअरो मज्झ ।
एत्थ च्चिअ परिवसिमो तुम्हेहिँ समं जहिच्छाए ॥

२२६ तो तेण पुणो भणिअं अलमिमिणा जंपिएण तं तस्स ।
सीलण्णो ण महामइ तेणेम्वविहं पअंपेसि ॥

२२७ परिअरिओ रअणिअरो रअणिअरभडाण दससहस्सेहिँ ।
सो णिसिसमए दिअवर देवाण वि दुज्जओ समरे ॥३९

२२८ एत्थम्ह समासण्णं अच्झुंतमणोहरं सुकुसुमलअं ।
सुप्फलिअपाअवं वरविहंगरुअमुहलिअदिअंतं ॥

२२९ विविहतरुकणइकिसलअणिरंतरंतरिअतरणिकरणिअरं ।
जक्खमहेसिसुआणं कण्णाण तवोवणुज्जाणं ॥

२३० ता तत्थ महाणुमई णामं जक्खाहिवस्स पिअतणआ ।
तावसवेसणिसण्णा ण आणिमो केण कज्जेण ॥

२३१ बीआ वि तारिसि च्चिअ सुतावसी कुवलआवली णाम ।
विहिणो विण्णाणवडाइअ व्व धूआ महामुणिणो ॥

What can compare to the love shared between sun and day? From the very beginning, they have never known a moment's separation from each other. 222

"Well now, why get upset about it? In this world, no one, no matter how good, gets what they want without good karma.[84] So let me suggest something to you. While it's still daylight, I will show you to a place where you can stay in comfort." 223 224

"Your holiness," I said, "what could that night-stalker do to me? I will be pleased to stay right here in your company." 225

"Please do not speak like that," he answered. "If you knew what he was really like, wise one, you would not say such things. That night-stalker has a cohort of ten thousand demonic soldiers, and when they come out at night, good Brahman, not even gods can defeat them. But very close to us here is the ashram of two girls, one the daughter of a *yakṣa*, the other of a sage. It is stunning, covered in flowers and vines, and rich in fruit trees. The call of exotic birds echoes through the sky, and the sun's rays shoot through a dense tangle of sprouting trees and vines. One of the girls, the daughter of the *yakṣa* king, is named Mahanumai. Why she is staying there in an ascetic's garb, I do not know. The other, named Kuvalaavali, is just as beautiful, the creator's crowning achievement. She is the daughter of a great sage, and an impressive ascetic 226 227 228 229 230 231

२३२ ताणेक्कमेक्क दोण्हं पि णेहसंदाणणिअलिअमईणं ।
समसोक्खदुक्खसंभावणाए दिअहा अइक्कंति ॥

२३३ ता एहि जा ण रुज्झइ इमाण वअपरिणआण अच्छीण ।
तिमिरेण दिट्ठिपसरो ताव तुमं ताण देसेमि ॥

२३४ वसिऊण जेण वच्चसि रत्तिं सहस त्ति लद्धवेसंभो ।
हिअइच्छिअं पएसं कुमरीण तवोवणाहिंतो ॥

२३५ अह तेण समं णरवइ संपत्तो तं तवोवणुज्जाणं ।
जं पेच्छिऊण पम्हुसइ सुरवरिंदो वि सट्ठाणं ॥

२३६ तत्थुच्चफलिहपरिवेसविरइआणेअरअणराइल्लं ।
परिसरतरुकुसुमामोअवासिआसामुहाहोअं ॥

२३७ वेरुलिअखंभतोरणविणिवेसिअसालहंजिआणिवहं ।
वज्जेंदणीलमरगअमणिमंडिअथूहिआबंधं ॥

२३८ बहुविहमहग्धमाणिक्ककिरणविच्छुरिअदारमुहसोहं ।
विदुमविचित्तसोवाणराइसुणिबद्धसंचारं ॥

२३९ कलहोअविणिम्मिअवसहमंडवासण्णणंदिमहआलं ।
दिट्ठं अइदृउव्वं भवाणिभवभवणमइरम्मं ॥

in her own right. Their hearts are bound fast by their 232
love for each other. They pass their days sharing each
other's pleasures and pain. Let us go, then. I must 233
show you to them before night covers the vision of
these age-worn eyes with darkness, so that you can 234
stay the night there and immediately proceed, fully
rested, from the girls' ashram to wherever your heart
desires."

Then, Your Majesty, he and I reached the grounds of 235
that ashram. Indra himself would forget all about
heaven if he saw it. There I saw an absolutely beautiful 236
temple of Bhavani.* Its crystal-clear enclosing walls
were tall and shone with hundreds of inlaid jewels;
the fragrance of the flowers of the trees planted
around it wafted as far as the eye could see; a group 237
of *śālabhañjikās* were cut into the beryl pillars of the
outer gateway;[85] diamonds, sapphires, and emeralds
adorned its main tower; on the temple doorway 238
precious rubies scattered rays of light; steps decorated
with coral formed its entryway; Nandi and Mahakala† 239
took their place in a bull-pavilion made of gold.
I never saw anything like it.[86]

---

* Parvati, wife of Shiva.
† Two doorkeepers of Shiva.

जं तं

२४० उप्पअइ व पवणुद्धुअधअवडपेहुणअपरिसरंतेण ।
उहओवासविणिग्गअतवंगपक्खाविआणेणं ॥

२४१ वाहरइ अ पिअसहअरिपरिकुविआराहणेकमहुरेण ।
णीडब्भंतरपरिभमिरविविहपारावअरुएण ॥

२४२ णिव्ववइ व वरसरिजलतुसारपरिअड्ढिआणुभावेण ।
पुरओ पइण्णकमलोवआरपवणच्छडोहेण ॥

२४३ इअ तस्स कणअदेवालअस्स दाहिणदिसाए अणुलग्गं ।
गोलाणइवअणविसेसअं व रम्मं मढाअअणं ॥४०

२४४ तस्सिं च विविहवरकुसुमरेणुरंगावलीविराअंते ।
माहविलआविआणअलमणहरे मणिसिलावट्टे ॥

२४५ उवविट्टं दिट्टं तावसीअणं हरहुआसखविअस्स ।
अंतेउरं व कुसुमाउहस्स विरहम्मि गहिअवअं ॥

२४६ तेणं च परिगआओ तावसवेसेण दो वि दिट्ठाओ ।
अविरिक्कासणसुहसंठिआओ जक्खेसिधूआओ ॥

२४७ एस त्ति महाणुमई एसा सा कुवलआवली एत्थ ।
इअ एव विअप्पंतो अल्लीणो ताण पासम्मि ॥

With the balconies extending on either side like   240
    outstretched wings, their pennants along its edges
    fluttering in the wind like feathers, it seemed to be
    taking flight.[87] With the cooing of so many pigeons   241
    scurrying between their nests while trying to soothe
    the anger of their mates, it seemed to be talking.
    With the gusts of wind that scattered flowers before it   242
    and a cool mist from the nearby river heightening its
    solemnity, it seemed to be making an oblation.

Situated on the southern side of this golden temple was   243
    the ashram, a charming henna decoration, as it were,
    on the face of the Godavari River.

In it was a jewel-studded slab, resplendent with colorful   244
    arrangements of the pollen of so many flowers, and
    shaded by a canopy of white-blossomed lianas. There   245
    I saw seated a group of female ascetics observing their
    vows, like a harem without the flower-arrowed god of
    love—he was incinerated, after all, by Shiva's fire.

And in their midst, in the garb of ascetics, I saw two   246
    of them sharing the same seat, one the daughter
    of a *yakṣa,* the other of a sage. I guessed that the   247
    former was Mahanumai, and that the latter must be
    Kuvalaavali, and so I approached them.

२४८ तो तं तहा मुणिंदं सहसा दट्ठूण ताहिं दोहिं पि ।
आमुक्कासणसमुहं दोतिण्णि पआइँ अणुसरिअं ॥

२४९ दूरोणसिरकमलाहिँ ताहिँ तह पणमिऊण पक्खिवत्तो ।
चलणकमलाण पुरओ सुहासणत्थस्स से अग्घो ॥

२५० एवमहं पि णराहिव वाआसंमाणजणिअपरिओसो ।
उवविट्ठो दूरासण्णमणहरे मणिसिलावट्टे ॥४१

२५१ णिव्वण्णिऊण दोण्णि वि णरवइ परिचिंतिअंम्हि हिअएण ।
स कअत्थो णअणसहस्सपेच्छिरो एत्थ सुरणाहो ॥

२५२ अणिमिसणअणालोओ सुरलोओ सहइ संपइ इमाण ।
णिव्विग्धदंसणं पाविऊण जक्खेसिधूआण ॥

२५३ सारअमिअंकजोण्हाविआणसरिसेहिँ वक्कलजुएहिं ।
किंत्तिकमलाओ णज्जइ एक्कठिआओ व्व दीसंति ॥४२

२५४ तक्कालमंथणुत्तिण्णसिंधुफेणोत्था णिराहरणा ।
सा एक्क च्चेअ सिरी णज्जइ दोहाइआ एत्थ ॥

२५५ जं ण पहुत्तं से अवअवेहिँ विहिणो विणिम्मअंतस्स ।
तं थणणिहेण पुंजीकअं व बालाए लाअण्णं ॥४३

As soon as the two of them saw the great sage, they rose   248
    from their seat and took a few steps toward him. They   249
    bowed their lotus heads low in reverence to him, and
    once he was seated, they presented a welcome offering
    before his feet.[88]

In the same way I too was gratified to be honored by   250
    their words, Your Majesty, and I took my seat on that
    charming jewel-studded slab at some distance from
    them.[89]

I hardly know how to describe the two of them, Your   251
    Majesty. In this case Indra could have put his
    thousand eyes to good use.[90] Divine beings are   252
    said to have an unblinking gaze—which they could
    certainly have used then to look unhindered upon
    the daughters of the *yakṣa* and the sage. Clad in two   253
    bark garments that looked like a flood of autumnal
    moonlight, it seemed that Fame and Prosperity
    had appeared in one place.[91] Since they wore no   254
    adornments, they looked like Lakshmi at the moment
    she emerged from the ocean's foam at the time of its
    churning—except doubled.[92] It was as if the creator   255
    had balled up the loveliness that was left over from
    fashioning each girl's other parts to make her breasts.

२५६ अह एवं विम्हअगअमणस्स मह तेण ताओ भणिआओ ।
वरतावसीओ मुणिणा भणामि अम्हाण भणिअव्वं ॥४४

२५७ एसो गुणरअणमहामहोअही सअलसत्थविइअत्थो ।
विजआणंदो णामं वरविप्पसुओ सुई सुअओ ॥

२५८ एत्येक्कदेसवसिओ तुम्ह पसाएण वच्चइ पहाए ।
हिअइच्छिअं पएसं णिव्वुअहिअओ इमाहिंतो ॥

२५९ भणिअं च ताहिँ भअवं स च्चिअ भूमी सुहेहिँ सच्छविआ ।
णिमिसं पि जत्थ एए वसंति जे तुम्ह पडिवण्णा ॥

२६० तो सो दिण्णासीसो संतुट्टो पडिवहं गओ गुरुओ ।
विणएण ताण पुरओ अहं पि सुविसत्थमासीणो ॥

२६१ तो ताहिँ समं बहुसो जहोइअं पेसलं पअंपंतो ।
ताव ट्ठिओ णराहिव जाव त्थइरिं गओ सूरो ॥

२६२ केत्तिअमेत्तं संझाअवस्स सेसं ति दंसणत्थं व ।
आरूढा तिमिरचर व्व वासतरुसेहरं सिहिणो ॥

२६३ भणिअं म्ह महाणुमईए साअरं भट्टउत्त णिसुणेसु ।
एसो समाहिसमओ संपइ समुवट्ठिओ अम्ह ॥

२६४ ता तुम्हेहि महामइ सुविसत्थं कुवलआवलीए समं ।
अच्छह मुहुत्तमेत्तं धम्मकहासुहविणोएण ॥

As I sat lost in amazement, the sage addressed the two   256
    beautiful ascetic girls: "I have something to tell you.
    This man here is a great ocean, and virtues are his   257
    jewels. He knows the meanings of all the sacred texts.
    His name is Vijaananda. He is a good man, pure, son
    of an excellent Brahman.[93] He will find a place here   258
    for the night, thanks to your kindness, and in the
    morning he will proceed with a happy heart from here
    to wherever he desires to go."

"Your Holiness," they said, "if someone is a guest of yours,   259
    wherever they stay, if even for a brief moment, we
    happily regard as the entire world."[94]

Pleased, the guru gave his blessing and started on his   260
    way back. As for me, I remained seated before them
    politely, and I began to feel more relaxed.

Then, Your Majesty, I made conversation with them on   261
    various topics for quite a while, until at last the sun
    reached the western mountain. The peacocks flew up   262
    into the tops of the nearby trees, as if they were spies
    of the darkness sent to see how much twilight was left.

Mahanumai spoke to me courteously: "Please listen, good   263
    sir. This is now the hour of my meditation.[95] So please   264
    feel free, wise one, to stay here with Kuvalaavali for a
    while, and entertain each other with religious stories."

२६५ एवं भणिऊण गआ समाहिभवणोअरं महाणुमई ।
सविसेससमप्पिअहिअअभावज्झाणट्ठिआ तत्थ ॥

२६६ अह सा मए नराहिव विणओणअवअणदाविअमणेण ।
परिसंठिअवेसंभं सब्भावं पुच्छिआ सुमई ॥

२६७ भअवइ विरुद्धमेवंविहं म्ह सहस त्ति तुम्ह पच्चक्खं ।
गुरुअणकओवहासं भणिउं फरुसक्खरं वअणं ॥४५

२६८ तह वि हु तुवरेइ पणट्टसुमरणा लहुइआसअं हिअअं ।
ता जइ खेअं ण मणम्मि होइ ता कहसु किं णेअं ॥

२६९ एम्वविहे वअविहवे एम्वविहाए वि रूअसोहाए ।
एम्वविहं तवचरणं एम्वविहो तवोवणो वासो ॥

२७० तो तं सोऊण ममाहि तक्खणं खुहिअलोअणजलेण ।
सिप्पंतथणहरुच्छंगवक्कलं तीए उल्लविअं ॥४६

२७१ भाउअ किं तुह इमिणा दुस्सोअव्वेण संपइ सुएण ।
अणहिअकम्माणम्हाण हअकहासंविहाणेण ॥४७

With this, Mahanumai entered the meditation hall. There   265
    she remained, giving her heart over to concentration
    with particular skill. At that point, Your Majesty,   266
    I kept my face turned down in modesty but could not
    help but disclose what was in my heart. I put the wise
    girl at ease, and then asked her the truth.

"Your Holiness, I know that it is rude, and perhaps   267
    disrespectful to your parents, for me to speak right
    in front of you like this, all of the sudden and in such
    a rough way. Yet my heart seems to have forgotten   268
    its manners and now basely urges me to ask. So if it
    would not cause you much trouble, please tell me:
    What is this? Such a beautiful girl, at such a tender   269
    age, practicing such austerities and living in such a
    retreat—I simply do not understand."

When she heard me speak, tears at once welled up in   270
    her eyes and began to spill over onto the bark dress
    covering her breasts. She said: "Brother, what good   271
    would it do you right now to listen to the sad tale of
    two ill-fated girls, so painful as it is to hear?"[96]

२७१क भणिऊण तीए भणिअं भाउअ पढमम्मि दंसणे च्चेअ ।
तीरंति णेअ कस्स वि सहसा कहिउं रहस्साइं ॥४८

२७२ णिअसुहदुहगुणदोसा तह अ विसेसेण णिअअगुज्झाइं ।
अमुणिअसीलसहावे जणम्मि किं कह कहिज्जंति ॥४९

After saying this, she continued: "Brother, it is not as if   271a
    secrets can be told to just anyone right away, after only
    having met the person. What gives you pleasure and   272
    what gives you pain, your virtues and vices, and most
    of all your secrets—would you really speak of any of
    these to someone whose true character you do not
    know?"

२७३ तह वि जइ महसि सोउं ता सुव्वउ अत्थि तिअससुहवासो ।
कुलमहिहराण पढमो मेरु त्ति तिलोअविक्खाओ ॥

२७४ कणअसिलाअडपक्खलिअसंदणुप्पाअविम्हलंगेहिं ।
दुक्खेहिं जस्स कीरइ पआहिणं रवितुरंगेहिं ॥

२७५ हरवसइसिंगविलिहणवसपसरिअकणअरअपिसंगेहिं ।
अविहाविएक्कमेक्कं णिवसिज्जइ दिग्गइंदेहिं ॥

२७६ गरुलणहकुलिसविउडिअकणअसिलावट्टसुहणिसण्णेहिं ।
परिपिज्जइ जत्थ जहिच्छिआसवं सिद्धमिहुणेहिं ॥

२७७ छम्मुहसिहंडितंडवमणोहरुज्जाणकअणिवासेहिं ।
गिज्जइ मारुअमअमुइअमाणसं किंनरगणेहिं ॥५०

२७८ णिसुणिज्जइ जत्थ विरिंचिहंससंलावसद्दसंवलिआ ।
सत्तरिसिसामणिग्धोसमासला तुंबुरालत्ती ॥

२७९ सुविसट्टपारिआअअपसूअमअरंदमउइअपहम्मि ।
तुरिअं पिअसंगमलालसाहिं सइ गम्मइ पिआहिं ॥५१

२८० मज्जंतेरावणदाणगंधलुद्धाअआलिमुहलेहिं ।
कंचणकमलेहिं जहिं परिहावं लहइ णवर सिरी ॥

KUVALAAVALI:
THE BIRTH OF MAHANUMAI

If you still want to hear, then listen. There is a place   273
   where the gods live in peace, the foremost of the
   Family Mountains, known throughout the world as
   Meru.[97] It is encircled by the sun's horses, their bodies   274
   straining to pull his bouncing chariot as it skates over
   its golden slopes. There reside the elephants of the   275
   directions, who can hardly make out each other's
   reddish bodies amid the clouds of gold dust that
   Shiva's bull keeps spearing with his horns.[98] There the   276
   siddha couples drink as much liquor as they desire,
   relaxing on golden rock faces scored by the blades of
   Garuda's claws. There the *kinnaras,* who make their   277
   homes in the gardens where the peacock of six-faced
   Skanda dances, enchant the prancing deer with their
   singing.[99] There you could hear Tumbura improvising   278
   a tune to the accompaniment of the deep Vedic
   chanting of the seven sages, joined by the honking of
   Brahma's goose.[100] There women are always hurrying   279
   to meet their lovers along roads that are sticky
   with honey from flowers of the *pārijāta* tree in full
   bloom.[101] The golden lotuses only intensify its beauty,   280
   abuzz with bees that stop on their petals, greedy for
   the fragrant liquid flowing from the cheeks of Indra's
   elephant Airavata as he bathes.

२८१ तस्सिं पसंडिसेले दाहिणसाणूसु रिद्धिसंपुण्णा ।
सुलसा णामेण पुरी सुरेसवसईसमब्भहिआ ॥

२८२ तत्थ अ विजाहरेंदो हंसो णामेण तिअसविक्खाओ ।
तस्स वि चित्ताणुगआ पउमा णामेण पिअजाआ ॥५२

२८३ उअरुब्भवाओ तिस्सा दोण्णि सुधूआओ दंसणीआओ ।
एक्काए वसंतसिरी सरअसिरी णाम बीआए ॥

२८४ दोण्हं पि ताण गुरुअणसंपत्तसुहोवएससुहिआण ।
देवाराहणकअणिच्छआण दिअहा अइक्कंति ॥

२८५ एवं केलासमहीहरम्मि गोरीहराण सइ पुरओ ।
वीणाविण्णाणगुणोवलद्धपसराओ वच्चंति ॥

२८६ अण्णम्मि णिसाविरमे ताहिं तहिं चेअ भाउअ गआहिं ।
दिट्ठो पणच्चमाणो हेरंबो सरहसावअवो ॥

२८७ भुअइंदफणामणिकिरणजालविच्छुरिअविअडवच्छअलो ।
गंडअलपलोट्टद्दामदाणलुद्धालिरवमुहलो ॥

२८८ विसरिसकरणवसुक्खित्तथोरकरकलिअपरसुबीहच्छो ।
सवणावअंससिअसप्पविड्डुरिल्लाणणाहोओ ॥५३

२८९ णवपारिआअपल्लवपसूणमंडलिअविअडकुंभभअडो ।
दसणेक्ककोडिसंपत्तपोक्करामुक्कसुंकारो ॥५४

२९० तड्डुविअकण्णपल्लवपच्छाइअदसदिसावहाहोओ ।
पअभरपासल्लिअमहिहरेक्कदेसट्ठिअगणोहो ॥

Along the southern ridges of that golden mountain is   281
    a city named Sulasa, full of riches, surpassing even
    Indra's capital city. There lives Hamsa, king of the   282
    vidyādharas, far-famed among the gods, and his dear
    wife Pauma, who attends to all his wishes.[102] She was   283
    the mother to two beautiful daughters, one named
    Vasantasiri, the other, Saraasiri.

The two daughters lived happily under their parents'   284
    sage guidance, and they passed their days resolved
    to worship the gods. Thus they would always present   285
    themselves to Shiva and Parvati on Mount Kailasa,
    gaining access through their skill at playing the vina.

Once at dawn, brother, they went there and saw elephant-   286
    faced Heramba dancing, his arms and legs wildly
    flailing.[103] Gems in the hoods of serpents scattered   287
    beams of light across his broad chest, and he hummed
    with the sound of the bees swarming over him to taste
    the liquid running down his cheeks. He was terrifying,   288
    wielding his ax in his sturdy trunk that flew upward in
    his unseemly contortions. The white snake that hung
    from his ear made his whole face horrifying. He wore   289
    a crown around his head made from fresh shoots and
    blossoms of the *pārijāta* tree, and his trunk, glancing
    the tip of his one tusk, let out a hiss. His flapping   290
    ears covered the whole expanse of the sky, and his
    pounding feet pushed down the mountain and forced
    all of Shiva's attendants to the opposite side.

२९१ तो तं सव्वाअरसुहपणट्टिरं भअवअं गणाहिवइं ।
उवहसिउं सरअसिरीए सणिअसणिअं समुल्लविअं ॥५५

२९२ उअ अम्महे इमाए विरूअसोहाए णच्चइ गणेसो ।
देवा वि अप्पसंभावगव्विआ केण वि गुणेण ॥५६

२९३ तो तेण सोवहासं वअणं उवलक्खिऊण कुविएण ।
सरअसिरीए अदअं दिण्णो सावो गणेसेण ॥

२९४ जह वच्चु दुव्विणीए णिवससु पच्चंतमाणुसे लोए ।
पावेसु जोव्वणुम्माअतुंगतरुणो फलं पावे ॥

२९५ तं वज्जवडणसविसेसदूसहं गअमुहाहि सोऊण ।
दुव्वअणं भअवसवेविराहिँ सो ताहिँ विण्णत्तो ॥

२९६ भअवं तिलोअपूइअ मा कुप्पसु परिअणो खु णे तुम्ह ।
ता किर कुडिलेण विणा ण विरुज्झइ गुरुअणे हासो ॥

२९७ णेत्थम्ह भावदोसो उवहसणिज्जो तुमं ण लोअस्स ।
कीस मुहा णिअसंकप्पलहुअभावं समुव्वहसि ॥

२९८ कस्स तुमं उवहासो को वा सो तिहुअणे वि जो तुम्ह ।
अहिअअरो अहिभूसण जेणम्हविहाओ सावेसि ॥

२९९ जह णम्ह भावदोसो ईसिं पि सुरासुरेंदणअचलण ।
तह होज्ज साणुअंपो जम्मे जम्मे तुमं चेअ ॥

When Saraasiri saw Lord Ganesha giving himself over   291
     completely to his wild dance, she laughed and
     whispered: "Do you see the way Ganesha is dancing?   292
     He looks so strange! Even the gods, it seems, will
     think they are great at anything they do."

Her insult did not escape Ganesha, who flew into a rage   293
     and put a cruel curse on Saraasiri: "How rude!" he   294
     said. "Go and live in the world of wicked men below,
     where you can reap the fruit of the tree of wanton
     youth."

Hearing these dreadful words of Ganesha, more   295
     unbearable than a lightning bolt, they addressed him,
     trembling with fear: "Your Holiness, revered in all   296
     three worlds, do not be angry. Indeed, we are your
     servants, and they say there's nothing wrong with
     having a laugh with one's betters, so long as there's
     no malice. We certainly have no such feelings, and it   297
     is impossible to ridicule you in any case. It would be
     pointless for you to bear such meanness in your heart.
     Who would ridicule you? Or who in all three worlds,   298
     lord adorned with snakes, could surpass you, that you
     should curse girls like us? The gods and demons alike   299
     bow down to you. Since we have no hurtful feelings
     at all toward you, we beg you, show us mercy in birth
     after birth."

३०० अह ताण दोसरहिअं हिअअं उवलक्खिवऊण तक्कालं ।
तक्खणणिअत्तरोसेण पभणिअं विग्घणाहेण ॥

३०१ जह वच्च मच्चुलोए वि तंसि हिअइच्छिआइँ सोक्खवाइं ।
पाविहिसि माणुसाओ सरअसिरि मह प्पसाएणं ॥

३०२ जइआ विज्जाहरसिद्धजक्खवगंधव्वमाणुसाणं च ।
एक्कत्तो संवलिआण वअणकमलाइँ पेच्छिहिसि ॥

३०३ तइआ विमुक्कसावा पुणोवि विज्जाहरत्तणं पुत्ति ।
लहिहिसि एवं भणिए अद्दंसणमुवगआ बाला ॥

३०४ इअरा वि भअवआ गअमुहेण भणिआ मअच्छि मा रुअसु ।
हिअइच्छिअं वरं तं पि मह पसाएण पाविहिसि ॥

३०५ एवं सा लद्धवरा वि कुलहरं णिअसहोअरीविरहे ।
दुक्खेहिँ सदुक्खं भट्टउत्त रुइरी गआ बाला ॥

३०६ दूराओ च्चिअ दट्ठूण सहिअणं गुरुअणं च रुइरीए ।
सिट्ठं माआपिउणो णीसेसं गअमुहुल्लविअं ॥

३०७ तं तह सोऊण विमुक्कबाहधारं सुपडिरुअंतेण ।
भणिअं हंसेण अहो ण तेण जुत्तं कअं पहुणा ॥

३०८ जं तीए बालभावाविसट्टबुद्धीए मुद्धकुमरीए ।
उवरि णिहित्तो सावो जाणंतेणावि गणवइणा ॥

३०९ अहवा ण तस्स दोसो एअं सहस त्ति दुकअकम्मफलं ।
परिणमिअं सरअसिरीविओअदुक्खच्छलेणम्ह ॥

Recognizing their hearts were pure, Ganesha, lord of 300
obstacles, his anger at once assuaged, said to them:
"Go to the world of mortals, Saraasiri, and there by 301
my favor you will obtain the happiness your heart
seeks from a man. When you look upon the lotus faces 302
of *vidyādharas, siddhas, yakṣas, gandharvas,* and men,
all gathered in one place, then you will be freed from 303
this curse, my child, and become a *vidyādhara* once
again." When he finished speaking, the girl vanished.

Lord Ganesha then addressed the other one: "Doe-eyed 304
girl, do not cry. By my favor you will obtain the wish
you most cherish in your heart."

Despite the gift of a wish, good sir, she returned to her 305
house weeping, deeply pained by separation from her
sister. From a distance she saw her friends and elders, 306
and through her tears she told her mother and father
everything Ganesha had said.

When he heard her tale, King Hamsa, too, broke into tears 307
that streamed down his face. "Oh!" he cried, "what
the lord has done is not right. Ganesha knew full well 308
that his curse fell on a simple girl, a child, really, when
it comes to her judgment. Or perhaps it is no fault of 309
his, but rather the effects of our bad karma, coming
due in the form of painful separation from Saraasiri."

३१० एवं भणिऊण चिरं सच्चुविअं बाहमइलिअकवोलं ।
वअणं घणघडिअमिअंकबिंबसरिसं सजाआए ॥

३११ भणिअं च पिए किं सोइएण इमिणा असोअणीएण ।
जं जह भविअव्वं होइ तं तहा देव्वजोएण ॥

३१२ किंतु अजुत्तं कीरइ तं चिअ अम्हेहिँ मूढहिअएहिं ।
अणुसीलिअं फलं तेण अज्ज एवंविहं पत्तं ॥

३१३ सव्वाउ च्चिअ कुमरीओ कुलहरे जा ण होंति तरुणीओ ।
ताव च्चिअ सलहिज्जंति ण उण णवजोव्वणारंभे ॥

३१४ ता देमि वसंतसिरी कस्स व सच्चुविअगुणविसेसस्स ।
वामाहि वि वामअरो वच्चइ जा णम्ह हअदेव्वो ॥

३१५ ण उणो धूआए समं चित्तक्खणअं जणस्स जिअलोए ।
हिअइच्छिओ वरो तिहुअणे वि दुल्हो कुमारीणं ॥५७

३१६ एवं बहुसो परिजंपिऊण सविसेसवड्ढिअविसाओ ।
गहिओ सुलसाहिवई वरलंभोवाअचिंताए ॥५८

३१७ तो तं विसण्णवअणं वरलंभोवाअवड्ढिअविसाअं ।
दट्ठूण वसंतसिरीए चिंतिअं ताव णिअहिअए ॥

३१८ ओ गरुअसिणेहोसरिअसोक्खवसकाअरेण हिअएण ।
चिंताभरं समुव्वहइ मज्झ दोसेण जं ताओ ॥५९

३१९ ता किं इमिणा दुसमीहिएण वीवाहमंगलेणम्ह ।
सव्वाइँ मि एवविहाइँ होंति सुहिआण सोक्खाइं ॥

३२० को हसइ को व गाअइ को णच्चइ को सवेइ मेहुणअं ।
सरसिसिरीए विउत्तो विरसो एसो म्ह वीवाहो ॥

With this he stared into his wife's face, her cheeks wet 310
    with tears, like the orb of the moon obscured by
    clouds. "My love," he said, "why should we grieve over 311
    what is beyond grief? Things have turned out just as
    fate would have it. It is not what Ganesha has done 312
    that is wrong, but rather what we keep doing with
    careless hearts. The results we met with today were
    long in coming.

"All girls are a credit to their parents' house until the 313
    moment they become teenagers. When that age
    arrives, it's all over. I need to bestow Vasantasiri on 314
    someone of manifest good character, lest our accursed
    fate go from bad to worse. Nothing in the whole world 315
    will drive a person quite so mad as a daughter, and
    nothing is harder to find than a man who meets with
    his daughter's approval."

After going on like this at length, the king of Sulasa was 316
    gripped with anxiety over finding a husband, and
    he fell into a deep despondency. When Vasantasiri 317
    saw his downcast face, despairing of finding her a
    husband, she thought to herself:

"Oh dear! It's my fault that my father is burdened with 318
    anxiety. His heart is apprehensive, with no room
    for happiness alongside parental love. Why should 319
    he bother with this wedding? I don't even want it
    in the first place. Joyful occasions like those are for
    people who can enjoy them. Who will laugh? Who 320

३२१ तह वि हु अप्पवसाओ ण हवंति कुमारिआओ अलमहवा ।
णिच्छिंतो ताओ दे करेमि हेरंबवअणेण ॥

३२२ जं तं तइआ भणिअं देवेण दआलुणा गणेसेण ।
तस्सेसो संपइ वरसमीहणोवट्टिओ कालो ॥

३२३ ता किं बहुएहिँ मि चिंतिएहिँ णलकूवरो वरो होउ ।
वित्ताहिवस्स तणओ गअमुह मह तुह पसाएण ॥

३२४ तो सो हेरंबवरप्पहावपक्खित्तविअसिअमुहस्स ।
हंसस्स धणअतणओ सहस त्ति उवट्ठिओ हिअए ॥

३२५ तो मित्तबंधुपरिअणमएण सा तेण तस्स णिअतणआ ।
णलकूवरस्स दिण्णा समुअं विज्जाहरेंदेण ॥

३२६ तेणावि तस्स पिउणा सप्परिओसेण वित्तणाहेण ।
पडिवज्जिऊण बहुसो पडिच्छिआ कुसुममाल व्व ॥

३२७ अण्णम्मि दिणे बहुविहविमाणमालाउलंबरसिरीए ।
अणुसप्पंतो सहसा सुलसं णलकूवरो पत्तो ॥

३२८ तत्थ सुरसिद्धकिंणरविज्जाहरजक्खरमणिणिवहेण ।
परिआलिओ पगिज्जंतमंगलो सुमइ परिणीओ ॥६०

३२९ अह णिव्वत्तविवाहो पडिवहगमणेक्कवट्टिअजवेण ।
कलरवरणंतकिंकिणिमुहलविमाणाण णिवहेण ॥६१

३३० संपत्तो णिअवसइं तत्थ जहिच्छं सुहं वसंतस्स ।
एस त्ति महाणुमई णामं धूआ समुप्पण्णा ॥

will sing? Who will dance? Who will tell the risqué
jokes?[104] I could not possibly enjoy the festivities
without Saraasiri. Still, it is not up to us girls whether   321
we marry or not. Enough of this. I'll use Ganesha's
promise to put my father's cares to rest. The merciful   322
lord Ganesha promised me whatever I desired, and
now is the time to use it. Why all these worries, then? I   323
choose Nalakubara, the son of Kubera, lord of wealth!
Ganesha, by your favor, let this come true!"[105]

Ganesha's promise worked its effects, and King Hamsa's   324
face lit up as Kubera's son suddenly came into his
mind. Then, with the consent of his friends, relatives,   325
and attendants, the king of the *vidyādharas* joyfully
bestowed his daughter on Nalakubara. His father,   326
the lord of wealth, gladly agreed and accepted her
like a garland of flowers. The next day, Nalakubara   327
quickly reached Sulasa, adorning the sky with all the
vehicles that followed behind him. There, good sir, he   328
celebrated the wedding, amid crowds of gods, *siddhas,*
Kinnaras, *vidyādharas, yakṣas,* and their wives, who
were all singing their blessings. Then, when the   329
wedding was over, he rushed back with even greater
speed, with a fleet of vehicles all humming, rattling,
and ringing, and reached his home. There they lived   330
together for a long time, and they had a daughter—
Mahanumai here.

३३१ किं भणइ धणअकुलसंभवा वि एवंविहे वि वअविहवे ।
णिअआआरविरुद्धं अणुहवइ इमं महादुक्खं ॥

३३२ तं जाणिसि च्चिअ तुमं सव्वाण वि दुद्धगंधिअमुहीण ।
जाअंति जहिच्छाआरमणहरा कुलहरे दिअहा ॥

३३३ जहसंठिआ जहपरिभमिअ रमिअ जच्छंद जंपिअ जहिच्छं ।
जह तह सव्वत्थ सलाहणिज्ज बालत्तण णमो ते ॥६२

३३४ जेणेसा वि जहिच्छं कणआअलमणहरेसु देसेसु ।
सहिआअणेण समअं दिअहं ण विरज्जइ रमंती ॥

३३५ अण्णम्मि णिसाविरमे भणिआहमिमीए पिअसहि अउव्वो ।
मलआअओ वि अम्हाण ता तहिं किं ण वच्चम्ह ॥

३३६ चंदणअरुसिहरारूढमाहवीवरलआअलंदोले ।
सिद्धकुमारीहि समं रमिऊण समागमिस्सामो ॥

३३७ भणिअं च मए पिअसहि इमाउ अलआउरीसआसाओ ।
अण्णो वि कोवि बहुगुणमणोहरो अत्थि उद्देसो ॥

३३८ तद्दिअसासण्णपरूढहिअअवेसंभवड्ढिअरसाए ।
सग्गो च्चिअ लहुओ सहि भणामि णिअजम्मभूमीए ॥६३

३३९ तह वि जइ महिसि गंतुं जलणिहिजलभरिअकंदराहोअं ।
लवलिलवंगेलालअवणगहणमणोहरं मलअं ॥

३४० ता जाण सुरेसदिसावहूए सूरो वि राअमुव्वहइ ।
ता वच्चम्ह पहुप्पंति जेण सव्वाइं रमिआइं ॥

KUVALAAVALI:
THE FIRST TRIP TO MOUNT MALAYA

You might ask why a girl born in the family of Kubera,   331
in the springtime of her youth, is experiencing this
enormous grief, which does not accord at all with her
position.[106] You know, of course, that young girls, the   332
scent of milk still on their breath, spend their days
at their parents' home, doing whatever they feel like
doing. Childhood, you are enviable in every respect: 333
you stay where you want, wander where you want,
play as much as you want, and say whatever you want.
Now this girl would spend the whole day playing with   334
her friends on the pleasant golden slopes.

One day, just before dawn, she told me: "Friend, we have   335
never seen Mount Malaya. Why don't we go there?
There are swings made out of *mādhavī* vines hung   336
from the tops of sandalwood trees. We can play with
the *siddha* girls there and then come back."

"My friend," I said, "could there be any place more   337
completely charming than this city of Alaka? I will   338
tell you, dear friend, that heaven itself can't compare
to the place you were born. Since that day, when
your company put my heart at ease, my enjoyment of
this place has only grown. Still, if you want to go to   339
Malaya, surrounded by coastal caves filled with the
ocean's waters, and with charming groves of *lavalī*,
cloves, and cardamom, let's go before the sun reddens   340
the eastern sky, so we can play all day."[107]

३४१ तो तोरविअविमाणाउ तक्खणं णिअसहीअणेण समं ।
संचलिआओ णहंगणसमीरविहुआलआलीओ ॥

३४२ पत्ताओ णिअअपरिणाहभरिअदक्खिणदिसामुहाहोअं ।
जलणिहिवेलारअणोवआरकअपरिअरं मलअं ॥

३४३ दिणअरफुरिअणिअंबं सिहरपहोलंतबहलतमधूमं ।
डहिऊण जअं पुंजइअ संठिअं पलअजलणं व ॥

३४४ चंदणकप्पूरलवंगसंगसिसिरेहिँ णिज्झरजलेहिँ ।
वडवाणलपज्जलिअस्स जलहिणो कुणइ सेअं व ॥

३४५ गुरुसिहरावडणविसट्टुणिज्झरप्पवहसीअरच्छाओ ।
सहइ सिलाअलसंघाअघोलिरो तारआणिअरो ॥६४

३४६ अंतोरमंतसुरसिद्धमिहुणमहुलेसु जत्थ ण विसंति ।
पत्तललआहरेसुं लज्जाअंति व्व रविकिरणा ॥

३४७ सेविज्जंति विअंभिअणिअडाअवभअभुअंगमामुक्का ।
आसण्णदिणहरोहंसपाअवा सिद्धमिहुणेहिं ॥६५
अवि अ ।

३४८ सुरवहुकड्ढिअहिअकुसुममुक्कपलहूससंतकप्पलअं ।
चंदणविडवंदोलणसुहसीअलपसरिअसमीरं ॥६६

३४९ मरगअकडअविणिग्गअजरढत्तणणिव्वडंततणणिवहं ।
फलिहसिलाअलपसरिअफंसमुणिज्जंतणइसोत्तं ॥

३५० जलहरजलविच्छोलिअसुहिअसुहासीणमुणिअणसमूहं ।
सिहरंतरिअणहंगणपच्छाइअदसदिसाहोअं ॥६७

So we set out that very moment with all our friends, our   341
    vehicles speeding, and our hair blowing in the wind
    of the open sky. We reached Mount Malaya, which   342
    occupied the whole expanse of the southern sky and
    which was surrounded by gems scattered upon the
    ocean's shore.[108] With the sun blazing at its base, and   343
    its peaks like rolling pillars of dark smoke, it seemed
    as if the fire of doomsday stood in a ball after burning
    up the world. As the submarine fire heated up the   344
    ocean, Mount Malaya seemed to be cooling it down,
    spraying the essence of sandal, camphor, and cloves
    from its waterfalls.[109] The stars that swirled around   345
    its rocky ridges seemed like mist from the streams
    cascading down from its massive peaks. The rays   346
    of the sun couldn't break into its leafy bowers, as if
    ashamed to hear the moaning of the divine *siddha*
    couples within. As the sun fell on its sandal trees, the   347
    intense heat drove out the snakes within, leaving the
    siddha couples free to enjoy them.[110]

What's more, the wishing-trees were stripped bare no   348
    sooner than they blossomed by *apsarases* who made
    off with all their flowers; the wafting breeze, after
    coursing through bowers of sandal trees, was cool to
    the touch; its grassy meadows, growing in emerald   349
    valleys, could be seen only when they dried up; its
    rivulets, running over riverbeds of crystal, could
    be known only by touching them; sages gathered to   350
    perform group sacrifices, taking their ritual baths
    in the cool water of the clouds; its peaks blocked

३५१ इअ विविहमणहरुज्जाणकणइभवणालिरइअपेरंतं ।
सुरसिद्धसुहणिवासं अच्छंतमणोहरं मलअं ॥

३५२ अह तस्स महागिरिणो णिअंबभाएक्कदेसकअसोहं ।
बहुविहतरुकुसुमामोअवासिआसं वरुज्जाणं ॥६८

३५३ सुपसत्थविविहविहगउलरावसंवलिअभमररवमुहलं ।
मुहलालिमुहविसट्टंतकुसुमवससुरहिगंधवहं ॥६९

३५४ गंधवहपरिमलालिद्धपूगसंदोहमंदवइवेढं ।
वइवेढासण्णणवंबलुंबिलंबंतकइणिवहं ॥७०

३५५ कइणिवहविहंडिअपउरफलरसासारसित्ततरुमूलं ।
तरुमूलपइट्ठिअपुप्फलाइपरिपूइआणंगं ॥

३५६ इअ विविहवेलिवेलहलपल्लवंतरिअतरणिकरणिअरं ।
रइवम्महवासहरं व मणहरं महिहरुज्जाणं ॥

the open sky and obstructed the horizons in all
directions.[111] Such was Mount Malaya, encompassed   351
by all kinds of beautiful gardens and bowers of vines,
where gods and *siddhas* lived, charming beyond
measure.

Adorning one of the slopes of that vast mountain was a   352
wonderful garden that filled the sky with the fragrance
of flowers of trees of all kinds.[112] It was alive with the   353
calls of the most brilliant birds joining the humming
of bees, bees humming as they opened up blossoms
with their mouths and perfumed the breeze, the   354
breeze bringing a scent that hung over the stands of
areca trees that formed an enclosing fence, and atop
this fence were heavy bowers of mango trees where
troops of monkeys hung, and these troops of monkeys   355
were breaking open the mango fruits and raining juice
on the base of the tree, and at the base of the tree
some girls, while out picking flowers, had set up an
image of the god of love to worship.[113] Such was the   356
mountain's charming garden, where the sun cast its
beams through the soft and tangled vines. It was as if
the god of love and his wife, Rati, made it their home.

३५७ तस्स वि मज्झुद्देसे विचित्तमणिकुट्टिमंगणं भवणं ।
जं पेच्छिऊण देवा वि णिअघराणं विरज्जंति ॥

३५८ तस्स भवणस्स पुरओ मणहरमणिकुट्टिमे सुहासीणा ।
उज्जाणवणसिरी विव एक्क च्चिअ बालिआ दिट्ठा ॥७१

३५९ वीणाविणोअवसवलिअकंधरुद्धच्छिपेच्छिरीए तहिं ।
सच्चविअं म्ह विमाणं णहमग्गपरिट्ठिअं तीए ॥

३६० भणिअं च णिबद्धंजलिपणामपडिवण्णहिअअसब्भावं ।
अब्भुट्ठाणमविम्हरिअविणअमहुरक्खरं वअणं ॥७२

३६१ अवअरह भअवईओ णिअपअकमलोवआरकअसोहं ।
पेच्छह एअं उज्जाणभवणं णंदणवणं व ॥

३६२ तो तीए वअणपरिओसवसविअंभंतभाववेसंभं ।
हिअअं चिअ अवअरिअं पच्छा सणिअं विमाणं म्ह ॥

३६३ अह तत्थ सुहासणकअपरिग्गहं भट्टउत्त अम्हेहिं ।
सा पुच्छिआ जुआणी सुंदरि साहेह का तं सि ॥

३६४ कस्सेसो विविहविचित्तपत्तविच्छित्तिपलहुओ हत्थो ।
कस्स व इमाउ वरवलईओ सुसराउ दीसंति ॥७३

३६५ कस्स व णीसेसकलाकलावसंसूअआइं एआइं ।
वत्तणफलआइं विचित्तवत्तणावट्टलिहिआइं ॥७४

३६६ कस्स व इमाइं दरिआरिदप्पदलणोइआइं दीसंति ।
विविहाउहाइं सुंदरि चंदणचच्चिक्करइआइं ॥

In the center of the garden was a building, its courtyard 357
   paved with colorful precious stones. Even the gods
   would forget about their homes if they saw it. And 358
   sitting in the charming courtyard in front of this
   building I saw a girl who could have been that garden's
   forest goddess. At that moment she was playing the 359
   vina. As she turned her neck and cast her glance
   upward, she saw our vehicle stopped midair. She 360
   showed her goodwill to us by bowing with folded
   hands, then rose and said these words, sweet and by
   no means lacking in politeness:

"Your Holinesses, please come down and visit this garden 361
   home, which is like the Nandana grove in heaven
   itself. You will make it even more beautiful with the
   offerings of your lotus feet."

So pleased we were to hear her words that our hearts, 362
   swelling with friendship, descended even before our
   vehicle.

Then, good sir, we accepted the comfortable seats that 363
   were offered to us and asked the young woman:
   "Please tell us, beautiful girl. Who are you? Who 364
   does this hand belong to, skilled in drawing intricate
   henna designs? Who do these beautiful lutes we see
   here belong to, with their lovely notes? Who do these 365
   gaming boards belong to, their surfaces painted with
   intricate patterns, which hint at mastery of all the fine
   arts? Who do all these weapons we see here belong to, 366
   beautiful girl, daubed with sandal paste and capable

३६७ कस्स व एसो दीसइ सरजंते सुअणु पोत्थअणिहाओ ।
कस्सेअं साहसु विस्सअम्मवासं व वरभवणं ॥

३६८ तं तह सोऊण ममाहि तीए भाउअ पुणो समुल्लविअं ।
भअवइ सुणेह सीसइ जइ तुह कोऊहलं एअं ॥

३६९ एत्थत्थि मलअमहिहरिसिहरोवरि सुप्पबद्धपाआरा ।
बहुविहतरुकुसुमामोअवासिआसेसपेरंता ॥

३७० सिद्धंगणाणणंबुरुहसिरिविलासोवसोहिअणिवेसा ।
अमरजणलोहणिज्जा महापुरी केरला णाम ॥

३७१ तत्थ सुराहिवई विव सिद्धाहिवई तिलोअविक्खाओ ।
मलआणिलाहिहाणो मेरु व्व अलंघिअत्थामो ॥

३७२ तस्स वि चित्ताणुगआ कमला णामेण पढमपिअजाआ ।
तिस्सा एक्को च्चिअ माहवाणिलो णाम पिअतणओ ॥७५

३७३ तस्सेअं उज्जाणं विज्जाभवणं विणिम्मिअं पहुणा ।
मलआणिलेण पिअसुअसिणेहसंबद्धहिअएण ॥७६

३७४ अहमेत्थ तस्स उज्जाणवालिआ माहवीलआ णाम ।
आजम्ममेक्कपंसूपकीलिआ णवर तेण समं ॥७७

३७५ एवं सोऊण मए भणिआ सा भट्टउत्त धण्णासि ।
जिस्सा मलअणिवासम्मि एरिसी सामिसंपत्ती ॥

३७६ भणिअं पुणो वि माहविलआए भअवइ तुमं पि साहेह ।
के तुम्हेत्थम्हाणं सहलीकअजीअलोआओ ॥७८

of destroying an enemy's pride? Who does this 367
collection of books here on the stand belong to, lovely
girl? Tell us, who does this excellent house belong
to, which seems like the home of Vishvakarman,
craftsman of the gods, himself?"

When she heard this, brother, she addressed me: "Listen, 368
Your Holiness, and I will tell you, since you are so
eager to know. Here, above the peaks of Mount 369
Malaya, there is a large and well-fortified town which
makes all the surrounding areas fragrant with the
scents of various plants, where homes are beautified 370
by the flirtatious looks upon the *siddha* women's faces,
and which even the gods long for. It is called Kerala.[114]
There reigns Malaanila, king of the *siddhas,* who is 371
as famous throughout the three worlds as the king of
the gods, and steadfast as Mount Meru itself. His first 372
and dearest wife, who is close to his heart, is called
Kamala, and she has just one son, called Mahavanila.
King Malaanila's heart is full of affection for his 373
beloved son, and so he built for him this garden and
house of learning. My name is Mahavilaa, and I am the 374
keeper of his garden. He and I used to play together
from our earliest days."[115]

When I heard this, good sir, I told her she was lucky to 375
live on Mount Malaya with such a master. "Your 376
Holiness," Mahavilaa continued, "please tell me now
who you are, who have made this life of mine worth
living."

३७७ सिट्टुं च मए तिस्सा सुंदरि एवंविहाउ अम्हे वि ।
अंदोलणसुहकोऊहलेण मलअं पवण्णाओ ॥

३७८ तो तीए सरहसुप्फुल्लणअण्णवअणाए अम्ह उल्लविअं ।
एसो सो दोलहरो रमह जहिच्छाए ता एणिहं ॥७९

३७९ ताव महाणुमईए सहसा भणिआओ णिअवअंसीओ ।
अंदोलह ता तुम्हेत्थ होइ जेणम्ह परिवाडी ॥

३८० तो पढमअरंदोलणदोहलआलुंखिएक्कभावाहिं ।
परिआलिज्जइ छणवम्महो व्व बालाहिं दोलहरो ॥

३८१ कीए वि पढमसंगममणोरहुक्कंठिआए व पिआए ।
अक्कम्मइ पेम्मपरव्वसाए दइओ व्व दोलहरो ॥८०

३८२ सो तीए सुरअरसलालसाए मज्जाविऊण तह रमिओ ।
जह अण्णाण वि बहुसो विसेसरमिअव्वओ जाओ ॥

३८३ इअ वारोसारंदोलिरीहिं भणिअं चिरेण अम्हं पि ।
रमिअं एत्थ जहिच्छं संपइ दे रमह तुम्हे वि ॥

३८४ ता अम्हेहिं वि भाउअ तत्थ जहिच्छाए कीलिऊण चिरं ।
आसीणाओ तहिं चिअ पुणो वि मणिकुट्टिमुच्छंगे ॥

"Beautiful girl," I said to her, "We are just as you see. We   377
    came to Mount Malaya because we were eager to
    enjoy a ride on the swing."

At this, her mouth and eyes immediately opened wide.   378
    "The swing is right here!" she told us. "Please enjoy it
    as long as you like."

Mahanumai wasted no time in telling her friends: "Go   379
    ahead and play, and we'll take turns!"

Then all of the girls suddenly wanted nothing more than   380
    to be the first to have a ride. They gathered around the
    swing and pushed it back and forth, as if it were the
    god of love at the spring festival.[116] One girl seemed   381
    as if she were impatient to make love for the first time:
    She climbed up on the swing like a woman mounting
    her partner, beside herself with desire. The way she   382
    played with the swing—bringing it down and back up
    again, completely lost in ecstasy—made the others
    want to play with it all the more. Thus they took   383
    turns on the swing. "We've been playing for a long
    time," they said. "Now you should play for as long as
    you want!" Then I took my own turn on the swing,   384
    brother. I played to my heart's content, then sat down
    again on the jeweled mosaic floor in the courtyard.

३८५ जा इर मुहुत्तमेत्तं वीसमिउं पडिवहं पवज्जामो ।
तो सो सिद्धकुमारो तत्तो च्चिअ आगओ सहसा ॥

३८६ तो सव्वाहिं मि सव्वाअरेण एसो त्ति सो भणंतीहिं ।
सच्चविओ जक्खकुमारिआहिं कोऊहलेण चिरं ॥

३८७ तो पढमपरोक्खणुराइरीहिं बालाहिं सच्चविज्जंतो ।
अल्लीणो मह माहविलआए समअं समीवम्मि ॥८९

३८८ तो दूरकअपणामो भाउअ भणिओ मए वि सो तत्थ ।
होहि जहिच्छिअकामो जिअसु चिरं बंधवेहिं समं ॥

३८९ भणिअं च तेण भअवइ जं महसि तुमं म्ह किं पि तं होउ ।
णूणं सव्वाइँ मि मंगलाइँ अज्ज म्ह जाआइं ॥

३९० अज्जे अज्ज कअत्था एसा तिअसेसरस्स वि दुलंघा ।
जो तुम्ह चलणकमलोवआरराअंकिआ भूमी ॥

३९१ एवं तेण भणंतेण तत्थ वलिअच्छिणा मुहं दिट्ठं ।
सहस त्ति महाणुमईए साहिलासच्छिविच्छोहं ॥

३९२ ववएसविवत्तंतेक्खणेत्तपेरंतपेच्छिअव्वेहिं ।
पुणरुत्तं तेण सकोउएण दिट्ठा महाणुमई ॥

३९३ तं च सविलासकोमलघडंतपडिलक्खलोअणं दिट्ठं ।
दट्ठूण महाणुमईए रूवसोहा समारूढा ॥

३९४ ता फुरिअविलासं सुंदरं पि सविसेससुंदरं जाअं ।
किसलअपसाहिआए सकुसुममंगं लआए व्व ॥

३९५ आणंदबाहपरिपूरिआइँ जाआइँ तक्खणं चेअ ।
अवसाअसलिलसित्ताइँ कुवलआइं व णअणाइं ॥

After resting for a bit we started on our way back, when at   385
    that moment, and from that very direction, the *siddha*
    prince appeared. The *yakṣa* girls all took notice. "It's   386
    him!" they said earnestly, and they fixed their eager
    gaze on him for a long while. The girls were staring   387
    at him as if they had fallen in love even before seeing
    him. He came straight to me and Mahavilaa.

Then, brother, I bowed to him at a distance and said: "May   388
    all your wishes be granted, and may you and your
    relatives live long!"

"Your Holiness," he said, "may what you have wished for   389
    me really happen. As a matter of fact, everything that
    could go right for me today already has. My lady, this   390
    land is difficult to reach even for Indra, the lord of the
    gods. But today your feet have blessed it, transferring
    their color, red like an offering of lotuses, to its
    surface."[117]

As he spoke, his eyes turned to the side, and at that instant   391
    he saw Mahanumai's face, her eyes darting nervously
    with desire. He managed to sneak eager glimpses of   392
    Mahanumai from time to time, glancing at her out of
    the corner of his eye on some pretext or other. And   393
    when he saw Mahanumai return his glances, her gaze
    gracefully and delicately meeting his own, she looked
    even more lovely. She was beautiful, but this flash of   394
    playful grace made her far more so, like a flowering
    bud on a tendril-laced vine. At that moment her eyes   395
    suddenly filled up with tears of joy, like water lilies

३९६ पसरइ विसट्टपम्हंतरालपरिलुलिअतारआहोआ ।
हिअआहिलाससुहतरुलअ व्व परिकोमला दिट्ठी ॥

३९७ पुणरुत्तमुम्मुहा होंति सज्झसूसासपाविअविसेसा ।
थणआ लज्जोणअवअणकमलउण्णामणत्थं व ॥

३९८ णिअआवेअपणोल्लणविसमसमुव्वेल्लमाणपाउरणा ।
पअडंति दंसणत्थं व थणजुअं सरलणीसासा ॥

३९९ अंगं पविअंभिअपुलअजालसंगलणमासलं सहइ ।
अंतोसव्वंगविसंतदइअदिण्णुण्णइगुणं व ॥८२

४०० सेअकणोहो रेहइ भंगुरतिवलीतरंगरिंगंतो ।
लाअण्णसलिलणिब्भरथण अलसाणं व णीसंदो ॥

४०१ परिसरपरिसंठिअसहिसमूहलज्जाणिरोहणित्थामा ।
तंसवलिआ किलम्मइ वम्महपडिपेल्लिआ दिट्ठी ॥८३

४०२ पडिलक्खभग्गपसरं तस्स वि णिमिसंतरं जुआणस्स ।
पडिरक्खिअअहिअआवेअलाहवं घडइ णअणजुअं ॥

४०३ तो सो इमीए मुहअंदचंदिमासारसलिलसिप्पंतो ।
सव्वंगं रोमंचच्छलेण णेहो व्व अंकुरिओ ॥

४०४ ता दोण्हं पि परोप्परमणरक्खणधीरसंणिरुद्धाइं ।
असमत्तालोअणदोहलाइँ तम्मंति णअणाइं ॥८४

४०५ दोण्हं पि पढमदंसणवसपसरिअसरसकोमलविलासं ।
दोलाअमाणसंगममणोरहं वेवए हिअअं ॥

in the morning dew. Her delicate eyes gradually   396
opened—eyelashes spreading apart and pupils rolling
restlessly between them—as if the desire within her
heart were putting forth shoots of pleasure. With   397
each heaving, nervous breath, her breasts rose, as if
to support her lotus face cast down in modesty. She   398
was only breathing—but these breaths, heavy and
irregular, made her saree slip down and reveal her
breasts, as if she intended to show them to him. Her   399
whole body seemed enveloped in waves of sensation
that made her hair stand on end, as if expanding to
contain him as he entered into her from head to foot.
The beads of sweat trickling over the curving folds of   400
her stomach made it look as though her breasts were
pots overflowing with the water of loveliness. Though   401
the god of love was directing her gaze, it faltered and
fell to the side, unable to break through the shield of
modesty formed by her friends gathered around her.

His gaze, too, could go no further than the girls who   402
stood between them, and the very next moment it
quickened with the excitement held in his heart. He   403
felt a thrill all over his body as if love itself, watered
by the light of her moon-like face, were putting forth
its shoots. The eyes of both were gasping, yearning   404
to behold each other in full, but held back by their
resolve to keep their feelings hidden. Both of their   405
hearts skipped, filled with the sensual and delicate
play of love at first sight, but anxious about its
fulfillment.

४०६ इअ एव मए उवलक्खिऊण भणिआ हला महाणुमई ।
परिणमइ दिणं गमणम्मि सुअणु किं कीरइ विलंबो ॥

४०७ एवं भणिऊण विचिंतिअम्हि अण्णोण्णसाणुराआण ।
कज्जुज्जुआण हिअए अण्णं पासट्टिआणम्ह ॥

४०८ अह सो मए वि भणिओ कुमार एसोम्ह परिणओ दिअसो ।
को लहइ तुम्ह दंसणसुहस्स अमअस्स व पमाणं ॥

४०९ धण्णा ते जाण तुमं अहिणिसि पच्चक्खदंसणो सि सआ ।
अम्हं पि इहागमणेण अज्ज सहलो इमो जम्मो ॥

४१० ता एक्कमेक्क तुम्हम्ह वसइगमणागमेण एत्ताहे ।
अणुसीलिओ पवड्ढइ णेहो जह तह करेअव्वो ॥

४११ एत्थम्ह महादिट्ठिविसेहिं णाएहिं वोमआरीहिं ।
दूसंचारो मग्गो होही अत्थंगए सूरे ॥

४१२ तेण भअं मह हिअए परिणमिओ वासरो विसज्जेह ।
दिअसस्स को वि कालो कुमार णे संभरेज्जासु ॥⁵

४१३ भणिअं च तेण भअवइ तुम्हेहिं समं असंकिआलावो ।
पुण्णमइआण काण वि जाअइ इह जीअलोअम्मि ॥

४१४ ता अलमवरेण पअंपिएण एअं म्ह जं तए सिट्ठं ।
ता सोहणं कअं विसहराण मा भाह एत्ताहे ॥

Seeing all this, I said to Mahanumai, "Sister, the day is   406
    turning into night. What is keeping us from going
    back, my dear?"

On saying this it occurred to me that those two standing   407
    next to us, having fallen in love with each other,
    had something quite different on their minds
    and were ready to take the next step. Then I   408
    addressed him: "Prince, our time here has come to
    an end. The pleasure of seeing you is like nectar.
    Who is lucky enough to have its full measure? The   409
    ones who get to see you right before their eyes, day
    and night, are truly blessed. And we too, just in
    coming here today, have achieved our lives' purpose.
    So please, from now on, let us take great care that we   410
    visit each other to tend this love so that it will grow.
    Right now, however, the sun is setting and the sky is   411
    starting to crawl with flying serpents, the very sight
    of which is poisonous, which will make the journey
    back impossible for us. That is why there is fear in my   412
    heart. Evening is coming. Please bid us farewell while
    there is still time left in the day, prince, and take care
    to remember us."

"Your Holiness," he said, "speaking with you freely is   413
    a privilege accorded to few in this world of living
    beings, and only those who have stored up reserves of
    good karma. But enough of these formalities. What   414
    you have said has given me great pleasure. Right
    now you should have no fear of poisonous serpents.

४१५ एसो खु पुरा भअवइ देवाण वि दुक्खसंचरो मलओ ।
आसि महाविसणाओवरुद्धचंदणवणाहोओ ॥

४१६ दुप्परिहोज्जाइँ विहाविऊण ताएण सिद्धलोअस्स ।
चंदणवणाइँ अहिलंघिआइँ आराहिओ गरुलो ॥

४१७ तेणेसो मह पिउणो दिण्णो णाआरि णाम अंगुलिओ ।
गेण्हह पहवंति ण जेण तुम्ह ते विसहरा गअणे ॥

४१८ अच्छंतु ताव ते वोमआरिणो जे रसाअले णाआ ।
ताण वि विसं पणासइ दंसणवहसंठिओ एसो ॥

४१९ भणिअं च मए ओप्पह कुमार एसो इमीए कुमरीए ।
हत्थाहत्थुवणीओ णीसेसविसावहो होइ ॥

४२० एवं सोऊण सलज्जवअणसंगलिअसेअसलिलेण ।
उवलक्खवासंकणिरुद्धभावणिहुअं मणे हसिअं ॥८६

४२१ तो हत्थफंससुहलालसेण अप्पा समप्पमाणेण ।
वामेण दाहिणं पीडिऊण हत्थेण से हत्थं ॥

४२२ णिमिओ कणिट्ठजेट्टंगुलिए सुइरेण तेण अंगुलिओ ।
तह जह अम्हेहिँ मि एक्कमेक्कणिहुअं मणे हसिअं ॥८७

४२३ तो तस्स मिअंकस्स व करफंससमुग्गएण सेएण ।
ससिमणिघडिआ वाउल्लिअ व्व वारीमई जाआ ॥

४२४ तो तक्खणविविहविलाससोहसुपसाहिअं सरीरं से ।
अममअं पिव घडिअं विअंभमाणेण मअणेण ॥८८

४२५ तो सज्झसवसपरिवेविरीए अवलंबिऊण कंठम्मि ।
सा माहवीलआ भट्टउत्त भणिआ इमीए तहिं ॥

Once, in fact, not even the gods could come to Mount 415
Malaya here, because its stands of sandal trees were
all filled with enormous serpents. My father felt that 416
the *siddha* people could not enjoy its sandal groves,
infested as they were with serpents, so he worshiped
Garuda. He gave my father this ring, called Nagari. 417
Take it. Those serpents in the sky will have no power
over you. Not only the serpents in the sky, but even 418
those in the underworld will lose their poison's power
once they see this ring."

"Please offer it to her, prince," I said. "Transferred from 419
your hand to hers, it will surely protect the princess
from every kind of poison."

Although the prince was anxious to conceal his feelings 420
out of modesty, hearing this made beads of sweat
form on his forehead, betraying the delight he felt in
his heart. Then he offered her his left hand, eager for 421
the pleasure of touching hers, and took hold of her
right. While he took his time putting the ring on her 422
finger, Mahanumai and I flashed a secret smile at each
other.

Then, at the touch of his hands, she almost melted, like a 423
statue made of moonstone at the touch of the moon's
rays.[118] Her figure, already beautified by the presence 424
of every grace at once, turned into nectar from the
love welling up within.

Then, good sir, she threw her arms around Mahavilaa's 425
neck and said, shaking with disquiet:

४२६ किं भणिमो सहि सव्वोवआरणिब्बाहिरं म्ह तइँ समअं ।
हिअअं तहा वि भण्णसि एक्कसि मं सच्चविज्जासु ॥

४२७ अह साअरेहिँ बहुसो सिणेहमइएहिँ सोवआरेहिँ ।
वअणेहिँ महाणुमईए णत्थि तं जं ण सा भणिआ ॥८९

४२८ भणिअं च तीए सामिणि मा एवं भणसु मह मणो चेअ ।
तुह चलणकमलदंसणसमूसुओ कीस गरुएसि ॥

४२९ इअ एवं भणिरीए लग्गइ कंठम्मि दढअरं जा से ।
ता सो सिद्धकुमारो मण्णइ आलिंगिओ त्ति अहं ॥

४३० तो अलआगमणसुहंकरेहिँ वअणेहिँ तोसिआए तहिं ।
दिण्णो इमीए तिस्सा भाउअ थूलामलो हारो ॥

४३१ एवं तं तत्थ विसज्जिऊण माहविलअं समुच्चलिआ ।
णिअअविमाणाहुत्तं सव्वेण वि परिअणेण समं ॥

४३२ सहिअणतोरविआए वि ण चलइ समअं पहाविआ तत्तो ।
अणिअत्तंतं चित्तं पडिवालइ अणुगआ दिट्ठी ॥

४३३ मा गम्मउ त्ति उअआरकमलसंकामिलंतमुहलेहिँ ।
चलणालग्गेहिँ खणं णिरुंभमाण व्व भमरेहिँ ॥

४३४ अल्लिअइ जा विमाणं अहं पि से तं तह च्चिअ कुमारं ।
आउच्छिऊण सुइरं सहस त्ति विमाणमारूढा ॥

४३५ हिअआणुवालणाधाविएहिँ णअणेहिँ तद्दिसाहुत्तं ।
अलअं उप्पुट्ठमुहीओ कह वि अम्हेहि पत्ताओ ॥९०

108

"What is there left to say, dear friend? My heart, beyond   426
    all formality, is one with yours. Still, I ask you to give
    me your attention just once."[119]

Then, in words that were considerate, full of affection, and   427
    courteous, there was nothing that Mahanumai did not
    tell her.

"Mistress," said Mahavilaa, "don't speak that way. My   428
    heart will always be eager to see your lotus feet. Why
    are you making the situation out to be so dire?"[120]

As Mahavilaa spoke, Mahanumai clasped her even more   429
    tightly around the neck, and the *siddha* prince felt
    he himself was the one she was embracing. Then,   430
    brother, Mahanumai happily gave Mahavilaa a
    necklace of large pearls, while gratifying her with
    an invitation to Alaka. In this way Mahanumai took   431
    her leave of Mahavilaa and started back toward her
    vehicle with all her friends. But even as her friends   432
    hurried her along, her gaze did not move from where
    it was: it kept waiting for her heart, which was not
    coming back. "Don't go," the bees seemed to say,   433
    mistaking her feet for fragrant lotus flowers and
    swarming around them, momentarily blocking her
    exit. As soon as our vehicle arrived, I too said a long   434
    farewell to Mahavilaa and the prince, then quickly
    boarded. My eyes ran off in that direction to keep   435
    watch over my heart, and with my head turned back,
    I somehow made it all the way back to Alaka.

४३६ ताव अ विअडणहंगणगमणवसाआसविअलिअंसुभरो ।
णित्थामो अवरमहीहरेंदसिहरं गओ सूरो ॥

४३७ आमुक्कगअणमग्गो जणस्स दिट्टीए लंघिओ सूरो ।
सिढिलिअणिअसंठाणा गरुआ वि पराहवमुएंति ॥

४३८ अत्याअंतो वि हु अत्थसिहरिणा धारिओ सिरेण रवी ।
सूरो वि पच्छिमाए दसाए जणवल्लहो होइ ॥९१

४३९ उव्वहइ अत्थसेलो परिसरपरिसेसपलहुअमऊहं ।
परिपिंगकेसरड्डुं कंचणकमलं व रविबिंबं ॥

४४० दंसणजोग्गं पि रहंगमिहुणदुव्विसहदंसणं जाअं ।
बिंबं विअडणहासोअकुसुमगुंछारुणं रविणो ॥

४४१ णवरि अ कमेण जलणिहिवेलाजलविलुलिओ समोसरइ ।
तडपूइअरुद्दजवापसूअपुंजो व्व दिवसअरो ॥९२

110

KUVALAAVALI:
THE SUNSET

In the meantime, the sun, exhausted by its journey   436
across the wide expanse of the sky, shed its rays like
garments and, dimmed, passed over the peaks of the
mighty mountain in the west.

The sun left its course in the sky and disappeared from   437
sight: Even the mighty can lose their position and fall
into obscurity.[121]

The mountain bore the setting sun on its crest: For the sun   438
in the west is like a brave warrior, beloved by all, being
carried in his final moments.[122]

Whatever was left of the sun's rays was stretched faint and   439
thin across the sky, so that the mountain seemed to
be wearing the round flower of a golden lotus strewn
with red filaments.

The sun came to resemble a cluster of bright red *aśoka*   440
blossoms in the wide expanse of the sky. Nothing
could be more beautiful, but the pairs of *cakravāka*
birds could not bring themselves to look upon it.[123]

Finally the sun slipped away, shimmering in the waters at   441
the ocean's edge, like Rudra being worshiped on the
beach with a handful of rose flowers.

४४२ रविणिवडणविहडिअजलहिसलिलपाअडिअरअणकंति व्व ।
संगलणमासला णहअलम्मि संझा समुल्लसिआ ॥

४४३ कालपरिणामसिढिलस्स सहइ णहतरुफलस्स दिणवइणो ।
अत्थइरिसिलावडणुच्छलंतरससच्छहा संझा ॥

४४४ जाअं पविरलतिमिराणुविद्धसंझापहापरिक्खित्तं ।
मअभिण्णसामलीगंडवासकसणारुणं गअणं ॥

४४५ ओहुत्तगरुअदिवसअरबिंबभरकड्ढिआ इव मिलंति ।
गोरेणुसंवलिज्जंततिमिरकलुसा दिसाहोआ ॥९३

४४६ मुहघडिअविअडरविकणअपिंडभारोणअग्गभाएण ।
कसणतुलादंडेण व तमेण गअणे समुल्लसिअं ॥९४

४४७ जामिणिवअणं वसुआअथोअपरिकसणकुंकुमच्छाअं ।
संझावसेससंवलिअविरलतिमिरप्पहं सहइ ॥

४४८ रविकण्णिअम्मि विअडे मउलाअंतम्मि दिवससअवत्ते ।
उड्डीणभमरणिअरो व्व पसरिओ तिमिरसंघाओ ॥

112

The twilight glimmered in the sky, intense in its profusion,   442
 as if the setting sun had cracked open the ocean and
 revealed its glistening jewels.

It was as if the fruit of the sky—the sun—had ripened over   443
 the course of the day, and its juice—the twilight—
 spilled out when it fell against the western mountain.

With the spreading twilight, interspersed here and there   444
 with blackness, the sky became dark red, like liquid
 oozing from the cheeks of a black elephant, or wine
 flushing the cheeks of a dark-skinned woman.

The darkness mixed with the cow dust on the dusky   445
 horizon, which seemed to contract, pulled down by
 the heavy orb of the setting sun.

The darkness took over the sky, as if the black bar of a   446
 scale had risen up, its other end weighed down by a
 heavy mass of gold in the form of the sun.[124]

The face of the night, where faint darkness blended with   447
 remnants of twilight, took on the complexion of a
 deep-blue crocus flower that has been dried out.[125]

The mass of darkness seemed like a swarm of bees flying   448
 upward as the enormous lotus that was the day, the
 sun as its pericarp, closed up.

४४९ वेढिज्जइ णिअडोसहिविडवे व्व रविम्मि कालपरिणमिए ।
णहचंदणरुक्खो कसणविसहरेणं पिव तमेण ॥

४५० सूराअवकमलवणम्मि मउलिए फुरिअतारआकुमुअं ।
दरदिट्ठतिमिरसलिलं जाअं सरसंणिहं गअणं ॥

४५१ रविणिवडणविहडिअजलहिसलिलमग्गुग्गएण णीसेसं ।
वडवाणलधूमेण व तमेण पच्छाइअं गअणं ॥

४५२ तो सजलजलहराहिँ व विणिम्मिओ अलिउलाहिँ उप्पण्णो ।
कलअंठिकंठकसणो पवट्टिओ तिमिरसंघाओ ॥

४५३ तममअमिव गअणअलं अंजणणिम्मज्जिआओ व दिसाओ ।
कोसिअरुआणुमेअं जाअं वणराइतरुगहणं ॥९५

४५४ अह दीसिउं पअत्ता सेलंतरिअस्स रअणिणाहस्स ।
पढमुल्लसंतपरिविअडधवलरहधअवडच्छाआ ॥

The sky looked like a sandalwood tree, and the darkness a   449
    black serpent encircling it, as the sun set, a thicket of
    herbs now withered.[126]

The sky was like a pond, and when the shining sun—its   450
    lotus bed—began to close, the constellations—its
    water lilies—began to open, altogether obscuring the
    darkness—the water below.

The whole sky was covered by the darkness, as if it were   451
    smoke billowing up from the submarine fire when the
    falling sun split open the ocean's waters.[127]

As if produced by heavy storm clouds, or fashioned by   452
    swarms of bees, the darkness, black as a cuckoo's
    neck, spread all over.

The sky seemed to be made of darkness and the horizon   453
    painted with lampblack, so much so that the dense
    growth of forest trees could be recognized only from
    the hooting of owls.

Then the white luster of the moon, lord of the night,   454
    began to appear from behind the mountains where
    it lay hidden, like a white flag fluttering ahead of his
    chariot.[128]

४५५ दीसइ पेरंते तमभरस्स परितलिणससहरालोओ ।
सअणट्टिअमहुमहरुद्धसेसदुद्धोवहिजलं व ॥

४५६ उम्मुहफुरंतपविरलससिकिरणालिहणकब्बुरो सहइ ।
तमणिवहो तंसोसरिअणिज्झरो विंझसेलो व्व ॥९६

४५७ तो जाआ उअअंतरिअससहरारुणमऊहविच्छुरिआ ।
कुविआहिसारिआअंबदिट्ठिभिण्ण व्व पुव्वदिसा ॥

A small trickle of light from the crescent moon appeared   455
    at the very edge of the darkness, as if Vishnu had
    displaced a few drops from the milk ocean as he
    slept.[129]

As the darkness was streaked by moonbeams stretching   456
    toward it, it came to look like the Vindhya mountains
    with waterfalls cascading from their peaks.[130]

Then the eastern sky was perforated by the red   457
    moonbeams, still hidden behind the mountains, as if
    pierced by the angry glares of women with midnight
    trysts.[131]

४५८ एत्थंतरम्मि एसा णीसेसं सहिअणं विसज्जेउं ।
वासहरमुवगआ मअणबाणपहराउरावअवा ॥९७

४५८ ताव अहं पि चिरागमणसंकपरिवेविरेण हिअएण ।
अंबाए वसंतसिरीए पाअमूलं समल्लीणा ॥

४६० भणिआ अ पुत्ति किं तुम्ह अज्ज णिअमंदिरं पि विरिअं ।
तो कहसु कत्थ रमिअं किं वा भमिअं चिरं जेण ॥

४६१ सिट्ठं च मए अंबम्हि अज्ज मलआअलम्मि रमिआओ ।
चंदणतरुसिहरारूढमाहवीकणइडोलहरे ॥

४६२ जं तुम्ह पाअमूलं एण्हिं ण समागआ महाणुमई ।
तं सुइरंदोलणखेअसंगसुढिआइँ अंगाइं ॥

४६३ एवं सोऊण अहं अंबाए विसज्जिआ तहिं चेअ ।
णवर ण दिट्ठा एसा तत्थ मए वासभवणम्मि ॥

४६४ परिचिंतिअंम्हि अव्वो कत्तो सा मअणबाणतविअंगी ।
अच्छइ विणा वि अम्हेहिँ जाणिअं अहव किं अण्णं ॥९८

४६५ जह एवं विवससरीरचलणवलिविसमभंगुरं सअणं ।
एवं च एत्थ कुसुमोवआरमलिअं कुदेसअलं ॥९९

४६६ तह सअणाओ भूमी भूमीओ पुणो वि संगआ सअणं ।
सअणाहि वि चंदमऊहसीअलं भवणमारूढा ॥१००

KUVALAAVALI:
CONFRONTING MAHANUMAI

Meanwhile our Mahanumai, grievously wounded by love's   458
arrows, took leave of all her friends and entered her
bedroom.

Meanwhile I went to touch the feet of her mother,   459
Vasantasiri, my heart pounding at how long it took us
to come back.

"What's wrong, child?" she said. "Did you forget where   460
you live? You could at least tell me where you were
playing, and why it took you so long to return."

"Mother," I said, "we were playing on Mount Malaya,   461
on a swing made from *mādhavī* vines hung from the
top of a sandalwood tree. Mahanumai has not come   462
here to touch your feet only because she is completely
exhausted from playing on the swing so long."

On hearing this, she let me go to Mahanumai's bedroom.   463
But to my surprise, I didn't find her there. "Oh no!"   464
I thought to myself. "Where could she be? Love's
arrow must be burning her body, and I'm not even
there to help her. Wait, I think I know. What else
could it be? The bed is disheveled from her helpless   465
body's tossing and turning, and the ground is littered
with flowers. She must have gone from the bed to   466
the ground, from the ground back to the bed, and
from the bed to the roof, to be cooled by moonbeams
there."

४६७ परिचिंतिऊण एअं सिणेहवसकाअरेण हिअएण ।
बहुसो परिभावंती मणिभवणमहं समारूढा ॥१०१

४६८ ताव अ उअअधराहरसिहरट्ठिअससिमऊहभिज्जंतो ।
पइसरइ गुहाविवरंतरेसु सो तिमिरसंघाओ ॥१०२

४६९ णिम्मलताराकुसुमोवसोहिअं उअअसेलसिहराहिं ।
पसरिअमऊहवक्खो ससिहंसो णहसरं विसइ ॥

४७० दीहमुणालेहिँ व पसरिएहिँ किरणेहिँ पिअइ हरिणंको ।
भुअणंतरालसरमज्झसंठिअं तमजलुप्पीलं ॥

४७१ पिअविरहे जलणाअंति ससिअरा इअ कहेइ अम्हाणं ।
घरदीहिआए संकुइअकमलमुहमंडला णलिणी ॥

४७२ पविरलदंसणसीलेण होइ पेम्मं सुदूसहं इमिणा ।
इअ कलिऊण व णलिणी ससिसंगपरम्मुही जाआ ॥१०३

४७३ तं वम्महबाणणिसाणवट्टअं ससहरं णिएऊण ।
परिचिंतिअंम्हि हिअए विसविसमो विरहिणीण इमो ॥

४७४ तो तत्थ मए एसा दुव्विसहाणंगबाणतविअंगी ।
फलिहमणिकुट्टिमुच्छंगसंगआ झत्ति सच्चविआ ॥

४७५ उवसप्पिऊण पासं हत्थेहिँ परव्वसाइँ अंगाइं ।
परिमासिऊण भणिआ पिअसहि कीसेरिसो ताओ ॥

४७६ कीस तुमं सहि एअं सेज्जाहरअं तहिं पमोत्तूण ।
इह फलिहसिलामणिकुट्टिमंगसंगं पवण्णासि ॥

With that in mind, I climbed up to the jeweled pavilion,   467
　　my thoughts racing, and my heart faint out of sisterly
　　love. That was just about the time when the darkness,   468
　　shattered by the rays from the moon atop the eastern
　　mountain, began to retreat into the openings of caves.
　　The moon, spreading its light, swooped down from   469
　　the eastern mountain into the broad heavens covered
　　with pure-white constellations: a goose spreading its
　　wings, swooping down from the treetops into a wide
　　pond covered with water lilies. With its spreading   470
　　beams like long lotus stalks, the moon drank up the
　　darkness—streams of water in that great pond, the
　　space between heaven and earth.

The moonbeams are burning her, separated from her lover: 471
　　so the stand of lotuses in the pond reported, their
　　face-like flowers closed into buds. *She cannot bear*   472
　　to love someone she rarely gets the chance to see: so the
　　stand of lotuses seemed to say in turning away from
　　the moon. When I saw the moon, whetstone for love's   473
　　arrows, I realized how deadly it could be for those
　　suffering separation.

It took no time at all to find her there, her body tormented   474
　　by the arrows of the irresistible love god, lying on
　　a crystal terrace inlaid with jewels. I stood alongside   475
　　her, laid my hands on her helpless body, and said:
　　"Why are you suffering like this, dear friend?   476
　　Why did you leave your bedroom and come up
　　to lie on this crystal terrace inlaid with jewels?

४७७ किं वा एअं उज्जाणकुसुमसंदोहसीअलं पवणं ।
अग्घाअंती पिअसहि ऊससिअव्वं पि विम्हरसि ॥

४७८ किं वा बहुकुसुमासवपाणपमत्तालिबहलझंकारं ।
सोऊण सज्जडक्कं व झत्ति अंगं समुक्खिववसि ॥

४७९ ससहरकरणिअरालुंखिआइँ सिसिरे वि सिज्जमाणाइं ।
णिच्चेट्टाइं पओसे पिअसहि किं वहसि अंगाइं ॥

४८० सासंकमुक्कणीसाससेससंरोहमोहविवसंगी ।
किं पुणरुत्तपवत्तणविसंठुलं कुणसि सअणीअं ॥

४८१ आसण्णपरिअणालावसंकिरी किं पअंपसि मअच्छि ।
अविहाविअक्खरत्थं पडिवअणमिणं असंबद्धं ॥

४८२ बहुविहविअप्पचिंताणिफ्फंदब्भंतरुग्गअंसुजलं ।
कीस उण अणिमिसच्छं अलद्धलक्खं पलोएसि ॥

४८३ अद्धुक्खित्तविसंठुलबाहुलआमूलफुसिअपत्तंकं ।
वअणं अइरुग्गअचंदबिंबसरिसं किमुव्वहसि ॥

४८४ सरसारविंदकेसरपराअपरिपिंजरे थणुच्छंगे ।
वसुआइ दिण्णमेत्तं मअच्छि हरिअंदणं कीस ॥

४८५ इअ कीस तुमं णूमेसि मज्झ णिअहिअअवेअणावेअं ।
सीसंतं लहुईहोइ होइ गरुअं असीसंतं ॥

Were you so busy taking in the breeze, cooled by all   477
the flowers in the garden, that you've even forgotten
to breathe? Perhaps you heard the loud buzzing of   478
the bees, wild to drink the nectar of all the flowers,
and straightaway collapsed, thinking you were stung?
Why are your limbs motionless and sweating in the   479
cool night, even when bestrewn by moonbeams?
Why are you rumpling your bed by constantly rolling   480
around, gripped with delirium and choking back
anxious sighs? Why is it, doe-eyed girl, that you   481
think these servants here are talking to you, and you
reply with babble they can't make out? And why are   482
your eyes constantly staring off into space? They
are welling up with tears from a heart seemingly
transfixed by all sorts of worry and care. Why have   483
you limply cast your delicate arms above your head,
only to let them fall and smear the makeup on your
face, so that it resembles the disc of the newly risen
moon? Doe-eyed girl, why is the sandalwood paste   484
drying out as soon as you put it on your chest, which is
red with pollen from the filaments of fresh lotuses?[132]
The grievous pain of one's heart grows light when   485
told, and heavy when not. Why, then, do you continue
to conceal it from me?"

४८६ तो तं इमीए आअण्णिऊण लज्जावसोणअच्छिजुअं ।
भणिअं ण णिण्हविज्जइ किं पुण एवंविहमसंतं ॥

४८७ जं अणुइअं कुमारीअणस्स लज्जापसाहिअकुलस्स ।
तं सविसेसं पिअसहि मह हअहिअएण पारद्धं ॥

४८८ तं कह णु तुम्ह सीसइ कह व ण सीसइ असाहणिज्जं पि ।
तह वि चिररक्खिअं पि हु कहिअव्वं तुज्झ ता सुणसु ॥

४८९ तं सिद्धकुमारं पेच्छिऊण एएहिँ सहि अणज्जेहिं ।
अविणअमग्गं हअलोअणेहिँ णीअम्हि किं भणिमो ॥

४९० जाणंती वि हु पिअसहि दूरविरुद्धं कुमारभावस्स ।
तह वि हअवम्महेणं अलज्जिराणं धुरे जुत्ता ॥

४९१ जं तेण मज्झ सहि एरिसो वि सअलाहिविसविणासअरो ।
गरुलपसाओ णिक्कारणं पि दिण्णो हसंतेण ॥

४९२ तं चेअ तस्स पिअसहि उअआरमहत्तणं भरंतीए ।
सहवड्ढिआणुराआ सिणिद्धअं भावअंतीए ॥१०४

४९३ सीलं कुलं सहावं विज्जाविणअं अणूणअगुणं च ।
बहुसो परिचिंतंती अविणअमग्गं समोइण्णा ॥

४९४ ता इह तुम्हं पि असाहिऊण लज्जापणट्टसब्भावा ।
एअं चंदाणिलसंगसीअलं किर समारूढा ॥१०५

४९५ ता एएहिँ दुपेच्छेहिँ तिक्खकरवत्तवअणसरिसेहिं ।
सविसेसं संतविआ खलेहिँ सहि चंदकिरणेहिं ॥

४९६ एआओ चंदकिरणेहिं अज्ज पज्जालिआओ व दिसाओ ।
उज्जाणे गंधवहा वि अज्ज विसलेविआ एंति ॥

At this, she lowered her eyes in embarrassment, and said: 486
"I wouldn't conceal anything from you, least of all
something as bad as this. It is with their modesty   487
that young women adorn their families. Yet what my
cursed heart has begun to feel is most opposed to
this. How could I tell you? How could I not tell you,   488
however unspeakable it may be? No, I must share
with you what I have kept secret for so long. Please
listen. No sooner did they see that *siddha* prince,   489
dear friend, than these shameful eyes of mine led me
down the road to immodesty. What can I say?[133] Even   490
though I know, my friend, that I am surely too young,
that wretched god of love has made me first among
girls without shame.[134] From the moment he smiled   491
and, without any prompting, gave me this wonderful
gift—the favor of Garuda that counteracts the poison
of all serpents—I've been thinking back on his great   492
courtesy toward me. And as my attachment to him
grew, I imagined that he was fond of me too.[135] Soon,   493
constantly thinking about the way he acted, his noble
birth, his character, his learning and modesty, and his
unparalleled good qualities, I was well on the road to
immodesty. That is why I climbed up here, where it   494
is cool from the moonlight and the breeze, without
telling even you, feeling as though shame has wrecked
my very existence. And so I was tortured all the   495
more, my friend, when the moonbeams turned out
to be as sharp as saw blades. I can't bear to look at
them! They now seem to have set the horizon ablaze,   496
and the breeze from the garden now blows poison.

४९७ ता साहसु संतावो कम्मि पएसम्मि फिट्टइ गआण ।
मअणमहाणलणडिआण दुकअकम्माण अंगाण ॥१०६

४९८ भणिअं च मए पिअसहि सव्वं एवं भणंति अण्णे वि ।
एसो मअणुम्माओ ण तरिज्जइ रक्खिअउं कह वि ॥

४९९ अण्णं तं णूमिज्जइ एअं पुण सुअणु वम्महरहस्सं ।
पअडिज्जंतं ण तहा गुप्पंतं जह फुडीहोइ ॥१०७

५०० एवं भणिऊण मए भाउअ सरिसेहिँ णलिणिवत्तेहिं ।
कप्पूरोहंसमुणालसीअलं विरइअं सअणं ॥१०८

५०१ तेण वि से संताओ जा ण गओ भट्टउत्त उवसामं ।
अवलोइअं सुभीआए तो मए दक्खिणाहुत्तं ॥१०९

So tell me, where can I go, wicked girl that I am, my   497
body tortured by the blazing fires of love, to finally put
an end to this pain?"

Then I said: "Dear friend, as others have truly said, there   498
is just no way to keep the madness of love a secret.
Anything else can be concealed, but the secret of love   499
is different: it is never so plainly visible when revealed
as when kept secret."[136]

With this, brother, I made her a bed of fresh lily pads,   500
made cool with camphor, sandalwood, and lotus
stalks. But even that pained her. And while I waited   501
for that pain to subside, good sir, I gazed anxiously
toward the south.[137]

५०२ ता झत्ति णहअलागमणखेअपरिसुढिअवअणतामरसा ।
सा माहवीलआ भट्टउत्त सहस त्ति संपत्ता ॥

५०३ तो सरहसाए वड्ढाविऊण आलिंगिआ मए पढमं ।
पच्छा इमीए भाउअ पुलअणिविच्चेहिँ अंगेहिं ॥

५०४ अह तं इमीए भुअजुअविक्खेवविहित्तपल्लवं सअणं ।
माहविलआए दट्ठूण सलहिओ ताव पंचसरो ॥

५०५ पच्छा सुरपाअवकुसुमसेहरो तालवत्तलेहो अ ।
परिउट्टवअणकमलाए अप्पिओ दइअदूईए ॥

५०६ अह सो इमीए पिअअमकरकमलपसंगलद्धमाहप्पो ।
सहस त्ति सहरिसाए पओहरोवरि परिट्टविओ ॥

५०७ अह सो मए वि सहसा परिओसुप्फुल्ललोअणमुहीए ।
अणिसामिअवअणप्पाहणाए सो वाइओ लेहो ॥

५०८ सत्थि मलआअलाओ सुंदरि तुह माहवाणिलो लिहइ ।
लेहं समुच्चअत्थं भावेज्जसु किं खु बहुएण ।

५०८ इमिणा वि णवपओहरपसंगसुहसीअलेण हारेण ।
ण समिज्जइ तुहदंसणसंव्वंगगओ अणंगग्गी ॥

128

KUVALAAVALI:
A MESSAGE FROM THE PRINCE

But just as I was looking in that direction, good sir,   502
Mahavilaa suddenly arrived, her lotus face faded from
her long journey through the sky. I rushed to greet and   503
embrace her, brother, and she returned my embrace
with a thrill coursing through her body. When   504
Mahavilaa saw the blossoms strewn on the bed by
Mahanumai's flailing arms, she immediately offered
praise to the five-arrowed god of love.

She was playing the role of a messenger from Maha-   505
numai's lover, for she presented us with a crown
of flowers from the divine tree* and a letter on a
palm leaf, her lotus face blossoming with delight.
Mahanumai took it at once and joyfully clutched it   506
to her breast, thinking it beyond price because it had
touched her lover's hands. At once she read it out   507
to me, her eyes and mouth both wide with delight.
She hardly even heard the words that came from her
mouth.[138]

"Hail! Mahavanila writes this to you, my dear, from   508
Mount Malaya. Please think of this letter as the sum
of all my feelings. To get straight to the point: Even   509
this necklace, which your young breasts have made
pleasantly cool by their touch, cannot put out the fire
of love that has raged since seeing you in person."[139]

———

* Probably the *pārijāta* tree, said to grow in Indra's heaven.

५१० तं सोऊण इमीए णिहुअणिबद्धंजलीए पंचसरो ।
हिअएणं चिअ णमिओ णमंतणअणुप्पलजुआए ॥

५११ ताव अ ममं पि माहविलआए सिट्ठो कुमारसंदेसो ।
जह तुम्ह सविणअं माहवाणिलो अंब विण्णवइ ॥

५१२ ण तुअं उवआरप्पाहणाण विसओ ण लोअवअणाण ।
तह वि हु भणामि णण्णो तुम्हाण पिअंकरो अम्ह ॥११०

५१३ सो सुपएसो सो च्चिअ सुवासरो सो सुलोअणालोओ ।
सो सुमुहुत्तो जत्थ अ पुणो वि तुम्हेहि दीसिहिह ॥१११

५१४ भणिअं च मए सहि माहवीलए कहसु केण कज्जेण ।
बहु मण्णिओ अणंगो तए वि तह विंभिअमणाए ॥

५१५ भणिअं च तीए भअवइ जेण कुमारो वि तम्मि सुपएसे ।
तुम्हगुणसंकहासत्तमाणसो अच्छिओ दिअसं ॥११२

When she heard this, she quietly pressed her hands   510
    together, lowered her eyes, and did reverence to the
    five-arrowed god of love in her heart.

Thereupon Mahavilaa related to me as well a message   511
    from the prince: "Mahavanila respectfully informs
    you, madam, that though you are not to be addressed   512
    with formalities or clichés, I must nevertheless say
    that no one is as dear to me as you, and it will be a   513
    wonderful place, a wonderful day, a wonderful sight
    for the eyes, and a wonderful moment when I see you
    again as well."

"Mahavilaa, my friend," I said, "tell me, why were you,   514
    too, so happy as to give thanks to the bodiless god of
    love?"

"Your Holiness," she said, "it is because the prince, too,   515
    in that lovely place of his, spent the whole day lost in
    thought about the virtues of you both."

५१६ ता अत्थसेलसंकेअसंगसुहसमिअदिअससंताओ ।
अणुराअणिब्भरो वारुणीए अवगूहिओ सूरो ॥

५१७ जाआ सिहरसमारूढविविहविहगउलबहलिअदलोहा ।
तामसगलंतपरितलिणबद्धतिमिरा तरुग्घाआ ॥११३

५१८ संझाअवदवदड्ढुं पलित्तणक्वत्तखण्णुअं सहसा ।
तिमिरमसिमइलिआसं जाअं रण्णं व गअणअलं ॥

५१९ णिण्णासिअसअलासामुहेण उप्फुसिअलोअसोहेण ।
सहस त्ति अंतएण व तमेण गिलिअं व भुवणअलं ॥

५२० ता उवहिणिमज्जंतद्धतिअसगअकुंभविब्भमाहोअं ।
अड्डुग्गआरुणं ससहरस्स बिंबं समुल्लसिअं ॥

५२१ सुरसुंदरिसमअकवोलवासपरिपिंजरारुणच्छाआ ।
पसरइ थोआरुणमंडलस्स जोण्हा मिअंकस्स ॥

MAHAVILAA:
THE SUNSET

Then the sun's daytime burning was relieved by the 516
pleasure of meeting his beloved, the lady of the west,
at their secret meeting-place, the western mountain,
where she embraced him.[140]

Thickets of trees were filled with all kinds of birds who 517
crowded among the leaves in the upper branches, and
their shadows grew thinner until they blended in with
the darkness.[141]

At that moment the sky was like a forest burned by the 518
fire of twilight, the stars its smoldering trunks, the
horizons blackened by the ash of darkness.

Suddenly the surface of the earth seemed to be swallowed 519
up by darkness, wiping out all the directions and
snuffing out the sky's beauty, as if by death, destroying
all hope and snuffing out the beauty of mankind.[142]

Meanwhile the moon glimmered, red and half-risen, its 520
shimmering orb the cheek of the Airavata, Indra's
elephant, half-submerged in the ocean.

The disc of the moon was reddish, and the light diffusing 521
from it had the pale red glow of the cheeks of a
beautiful *apsaras* drunk on wine.

५२२ मंदरधुअजलणिहिफेणपुंजभिण्णं तमालगहणं व ।
जाअं फुरंतपविरलमिअंककरकब्बुरं तिमिरं ॥

५२३ दीसइ परिकोमलससिमऊहदंतुरिअतलिणिअतमोहं ।
कलहोअरसिअमरगअकुट्टिमभूमिप्पहं गअणं ॥

५२४ दीसइ उअअधराहरसिहरट्ठिअससिमऊहभिज्जंतो ।
दरसिढिलिअणिम्मोओ कसणभुअंगो व्व गअणवहो ॥

५२५ ताव अ सिअजरढाअंतससिअरुप्फुसिअतिमिरवडलाओ ।
जाआओ दुद्धसाअरवेलाधोआओ व दिसाओ ॥११४

५२६ दरविहडिअवअणविणिंतगंधलुद्धालिंगणसणाहाइं ।
कुमुआइँ ससहरक्कंततिमिरभरिआइं व फुडंति ॥

५२७ रअणिअरकरोवग्गणभिज्जंतुव्वरिअतिमिरसेसाइं ।
सरणागआइँ मलओ रक्खइ व गुहाहरुत्थाइं ॥११५

५२८ सअलेण भुवणपरिपाअडेण णिव्वविअसअललोएण ।
अकुणंती णलिणी चेअ वंचिआ संगमं ससिणा ॥

The darkness, broken here and there by the shining rays of   522
the moon, was like a thicket of *tamāla* trees on Mount
Mandara, covered in foam spewed from the churning
of the sea.[143]

As the soft rays of moonlight fell in thin, uneven patterns   523
through the darkness, the sky looked like an emerald
floor laced with gold.

As rays of light from the moon, standing atop the eastern   524
mountain, broke through the expanse of the sky, it
looked like a black snake in the midst of sloughing off
its skin.

Meanwhile, the thick darkness was being blotted out by   525
the rays of the steadily whitening moon, making the
horizons seem washed clean by the waves of the milk
ocean.

The night lilies began to open, as if they themselves were   526
filled with the darkness the moon had overrun, while
bees swarmed around them in pursuit of the fragrance
that came from within their still half-closed petals.

The remnants of darkness left from the moonbeams'   527
onslaught seemed to shelter in the caves of their
protector, Mount Malaya.

The day lotus alone was cheated of a reunion with the full   528
moon, seen throughout the world and showering its
beams on everyone, as if with a perfect lover, skilled in
the arts, famous throughout the world, and a delight
to all people.[144]

५२९ ता दुल्लहलंभजणाणुराअरसमउइअम्मि ओअद्धा ।
हिअअम्मि से कुमारस्स ससिअरा कुसुमबाण व्व ॥

५३० तो सो विसट्टवरकुसुमगंधविसधारिओ विअ कुमारो ।
तत्तो च्चिअ तुम्हालुंखिआए भूमीए सुणिसण्णो ॥११६॥

५३१ दूसहसंतावपरव्वसो वि तब्भूभिफंससुहलुद्धो ।
सव्वंगिअं णिसण्णो णेच्छइ णलिणीदलत्थुरणं ॥

५३२ णिज्जइ णिसाए चंदो णिसा वि चंदेण दोहि मि अणंगो ।
मअणेण वि से विरहो दूरं तेणावि संतावो ॥११७॥

५३३ सो वम्महसरपसराउरम्मि हिअअम्मि विणिहिओ हारो ।
णिव्वूढसरेण व वम्महेण पासो व्व से खित्तो ॥

५३४ इमिणा णिसाअरेण व णिसाअरेणज्ज से णिसंसेण ।
अंगाइँ तक्खणं चिअ कआइँ चम्मट्ठिसेसाइं ॥

५३५ तो सो अणिमिसिअच्छं अलद्धलक्खं चिरं पलोअंतो ।
अब्भत्थेइ मिअंकं पवणं तं चेअ उज्जाण ॥

५३६ हंहो मिअंक हो पवण हो वरुज्जाण रक्खह पिआए ।
अंगाइँ सरसतामरसपम्हमउआइँ मह हिअए ॥

५३७ तं तह सोऊण मए भणिअं सहसा कुमार अलमिमिणा ।
असमंजसेण भणिएण कत्थ सा पिअअमा एत्थ ॥

५३८ कीस तुमं अप्पाणं विम्हरिओ जेण जंपसि असंतं ।
दुल्लहलंभाइँ समावडंति कालेण पेम्माइं ॥

५३९ अण्णं च एत्थ सुव्वइ कामावत्था वि बहुविहा होइ ।
सा इर कमेण कामीअणस्स अंगे समारुहइ ॥

MAHAVILAA:
THE PRINCE IN LONGING

When the prince's heart was softened by feelings of love   529
for his far-off beloved, the moon's rays entered it like
the flower-arrows of the god of love. The fragrance   530
of the just blooming night lotuses was like poison to
the prince, and he collapsed on the ground where you
walked—ground he longed to touch though in the   531
grip of overwhelming pain. Without even spreading
a bed of lotus petals, he laid his whole body down on
it. The night brought on the moon, and the moon   532
the night, both brought on his desire, and his desire,
longing, and his longing, at last, vast pain. His heart   533
was wounded by the arrows of love, and the necklace
he wore upon it was like a net that the god of love cast
over him after running out of arrows. Then it was the   534
cruel moon that, like a demon, reduced his body to
skin and bones in an instant.

For a long time he stared with unblinking eyes into the   535
expanse, and then begged the moon, the breeze, and
the garden he was in: "Oh moon! Breeze! Beautiful   536
garden! Please keep my beloved's body, soft as fresh
lotus filaments, safe in my heart!"

At this I said: "Prince, stop this incoherent talk at once.   537
Where is that beloved of yours now? Really, have you   538
lost your mind, that you are babbling to someone who
isn't there? In time, even the most impossible love will
find fulfillment. And besides, they say that love has   539

५४० पढमण्णोण्णालोअणसंदीविअमणहिलासपरिओसो ।
परिओसाहि वि जाअइ आलावो को वि उहआण ॥

५४१ आलाववइअराणंतरं च चिंता मणम्मि संठाइ ।
चिंतिज्जंतो पसरइ सज्जीवधणुद्धरो कामो ॥

५४२ तक्कालुक्कंठाणिब्भरेहिँ परिआणिऊण कज्जगइँ ।
हिअआइँ दूइवअणेहिँ दिण्णगहिआइँ कीरंति ॥

५४३ दूइसमागमसंतुट्टुहिअअपरिभाविओ गुणुग्धाओ ।
तद्दिअसिअं गुणिज्जइ सहीहिँ समअं अणिट्टुंतो ॥

५४४ गुणकित्तणाणुराओसुआण मिहुणाण मुक्कसंदेहो ।
जो तह समागमो सो भणामि किर कस्स सारिच्छो ॥

५४५ सव्वंगणिव्वुइअरो सो अण्णो सत्तमो रसो को वि ।
आसाइज्जइ जो पढमपेमपिअसंगमाहिंतो ॥

५४६ तं सत्थेसु ण सुव्वइ अगोअरं तं महाकईणं पि ।
जं किं पि सुहं णवसंगमम्मि दइओ जणो कुणइ ॥

५४७ तह संभोअसुहाहिं मि वेसंभो होइ एक्कमेक्काण ।
वेसंभाओ णेहो णेहाओ पवड्डुए पणओ ॥

५४८ पणअम्मि पमाणपवड्डिअम्मि केणावि दिव्वजोएण ।
जो होइ विप्पलंभो सो दुसहो पेम्मपरिणामो ॥११८

५४९ तं सि उणो इह दंसणमेत्तेणं चेअ एरिसावत्थो ।
जाओ मअणमहाणलसंतावपरव्वसावअवो ॥

many stages, and one by one they overtake a lover's
body. Delight is when the glances first exchanged   540
between two people cause their hearts to glow with
a feeling of attraction. It gives rise, in both of them,
to affectionate words. After exchanging affectionate   541
words, concern arises in their hearts, and this ushers
in the love god, who arrives with his bow strung taut.
Once they are full of longing for each other, they   542
figure out their next steps, and encourage each other
by sending and receiving words through go-betweens.
In their hearts, delighted by the go-between's arrival,   543
they imagine all the good qualities of their lover, and
then they recount them ceaselessly to their friends,
day after day.[145] Constantly recounting a lover's good 544
qualities puts all doubt to rest and when the two are
finally united—what can I possibly compare it to?
What is savored when two lovers first unite in love   545
is the seventh *rasa,* something special and unique,
that produces total satisfaction.[146] The special kind   546
of pleasure a lover gives at the first union is not
described in our traditional texts, and lies beyond the
scope of even the great poets.[147] After the pleasure   547
of union, they start to feel comfortable with each
other. From comfort fondness arises, and from
fondness attachment grows. When affection reaches   548
its peak, however, some device of fate will bring about
separation, and that is the stage of love most difficult
to endure. I can tell just by looking at you that you're 549
in just such a stage right now. You have lost control of
your body to the searing pain of love's fire."

५५० तो तेणाहं भणिआ बहुजंपिरि भणसु तं सि ण गआ सि ।
थिमिआलसवलिअद्धच्छिपेच्छिअव्वाण दिट्ठिवहं ॥११९॥

५५१ जं तीए तुज्झ भणिअं तं जइ मणअंपि किं पि संभरसि ।
ता वच्च मा हु एवंविहाइँ उल्लवसु एत्ताहे ॥१२०॥

५५२ इअ एवमहं भणिऊण तेण भअवइ विसज्जिआ एत्थ ।
संपइ दिट्ठं वच्चामि तुम्ह पअपंकअचउक्कं ॥

"Keep talking, since you clearly love to talk," he said.   550
    "Here is something you haven't done: go to her
    presence, where sidelong glances fall from her glassy
    and languid eyes. Go and see if you can relate back   551
    to me anything that she tells you. In the meantime,
    please stop talking about such things."

That is what he told me, Your Holiness, when he sent me   552
    here. And now that I have seen your lotus feet, ladies,
    I will be on my way.

५५३ भणिअं च मए सुंदरि एवं णिअसामिणो भणिज्जासु ।
मज्झ वअणेण बहुसो जह सो णण्णं विअप्पेइ ॥

५५४ भण्णसि णीसेसपसिद्धसिद्धसिरमउडघडिअचलणस्स ।
मलआणिलस्स तणओ सज्जणणिसमुब्भवो तं सि ॥

५५५ एसा वि महाणुमई जम्मि कुले जाणसि च्चिअ तुमं पि ।
कं सेसं जं सीसइ वअविहवाआरसीलाण ॥

५५६ ता एसो अण्णोण्णाणुसरिसविण्णाणराअसंवाओ ।
पुण्णमइआण काण वि जाअइ इह जीअलोअम्मि ॥१२१

५५७ ता णिअताअं पडिबोहिऊण एअं कुमारिआरअणं ।
सव्वाअरं वरिज्जउ उहआण वि उहअलोअसुहं ॥

५५८ भणिअं च तओ माहविलआए अंबम्ह तुम्हि जं भणह ।
एत्ताहे देवी देउ किं पि संदेसअं पइणो ॥१२२

५५९ भणिअं च महाणुमईए ईसिलज्जापरत्तिअमुहीए ।
अइउज्जुआसि पिअसहि किमहं जाणामि संदिसिउं ॥

५६० सोक्खाइँ तुमाहिंतो तत्तो णिद्धा तुमाहि मे जीअं ।
पिअसंगमं तइंतो जं जाणसि तं कुणिज्जासु ॥

KUVALAAVALI:
A MESSAGE FOR MAHAVANILA

"Beautiful girl," I said, "please convey the following   553
message to your lord in full, and make sure that he
knows I said it, so he does not get the wrong idea:
'We are told you are the son of Malaanila, whose feet   554
are adorned by the crowns on the heads of all the
famous *siddhas,* and you are born from a respectable
mother. You already are fully aware of the family   555
into which our Mahanumai was born. What needs
to be told of the glory of her youth, her conduct,
and her character? Hence this is a perfect match of   556
intelligence and affection, a privilege accorded to few
in this world of living beings, and only those who have
stored up reserves of good karma. Therefore speak   557
to your father and marry this gem of a young woman
with all due ceremony, a source of pleasure in both
worlds for you both.'"

Then Mahavilaa said: "As madam commands us. Now do   558
you, my lady, have any message to give your husband-
to-be?"

"My dear friend," said Mahanumai, turning her face down   559
slightly in embarrassment, "you are too forward.
What message could I possibly send? On you depends   560
my happiness, my ability to sleep, my life. On you
depends my union with my beloved. You know what
you need to do."

५६१ अह एवं गहिअत्था अम्हसआसाओ सा गआ दूई ।
अम्हे वि अ तिस्सा गुणगणाणुगहणे पअत्ताओ ॥

५६२ तो ववगआए तीए बहुविहचिंताविअप्पसंधिमिओ ।
सविसेसं पज्जलिओ इमीए हिअए अणंगसिही ॥

५६३ तत्तो मुहुत्तमेत्तं णिरुद्धणीसासणिच्चलच्छीए ।
णिव्वाहिऊण भाउअ इमीए संपइ समुल्लविअं ॥१२३

५६४ सहि सिट्टं जं माहविलआए जं चम्ह तेण संदिट्ठं ।
तस्स तए अणुसरिसं ण किंचि अप्पाहिअं वअणं ॥

५६५ मा मह हआए दोसेण दूसहं माणसं वहंतस्स ।
अण्णं पि किंपि होही सविसेसं जं इमाओ वि ॥

५६६ तेणाहं पज्जाउलिअमाणसा एहि मलअसेलम्मि ।
वच्चम्ह देमि अप्पाणमप्पणो च्चेअ सहि तस्स ॥

५६७ ण सहइ कालक्खेवो हिअअं मह मअणहुअवहपलित्तं ।
तस्स वि संदेहगअं जीअं णिसुअं चिअ तए वि ॥१२४

५६८ भणिअं च मए पिअसहि णिसुअं दिट्ठं सअं च अणुहूअं ।
दुच्चरिअं हअकुसुमाउहस्स किं मज्झ साहेसि ॥

५६९ पेरिज्जंतो पुव्वक्कएहिं कम्मेहिं केहि मि वराओ ।
सुहमिच्छंतो दुल्लहजणाणुराए जणो पडइ ॥

५७० दुल्लहसमागमुद्दूमिआण कामीण जं समावडइ ।
दुक्खेण तेण परवसणपेच्छिरो डज्झउ अणंगो ॥१२५

५७१ जेहिं दइअं ण णाअं अणाअदुक्खा सुहीण ते पढमा ।
जाणं चिअ पिअविरहो जाणसु दुक्खीण ते पढमा ॥१२६

144

Then, keeping our words in mind, our messenger left our   561
    presence, and we appreciated deeply all her good
    qualities. When she had gone, the fire of love burned   562
    all the more fiercely in Mahanumai's heart, fanned by
    various worries and doubts. Then for just a moment,   563
    brother, she managed to hold back her sighs and keep
    her eyes still just long enough to say:

"Oh my friend, the message you sent back to the prince   564
    pales in comparison with what Mahavilaa said and
    the message he sent us.What a wretch I am! He is   565
    suffering this anguish because of me! I hope that
    nothing even worse than this will happen to him! I   566
    am utterly heart-sick over it. Come, let's go to Mount
    Malaya! I will give myself to him in person.The fire of 567
    love is burning my heart, and I can't bear to waste any
    time. You heard it yourself. His life, too, hangs in the
    balance."[148]

"Dear friend," I said, "I have heard and seen and   568
    experienced myself the awful things that can be done
    by the cursed god of flower-arrows. What more could
    you tell me about them? Wretched indeed is he who,   569
    only seeking his own happiness, is driven by karma
    to fall in love with someone unattainable.[149] Too bad 570
    the bodiless god himself cannot burn with the pain he
    inflicts on those tormented by unattainable unions.
    Happiest of all are those who have never known   571
    love, for they have never truly known pain. And the
    unhappiest, you must know, are those separated from

५७२ दुक्खघडिराण खणविहडिराण विरहावसाणविसमाण ।
दुप्परिअल्लाण रसं धण्णा ण मुणंति पेम्माण ॥

५७३ तह वि हु मा तम्म तुमं मा झूरसु मा विमुंच अप्पाणं ।
को देइ हरइ को वा सुहासुहं जस्स जं विहिअं ॥१२७

५७४ जह संबज्झंति गुणा अणुरज्जइ परिअणो जणो जह अ ।
जह गुरुअणो पसंसइ तह कीरउ एरिसं कज्जं ॥१२८

५७५ विरसाइँ जाइँ पमुहे अमअरसाअंति जाइँ परिणामे ।
कज्जाइँ ताइँ सुविआरिआइँ ण जणे हसिज्जंति ॥

५७६ तेण हि भणामि पिअसहि सच्छंदा होइ जा जए कण्णा ।
सा लोअणिंदणिज्जा अम्हारिसिआ विसेसेण ॥१२९

५७७ णलकूवरस्स धूआ वसंतसिरिउअरसंभवा तं सि ।
ता कह काहिसि पिअसहि जणवअणिज्जं असावण्णं ॥१३०

५७८ अप्पाणमप्पण च्चिअ दिज्जइ अपरिग्गहाहिँ वरईहिँ ।
कुमरीण महाकुलसंभवाण मग्गो च्चिअ ण होइ ॥

५७९ किं जह मए वि एअं अणुहूअं चेअ तुज्झ साहेमि ।
अवसरवडिअं पिअसहि अवहिअहिअआ णिसामेह ॥

146

their beloved. Lucky are those who have never known 572
the taste of impossible love, where lovers meet with
great difficulty, only to be torn apart in an instant and
then to suffer separation.[150] But still, you mustn't 573
give in to this anguish. Don't surrender yourself to it.
A person's pain and pleasure are preordained: who
can give it, and who can take it away? Things like this 574
should be done in such a way that your virtues will
not be compromised, your family will be pleased, and
your parents will give their approval. They should be 575
done with careful planning, so that, as distasteful as
they seem in the beginning, in the end they have the
savor of pure nectar, and they will never come in for
censure.[151] That's why I have to tell you, dear friend, 576
that girls who do whatever they feel like, especially
those of our station, will be exposed to public shame.
You are the daughter of Nalakubara, born from 577
Vasantasiri. How, then, could you do something that
goes against your birth? People will say things, dear
friend.[152] Offering yourself in marriage? That's what 578
miserable creatures do who have no prospects, not
girls born into great families. Let me tell you about 579
what I personally had to go through. The occasion has
finally presented itself, dear friend, so please listen
attentively."

५८० आसि पसाहिअचउजलहिवलअरसणावसुंधराणाहो ।
आसि पसाहिअचउजलहिवलअरसणावसुंधराणाहो ।
णिण्णासिआरिवक्खो राआ विउलासओ णाम ॥१३१

५८१ आसाअरेक्कछत्तंकवसुमई आदिवंगणालच्छी ।
आभुअणजअसिरी जस्स खग्गमग्गे चिरं वसिआ ॥१३२

५८२ सो तीए असंतुट्ठो णरणाहो एक्कभुवणलच्छीए ।
दाऊण णिअअरज्जं णीसेसं दिअवराण गओ ॥

५८३ सुरसरिजलसिसिरतुसारसित्ततरुकुसुमवासिअदिअंते ।
तुहिणाअलस्स कडए महातवं चरिउमाढत्तो ॥१३३

५८४ तत्थासंखं कालं मूलफलाहारणिव्वुअसरीरो ।
मअविहगउलसहावो वक्कलवसणो सिलासअणो ॥

५८५ पत्तहरकअणिवासो णीसंगो जा तहिं तवं चरइ ।
ता भीएणाणत्ता सुरवइणा सुरवहू रंभा ॥

५८५क रंभे वणगहणपरिट्ठिअस्स वेत्तासणस्स वरमुणिणो ।
गंतूण कुणसु विग्घं उग्गतवासत्तहिअअस्स ॥१३४

५८५ख सुरवइलद्धाएसा वरवअणा झत्ति सहरिसावयवा ।
संपत्ता वणगहणे कअणिअमो वरमुणी जत्थ ॥

५८५ग ता सुरवहुदंसणचालिअम्मि मुणिवरमणम्मि मअणग्गी ।
पज्जलिओ तवतरुडहणलालसो मोहघअसित्तो ॥

KUVALAAVALI:
HER OWN STORY

Once there was a king, lord of the earth girt by the four   580
  oceans, destroyer of his adversaries, named Viulasaa.
  Along the path cut by his sword, three made their   581
  dwelling: earth, beneath one parasol all the way to
  the ocean's shore; wealth, all the way to the courtyard
  of heaven; martial victory, all the way to the ends of
  earth.

But the king was not satisfied with the royal splendor of   582
  merely one world. He transferred the cares of state
  to his ministers and then departed. He started to   583
  practice harsh austerities on the slope of a snowy
  mountain, where flowers perfumed the air and ice
  from the waters of the celestial Ganga clung to the
  trees. For an inconceivable time there he kept his body   584
  alive on roots and fruits, living like the beasts and
  birds, wearing bark cloth and sleeping on bare stone.

While he lived there without attachment in a leaf hut and   585
  practiced austerities, Indra grew apprehensive, and
  sent forth Rambha, an *apsaras*.[153]

"Rambha, there is a great sage deep in the forest seated on   585a
  a cane stool, his heart set on fierce austerities: go and
  disrupt him." When she was given this command from   585b
  Indra, her body shivered with delight. At once she set
  out for the forest grove where the sage was practicing
  his vows. At the sight of the celestial maiden, the great   585c
  sage's heart was shaken. The fire of lust was ignited,

५८६ सा किअचिरं पि कालं तेण समं मअणमोहिअमणेण ।
अच्छंती उअरवई जाआ परिओसिअसुरेसा ॥१३५

५९८ तिस्साहं तिहुअणसुंदरीए रंभाए उअरसंभूआ ।
सा मं पसूइसमए मोत्तूण दिव समारूढा ॥

५८८ अह ताएण वि पिअसहि जणणिविउत्तं ति मं कलेऊण ।
अब्भत्थिआओ वणदेवआओ सव्वाअरेण तहिं ॥१३६

५८९ तो ताहिँ फलरसामअरसेण संतप्पिआ अहं ताव ।
जा जाआ तम्मि तवोवणम्मि पअचारिणी णिरुआ ॥

५९० वक्कलकुप्पासावरिअविग्गहा पोत्तजीविविआहरणा ।
मअसावएहि समअं बालकीलासुहं पत्ता ॥१३७

५९१ दिअहेहिँ केत्तिएहिँ वि मुक्काहं तेण बालभावेण ।
ताअपअपंकआराहणम्मि उवसप्पिआ बुद्धी ॥

५९२ आणेमि कंदमूलप्फलाइँ विविहाइँ तरुपसूआइं ।
संमज्जणोवलेवणकम्मक्खणएण संतुट्ठा ॥१३८

५९३ अण्णम्मि णिसाविरमे बहुविहवरविडवकुसुमलोहेण ।
सुविसटृपाअवं वरविहंगरुअमुहलिअदिअंतं ॥१३९

५९४ महुमत्तमहुअराविलिझंकारुग्गीअपाअवणिउंजं ।
कप्पतरुकणइकिसलअणिरंतरंतरिअरविकिरणा ॥१४०

accelerated by the ghee of delusion and ready to burn
down the tree of his austerity.

For a good while she stayed with him, his mind clouded 586
with lust, and became pregnant, much to Indra's
delight. I was born from the womb of that Rambha, 587
the most beautiful woman in the three worlds. After
my birth, she left me and returned to heaven.

Then, dear friend, my father humbly sought the aid of the 588
forest goddesses in that place, seeing as my mother
had left me. They nourished me with the nectar of 589
fruit juices, and soon enough I was walking on my
feet and in good health in that forest retreat. With my 590
body covered in a bark garment, I was sustained by
the forest animals, and I experienced the pleasures of
childhood playing with the fawns. As the days wore 591
on and I left childhood behind, my thoughts turned to
doing service at my father's feet. I would bring all the 592
different kinds of bulbs, roots, and fruits that the trees
produced, and I was happy with the occasional tasks
of sweeping and polishing up.

Once, as night was turning into day, I was keen to gather 593
flowers from many different types of trees, so I set
out for a mountain forest: the trees there were in full
bloom, and the sky echoed with the calls of all kinds
of birds; copses resonated with buzzing swarms of 594
nectar-frenzied bees, and the sun's rays pierced the
thick cover of the vines and stalks of wish-granting

५९५ सुस्साअफलभरोणमिअवच्छपालंबचुंबिअधरंकं ।
हिमसेलसिहरणिज्झरतुसारपरिसित्तपेरंतं ॥

५९६ सुरवहुचलणालत्तअचिंचिल्लिअमणिसिलाअलुच्छंगं ।
गंधव्वगेअरवदिण्णअण्णमअजूहसंघाअं ॥

५९७ इअ एवविहं पिअसहि साणुवणं तेण कुसुमलोहेण ।
उवसप्पिअंम्हि अमुणिअविहिपरिणामं हआसाए ॥

५९८ ता तत्थ सुरहिकुसुमोज्झआविहिअहिअअभावपसराए ।
वामणअरुकणइवलंबिअग्गहत्थाए सब्भविअं ॥

५९९ धुव्वंतधअवडाडोअडंबरं सिरिणिवेसपरिवेसं ।
पवणपहल्लिरकिंकिणिरवमुहलिअणहअलाहोअं ॥

६०० विप्फुरिअविविहवररअणकंतिसंजणिअसुरधणुसमूहं ।
गअणाहि अवअरंतं दिव्वविमाणं सुहालोअं ॥

६०१ ता तत्थ पढमजोव्वणविअंभिआरंभभूसिआवअवो ।
विअडोरअडपहोलंतकुसुममालाकआहरणो ॥

६०२ मंदाणिलवसपसरिअसव्वंगामोअवासिअदिअंतो ।
लावण्णपहाविच्छुरिअसअलवणकाणणाहोओ ॥१४१

६०३ लीलाकमलणिवारिअवअणिलीणालिपअडिअच्छिजुओ ।
पेच्छंतो मह वअणं दिव्वकुमारो समल्लीणो ॥

trees; the trees, bent low with the burden of delicious   595
fruits, leaned down to kiss the earth, and water
cascading from the snowy peaks of the mountain
sprinkled a cool mist on the outskirts; the lac foot-   596
prints of the *apsarases* mingled with the gems that
studded the rocky slopes, and all the herds of animals
gave ear to the music of the *gandharvas*—such, my   597
dear friend, was the mountain forest I sought in the
hope of picking flowers, completely unaware how this
poor girl's fate was soon to change.

Just then, when my heart was set on collecting fragrant   598
flowers and my fingers were resting on the creeping
vine of a small tree, I spotted something with a flag   599
flapping loud and furious, with a nimbus of radiance
clinging to it, fitted out with bells that rang from
gusts of wind and filled the expanse of sky with their
jingling—a celestial vehicle descending from the   600
sky, leaving in its wake rainbows made by the light
streaming from glimmering jewels, a beautiful sight to
behold.

Then a heavenly prince emerged from it. His body was   601
adorned with the first signs of youth and by a garland
of flowers that fell over his broad chest. The air was   602
suffused with his body's fragrance as the gentle breeze
blew over him, and the entire forest grove sparkled
with the coruscating radiance of his beauty. I could   603
see his eyes only when he used a lotus flower to ward
off the bees gathering around his face—and he was
looking at me.

६०४ तो तं दट्ठूण मए सच्छरिअं साअरं सविणअं च ।
तब्भावभाविआए खित्तो कुसुमंजली पुरओ ॥

६०५ परिचिंतिअंम्हि हिअए अज्ज कइच्छाइँ पुण्णमइआइं ।
सच्छविअउहअलोआइँ लोअणाइं इमे दिट्ठे ॥१४२

६०६ अह तेण पुच्छिआहं समीवमुवसप्पिऊण कोहलिणा ।
मउएहिँ मुद्धमहुरक्खरेहिँ वअणेहिँ सच्छरिअं ॥१४३

६०७ पुप्फलाइ णवकणइविआणणिउंजए
        गुंजिरालिउलवलअमणोहररावए ।
कासि तं सि तिअसवहुविलासविणोअअं
        काणणम्मि परिभमसि असंकिरि णिब्भअं ॥१४४

६०८ तो तं सोऊण मए पिअसहि पढमं पिअंकरं वअणं ।
वज्जरिअं तस्स फुडं णिअअणिवासं कुलं णामं ॥

६०९ तो तेण साहिलासं सप्परिओसं ससंभमं समुअं ।
सासंघं ससिणेहं सविलासमहं पुणो भणिआ ॥

६१० सुंदरि ता अविरुद्धं एक्केक्कमदंसणं म्ह किं जेण ।
गंधव्वेसाण कुले अहं पि विमले समुप्पण्णो ॥१४५

६११ चित्तंगआहिहाणो तुह दंसणकोहलेण अवअरिओ ।
जह होसि सप्पसाआ ता जुत्तं वम्महेण कअं ॥१४६

I was astonished to see him, and with politeness and   604
    modesty I extended to him a handful of flowers,
    eager to know what he had in mind. I thought to   605
    myself, when I saw him, that my eyes were blessed,
    had fulfilled their sole purpose, had beheld both this
    world and heaven.

Then to my surprise he eagerly stepped forward and   606
    addressed me in soft words, syllables tender and
    sweet:

"Flower gatherer,   607
    you are wandering in this grove,
    with bowers and canopies formed by young vines
    and the charming sound of buzzing bees,
    without fear or hesitation
    like a graceful *apsaras* at play.
    Who are you?"[154]

When I heard those first enthralling words, dear friend,   608
    I told him plainly of my home, my family, and my
    name. Then he addressed me once again, with   609
    longing, delight, eagerness, joy, affection, and charm.

"Well then, beautiful girl, there is nothing to stop us   610
    from looking upon each other, is there? I too was born
    into a spotless family, that of the *gandharvas*.
    My name is Chittangaa. I came down to earth eager to   611
    have a look at you. If you would oblige me, then
    the god of love will have done the right thing.

६१२ अज्जदिअसाउ रज्जं कोसं जीअं सुहं सरीरं च ।
अण्णं पि किंपि जं मज्झ तं असेसं तुमाअत्तं ॥

६१३ ता पसिअ देहि मे पाणिपल्लवं मा विलंब एत्ताहे ।
ण सहइ कालक्खेवो मह हिअअविअंभिओ मअणो ॥१४७

६१४ एवं तं चाडुसआणुसंधिअं वअणं सुणेऊण ।
हिअअं आगअणरसाअलं म्ह पप्फुल्लिअं सहसा ॥१४८

६१५ आणंदबाहपडिपूरिएहिं सहि मणसिणिद्धआ तस्स ।
अच्छीहिं विअ सिट्ठा पडिवअणमसंभरंतीए ॥१४९

६१६ अइगरुअसज्झसाआसवसविसट्टंतमुहपअट्टेहिं ।
णीसासेहिं सअं चिअ दिण्णो अंतग्गओ भावो ॥१५०

६१७ अंगेहिं मि अणवत्थिदिएहिं असहीरणा समुद्दिट्ठा ।
लज्जोणएण वअणेण अप्पिओ हिअअसब्भावो ॥

६१८ कं जं ण सेअपुलउग्गमेण पिअसहि ण पिसुणिअं तस्स ।
पअडीकआ हआसेण लहुइआ ऊरुकंपेण ॥

६१९ इअ एमविहं पोरत्थिएहिं अंगेहिं मअणणडिएहिं ।
लज्जालुआणुरूआ अवणीआ गुणमई बुद्धी ॥१५१

६२० तो वामपअंगुट्ठेण तत्थ धरणीअलं लिहंतीए ।
भणिअं अणुच्चसद्दं अहोमुहच्छं च सहि तस्स ॥

From now on, my kingdom, my treasury, my life,   612
happiness, and body—everything that belongs to me
will be at your disposal. So please give me the flower   613
bud of your hand without delay. I cannot bear to wait.
My heart is bursting with love."

Thus he spoke to me with coaxing words by the hundreds.   614
In no time at all my heart seemed to fill the whole
space from heaven above to hell below. Only the   615
tears of joy that filled my eyes, dear friend, told of my
heart's affection for him—I myself completely forgot
to say anything in response. The sharp sighs escaping   616
from my gasping mouth, as I was overcome with
agitation, gave away what I felt inside. My restless   617
quivering showed how impatient I was, and my face,
turned down in embarrassment, gave up what my
heart really felt. Is there anything, dear friend, that   618
my sweat and my hair standing on end did not betray
to him? My legs trembled hopelessly. It was perfectly
clear that I was undone. Thus my mind, modest,   619
decorous, and virtuous, was dragged down by my
treacherous body, which lust took advantage of. Then,   620
my friend, I drew a line on the ground with the toe
of my left foot and spoke to him softly with my eyes
lowered:[155]

६२१ को एअं ण पसंसइ कस्स व इमिणा ण होइ परिओसो ।
को तुम्ह ण संबज्झइ कह व ण दीसइ तुमाहिंतो ॥१५२

६२२ इअ जइ मं महसि महाणुभाव वण्णतावसिं पि णाऊण ।
ता गंतूणं म्ह तवोवणम्मि ताअं चिअ भणेसु ॥१५३

६२३ तो तेण पुणो भणिअं अलमिमिणा केचिरं विलंबेसि ।
ण सहइ तुह दंसणसुहसमुग्गओ मह मणे मअणो ॥

६२४ कालंतरपरिवसिए अवसरचुक्कम्मि मअसिलिंबच्छि ।
विग्घसहस्साइँ समावडंति हिअइच्छिए कज्जे ॥१५४

६२५ एवं भणिऊण वअंसि तेण पुलइअपओट्टहत्थेण ।
गहिओ मे मुणिअ मणाहिलासमवसारिओ हत्थो ॥

६२६ तो तेण मज्झ पिअसहि सहसा णिव्वत्तिओ सवीवाहो ।
पम्हुसिआसेसकुलक्कमाए हअमअणणडिआए ॥१५५

६२७ तह तत्तो चिअ पिअसहि कुसुमासवमत्तमहुअरुग्गीए ।
कलअंठिकलअलारावमुहलिए दसदिसावलए ॥१५६

६२८ णिव्विच्चलआपल्लवणिरंतरंतरिअअतरणिकरणिअरे ।
बहुविहपसूअपरिमलपरिवासिअअतरुणिउंजम्मि ॥१५७

६२९ सत्तच्छअसुहपाअवतलम्मि इच्छाए अच्छिऊण चिरं ।
दिवसावसाणसमए संभरिओ सहि मए अप्पा ॥

"Who could withhold approval? Who could hide their 621
delight? Who could resist making love with you?
Why should I not be the object of your gaze?[156] So if, 622
despite knowing that I am a forest-dwelling ascetic,
you still long for me, noble sir, then please go and
speak to my father who lives in the ashram."

At that point he said, "Enough of this! How long are you 623
going to take? After having had the pleasure of seeing
you, the love in my heart cannot bear to wait! Fawn- 624
eyed girl, if time slips by, or if the moment is missed,
thousands of obstacles will fall in the way of the heart
getting what it wants."

As he spoke these words, my friend, the hair on his arms 625
stood on end, and once my hand slipped to the side,
he grabbed it, knowing my heart's desire.[157] Then 626
he quickly consummated his marriage with me, dear
friend, and I, tricked by accursed love, just as quickly
forgot everything that concerns the proper order of
family life.

After that, as the whole area around us buzzed with bees 627
crazed for the nectar of flowers, echoing with the
clamor of cuckoos, where the rays of the sun were 628
blocked by a thick growth of vines and shoots and the
bowers of trees were perfumed by the fragrance of
all kinds of flowers, I stayed with him for a long time 629
under the pleasing shade of the *saptacchada* tree, and
then, my friend, when the day was almost over, I came
to my senses.

६३० भणिअं च मए पिअअम ण हु एसो दुण्णओ सुहेणम्ह ।
वोलेइ जइ ण देव्वो अणुकूलो होइ एत्ताहे ॥१५८

६३१ अइगरुओ अवराहो विसमो ताओ असंकिरो मअणो ।
अविमरिसिअं च कज्जं ण आणिमो कह विपरिणमइ ॥१५९

६३२ ता तेणाहं भणिआ मा भाअसु एहि ताव णिअवसइं ।
वच्चम्ह विगअरोसो होही कालेण तुह ताओ ॥१६०

६३३ दिण्णाण अदिण्णाण अ आहवगहिआण सइँवराणं च ।
परिणीआण कुमारीण णत्थि अण्णं भणेअव्वं ॥१६१

६३४ अह एरिसे समुल्लाववइअरे सुअणु एक्कसरिआए ।
सुइरण्णेसणसुढिओ तत्तो च्चिअ आगओ ताओ ॥

६३५ ता तेण समं पिअसहि सहसा गंधव्वराअतणएण ।
एक्कविमाणासीणा सच्चविआ णवर ताएण ॥

६३५क भणियं च महामुणिणा पावसु रे पाव रक्खसालोयं ।
दुहिया मे अवहरिया कामासत्तेण अइरहसा ॥१६२

६३५ख वुत्तं च तओ तेण वि गंधव्वेण वि कयावराहेण ।
भयवं इमस्स होही कइया आउस्स पज्जंतो ॥१६३

६३५ग भणियं च तओ इसिणा णियत्तरोसेण पुत्तिणेहाओ ।
अइदुसहसुहडपारद्धसंगरे जाव सिरसि हओ ॥१६४

"Beloved," I said, "this was wrong of us. If fate is now 630
    unfavorable to us, it will really not end well. It is a 631
    serious offense; my father has a temper; we didn't
    second-guess our feelings or think through our
    actions. I don't know what will happen next."

Then he said to me, "Don't be afraid. Just come home 632
    with me. Your father's anger will fade in time.
    When women are taken in marriage in war or in a 633
    svayaṃvara, it doesn't matter whether or not their
    fathers have bestowed them. They have no say in the
    matter."[158]

Just as we exchanged these words, lovely girl, who should 634
    arrive but my father, exhausted from searching
    everywhere for me. At that moment, my father simply 635
    saw me sitting in the same vehicle as the *gandharva*
    prince.[159]

"Wicked man!" said the great sage. "Off with you to the 635a
    world of demons! You have stolen away my daughter
    in your reckless craving for sex!"

Then the blameworthy *gandharva* said: "Your Holiness, 635b
    when will that life you have cursed me to come to an
    end?"

The sage's anger then subsided, and out of love for his 635c
    daughter, he said: "When your head is struck off in a
    battle fought by invincible warriors."

६३५घ ता सोयमज्जिअविसट्टगयणपसरेण पेच्छमाणाए ।
सावपवणेण हरिओ णवरि पिओ कत्थ वि पएसे ॥१६५

६३६ तो मे झसत्ति पडिअं अविणअगिरिगरुअतुंगसिहराहि ।
हिअं लज्जाभअकुलिसताडिअं पिव णिरालंबं ॥

६३७ अह अअसमहासीहेण तासिआ पलइऊण वेएण ।
एक्कं णिउंजकणईविआणगहणं समल्लीणा ॥

६३८ ता तत्थ मं णिलुक्कं अविणीअं पेच्छउ त्ति मा ताओ ।
इअ कलिऊण व सूरो णीओ लज्जाए अत्थमणं ॥

६३९ महदुक्खदुक्खिआहिं व दिसाहिं अंधारिआइं वअणाइं ।
महभअभीआइं व संकुअंति वणअरसमूहाइं ॥

६४० ता रविरहवडणविसट्टजलहिमग्गुग्गएण व तमेण ।
पाआलाहिं व समअं विलुंपिओ णहअलाहोओ ॥१६६

६४१ ता हं कणइविआणाओ सणिअसणिअं महाभउप्पेत्था ।
अण्णण्णतरुवणंतरणिलुक्कमाणी समल्लीणा ॥१६७

६४२ ता ण पिओ ण विमाणं ण अ ताओ णेअ किं पि तं चिण्हं ।
जं पेच्छिऊण जीअं मुहुत्तमेत्तं विमालेमि ॥१६८

६४३ अह तं दट्ठूण मए सज्ज मसाणं व झत्ति दुप्पेच्छं ।
चिरमोहलद्धसण्णाए मुक्कअंठं चिरं रुण्णं ॥१६९

Then, as I stood by watching, the winds of the curse   635d
    silently filled the sky, drowning me in despair, and
    took my love, just like that, off to some other place.

So, all of a sudden, the ax of shame and fear struck at my   636
    heart, and it helplessly tumbled off the peak of the
    tall mountain of my immodesty. I ran off, put to flight   637
    by the great lion of scandal, and reached a thicket
    covered over with a dense growth of vines.

Then, as if to prevent my father from finding his   638
    wayward daughter hiding there, the sun absconded
    in embarrassment. The horizon's face darkened as   639
    if pained by my pain. The creatures of the forest
    all withdrew, as if frightened by my fear. Then   640
    the darkness, as if coming up from a breach in the
    ocean opened up by the descent of the sun's chariot,
    emerged from the netherworld to plunder the curving
    plane of the sky.

Then, still gripped by terror, I slowly emerged from the   641
    thicket of vines and made my way back, taking cover
    among the trees in one patch of forest after another.
    Then—no lover, nor his vehicle, nor my father, nor   642
    any sign of anything at all. At this sight, it was all I
    could do to stay alive just a moment longer. As all of   643
    this at once came into view, as awful to look upon as a
    cremation ground, I fainted for a long time, and when
    I came to I sobbed uncontrollably for just as long.

६४४ हा ताअ गअसिणेहो कीस तुमं तक्खणेण मह जाओ ।
अविणीए वि अवच्चे हवंति कलुणासआ मुणिणो ॥१७०

६४५ हा अज्जउत्त तुह णेहबंधणोबद्धजीविआ विहिणा ।
वोच्छिण्णा विसवल्लि व्व विअडकप्पदुमाहिंतो ॥

६४६ हा अंब तए वि अहं हअणामा जम्मवासरे मुक्का ।
एण्हिं असरणहिअआ कं जं सरणं पवज्जिस्सं ॥१७१

६४७ हा भअवईओ वणदेवआओ दंसेह पिअअमं मज्झ ।
तुम्हं सरणपवण्णा वि उअ अणाहा विवज्जामि ॥१७२

६४८ इअ एवं बहुसो विलविऊण परिचिंतिअंम्हि हिअएण ।
किं मह हआए इमिणा अप्पडिआरेण रुण्णेण ॥१७३

६४९ दुक्खावगमोवाओ णण्णो मरणाउ दीसइ कहिं पि ।
ता इह सत्तच्छअपाअवम्मि पासं णिबंधिस्सं ॥१७४

६५० एवं हिअए परिभाविऊण वलिअंम्हि वक्कलवरिल्लं ।
सच्चविआ जमहरवत्तणि व्व हिअइच्छिआ साहा ॥१७५

६५१ भणिअं च णिबद्धंजलिपणामपुव्वं मणंम्मि झाऊण ।
भअवं विस्सपआवइ जइ किं पि मए कअं सुकअं ॥१७६

६५२ ता अण्णंम्मि वि जम्मे सो च्चिअ मह पिअअमो हविज्जासु ।
मा होज्ज पुणो एवंविहाण दुक्खाण संभूई ॥

"Father! How could you lose all your love for me in an   644
   instant? Sages ought to be full of compassion, even
   if their children go astray. My husband! As soon as   645
   the bond of love had tied my life to yours, fate cut
   me loose, like a choking vine cut from a great wish-
   granting tree. Mother! I must be cursed, since you   646
   too left me the very day I was born. Now that my
   heart has no refuge, where am I to seek it? Holy forest 647
   goddesses! Show me my beloved! I turn to you for
   refuge. I have fallen into disaster without my beloved
   to protect me."

I wailed like this unceasingly until I thought to myself: 648
   "What use is this wretched crying? It won't do
   anything to help. There seems to be no way to escape   649
   this suffering besides death. So I will hang a noose
   from this *saptacchada* tree here." My heart thus   650
   surrendering, I twisted my bark clothing into a rope
   and fixed my gaze onto what I most desired: a branch
   that seemed like a path to the house of Yama.*

I joined my hands in reverence and, in deep concentration, 651
   I said, "Holy creator of all, if I have ever done
   anything good, then let the same person be my lover in 652
   another birth. But please do not let anything come to
   pass which would give rise to such suffering as this!"

---

* God of death and the underworld.

६५३ एवं भणिऊण मए उवबद्धो जा तहिं दुमे अप्पा ।
तो अद्धट्ठुडीणे जीविअम्मि गअणे सुओ सद्दो ॥

६५४ अइ अलमलमिमिणा तुज्झ पुत्ति ववसाअसाहसरसेण ।
वीसत्था होहि अहं खु तुज्झ जणणी बले पत्ता ॥१७७

६५४क ता झत्ति णहयलाओ अवयरिऊणम्ह सहि सुजणणीए ।
तं तोडिऊण पासं गहियाहं सुयणु उच्छंगे ॥१७८

६५५ जाणामि तेण मुणिणा णिरावराहा वि मुक्कसंगेण ।
परिसेसिआ सि बाले दूरं णिक्करुणहिअएण ॥१७९

६५६ ता तुज्झ सो अगम्मो सुरलोओ जत्थ सइ णिवासो म्ह ।
अत्थि मह हिअअदइओ जक्खो णलकूवरो णाम ॥

६५७ वित्ताहिवस्स तणओ सुअणो सच्चव्वओ पिआहासी ।
पडिवण्णवच्छलो सइ परोवआरेक्कपत्तट्टो ॥

६५८ तस्स समप्पेमि सुहेण जेण पिअविरहदुक्खमइआ वि ।
सुवअंसिआहिँ समअं वच्चंति अलक्खिआ दिअहा ॥

As I was saying this and tying myself to the tree, half of   653
    my life had already left me when I heard a sound in
    the sky.

"No! No more, my daughter, of such reckless decisions.   654
    Be still. It is I, your mother, who have come."

Then all at once, friend, my mother came down from the   654a
    sky, cut the noose, and clasped me to her bosom.

"I know the sage has left you, blameless though you are,   655
    and now you are all alone. Compassion, my child,
    is the last thing on his mind. At the same time, you   656
    cannot come to the place where I live, the realm of
    the gods. But I have a close friend, a *yakṣa* named
    Nalakubara. He is the son of Kubera, the lord of   657
    wealth, a good person, devoted to truth, kind in
    speech, fond of those who come into his care, with an
    uncommon skill for helping others. I will commit you   658
    to his care, and the days will happily pass by unnoticed
    in the company of friends, despite the torment of
    separation from your lover."

६५९ एवं भणिऊण चिरं अंबाए सिणेहसंगअमणाए ।
एत्थाणिऊण पिअसहि समप्पिआ तुज्झ ताअस्स ॥

६६० तो तद्दिअसाहिंतो तुम्हं अंबाए तह अ ताएण ।
तुम्हाहिँ वि सविसेसं सञ्चविआ एचिरं जाव ॥१८०

६६१ तेणेत्तिअं पि कालं तुह णेहणिबद्धजीविविआसाए ।
सब्भावसमप्पिअमाणसाए दुक्खं चिअ ण णाअं ॥१८१

६६२ तुह सुहसुहिआ तुह दुक्खदुक्खिआ तुज्झ हिअअगअहिअआ ।
तेण णिवारेमि इमं गुरुअणमणबाहिरं कज्जं ॥१८२

६६२क इय गुरुजणमणरहिअं कज्जं जो कुणइ सुयणु सच्छंदो ।
सो दुक्खवहरं जाअइ जह जाया हं खु सच्छंदा ॥१८३

६६३ जइ णिच्छएण एअं तुह हिअए संठिअं कुरंगच्छि ।
ता अंबाए सीसइ स च्चिअ सव्वं समाणिहइ ॥

६६४ अहवा सअं पबोहेमि तत्थ गंतूण तं चिअ कुमारं ।
जेण वरेज्जसि दिज्जसि एक्केक्कमकुलहरीसेहिँ ॥

६६५ इअ एवविहो धम्मो सिट्ठो देवेहिँ दिअमहेसीहिँ ।
अविरुज्झंतो पिअसहि उहआण वि उहअलोगसुहो ॥१८४

For a long while my mother spoke to me with words like   659
    this, her heart filled with love, and then brought
    me here, dear friend, and put me in the care of your
    father. And from that day on, your mother and father,   660
    and you yourself, have taken extraordinary care of
    me, right up until now. This whole time, you see, your   661
    love strengthened my will to live, and with my heart
    entrusted to your kindness, I felt no sorrow at all.
    Happy in your happiness, and pained at your pain, my   662
    heart has followed yours. That is why I must stop you
    from doing this deed, which is against the wishes of
    your parents.

Lovely girl, whoever willfully does a deed of which their   662a
    parents disapprove will become a house of pain, sure
    as I have by my willfulness.

If this is completely settled in your heart, doe-eyed girl,   663
    then tell your mother. She will arrange everything.
    Otherwise I myself will go there and tell the prince,   664
    so that you may be requested and given in marriage
    by the heads of each household. This is the dharma   665
    that the gods, Brahmans, and great sages have
    taught. When you abide by it, dear friend, it leads to
    happiness in this world and the next.

६६६ एवं भणिआए इमीए पभणिअं णिव्वहिज्ज जइ एवं ।
ता केत्तिअमेत्तं हअणिसाए सेसं म्ह साहेसु ॥

६६७ भणिअं च मए पिअसहि कीस तुमं एरिसं पि ण णिएसि ।
अरुणकराहअतिमिरं पुव्वदिसापंडुरं गअणं ॥

६६८ पेच्छेअं सुहमारुएण पहअं दुल्लक्खताराअणं
आमोअं ण जणेइ कामिणिअणे बालाअवालिद्धअं ।
दूरच्छिण्णदिसं सहावधवलं ओलग्गचंदाअवं
आलिक्खालिहिअं व छाअरहिअं जाअं णहोमंडलं ॥

६६९ दीसइ पसरंतणवारुणप्पहापहअतिमिरपब्भारं ।
हरणक्खुक्कत्तिअगअदइच्छदेहारुणं गअणं ॥१८५

६७० एसा वि सुअणु घरदीहिआए चिरविरहवेअणुक्कंठं ।
वाहरइ चक्कवाई णलिणोवरि संठिअं दइअं ॥१८६

६७१ संमिल्लंति सुहासाअजणिअपरिओसदुव्विसट्टाइं ।
इंतखरदिणअराअवसंकाइ व कुमुअगहणाइं ॥१८७

KUVALAAVALI:
THE RETURN TO MOUNT MALAYA

When I had told her all this, she said: "If that is so, then   666
let's bring this matter to an end. Tell me one thing.
How much of this wretched night do we have left?"

"Why, dear friend," I said, "don't you see how these red   667
rays are encroaching on the darkness of the sky, now
growing pale in the east?

"See how a pleasant breeze is now coursing through it,   668
with its innumerable stars.
Doesn't it gladden those who are in love?
The young glow of the day clings to it,
the horizon opens up in the distance, and its natural white
returns as the moonlight dims.
The expanse of the sky is fast losing its darkness,
as a painted figure has no shadow.[160]

"As the spreading streaks of red light push back on the   669
mass of darkness, the sky looks as red as the body of
the elephant demon flayed by Shiva's claws.[161] And   670
here, my lovely girl, is a female *cakravāka* bird in the
pond at your house, calling to her mate in the stand
of lotuses nearby, while he cranes his neck in the pain
of their long separation. The thickets of night lilies,   671
which were slow to open because there was so much
pleasure for them to enjoy, are now closing again, as if
in fear of the approaching sun's harsh heat."[162]

६७२ इअ जा ममाहिँ सोउं पेच्छइ अरुणारुणं नहाहोअं ।
ता उअअधराहरसिहरसंठिओ झत्ति दिणणाहो ॥

६७३ तो मह इमीए भणिअं एसो सहि उअअसेलसिहरम्मि ।
लक्खारसरत्तो विअ सहस त्ति समुग्गओ सूरो ॥१८८

६७४ कणअकविलम्मि सहसा दिट्ठे गरुले व्व दिअसणाहम्मि ।
ओसरइ कसणविसहरणिवहो व्व णहाहि तमणिवहो ॥१८९

६७५ णलिणोअरपरिवसिआइँ अलिउलाइं करेहिँ विउडिंतो ।
उक्खणइ व तमबीआइँ पेच्छ रोसारुणो सूरो ॥१९०

६७६ बालाअवो ण णिवडइ रहसमिलंतेसु चक्कवाएसु ।
विअसिअकमलसमुच्छलिअरेणुकविसासु सरसीसु ॥१९१

६७७ दीसंति फुरिअरविअरकरवालोलुंपिअस्स तमतरुणो ।
महिवेढणिवडिआओ छल्लीओ व रुक्खछाआओ ॥१९२

६७८ एसो सो सूराअवसंगसमुप्फुसिअचंदिमापसरो ।
धवलब्भदलसरिच्छो जाओ गअणंगणे चंदो ॥१९३

६७९ ता वच्चु मलअसेलं जीविअमरणाण बहुगुणं जं म्ह ।
तं जाणिऊण पिअसहि कुणसु सअं चेअ किं अण्णं ॥

६८० अविरुज्झंतं जं गुरुअणम्मि उइअं च जं सिणेहस्स ।
तं जाणसि च्चिअ तुमं सेसं किमहं पवोच्छामि ॥

172

While she was listening to my words, and gazing at the   672
sky's deep red expanse, the lord of the day suddenly
appeared on the peak of the eastern mountain.

"Friend," Mahanumai then said to me, "here comes the   673
sun as we speak, appearing on the peak of the eastern
mountain, as if it had been dyed with lac. The dense   674
darkness is retreating from the sky in the presence of
the lord of the day, like a pit of black serpents at the
sight of the golden-red eagle Garuda. Look how the   675
sun, with its rays, is scattering the bees that had spent
the night locked within day lotuses, as if, red with
anger, it were digging out with its hands the seeds of
darkness.[163] *Cakravāka* birds rush to reunite in ponds   676
already red with pollen blown from newly opened
lotuses—the morning sunlight doesn't even get a
chance to fall there.[164] The trees' shadows look like   677
bark fallen on the ground after the sun has sheared
them from the tree of darkness with the glistening
sword of its rays. And here is the moon. Now that   678
the sun's brilliance has dimmed its profuse light, it
resembles a wisp of a white cloud in the sky.

"So go to Mount Malaya. You will know what is best for   679
me, whether life or death, and I entrust you to do
it yourself, dear friend. How could it be otherwise?
You will just know what to do: something my parents   680
would approve of, and befitting the love I have. What
is left for me to say?"

६८१ एवमहं आढत्ता भाउअ सुजवेण सुहविमाणेण ।
तं चेअ मलअभवणं संपत्ता जत्थ सो दिट्ठो ॥१९४

६८२ तो तं पणट्टसोहं अणिमज्जिअकुट्टिमं अणुब्भिअवडाअं ।
अपसाहिअवंदणमालतोरणं अरइअद्दारं ॥१९५

६८३ अकअकुसुमोवआरं अप्पत्तविलेवणं अदिट्ठिवत्तं ।
अविहाविअचिरसोहं अपेच्छणिज्जं च अच्छीण ॥१९६

६८४ तं तारिसं दुपेच्छं दट्ठूण हु भवणं हआसाए ।
परिचिंतिअंम्हि हिअए हद्धी किं णेरिसं एअं ॥१९७

६८५ हअबंभरक्खसुव्वासिअं च दूरोसरंतचिरसोहं ।
अज्जेअं किं माहविलआए परिसेसिअं भवणं ॥

६८६ अलमहवा इह दुच्चिंतिएण वच्चामि केरलं ताम ।
तत्तो च्चिअ जाणिस्सं एअं एवंविहं कज्जं ॥१९८

६८७ परिभाविऊण एअं संपत्ता केरलाउरिदुवारं ।
तत्थ मए अक्कंदिअसद्दो णिसुओ असोअव्वो ॥

६८८ तो णिवडिअहिअअविहीरणाए उवसप्पिऊण पासंमि ।
एक्को पओलिवालो णिहुअं चिअ पुच्छिओ सभअं ॥

६८९ भद्द किमेसो सुव्वइ जणणिवहक्कंददूसहो सद्दो ।
अइगरुअदुक्खपरिभूअबंधवो तुम्ह णअरीए ॥१९९

With this, brother, I started out at high speed in my   681
  comfortable vehicle, and I arrived at the house on
  Mount Malaya where we had met Prince Mahavanila.

Then I looked at that house—terrible as it was to look   682
  upon—and saw that its beauty was gone, its floors
  no longer swept, flags no longer flying above it, no
  longer festooned with garlands above the doors, its
  doorways no longer decorated, welcome flowers no   683
  longer arrayed, no longer daubed with ointments, no
  one to take care of it, not having been taken care of
  for some time, impossible for my eyes to behold.[165]
  I thought to myself, "Dear god, it can't really be like   684
  this, can it? Has Mahavilaa really abandoned this   685
  house? The beauty it once had is now long gone, and it
  seems infested with accursed *brahma-rākṣasas*.[166] No,   686
  there's no point in speculating about it. I'll leave for
  Kerala at once and learn from there what this business
  is about."

I reached this decision, then reached the gates of the city   687
  of Kerala. There I heard something I wished I had
  not: the sound of lamentation. With my heart sinking   688
  in anticipation, I made my way to a gatekeeper and
  asked, my voice bated in fear:

"Sir, why is it that, in your city, the dreadful sound of   689
  so much lamentation can be heard, overwhelming
  friends and relatives with grief beyond measure?"

६९० भणिअं च तेण अज्जे अज्जकुमारो अणज्जणिसिसमए ।
वसिओ विज्जाभवणे असहाओ देव्वजोएण ॥

६९१ सो अम्ह अउण्णाणं कत्थ व केहिं पि दुट्ठसत्तूहिं ।
अवहरिओ मलअमहीहराहि णिक्करुणहिअएहिं ॥

६९२ मलआणिलो वि पिअसुअसिणेहवसकाअरेण हिअएण ।
अण्णेसिऊण सुइरं जाआए समं गओ मोहं ॥

६९३ मुच्छाविरामसंभरिअगुणगणुक्कंठिएहिँ तह रुण्णं ।
जह मलअवणगएहिँ वि गएहिँ ण विहाविअं जूहं ॥

६९४ हा वच्छ माहवाणिल हा बालअ हा अणोवमाआर ।
हा गुणरअणमहोवहि हा अविणअभीरु कत्थ तुमं ॥

६९५ दीसिहिसि पुणो वि मए सुअणजणसलाहिएहिं सुमईहिं ।
कीलंतो मलअमहीहरम्मि समअं वअंसेहिं ॥२००

६९६ एवमवरं पि बहुसो रोत्तूण चिरं पअंपिअं पहुणा ।
एहि पिए किं इमिणा जरहरवासेण एत्ताहे ॥

६९७ जस्स कए पालिज्जइ रज्जं जीअं धणं परिअणं च ।
सो च्चेअ णत्थि संपइ किं इमिणा रज्जभारेण ॥

६९८ तुह भाउणो समप्पेमि पिअअमे परिअणं च रज्जं च ।
वच्चामि वणं परलोअकज्जदिण्णेक्कमणभावो ॥

१७६

"My lady," he said, "our prince spent the night—a terrible   690
night it would turn out to be—alone in his house of
learning, and as fate would have it some awful and   691
cruel-hearted enemies of ours, lacking in good karma
as we are, took him away from Malaya Mountain to
who knows where. Malaanila searched for him for   692
a long time, his heart terror-stricken out of love for
his dear son, but soon fainted, together with his wife.
When they had regained consciousness, their son's   693
many virtues came to mind, and they wept so much
from missing him that even the elephants in the
Malaya forests left their herds behind.

"'Mahavanila, dear child, incomparable son, ocean full   694
of virtues like perfect jewels, afraid to do anything
wrong! Where can you have gone? Will I ever see you   695
again, amusing yourself on Mount Malaya with those
kind friends of yours, always praised by good people?'

"With words like these, and many more besides, his   696
father wept for a long time, then said: 'Come now,
beloved wife. What good is domestic life now that it
is in ruins? The one for whose sake we guarded our   697
kingdom, our lives, our wealth, and our retinue is no
more. What use now is this burdensome kingdom?
Beloved, I will make over our retinue and kingdom   698
to your brother and withdraw to the forest. My heart
will be then completely given over to the duties of the
world beyond.'

६९९ तो परिसेसिअरज्जे राए वणगमणगहिअसंकप्पे ।
सविसेसं रुअइ जणो पसाअसुहसुमरणासत्तो ॥२०१

७०० इअ एमविहं भाउअ दुस्सोअव्वं तहिं सुणेऊण ।
अफुडिअहिअआ अविवण्णजीविआहं पि विणिअत्ता ॥२०२

७०१ जीविअमरणाण मणे चिंतंती बहुगुणं म्ह किं एत्थ ।
मह जीविएण सा जिअइ मरइ मरणे महाणुमई ॥२०३

७०२ ता जीविअं चिअ वरं मरणाहिंतो मणम्मि धरिऊण ।
सुइरेणोरुण्णमुही णिअवसइं कह वि संपत्ता ॥

७०३ तो बाहजलोल्लिअलोअणाए दीणाणणाए दूराओ ।
एसा मए अहव्वाए दंसणे च्चिअ विसंणविआ ॥

७०४ सिट्टं तं किं पि मए दुव्वोच्चं वज्जकढिणहिअआए ।
जं तुम्ह वेरिआण वि सवणवहं मा हु वच्चेज्ज ॥२०४

७०५ अह तं सहस त्ति णिसामिऊण मम्माहा इव णिसण्णा ।
पडिआ धरणीवट्टे हा किं णेअं पअंपंती ॥

७०६ ताव मए से गुरुअणसंवाआसंकिरीए घेत्तूण ।
सीसं णिअउच्छंगे सुइरेणासासिआ एसा ॥२०५

७०७ णिहुअं गुरुअणसंकालुईए विअलंतबाहपिहिअच्छं ।
रुण्णं रुअंतपरिअणपरिसेसिअजीविआसाए ॥

"When the king had made up his mind to leave his   699
    kingdom behind and go to the forest, the people began
    to weep all the more, clinging to the memory of the
    happiness they had experienced by his favor."

Such were the words, brother, terrible words, that I   700
    heard there. When I returned, I was somehow still
    alive, although my heart was shattered. As I reflected   701
    whether in the circumstances it would be better to live
    or die, I was persuaded that Mahanumai would live
    if I lived, and die if I died, and for that reason it was   702
    better for me to live than to die. With tears streaming
    down my face all the while, I made it home with great
    difficulty. At the mere sight of me, even at a distance—   703
    miserable as I was, my eyes flooded with tears, and
    the awful expression on my face—she fainted. I told   704
    her a thing so terrible to tell with a heart as hard as
    diamond. May such news never reach the ears of your
    worst enemies.

No sooner had she heard my words than she sank to the   705
    ground as if wounded to the quick: "Oh god, can you
    really be telling me this?"

I immediately took her head into my lap, afraid of letting   706
    her parents know, and spent quite a while consoling
    her. She wept quietly out of fear of her parents, her   707
    eyes streaming with tears. Her servants were weeping,
    too, despairing of her very life.

७०८ हा जीविएस हा सुअणु हा अणंतगुणभूमि हा दइअ ।
हा णिक्कारणवच्छल कत्थ पुणो तं सि दीसिहिसि ॥२०६

७०९ जं पढमदंसणाणंदबाहपडिपूरिएहिँ अच्छीहिं ।
सच्चविओ सि ण सुइरं तं एणिहं किं णिअच्छिस्सं ॥२०७

७१० जं तंगुलिआहरणच्छलेण सुइरं णिपीडिओ तुम्हि ।
सो मे तह लग्गो च्चिअ अज्ज वि हत्थो ण वीसरइ ॥

७११ दिण्णाइँ जाइँ माहविलआए जह तुह सहत्थलिहिआइं ।
अमअमआइँ व लेहक्खराइँ एणिहं विसाअंति ॥

७१२ इअ एवं बहुसो पलविऊण भणिअं इमीए मह हुत्तं ।
असमत्थाहं पिअसहि तेण विणा जीविउं एणिहं ॥

७१३ ता जुत्तमजुत्तं किं पि जं मए लंघिआसि पणएण ।
तं मरिसेज्जसु पिअसहि मरणमआले कअं विहिणा ॥

७१४ ण अ लज्जा ण अ विणओ ण कुमारिजणोइअं अणुट्ठाणं ।
ण अ सो पिओ ण मोक्खं तो किं हअजीविएणम्ह ॥

७१५ इमिणा असुहज्जिअकम्मकलुसिएणम्ह किं सरीरेण ।
तह कह वि विवज्जिस्सं जह पुण जम्मो च्चिअ ण होइ ॥

७१६ भणिअं च मए पिअसहि मा एवं भणसु किं ण आणासि ।
जो जस्स हिअअदइओ मिलइ जिअंतो जिअंतस्स ॥

७१६क चिरपवसिओ वि आवइ वाहिग्गहिओ वि णिव्वुओ होइ ।
बंधणगओ वि मुंचइ मओ त्ति झीणा कहा लोए ॥२०८

"Lord of my life, handsome man, source of endless good   708
    qualities, my love! You showed me such selfless
    kindness. How will I ever get to see you again? How   709
    brief was the sight when I first saw you, my eyes filled
    with tears of joy at the very first glance. Now will I
    ever get to see you at all? You held my hand in yours   710
    and squeezed it for a long time under the pretext
    of giving me a ring. And still today my hand cannot
    forget: it remains clasped as ever. The letters that   711
    Mahavilaa gave me, the way you had written them
    with your own hand—they once seemed made of
    nectar, and now they are poison."

She went on like this at length, and then said to me: "Dear   712
    friend, I just cannot live without him now. So if, out   713
    of love, I have done anything to offend you, whether
    right or wrong, please forgive me, dear friend. Fate
    has assigned me an untimely death. I have no shame   714
    and no modesty. I haven't done the things young
    women ought to do. My beloved is gone, as is my hope
    of liberation. So what good to me is this accursed life?
    What good is this body of mine, defiled as it is with   715
    bad karma? I must find a way of reaching my end so
    that I am not reborn at all."

"Dear friend," I said, "don't you know? If you're ever to   716
    meet your beloved again, both of you have to be alive!
    One who goes off on a long journey comes back, one   716 a
    who is struck with illness recovers, and one who is
    imprisoned is released—and the rumor that he is

७१७ जीअं तिवग्गसिद्धीए कारणं दुल्लहं च जिअलोए ।
ण हि तेण विणा पिअसहि हवंति हिअइच्छिआ भोआ ॥

७१८ सो तुज्झ पिओ पिअसहि ण विवज्जइ णूण जुअसएहिं पि ।
सच्चविअं तस्स मए दीहाउअलक्खणं तइआ ॥

७१८ जइ बहुगुणं च मरणं ण जिअइ मलआणिलो वि ता पढमं ।
जणणी वि ण पिअसुअविप्पलंभदुक्खं पवज्जंती ॥

७२० ता अलमिमिणा मरणाहिलाससमुहोवलग्गभावेण ।
अहवा सो होही तुज्झ सुअणु आराहसु भवाणी ॥२०९॥

७२१ एत्थं चिअ कुलभवणे णिच्चं णिअमट्ठिआए होहिंति ।
हिअइच्छिआइँ पिअसहि कीस तुमं मरणमहिलससि ॥

७२२ भणिअं च महाणुमईए तं तहा मह मुहाहि सोऊण ।
सहि जइ णेच्छसि मरणं ता किं पि भणामि णिसुणेसु ॥

७२३ किं काण वि कह वि कुमारिआण कुलहरणिवाससुहिआण ।
सिज्झंति देवआराहणेक्कचित्ताणुसाराइं ॥

७२४ इअ जइ मरणमसंतं मण्णसि एवंविहे वि पिअविरहे ।
मह मंदभाइणीए ता होउ तवोवणे वासो ॥

७२५ जह तं तणं व तुलिऊण सिद्धराएण उज्झिअं रज्जं ।
तह कुलभवणसुहाणं संकप्पो सहि मए वि कओ ॥

dead vanishes. It is life that allows you to achieve the 717
three goals, and such a life, in the world of human
beings, is a rare gift.[167] For without it, dear friend, the
enjoyments your heart seeks are not possible. That 718
lover of yours, dear friend, will surely not perish for
hundreds of years.[168] For I saw on him, on that earlier
occasion, the sign of a long life. If death were really the 719
better option, then Malaanila, to begin with, would
not be alive now, nor would his mother be subjecting
herself to the pain of separation from her beloved son.
So enough of this mood you're stuck in that makes 720
you wish you were dead! No, he will be yours, dear
girl. Ask a favor of Bhavani. If you are constant in your 721
vows, dear friend, then your heart's desires will be
fulfilled, even in your family home. Why should you
want to die?"

Mahanumai listened as these words tumbled from my 722
mouth, then spoke: "My friend, if you really don't
want me to die, then hear what I have to say. Is it 723
really possible for girls to achieve their heart's desires
by single-mindedly propitiating the gods, all while
living comfortably at home?[169] If you insist that 724
it would be bad for me to die, even when I am so
desperately separated from my beloved, then let me
go and stay in an ashram, unlucky as I am. The *siddha* 725
king relinquished his kingdom, considering it to be
worth less to him than a blade of grass. In the same
way, friend, I too have resolved to leave behind the
comforts of home."

७२६ इअ इह इमीए कअणिच्छिआए णिअगुरुअणं पबोहेउं ।
अणिअत्तमणाए कओ सहस त्ति तवोवणे वासो ॥२१०॥

७२७ एवं सोऊण चिरं णीसेसं कुवलआवलिमुहाओ ।
भणिअं णरणाह मए भअवइ किं वो भवाणीए ॥

७२८ ण कओ दुक्खावगमो एमविहाणं पि तुम्ह एमविहे ।
वणवासकिलेससमोसरंतसोक्खे तवच्चुरणे ॥

७२९ भणिअं च इसिसुआए कत्तो इह जम्मदुक्खवोच्छेओ ।
दीसइ पुव्वज्जिअअसुहकम्मओविग्गिआणम्ह ॥२११॥

७३० अण्णं पि तुम्ह सीसइ सविसेसं जं इमाओ इह जाअं ।
ण कअत्थो एत्तिअमेत्तिएण देव्वो कएणम्ह ॥२१२॥

184

With her mind thus made up, she informed her parents   726
    and straightaway took up residence in this ashram,
    and she has never since wavered in her decision.

VIJAANANDA:
A BRIEF INTERRUPTION

For this entire time, my lord, I had been listening to the   727
    whole tale that came pouring forth from Kuvalaavali's
    mouth. But at this point I spoke: "Your Holiness, has   728
    goddess Bhavani not given you both some reprieve
    from the sorrows you have described in such an
    ashram as this, where happiness commingles with the
    difficulties of forest life?"

"The bad karma we accumulated in the past has engulfed   729
    us," said the sage's daughter. "How can we ever hope
    to be completely freed from the suffering of this
    birth? I will tell you something else that happened,   730
    something even more striking than this. For fate was
    not yet satisfied with all that it has done to us already."

७३१ एत्थेक्कदिवसभाए णिसुओ गोलाणईए परतीरे ।
पडिराववपूरिआसो णराण गरुओ हलब्बोलो ॥२१३

जहा ।

७३२ एत्थुत्तरपुव्वपलोट्टभूमिभाए खिवेह पत्तोली ।
विच्छिण्णं कीरउ राउलस्स राअंगणुद्देसं ॥

७३३ परहुत्तं सारेज्जसु हट्टवहो जेण एत्थ संमाइ ।
इअरो वि हट्टणिवहो वेअडिअवणिद्धुरालग्गो ॥२१४

७३४ इह होउ पिंडवासो एत्थ णिओई हवंतु आसण्णे ।
इह वासो वारकरेणुआण एसो अणुग्गीण ॥

७३५ मोत्तुं भंडारमहाणसाण गोरीहरस्स पइरेक्के ।
मग्गो सुणट्टसालाए होउ जो जत्थ सो तत्थ ॥

७३६ कलुसिज्जइ जा ण जलं करेणुकरितुरअणरसमूहेहिं ।
ता भरसु मज्झणावेल्लमज्जणक्खण अदोणीओ ॥२१५

७३७ इअ जा सुव्वइ एसो हलबोलो ताण एक्कमेक्काण ।
ता दूसपट्टसालासएहिं आवासिओ लोओ ॥

७३८ एत्थंतरम्मि वरवाररमणिसंघाअसिट्टसिरिविहवा ।
विविहाअवत्तपरिपिहिअणहअलोरुद्धरविकिरणा ॥२१६

७३९ रमणिअणसमूहुग्घुट्ठमंगलारावपूरिअदिअंता ।
कंचुइअणुमग्गगआ राअकुमारी तहिं पत्ता ॥२१७

186

KUVALAAVALI:
THE PRINCESS'S ARRIVAL

One day we heard the sound of men on the far shore of the   731
Godavari River, making a commotion loud enough to
echo across the sky. It went: "Here, put up the gate on   732
this plot of land that has been cleared to the northeast!
Mark off this space for the courtyard of the royal
palace! Run the main market street in that direction,   733
so we can fit in another row of stalls right next to the
jewelers and merchants over here! Put the retinue   734
here, and have the officials stay in this area here! This
is where the gateway elephants will stay, and this is
for the guards![170] Have each path go where it needs   735
to: besides those of the storehouses and kitchens, and
that of the temple of Gauri in an isolated spot, there
should be one for the performance hall![171] Quick, fill   736
the golden tubs for the midday bath before all these
elephants, horses, and men muddy up the water!"

As we heard them shouting at each other like this, a group   737
of people set up camp with hundreds of tents. In the   738
meantime a princess arrived on the scene, following
the lead of her chamberlains. Crowds of beautiful
female attendants announced her high royal status.
The multitude of her parasols covered the sky and   739
shut out the sun's rays. The echoes of auspicious
songs sung by crowds of beautiful women filled the
horizons.[172]

७४० अह एत्थम्हतवोवणकुसुमामोआवलंबिअमणाए ।
भणिआओ णिअवअंसीओ कुणह कुसुमोच्चअं एत्थ ॥

७४१ तो खिण्णकरेणुसमोअरंतदरदाविओरुवेढाओ ।
परितलिणणिअंसणसिढिलगंठिसंजमणसीलाओ ॥२१८

७४२ विअलंबलपाउरणगगखलिअचरणारविंदगमणाओ ।
विअलंतमेहलावलिगुणकलणक्खलिअहत्थाओ ॥२१९

७४३ असमंजसपअणिक्खेववसविअंभंतणेउररवाओ ।
रंखोलिरहारविमूढकण अवलआवलिभुआओ ॥२२०

७४४ इअ विविहकुसुमपरिमलगंधवहुक्खित्तहिअभावाओ ।
एत्थम्ह समीवसमागआउ वरपुप्फलाईओ ॥

७४५ पारद्धं च सअण्हाहिँ ताहिँ कुसुमोच्चअं वणे काउं ।
एक्केक्कमजअकंखिअमणाहिँ परिउट्टुवणाहिँ ॥

७४६ तो सहसाअड्ढिअतरुणविडवपालंबचुंबिअथणाहिँ ।
करकमलकोमलंगुलिणहकिरणारुणिअगोच्छाहिँ ॥२२१

७४७ दूरुच्चाइअभुअजुअलवसविराअंततिवलिवलआहिँ ।
चलणअलग्गद्दिअथरहरंतथोरोरुवेढाहिँ ॥

७४८ णीसाससमीरुच्छित्तकुसुमरअतरलिअच्छिजुअलाहिँ ।
अलआवलिविवरविणिंतसेअतण्णाअतिलआहिँ ॥

७४९ णिविडलआहरसंचरणविलुलिआलअविढत्तसोहाहिँ ।
बंधुज्जिअकुसुमविमूढभमरडक्काहरिल्लाहिँ ॥२२२

Then her attention was captured by the smell of the   740
   flowers in our ashram. "Go pick flowers here," she
   told some friends. Approaching slowly like tired   741
   elephant cows, showing their thighs a little, constantly
   tightening the loose knots that held their sheer clothes
   in place, their lotus feet tripping on the hem of their   742
   long shawls as they walked, their hands struggling to
   keep tied the stubborn strings of their waistbands,
   the sound of their anklets amplified as their feet fell at 743
   irregular intervals, necklaces swaying, golden bangles
   ringing their arms, those expert flower pickers came   744
   to where we were, their hearts lifted up by the breeze
   that carried the fragrance of all kinds of flowers.[173]

They started picking flowers in the forest with great   745
   eagerness, each trying to outdo the others, delight
   manifest on their faces. They tugged on the young   746
   branches whose pendant sprouts grazed their breasts,
   and they reddened the bunches they collected with
   light from the nails of their tender fingers.
   They exposed the triple fold at their stomachs when   747
   they stretched their arms up high, and their thick
   thighs quivered when they stood on tiptoes.
   They squinted their eyes from the pollen their   748
   heavy breathing had stirred up, and the sweat that
   beaded between ropes of hair washed off their *tilakas*.
   Their hair was disheveled from plunging into thickets   749
   of overgrown vines, which only added to their beauty,
   and their lips were bruised from stinging bees that
   confused them with the *bandhujīva* flower.[174]

७५० इअ सुइरेण समाणिअ ताहिं सुरअं व कुसुमपरिअम्मं ।
पारद्धं गोलासलिलमज्जणं जणिअखेआहिं ॥२२३

७५१ तो विअडासोअतले संठविआहरणकुसुमवासाहिं ।
सच्चविअं विमलगहीरमणहरं वरसरीसलिलं ॥

७५२ ता विमलसलिलदंसणणिव्वविआरत्तभावरच्छीण ।
णहकोडिविरल्लिअचिहुरभाररुद्धावरोहाण ॥२२४

७५३ आमुक्काहरणपलहुइअंगपरिहत्थपअणिवेसाण ।
सविसेसगंठिसंजमिअविउणकच्छडअवेढाण ॥

७५४ इअ पढममज्जणारंभरहससंचालिअंबुणिवहाण ।
अण्ण च्चिअ का वि वरंगणाण सोहा समुल्लसिआ ॥२२५

७५५ कीए वि णिबुडुंतोरुमूलवसपसरिओ सरीरम्मि ।
रोमंचो जोव्वणकंदकुहरकरणिं समुव्वहइ ॥

७५६ कीए व जलपरिग्गहिअणाहिविवरुग्गआ समारुहइ ।
थणमूलासाइअतंतुकसणवल्लि व्व रोमलआ ॥

७५७ कीए वि विसमतिवलीतरंगपक्खलणवससमुच्छलिअं ।
णिमिसड्ढं सिअपट्टंसुअं व सिहिणोवरे सलिलं ॥२२६

७५८ कीए वि समंताअंतसलिलमज्झट्ठिअं रमंतीए ।
पवणाहअसरसंबुरुहविब्भमं होइ मुहकमलं ॥

७५९ रत्तुप्पलमहुसद्दालुएण कीए वि मुद्धभसलेण ।
परिमाणंतीए जलं डक्को उद्धट्ठिओ हत्थो ॥२२७

So they went about their flower gathering as if making   750
love, and when finished, they were exhausted, and
went off to bathe in the waters of the Godavari.

They piled their jewelry, flowers, and clothing at the foot   751
of a huge *aśoka* tree and set their sights on the clear
deep waters of the great river. When the mere sight   752
of it washed the redness from their beautiful eyes,
they paused their descent for a moment to comb
out their long hair with their fingernails, then they   753
removed their jewelry, and, planting their steps more
firmly with unencumbered limbs, they doubled over
their loincloths and tied them tight. Then they began   754
their bath with a huge splash, sending waves rushing
through the water, and all of a sudden the girls' rare
beauty appeared in a completely new light.

As one girl plunged into the water, the hair stiffening on   755
her thighs looked like sprouts bursting forth from
the bulb that was her youth. With water rushing   756
into another girl's navel, the line of down climbing
there was like a delicate dark vine creeping toward
her breasts. Waves crashed against the three folds   757
of another's stomach and splashed up like a bolt of
white cloth draped momentarily over her breasts. One   758
girl played in the middle of the water, which eddied
around and made her face seem like a bobbing lotus
pushed to and fro by the breeze. Another was holding   759
her hand up to measure the water's depth when it was
stung by a confused bee, avidly seeking the nectar of

७६० सो तीए तरलिअंगुलिविहुओ करपल्लवो रुअंतीए ।
तो से सहीहिँ मुहमारुएण कह कह वि णिव्वविओ ॥२२८

७६१ इअ वअणणअणथणहरकरअलपरिचुंबिरालिवाउलिओ ।
उत्तिण्णो सो गोलादहाहि वरकामिणीसत्थो ॥

७६२ मज्झम्मि ताण सा वरकुमारिआ मणहरेहिँ अंगेहिँ ।
महणुत्तिण्णाहिँ व अच्छराहिँ परिवालिआ लच्छी ॥२२९

७६३ तो सा अम्हेहिँ चिरं भाउअ णिव्वण्णिआ पअत्तेण ।
सुरवहुदंसणदूसिक्खिएहिँ अच्छीहिँ पुणरुत्तं ॥

७६४ णहमणिकिरणारुणकोमलंगुलीदलविराइआवअवं ।
णिग्गूढगुप्फसुपरिट्ठिअं च चरणारविंदजुअं ॥

७६५ पविरलतणुरोमसुवट्टिअंगसमसंधिबंधणं सहइ ।
लाअण्णसुवण्णविणिम्मिअं च वरजंघिआजुअलं ॥

७६६ रमणभरभंगभीअं व संगअं सिरिसकुसुमसोमालं ।
करिकलहकराआरं हरइ कुमारीए ऊरुजुअं ॥२३०

७६७ गंभीरणाहितणुतिवलिभंगुरं दरविसट्टरोमलअं ।
तुच्छं संसारसुहं व मणहरं मज्झएसं से ॥

७६८ णिव्विच्चुतुंगाहोअकक्कसं पिक्कसिरिहलसरिच्छं ।
होंतपरिणाहगरुअं अग्घइ णवथणहरुच्छंगं ॥२३१

७६९ कंकेलिपल्लवाअंबकरअलालंकिअं समुव्वहइ ।
मंदाइणिकणअमुणालिआणुसरिसं भुआजुअलं ॥

a red lotus. She cried out and shook her bud-like hand   760
with trembling fingers, and her friends tried hard to
ease her pain by blowing on it. The group of beautiful   761
young women was thrown into confusion by the bees
that kept alighting on their faces, eyes, breasts, and
hands, and so they finally came out of the deep waters
of the Godavari.

In their midst, surrounded by their lovely bodies, was   762
that beautiful princess, like Lakshmi surrounded by
apsarases churned up from the cosmic milk ocean.[175]
Then, brother, we kept trying to have a look at her,   763
but our eyes were unaccustomed to the sight of a
goddess. Her lotus feet glowed with petals of tender   764
toes turned pink by the light of her toenails and
pleasingly attached to delicate ankles. Her beautiful   765
legs were sparsely covered with down, with round
features and well-proportioned joints, and fashioned
from the gold of loveliness. The princess's thighs, soft   766
as *śirīṣa* flowers and tapering like a baby elephant's
trunk, came together as if afraid of being broken by a
lover's weight. Her fetching waist was slight, like the   767
pleasures offered by samsara, made shapely by a deep
navel and three subtle folds, and a line of hair just
peeking out. Her young breasts, precious and heavy,   768
were compact, curving up high, and firm, like ripe
bael fruits just reaching their full size. Her arms, with   769
hands red as the flowers of the *aśoka* tree, looked like
golden lotus stalks growing in the Mandakini River.*

* The celestial Ganga.

७७० सुविसिट्ठतिरेहावरणविरइओ मडहपरिअराबंधो ।
कलहोअकलसकंठावसाअणो कंधरणिवेसो ॥२३२

७७१ रइकणइकुसुमगोच्छो व्व ईसिमज्झुण्णओ सुहावेइ ।
दसणावलिपरिवेसो विद्दुमराआरुणो अहरो ॥२३३

७७२ अविसट्टपुडजुआणुब्भडुज्जुओ वअणकमलकअसोहो ।
णिण्णुण्णअमज्झत्थो विहरइ से णासिआवंसो ॥

७७३ चिरमज्जणसलिलकसाअपाडलावंगदेसदीहाइं ।
णअणाइँ बालरविअरछित्ताइं दीवराइं व ॥

७७४ सज्जीवकामकोअंडसच्छहं सवणपत्तपेरंतं ।
णअणुप्पलणालजुअं व सहइ भुमआवलीजअलं ॥२३४

७७५ अद्धेंदुबिंबसरिसं णिडालफलअं विहाइ णिप्पंकं ।
जोव्वणसिरीए मुहदप्पणं व विहिणा विणिम्मविअं ॥२३५

७७६ तणुकसणसिणिद्धाआममणहरो दूरदेसकअसोहो ।
पट्टिणिसण्णो से हरइ भंगुरो केसपब्भारो ॥२३६

७७७ इअ जो जो से दीसइ अंगावअवाण को वि उद्देसो ।
सो सो ण देइ चलिउं अणिमिसपेच्छीण अच्छीणि ॥२३७

७७८ तं तह सुइरं णिव्वण्णिऊण परिचिंतिअंम्हि हिअएण ।
अण्णो सो को वि विही जस्सेअं रूवविण्णाणं ॥

७७९ अण्णह कह वेअजडस्स तस्स विसआहिलासविमुहस्स ।
णिप्पज्जइ लोअपिआमहस्स एवंविहं रूवं ॥

७८० मण्णे चंदामअपरिआअवम्महवसंतमइराए ।
कोत्थुहसिरिसारसमुच्चआहिँ एसा विणिम्मविआ ॥२३८

Her neck, with three clear lines around it and thin in 770
circumference, matched the neck of a golden ewer.
Her lips, pleasantly swelling toward the middle and 771
hiding her teeth, were like a coral-red flower cluster
on the vine of sex. Her nose was the stalk that gave 772
beauty to the lotus of her face, coming right in the
middle of its upper and lower parts, straight, not too
pronounced, with nostrils that did not open too much.
Her eyes, large and rimmed with pink from her long 773
swim, were like blue lotuses touched by sunbeams in
the morning. Her eyebrows, extending to her ears, 774
looked like bows strung by the god of love, or stalks of
the lotuses that were her eyes. Her forehead was like 775
the disc of the moon, but without the spot, or like a
hand mirror fashioned by the creator for the beauty
of youth. Her hair fell in curls down her back, fine, 776
black, glossy, long, and entrancing, with a beauty that
shone for miles. Whatever body part one gazed at 777
held the eyes unblinking and stopped them from ever
leaving.[176]

For a long time we stared at her like this, and we thought 778
to ourselves: It must have been some other creator
who had fashioned her, to have such knowledge
of beauty, completely different from the one we
know. For how could beauty like that ever issue 779
from the grandfather of the world, who has grown
numb from Vedic study and spurns all desire for
sensual objects?[177] She must have been fashioned 780
by combining the essence of the *kaustubha* gem and

७८१ किं एसा णाअवहू णु होज्ज विज्जाहरी णु देवी णु ।
असुरजुआणी सिद्धंगणा णु मज्झं समोइण्णा ॥२३९

७८२ ताव अ से णामणिवासजम्मकोऊहलाविआणम्ह ।
भणिआ विचित्तलेहा णामेण वअंसिआ तीए ॥

७८३ हल सहि विचित्तलेहे अणुगमसु इमं तवोवणं ताव ।
जाव णिवत्तेमि अहं पूआअम्मं भवाणीए ॥

७८४ जो सा विचित्तलेहा भाउअ सहसा समागआ एत्थ ।
अब्बीअं पिव हिअअं तिस्सा उवलक्खिवअं अम्हि ॥२४०

७८५ सा दूरकअपणामा भणिआ अम्हेहि तुज्झ का एसा ।
सुंदरि वअंसभावाणुसंगआ अणुवमकुमारी ॥

७८६ कस्स व एसा धूआ केण व कज्जेण आगआ एत्थ ।
कत्थ व जाही साहसु किं णामं कत्थ व णिवासो ॥

७८७ भणिअं च तीए भअवइ एअं जइ अत्थि तुम्ह कोहलं ।
ता साहेमि णिसामेसु वित्थरत्थं कहेअव्वं ॥२४१

Lakshmi with the moon, the heavenly *pārijāta* tree,
the god of love, the spring, and wine.[178] Is this girl   781
a *nāga,* or a *vidyādhara* perhaps, or a goddess, or
maybe a young *asura,* or possibly a *siddha,* who has
descended to the world of human beings?[179]

While we were thus overcome with curiosity about her   782
name, her native place, and her birth, she called out
to one of her friends, who was named Vichittaleha:
"Vichittaleha, my friend! Please go and visit this   783
ashram while I make an offering to Bhavani."

Straightaway, brother, Vichittaleha arrived. We could   784
tell that she and the princess were one at heart. We   785
bowed to her at a distance and said: "Beautiful girl,
who is that incomparable princess, so like you in age
and disposition? Whose daughter is she? For what   786
purpose has she come here? Where is she going? Tell
us, please. What is her name? Where does she live?"

"Your Holiness," she said, "if you really are keen to know,   787
then I'll tell you. But pay attention, as the story I'm
about to tell is long."

७८८ अत्थि तिसमुद्दपुहईविक्खाअजसो अखंडिअपआवो ।
णामेण सिलामेहो सिंहलदीवाहिवणरिंदो ॥

७८९ सो एक्कम्मि सुदिअहे पारद्धिविणिग्गओ महारण्णे ।
रमिऊण चिरं रण्णाउ पडिणिअत्तो पुराहुत्तं ॥

७९० तो तत्थ एक्कपाइक्कतुरअगअसाहणेण संचलिओ ।
सहस त्ति विअडदाढो पुरओ कोलोसमुच्छलिओ ॥

७९१ तो एक्कहअसहाओ तस्स वराहस्स मग्गसंलग्गो ।
णरणाहो ताव गओ जा तरुविडवाउलं रण्णं ॥२४२

७९२ ता तत्थ कुररकारंडचक्ककलहंसकंककसंकिण्णं ।
भमरभरोणअपंकअरअरंजिअपिंगपेरंतं ॥२४३

७९३ एवविहं सो भअवइ कमलसरं राइणो णिअंतस्स ।
सहस त्ति संपइट्ठो अत्थाहजलं महाकोलो ॥२४४

७९४ ता गंभीरसरोवरपवेसविसमं गए वराहम्मि ।
सच्छरिओ स विलक्खो मुहुत्तमेत्तं ठिओ राआ ॥२४५

७९५ तो परिसुदिअतुरंगो सो सहसा विम्हआवहिअहिअओ ।
आसण्णमसोअवणं सिसिरच्छाअं समल्लीणो ॥

७९६ ता तत्थ उहअकरगहिअकुसुममाला मणोहरावअवा ।
एक्कसरिआइ पहुणो पुरओ परिसंठिआ बाला ॥

198

VICHITTALEHA:
THE STORY OF LILAVAI

There once was a king of the Island of Sinhala, named 788
Silameha, whose fame had spread across the earth's
three oceans and whose might was irresistible. One 789
fine day he went out to the great forest to hunt, and
after spending some time there, he started back
toward the city. Just then a large-tusked boar, finding 790
itself harried by a force of men on foot, horse, and
elephant, suddenly ran out in front of him. That 791
very moment the lord of men, his horse his only
companion, was suddenly gripped by a desire to hunt
down that boar, and set off into the forest overgrown
with trees and thickets. In the forest was a lotus pond, 792
filled with ospreys, ducks, *cakravākas,* geese, and
herons, its edges tinged red by the pollen of lotuses
weighed down by bees, and there, Your Holiness, right 793
before the king's eyes the great boar suddenly plunged
into the water's depths. Once the boar had gotten out 794
of range by immersing itself in the deep waters of the
pond, the king stood there a moment, both amazed
and disappointed. Then, his horse exhausted and his 795
heart transported by wonder, he withdrew to a nearby
grove of *aśoka* trees to enjoy their cool shade. And 796
there a girl suddenly appeared before him, stunning in
body and holding a garland of flowers in each hand.

७९७ राएण तओ भणिआ कासि तुमं एरिसे महारण्णे ।
सच्छंदा वरमालं अप्पसि मह केण कज्जेण ॥२४६

७९८ भणिअं च तीए णरवइ किं इमिणा पुच्छिएण तुह ताव ।
परिणेसु मं णिसंको जाणिहिसि गएहिँ दिअहेहिँ ॥२४७

७९९ तं तह सोऊण णराहिवेण सा बालिआ पुणो भणिआ ।
सुंदरि णराहिवाणं एसो मग्गो च्चिअ ण होइ ॥

८०० अपरिग्गहा कुमारी अमुणिअगोत्तक्कमा अइट्ठसुआ ।
कह परिणिज्जसि बाले कहसु तुमं चेअ मह एअं ॥२४८

८०१ भणिअं च तीए णरवइ एसो च्चिअ सुपुरिसाण सद्धम्मो ।
ता साहेमि णिसामेसु कुलहरं जं म्ह एत्ताहे ॥२४९

८०२ अत्थि कणआअलुच्छंगसंगआ तिअसलोअविक्खआआ ।
सुलसा णामेण पुरी अब्झंतमणोहरा रम्मा ॥२५०

८०३ तत्थ अ विजाहरेंदो हंसो णामेण तिअसविक्खाओ ।
तस्सम्हेहि णराहिव दो च्चिअ धूआओ जाआओ ॥२५१

८०४ एक्काए वसंतसिरी मज्झ महल्लाए णाम णरणाह ।
वाहित्ता सरअसिरी अहं पि णिअगुरुअणेण तहिं ॥२५२

८०५ एवं णे दो वि पहाअसमअसंगीअअप्पसंगेण ।
देवीहराण पुरओ केलासगिरिं पवण्णाओ ॥

८०६ तत्थम्हेहि णराहिव हरिसवसुप्फुल्ललोअणो दिट्ठो ।
गोरीहराण पुरओ पणच्चमाणो गणाहिवई ॥२५३

८०७ अह सो मए गणेसो चिरपरिचअविम्हआए सामि तहिं ।
उवहसिओ तेणाहं पक्खित्ता मच्चुलोअम्मि ॥२५४

The king asked, "Who are you, roaming such an immense   797
    forest as this? And why are you offering me these
    beautiful garlands?"

"Your Majesty," she said, "why are you asking me these   798
    silly questions? Put your doubts aside and be my
    husband. In time you will come to understand it all."

To this the king replied, "Beautiful girl, this is most   799
    assuredly not the path kings follow. How could I   800
    marry a young woman without a wedding ceremony,
    about whose family I know nothing, whom I have
    never seen or heard of before? It is you who must
    answer me, girl."

"Your Majesty," she said, "this is indeed the true dharma   801
    of good men. So I will tell you now about my family.
    Listen closely.

"There is a lovely, utterly captivating city on the slopes   802
    of Golden Mountain, well known in the divine
    realm, named Sulasa. There lives Hamsa, king of   803
    vidyādharas, famed among the gods. I am one of
    his two daughters, Your Majesty. The other one,   804
    my elder sister, is called Vasantasiri. As for me, my
    parents called me Saraasiri. The two of us went   805
    before the goddess and Hara on Mount Kailasa to
    sing songs fit for the dawn. There, Your Majesty, we   806
    saw Ganesha dancing before Gauri and Hara, his
    eyes wide with joy. I had known him so long that I   807

८०८ एसो मह तेणं चिअ सूअरवेसो दआलुणा दिण्णो ।
णिअदूओ जेण तुमं अणुग्गहत्थं म्ह उवणीओ ॥

८०९ ता तेणं चिअ दिण्णो तं सि वरो भअवआ गणेसेण ।
परिणेसु णिरासंको एवविहं तुम्ह अविरुद्धं ॥२५५

८१० एवं सोऊण णराहिवेण परिओसविअसिअमुहेण ।
तक्कालोइअविहिणा परिणीआ तेण सा तत्थ ॥

८११ ताव अ तुरंगखुरखोज्जपवहलग्गेण साहणेण तहिं ।
सच्छविओ णरणाहो सरअसिरीलंभपरिउट्ठो ॥

८१२ तो सरअसिरीदंसणपहिट्ठपरिवारपरिलिओ राआ ।
संपत्तो णिअभवणं बंदिणजअसद्दहलबोलं ॥२५६

८१३ अह तिस्सा तेण तहिं एसा लीलावइ त्ति णामेण ।
उप्पण्णा पिअतणआ किं भणइ इहागआ कीस ॥

८१४ तं तुम्ह सीसइ च्चिअ इमीए जं जम्मवासराहिंतो ।
अज्जदिअसंतरं जाव वित्थरत्थं कहेअव्वं ॥

८१५ केणावि जम्मदिअहे इमीए असरीरिआए वाआए ।
दिव्वेण समाइट्ठं सिट्ठं देवण्णुएहिं पि ॥२५७

८१६ जह तो इमीए वरबालिआए होही वरो त्ति वरसमए ।
सो सअलपुहइणाहो लहिही दिव्वाओ सिद्धीओ ॥

८१७ एवं सोऊण कअं वद्धावणअं म्ह राइणा तत्थ ।
पहआइं संखकाहलरवसंवलिआइं तूराइं ॥२५८

made a lapse in judgment: I laughed at him, Your
Majesty, and he cast me down into the world of men.
He was compassionate enough, however, to give me a   808
personal attendant disguised as a boar—the very boar,
in fact, which has done me the favor of leading you to
me. So Lord Ganesha himself has delivered you to be   809
my husband. Put aside your doubts and marry me.
A union of this sort is not forbidden you."

At this the king's face blossomed with delight, and he   810
married her then and there with the rite appropriate
to the occasion. The very same moment, the king,   811
pleased to have gained Saraasiri as his wife, was
spotted by his forces, who had been following the
trail of his horse's hoofprints. Then the king and   812
his attendants, who were all delighted by the sight
of Saraasiri, returned home to the loud sounds of
panegyric hymns. To her was born a beloved daughter,   813
this girl here, named Lilavai. Why has she come here,
you ask?

Let me set out for you in full detail everything there is   814
to tell, from the day of her birth to the present. On   815
the day of her birth, a god foretold in a disembodied
voice, interpreted by the soothsayers, that whoever   816
this beautiful girl chooses as her husband will,
when the time comes, rule the whole earth and
gain supernatural powers. When the king heard   817
this prophecy, he performed her *vardhāpanaka*

८१८ उब्भीकिकआउ वरगुडिआओ हट्टेहिँ हट्टसोहाओ ।
देवालएहिँ देवंगधअवडाओ अ लोएण ॥२५९

८१९ परमपरिओसमुइओ पणच्चिओ वरविलासिणीणिवहो ।
दिण्णाइँ विप्पबंदिण बहुविहआइं च दाणाइं ॥२६०

८२० एवं णिव्वत्तासेसणामकरणाइमंगलीएहिँ ।
तद्दिअसं कीरंतेहिँ बालभावाउ उत्तिण्णा ॥

८२१ णिव्वडिआसेसविलाससोहसुपसाहिएहिँ अंगेहिँ ।
आरंभो णवजोव्वणसिरीए गहिओ अआलेण ॥

८२२ ताव अ लावण्णामअपूरिज्जंताइँ से णिएऊण ।
अंगाइँ सिलामेहेण चिंतिअं को वरो होज्ज ॥

८२३ अण्णम्मि दिणे बहुसिक्खिआण सुमईण विद्दुकुसलाण ।
णिअणअरचित्तआराण अप्पिओ राइणा णिअमो ॥

८२४ जह वच्चह हे उज्झाअसीसहा एत्थ पुहइविक्खआ ।
वसुहाहिवा लिहेऊण मज्झ दावेह जे के वि ॥२६१

ceremony* with the loud sounds of conches and bass
drums combined with the beating of tabors. The   818
marketplaces raised up wonderful decorative poles,
the temples raised up the beauty of the markets,
and the people raised up the flags in the temples.[180]
Troupes of beautiful women danced with the utmost   819
delight. Gifts of all kinds were presented to Brahmans
and bards. With all of the auspicious ceremonies,   820
such as the naming ceremony, being thus brought
to completion on that same day, she crossed over
from infancy to the next stage of life. Her body, well-   821
adorned with every kind of grace and beauty that
developed in her, reached the beginning of youth's
splendor well before its time. And the whole time   822
Silameha, observing how the nectar of allure was
filling the vessel of her body, kept wondering who
might eventually wed her.

One day the king gave a command to the artists of his   823
city who were very learned, wise, and mature in skill:
"Teachers and students, I want you to go and draw all   824
of the kings who are far-famed on this earth and show
them to me."

---

* The cutting of the umbilical cord.

८२५ तो तेहिँ चित्तआरेहिँ ते णरेंदा बहूहिँ दिअहेहिँ ।
लिहिऊण जहाइट्ठा सुहदिअहे दाविआ पहुणो ॥२६२

८२६ तेणावि चिरं णिव्वण्णिऊण लीलावईए वासहरे ।
संठविआ सुपइत्तेण किं पि हिअए धरेऊण ॥

८२७ तो जद्दिअसाहिंतो दिट्ठा वसुहाहिवा इमीए तहिं ।
तद्दिअसाओ दीसइ दिअहे दिअहे किसाअंती ॥

८२८ ण रमइ सहीहिँ समअं ण देइ सुअसारिआण परिवाडिं ।
णाहरणं पडिवज्जइ ण सुणइ गेअं पि गिज्जंतं ॥२६३

८२९ कुसुमोच्चअं पि ण कुणइ भवणुज्जाणम्मि विअसिअलअम्मि ।
ण अ भवणदीहिआमज्जणम्मि चित्तं समप्पेइ ॥

८३० ण अ रज्जं बहु मण्णइ ण रमइ वाउल्लिआहिँ अविअण्हं ।
णिद्दं विणा वि सअणं ण अ मुंचइ अद्धणिमिसं पि ॥२६४

८३१ ण अ विसइ णट्टसालं ण अ कीलापव्वअं समारुहइ ।
धाराहरे वि ण रमइ णाहारे आअरं कुणइ ॥२६५

८३२ इअ एव मए उवलक्खिऊण एक्कम्मि वासरविरामे ।
काऊण रहस्सं णवर पुच्छिआ सहि णिसामेसु ॥२६६

८३३ कीस तुमं तद्दिअसं जोआभासं गआ इव दुपेच्छं ।
संकप्पालिहिअं पिव पेच्छंती णालसं जासि ॥२६७

८३४ ण रमसि केणावि समं दिट्ठं पि ण परिअण समालवसि ।
अम्हं पि ण वेसंभसि अलमहवा पुच्छिआए तए ॥२६८

The artists then drew the kings, as ordered, over many   825
    days, and then on an auspicious day showed them
    to the king. He, in turn, looked them over for a   826
    while, and, keeping his plans to himself, he carefully
    displayed them in Lilavai's bedroom. From the very   827
    day she first beheld the kings there, she started
    growing thinner day by day. She no longer played   828
    with her friends, no longer spoke her usual phrases to
    her parrots and mynas, no longer got dressed up. She
    wouldn't even listen to songs when people would sing.
    She didn't pick flowers, either, in the house gardens,   829
    where the vines were all in bloom, nor did she set her
    heart on swimming in the house pond. She didn't   830
    respond to consolation, or find any satisfaction in
    playing with her dolls. Even though she couldn't sleep,
    she never left her bed for even half a second.[181] She   831
    didn't set foot in the dance hall, didn't climb up the
    play mountain, didn't spend any time in the fountains,
    didn't even care about food.

I noted all this until one day, as evening fell, I went to her   832
    in private and asked her. "Tell me, friend, how is it   833
    that, ever since that day, you seem to have entered
    some sort of yogic trance, and never tire of staring at
    an image drawn in your mind, which no one else can
    see? You don't spend time with anyone. You haven't   834
    even been seeing your friends, must less talking to
    them. But why do I even bother asking you? You do
    nothing at all to reassure us."

८३५ तं तह सोऊण ममाहिँ पणअपरिकोअकक्कसं वअणं ।
लीलावईए भणिअं पिअसहि कह तुज्झ ण कहेमि ॥२६९

८३६ ण तहा जणंति सोक्खं कज्जविसेसा विसेसरमणीआ ।
दीसंता वि हु एक्केहिँ जह वअंसेसु सीसंता ॥

८३७ अणुहूआण वि एक्केहिँ दइअदंसणविसेससोक्खाण ।
पच्छा वअंसिसिट्ठाण पल्लवा ताण पसरंति ॥२७०

८३८ ता साहेमि णिसामेसु तुज्झ एआण पुहइवालाण ।
मज्झम्मि इमो जो तविअकणअसरिसप्पहो लिहिओ ॥

८३९ दीसइ तणुकसणसणिद्धकेसवल्लरिपसाहिआववअवो ।
विउलाणणारविंदो आरत्ततिहाअणअणुजुओ ॥२७१

८४० उण्णअणासावंसो सुपरिट्ठिअमडहकंधराबंधो ।
विअडोरत्थलदेसो आजाणुपलंबदीहभुओ ॥२७२

८४१ मच्छंकुसजवचक्कंककरअलो पीणपीवरपओट्टो ।
तणुमज्झो सीहकडी करिकरजंघोरु सुहचलणो ॥

८४२ एअं दट्ठूण महं जाअं कोऊहलं परं हिअए ।
धण्णाओ ताउ जाणं दइओ एसो णराहिवई ॥

८४३ धण्णाण वि धण्णअराओ ताओ दइआओ जाओ एअस्स ।
पेच्छंति मुहं णिच्चं ताणं पि णमो पुरंधीणं ॥

८४४ इअ एवं चिंतंतीए सो मए पुच्छिओ सुचित्तअरो ।
सिट्ठं च तेण एसो राआ सालाहणो णाम ॥

८४५ अक्खलिअपआअवपसरो उइओइअवंससंभवो सुअणो ।
सव्वकलापत्तट्ठो चाई सूरो सुहाराहो ॥२७३

When she heard these words of mine, which were harsh 835
   with anger but only out of love, Lilavai said: "Dear
   friend, why shouldn't I tell you? For there are some 836
   things that, exquisitely pleasant as they may be, just
   don't give as much pleasure when you experience
   them by yourself as when you tell them to friends.
   And the exquisite pleasure of looking at your beloved, 837
   although experienced alone, only sends forth shoots
   later, when you tell your friends about it. So listen and 838
   I will tell you. Among these kings there is one painted
   here whose skin is the color of heated gold, whose 839
   fine, dark, and glossy hair, in curling locks, enhances
   his body's beauty; whose lotus face is broad, and eyes
   red at the corners; whose nose has a prominent bridge, 840
   neck slim yet well-proportioned, chest very large, and
   arms hang down to his knees; who has marks shaped 841
   like a fish, an elephant-goad, barley, and a discus on
   the palms of his hand; with forearms swollen with
   muscle, a thin waist, hips of a lion, thighs like the
   trunk of an elephant, and beautiful feet—when I saw 842
   him, desire overwhelmed my heart. 'Lucky are those
   women who could be the beloved of such a king.[182]
   Even luckier those who, beyond just being his beloved, 843
   get to see his face forever. Reverence to those women!'
   With this in mind I went and asked the painter, who 844
   told me that the king's name was Salahana, that he 845
   is a good man, the scion of a family on the rise, who
   projects his power unfailingly, skilled in all the arts,
   a generous patron, brave, and easy to conciliate.[183]

८४६ अह तस्स मुहाहि णिसामिऊण सविसेसकोउहल्लाए ।
जाआ मणडोहलआ जइ एसो मह वरो होइ ॥२७४

८४७ एवं तद्दिअसपवित्थरंतचिंताभरोत्थअमणाए ।
बहुएहिं णवर दिअहेहिं मज्झ सहि आगआ णिद्दा ॥

८४८ ता सो जहसंभाविअरूवाइसओ णराहिवो तत्थ ।
जाणामि समासीणो आगंतूणम्ह सअणीए ॥

८४९ ता सहि पच्चक्खं पिव तद्दंसणसज्झसावहिअहिअआ ।
सहस त्ति समुट्टंती हत्थे चेत्तूण णे भणिआ ॥

८५० एएहिं अवंगेहुण्णमंतभुमआवलंतविसमेहिं ।
हरिऊण मज्झ हिअअं णअणेहिं कहिं खु चलिआ सि ॥२७५

८५१ ता तक्खणं पकंपंतहिअअपडिवण्णपणअपसरा वि ।
लज्जाए अहं पिअसहि णइंचि पडिजंपिआ तस्स ॥

८५२ तो तेण मज्झ सहसा थिमिआलसलोअणुण्णअमुहेण ।
दिण्णो पओहरोवरि ससेअविरलंगुली हत्थो ॥

८५३ अवगूहिऊण धणिअं णवर णिसण्णो पुणो तहिं चेअ ।
परिउंबिअम्हि वअणे णअणेसु कवोलपासेसु ॥२७६

८५४ एवं च चाटुआरेण तेण लज्जा अलज्जिरेणम्ह ।
अवहरिआ हिअआओ समअं कोमारभावेण ॥

८५५ एत्थुप्परं ण आणामि किं पि जं तुह कहेमि वाआए ।
हिअअं चिअ जइ जाणइ केत्तिअमेत्तं ण विम्हरइ ॥

   As soon as those words left his mouth my desire grew   846
all the more intense and longing arose in my heart.
What if he should be my husband?

"So it was many days before sleep came to me, my friend,   847
    as my heart was weighed down since that day by
    an ever-growing burden of anxiety. Then the king   848
    himself, I am sure of it, came and sat right next to me
    on my bed. He was even more handsome than I had
    imagined. Panic seized my heart, my friend, when it   849
    seemed that I was looking at him face to face. I quickly
    tried to get up, but he took me by the hand and said,
    'Where do you think you're off to, having stolen my   850
    heart with these eyes of yours that keep darting below
    your upraised eyebrows?'

"At that moment, dear friend, my heart was pounding   851
    and overflowing with love for him, but I was too
    embarrassed to say a single thing to him. Then he   852
    lifted his face, eyes still and calm, and placed his hand,
    moist with sweat and fingers limp, upon my breast. He   853
    embraced me tightly, and then he lay right down next
    to me, and kissed me on my mouth, my eyes, and my
    cheeks. By romancing me like this, with no shame at   854
    all, he drew the shame right out of my heart—and with
    it, my virginity. Beyond this, I don't know if there's   855
    anything I could tell you in words. It's my heart that
    knows, and what it knows, it won't forget.

८५६ ताव अ पहाअपडिहअतूरणिणाएण पडिविउद्धाए ।
सच्चविअं सअणीअं जा सो ण अणम्हि कत्थ गओ ॥

८५७ तद्दिअसाओ पिअसहि तं चिअ खलसिविणअं सरंतीए ।
पच्चक्खसोक्खतण्हालुआए परिवड्ढिआ चिंता ॥२७७

८५८ ता सुक्कपाअवब्भंतरुग्गओ हुअवहो व्व मह मअणो ।
चिंतासमीरणुद्दीविओ व्व हिअअम्मि पज्जलिओ ॥२७८

८५९ ता ण सुहं सअणीए ण अ धरणिअले ण बाहिरे ण घरे ।
ण अ दिणसमए ण णिसासु कह वि पावंति अंगाइं ॥२७९

८६० एआइ मि रमणीआइँ जाइँ भणिआइँ तुम्हि पुणरुत्तं ।
विवरीआइँ असेसाइं ताइँ जाआइं मह एण्हिं ॥

८६१ अह किं पुणरुत्तपअंपिएण बहुएण तुज्झ सहि पुरओ ।
उद्देसिअं पि जाणसि हिअअणिहित्तं म्ह सब्भावं ॥२८०

८६२ जइ सो एत्थ ण एही ताओ ण अ पेसिही ममं तत्थ ।
ता दूसहं सहंती मरणे वि सुहं ण पाविस्सं ॥२८१

८६३ तं तह सोऊण चिरं भअवइ भणिअंम्हि तह वि णूमेसि ।
एमविहो अणुराओ एमविहे वि हु वरे जाओ ॥

८६४ अंबाए इमं सीसउ स च्चिअ ताअस्स कहउ जं संतं ।
सो वि हु सुद्धसहावो काही हिअइच्छिअं तुज्झ ॥२८२

"As I woke to the sounds of the drums being played at   856
    dawn and looked at my bed, I had no idea where he
    had gone. Ever since that day, dear friend, I have held   857
    on to the memory of that dream, growing more and
    more distraught in my longing to have that pleasure
    in person. Then, like a fire exploding in the branches   858
    of a dry tree, desire ignited within my heart, inflamed
    by the wind of anxious thought. My body took no   859
    comfort at all, neither in my bed nor on the floor,
    neither outside nor at home, neither day nor night.
    All the pleasing things you would say to me, again and   860
    again, have now become quite the opposite, without
    exception. But why, my friend, should I repeat all   861
    this to your face? I have said what I can, but you must
    already know the truth that is hidden in my heart. If   862
    he won't come here, and if my father won't send me
    there, I just won't be able to bear it. Even death would
    give me no comfort."

I listened to her speak, Your Holiness, for quite a while,   863
    then said: "Why should you have hidden it for so long,
    with such love you have for so worthy a man? You   864
    should tell your mother, and she can tell your father
    whatever there is to tell. As for him, his nature is pure,
    and he will do what you desire."[184]

८६५ भणिअं पुणो वि लीलावईए किमहं ण आणिमो एअं ।
सिविणअदिट्ठम्मि जणे अणुबंधो पडइ उवहासे ॥

८६६ तह वि हु जह ण हसिज्जइ लक्खिज्जइ जह ण पोढिमा मज्झ ।
तह साहेज्जसु पिअसहि अंबाए णिज्जणम्मि तुमं ॥२८३

८६७ एवं भणिआइ मए भअवइ गंतूण णिज्जणुद्देसे ।
सिट्ठं माआपिउणो ण विरुज्झइ जह सलज्जाण ॥

८६८ तो गुरुअणेण एसा तं चिअ बहु मण्णिऊण मह भणिअं ।
सव्वाअरेण हालस्स पेसिआ वच्चउ पहाए ॥

Lilavai spoke again: "Don't you think I know this? They   865
would laugh at me for falling in love with someone I
saw in a dream! All the same, dear friend, please find a   866
private spot to go and tell my mother, but please do it
in such a way that she won't make fun of me, or realize
what I had the audacity to do."

At this, Your Holiness, I went and told her parents in   867
private, without going into the embarrassing details.
Her parents then told me how highly they thought of   868
Hala, and that she should be sent to him with all due
regard at dawn.

८६९ इअ एमविहं भाउअ विचित्तलेहाणणाहि सोऊण ।
सहस त्ति महाणुमईए पभणिअं सहरिसंगीए ॥

८७० पिअसहि विचित्तलेहे एसाहं इह वसंतसिरितणआ ।
तुम्हं माउसभइणी साहसु लीलावईए लहुं ॥

८७१ तो सा विचित्तलेहा एवं सोऊण पडिगआ तुरिअं ।
लीलावईए पासं हिअए णमाअंतपरिओसं ॥

८७२ ता तीए समं कंचुइपुरस्सरा परिअणेण परिअरिआ ।
लीलावई वि सहसा अम्ह सआसं समल्लीणा ॥

८७३ अह सहरिसाए भाउअ सहसा समइच्छिआ मए पढमं ।
तह अ महाणुमईए पुलअसणाहेहिं अंगेहिं ॥२८४

८७४ तो सा अम्हेहिँ तहिं अणिच्छमाणा वि कड्ढिऊण करे ।
उववेसिआ सलज्जा एक्कासणमज्झदेसम्मि ॥

८७५ अह एक्केक्कमकुलहरकुसलसुहालावदिण्णहिअआण ।
गलिअं णिरुंभमाणं पि बाहसलिलं कवोलेसु ॥

८७६ पुसिऊण कवंडलवारिणा मुहं मह मुहं णिअंतीए ।
लीलावईए भणिअं अज्जे एअं म्ह अच्छरिअं ॥

८७७ एसो जडाकलावो इमाइँ तरुवक्कलाइँ इह वासो ।
वअविहवाआरकुलक्कमस्स दूरं विरुद्धाइं ॥

216

KUVALAAVALI:
LILAVAI'S RESOLUTION

Having heard this, brother, from the mouth of   869
    Vichittaleha, Mahanumai shivered with joy, and she
    said: "Dear friend, Vichittaleha, go quick and tell   870
    Lilavai that I am here, the daughter of Vasantasiri, her
    cousin on her mother's side."

Vichittaleha heard this and quickly returned to Lilavai.   871
    Her heart could not contain her delight. Then Lilavai   872
    herself quickly came to where we were,
    in the company of Vichittaleha and her attendants,
    and preceded by a chamberlain. I was thrilled,   873
    brother, to be the first to embrace her. Mahanumai
    was next, the hair on her body standing on end.
    Then, although she was unwilling, shy as she was, we   874
    took her hand and made her sit down between the
    two of us on a single seat. Our hearts were completely   875
    given over to pleasant conversation, asking after the
    health of each other's families. And though we tried to
    hold them back, tears tumbled down our cheeks.

Lilavai dabbed her face with water from the pitcher,   876
    then looked me in the eyes and said: "This is really
    unbelievable, madam. These locks of matted hair,   877
    these tree bark clothes, your living here—how
    profound a contradiction with your youth, your
    wealth, your beauty, and your parentage."

८७८ सिट्टुं च मए तिस्सा एअं जं तुम्ह साहिअं पढमं ।
अमुणिअमणाइ भाउअ णीसेसं साअरं तीए ॥२८५

८७९ तं तह सोऊण ममाहि तक्खणं चेअ तीए उल्लविअं ।
अज्जदिवसाउ अज्जे ममावि वासो इह च्चेअ ॥

८८० सो हिअअसमीहिअवरसमागमो जेच्चिरेण संपडइ ।
तेच्चिरआलं तुम्हाण चलणसंवाहिआहोमि ॥

८८१ एवं च समुल्लविए भणिअं अम्हेइँ पडिहअं वअणं ।
एअं तुह बालमअच्छि कण्णकडुअं सुणंताण ॥

८८२ असुहज्जिअकम्माण वि हवंतु अम्हाण संपइ सुहाइं ।
तुह हिअअसमीहिअवरविवाहदंसणमहग्घाइं ॥२८६

८८३ भणिअं पुणो वि लीलावईए मा एरिसं समुल्लवसु ।
किं तुम्हेहि ण आणह जह भणिअं पुव्वपुरिसेहिं ॥२८७

८८४ इअ जेट्ठाणुक्कमबाहिराइँ कज्जाइँ जाइँ कीरंति ।
असुहाइँ ताइँ लोए पडंति उवहासपअवीए ॥२८८

८८५ जइ कह व अपेच्छंती वसणमिणं ववगआ गआ णाम ।
संपइ लोअविरुद्धं गमणं मा भणसु एत्ताहे ॥२८९

८८६ अह किं बहुणा तुह पिसुणिएण सा कह वि कह वि अम्हेहिं ।
विणिअत्तिउं ण तिण्णा इमाउ णिअणिच्छआहिंतो ॥२९०

८८७ इअ एवं वसणपरंपराए ओवग्गिआओ अम्हेहिं ।
ता किं पुच्छसि ण कओ तुम्ह पसाओ भवाणीए ॥

Then I patiently shared with her the entire story I just told 878
   you, brother. She had not known any of it. The very 879
   moment she heard it, she began to speak: "From this
   day forward, madam, I too will live right here with
   you. Until you both are reunited with the men your 880
   hearts desire, I will be here to wait on you hand and
   foot."[185]

To this I replied: "What you just said, fawn-eyed girl, 881
   pains my ears to hear. We may have bad karma from 882
   prior misdeeds, but for now let us have the invaluable
   pleasure of seeing your wedding with the man your
   heart desires."

Lilavai spoke again: "Don't talk like that. Don't you know 883
   what people long ago used to say? Follow the order of 884
   seniority in your affairs, for if you don't they will all
   fall through and make you the laughingstock of the
   world.[186] If I had gone off without knowing anything 885
   at all of this disaster, then I would have gone. But
   don't tell me to go now—that's not what people do."

Oh, why should I keep telling you about this? Try as I 886
   might—and I did—I couldn't get her to reverse that
   decision of hers. Such was the series of disasters that 887
   kept engulfing us. So why do you ask whether Bhavani
   has shown us any favor?

८८८ एवमसेसं सोऊण तत्थ तं कुवलआवलिमुहाओ ।
णरणाह मए भणिअं हिअए णमाअंततोसेण ॥

८८९ एसो हं भअवइ तस्स राइणो पणइआण मज्झम्मि ।
आबालसेवओ वरपसाअसुहसंगसंतुट्ठो ॥

८९० ता कहसु कत्थ सा अम्ह सामिणी वसइ जंणिएऊण ।
साहामि सहरिसं सुकअकम्मफलमप्पणं पहुणो ॥

८९१ भणिअं च इसिसुआए हरिसभरिज्जंतलोअणमुहीए ।
अमअवरिसो व्व भाउअ अज्ज तुमं आगओ अम्ह ॥

८९२ एत्थम्ह तवोवणतरुविणाससंकाणिरुद्धपरिवारा ।
लीलावई इमाओ णिवसइ अद्धोअणद्धम्मि ॥

८९३ अह एवं जा पिसुणेइ मज्झ सा कुवलआवली देव ।
ता तत्थ महाणुमई वि आगआ एक्कदेसाओ ॥२९१

८९४ सिट्ठं से सहि सालाहणस्स पिअपणइआण मज्झम्मि ।
एसो विजआणंदो आबालवअंसओ पेच्छ ॥

८९५ तो तं सोऊण ससंभमाए जक्खाहिवस्स तणआए ।
भणिअं अज्ज सुदिअसो भाउअ तुम्हागमेणम्ह ॥

८९६ तो गोसग्गे पेच्छसु तत्तो च्चिअ कुवलआवलीए समं ।
गंतूण सामिजाअं अमअरसोल्लेहिँ अच्छीहिं ॥

VIJAANANDA:
HIS MEETING WITH LILAVAI

When I heard all this from Kuvalaavali's mouth, my lord,   888
    I said, with joy my heart could not contain:

"Your Holiness, I am a companion of that king, in his   889
    service since childhood, and I am pleased to be in his
    favor. So please, tell me where our lady is staying.   890
    After I see her, I will be thrilled to tell my lord about
    the fruit his good karma has borne."

"Brother," said the daughter of the sage, wide-eyed and   891
    smiling, "your arrival here today is like a rain of nectar
    for us. Lilavai is staying a few miles from here. Her   892
    retinue was not allowed here, out of concern they
    might destroy the trees in our ashram."

Then, king, just as Kuvalaavali was saying this to me,   893
    Mahanumai, too, came from somewhere to join her.
    "Friend," she told her, "this man, Vijaananda, is one of   894
    the close companions of Salahana. Look! He has been
    his friend since they were children."

At this, the daughter of the *yakṣa* king spoke eagerly: 895
    "Brother, your arrival here has made this a truly
    auspicious day. Please go and behold your master's   896
    wife-to-be with your own eyes, drenched with nectar,
    leaving from here at dawn with Kuvalaavali."

८९७ भणिअं च मए भअवइ जं सि तुमं आणवेसि एत्ताहे ।
मह उण हिअअं असहीरणाए णीअं तहिं चेअ ॥२९२

८९८ एवं सा तुम्ह कहाविणोअसुहणिब्भराण वोलीणा ।
सव्वाण विणिद्दाणम्ह देव अइदीहरा राई ॥

८९९ तो गोससमाहिसुहावसाणसमअम्मि पेसिआ ताहिं ।
तावसकुमरी लीलावईए परिओसिरी पुरओ ॥

९०० अणुमग्गमुवगआ से अम्हे वि हु कुवलआवलीए समं ।
पत्ता अ करिकरेणूसमाउलं राउलं तत्थ ॥२९३

९०१ दिट्ठं च मए पढमं गहिआउहभडणिहाअणिव्विच्चं ।
बीअं पडिहारणिरुंभमाणजणसंकुलं दारं ॥२९४

९०२ तइअं च महुरमद्दलवेणुपगिज्जंतमंगलणिहोसं ।
रमणिअणाहरणमऊहजालबज्झंतसुरचावं ॥२९५

९०३ एवमहं तं तइअं कमेण कच्छंतरं कमेऊण ।
अब्भंतरकअकुसुमोववआरमणिकुट्टिमं विसिओ ॥

९०४ ता तत्थ फलिहमणिकुट्टिमम्मि विरइअपिसंडिपलंके ।
सहस त्ति समासीणा सच्चविआ सा मए कुमरी ॥

९०५ णाणाविहगहिअपसाहणेण सहिआअणेण परिअरिआ ।
विमलम्मि सरअसमए सरिक्खणवचंदलेह व्व ॥

९०६ अह सा सब्भुट्ठाणं णमिऊण पुणो वि तत्थ सअणीए ।
कुवलअमालाए समं जेट्ठकणिट्ठं समासीणा ॥२९६

९०७ ताव अहं पि णराहिव कअसत्थीवाअणो समासीणो ।
सव्वाअरोवणीए पुरओ कणआसणुच्छंगे ॥

222

"As you command, Your Holiness," I said. "My heart, 897
however, can't bear to wait, and has already gone
there ahead of us."

In this way, my lord, all of us passed the long night without 898
sleeping, instead pleasantly diverting ourselves with
stories about you.[187]

When the two girls had completed their dawn meditation, 899
they sent ahead to Lilavai an amiable ascetic girl.
Kuvalaavali and I went along after her, and in due 900
course we reached her palace, marked by a stable
full of bull and cow elephants. The first gate I saw 901
was packed with squads of armed guards, and the
second was full of people that the doorkeepers were
trying to keep in order. The third was very loud, 902
as pleasant *mardala* drums and pipes were playing
auspicious music, and cascading rays of light from
the jewelry of beautiful women had formed a rainbow
around it. The path I just described took me to the 903
third chamber, and once inside, I was seated on a
jewel-studded slab strewn with flower petals. There 904
I instantly recognized the princess, seated as she was
upon a golden palanquin set upon a crystal platform.
She was surrounded by attendants wearing all manner 905
of ornaments, like the crescent moon with the stars
on a clear autumn night. Then she rose courteously 906
to us, bowed, and sat down again on the couch with
Kuvalaavali, observing the order of seniority. For my 907
part, my lord, I spoke a blessing, and sat down in front

१०८ अह तत्थ सुहासणकअपरिग्गहो साअरं सलज्जेहिं ।
अच्छीहिं चिअ लीलावईए संमाणिओ त्ति अहं ॥२९७

१०९ ता णिहुअणिवारिअपरिअणाए पट्टिट्ठिआए बालाए ।
एक्काए कणअकलसो सिसिरो पल्हत्थिओ सीसे ॥

११० अण्णाए कंठमज्झे संजमिओ णिअउत्तरिज्जेणं ।
अण्णाए सिचअवट्टीए कड्ढिओ मज्जणाहुत्तं ॥

१११ अण्णाहिँ परमपरिहासपहरिसुप्पण्णगरुअथामाहिं ।
हक्खुविउं उज्जला खित्तो हं कणअदोणीए ॥२९८

११२ ता तुम्ह संकहालावपमुइआहिं पसण्णवअणाहिं ।
ण्हावेऊण जहेच्छं भोअणसालं समुवणीओ ॥

११३ तत्थ मणोज्जं सरसं विविहाहारं कमेण भोत्तूण ।
तंबोलकरविलेवणसंपत्तुक्किट्टसंमाणो ॥

११४ परिअरिओ वररमणीअणेण उवसप्पिओ पुणो वि तहिं ।
जाआए तुम्ह णरवइ सप्परिहासं हसिज्जंतो ॥

११५ अज्जेत्थ तुम्ह गरुओ सउणविसेसेण केण वि किलेसो ।
जाओ अविणअसीलाओ दुट्ठजुवईअणाहिंतो ॥२९९

of them on a raised seat of gold that had been brought
to me with great courtesy. Once comfortably seated,   908
I was met with due honor—by none other than
Lilavai's modest eyes.

Then one girl, having given a silent sign for the other   909
attendants to leave, stood behind me and poured cool
water from a golden ewer over my head. Another   910
held me with her upper garment around my neck,
and another dragged me to my bath by the hem of
my clothes. Some other girls had drawn superhuman   911
strength from their delighted giggling and picked me
up by force to throw me into a golden tub. Then, with   912
smiles on their faces as they spoke about you, they
gave me a very welcome bath and led me to the dining
room.

The food I enjoyed there, of various kinds and over several   913
courses, was delicious and very agreeable. I was then
given the great honor of receiving betel leaves and
hand ointments. When once again I came before your   914
wife-to-be, my lord, with all of those beautiful girls
surrounding me, she laughed and made a joke: "You   915
must have gotten a bad omen this morning, seeing the
great trouble these bad girls have given you with their
immodest behavior."

९१६ भणिअं च मए सामिणि एअं एएहिँ जं कअं अम्ह ।
तं सविसेसं होही दूणं तिउणं ममाहिंतो ॥

९१७ अम्हेहिं पि ण भद्दा जं जेण कअं कमेण तं तस्स ।
अकअं होही किं जंपिएण बहुएण एत्ताहे ॥३००

९१८ एवमवराइँ बहुसो परिहासपअंपिआइँ सोऊण ।
सप्परिओसा सा कुवलआवली ववगआ देव ॥३०१

९१९ एवमहं पि णराहिव तत्थ सुहं अच्छिऊण तद्दिअहं ।
गोसे धरेज्जमाणो वि ताहिँ तुरिअं समुच्चलिओ ॥

९२० पत्तो अविहाविअपहपरिस्समो अगणिएहिँ दिअसेहिँ ।
गरुएण महातोसेण तुम्ह पअपंकअच्छअं ॥

"Mistress," I said, "what they have done to me, I will have   916
    to do to them, two or three times worse. I am not such   917
    a nice guy that I would leave unpunished the wrongs
    that are done to me. But let's not get into details right
    now."

After listening to a few more jokes like these, my lord,   918
    Kuvalaavali returned home with satisfaction. As for   919
    me, Your Majesty, I had the pleasure of staying there
    the whole day. Although they tried to keep me longer,
    I slipped away the following morning.

Over the many days that it took me to reach the beauty of   920
    your lotus feet, my enormous delight prevented me
    from feeling any weariness from my travels.

९२१ एवमसेसं कुवलअदलच्छि सोऊण राइणा तत्थ ।
विजआणंदो तं चेअ पुच्छिओ फुल्लिअच्छेण ॥

९२२ हंहो सच्चं एअं सच्चविअं किं तए सअच्छीहिं ।
णिसुअं वा कत्थ वि सिविणअं व दिट्टुं णिसासमए ॥

९२३ भणिअं च तेण णरवइ सच्चं मोत्तूण सामिणो पुरओ ।
उल्लवइ को अलज्जो एद्दहमेत्तं फलं कज्जं ॥

९२४ तं तह सोऊण णराहिवेण उब्बिंबबालहरिणच्छि ।
भणिअं अज्ज वि अच्छइ ता किं सो पोट्टिसो तत्थ ॥

९२५ णूणं च सिलामेहो वि जेण दुच्चिंतिमा परिच्चअइ ।
आ जम्मं तेण समं एत्ताहे घरकुडुंबं म्ह ॥३०२

९२६ अण्णं च पुणो पुच्छामि साह जइ तं तए तहा दिट्टुं ।
ता सो सिद्धकुमारो कह उण ताणं समावडइ ॥

९२७ जइ होइ महाणुमईए सो वरो ता ममं पि पडिवण्णं ।
विहिणा जं तं लीलावईए सिविणंतरे दिट्टुं ॥

९२८ जइ सो तिस्सा ता सा वि अम्ह लीलावई सराआ वि ।
पत्थेज्ज अहं ता पिअवअंस वच्चेज्ज से पासं ॥

९२९ विसमा खलु कज्जगई णेसा दाणेण णेअ बुद्धीए ।
ण अ पोरिसेण सिज्झइ एक्कं देव्वं पमोत्तूण ॥३०३

९३० जं जीएण वि दुलहं दूरत्थं जं मणोरहाणं पि ।
तं मह विहिणा सव्वाअरेण सोक्खं समाइट्टुं ॥३०४

९३१ तह वि दुरासा एसा जीएण समं म्ह संपइ णिबद्धा ।
वच्चेज्जसु विजआणंद तं सि जा पोट्टिसो एइ ॥

THE POET:
VIJAANANDA'S SECOND MISSION

The king listened to all of this, my love with lily-petal   921
    eyes, and with wide eyes he asked Vijaananda about
    it: "Now tell me, is this really true? Did you see it with   922
    your own eyes? Or did you hear it? Or maybe you fell
    asleep, and saw it in a dream?"

"King," he said, "who could be shameless enough to speak   923
    anything but the truth before his master regarding so
    important a matter?"

When the king heard this, my fawn-eyed love, he said: 924
    "What about Pottisa? Is he still there? Silameha must   925
    surely have renounced any hostility to us, now that
    he has joined our house and family for life. And I have   926
    one more thing to ask. Tell me if you see any way at
    all for that *siddha* prince to be restored to them. If he   927
    can become Mahanumai's husband, then I too will
    have obtained what fate revealed to Lilavai in her
    dreams. Once he is hers, my dear friend, then Lilavai   928
    would set out again for me, the one she loves,
    or I would go to her myself. The course of affairs is   929
    difficult indeed. It can neither be accomplished by
    gifts nor by intelligence, acts of valor, nor indeed
    by anything except fate. Fate has destined me, with   930
    great consideration, for a happiness that human life
    very rarely attains, far beyond the reaches of even
    my desires. At all events, my life now depends on this   931
    hope, vain though it may be. Please go, Vijaananda,

९३२ जं तं णिसुअं सिट्टुं च तेण लीलावईए जम्मदिणे ।
असरीरिआए वाआए किं पि केणावि किर भणिअं ॥

९३३ तं पुच्छिज्जइ सो च्चिअ पुणो वि एवंविहे समावडिए ।
कह होज्ज अम्ह जाआ कह वा सिद्धाहिवो तिस्सा ॥३०५॥

९३३क एवं जा तेण समं विजआणंदेण अच्छइ णरिंदो ।
मंतंतो ता कुवलअदलच्छि सो पोट्टिसो पत्तो ॥३०६॥

९३४ तो से विजआणंदेण किं पि जं पाविअं दिसाविजए ।
तं उवणीअं पहुणो करिरअणसुवण्णसंघाअं ॥

९३५ तो तम्मि महाकोसे सच्चविओ राइणा अणग्घेओ ।
पाहुडजोग्गो लीलावईए थूलामलो हारो ॥३०७॥

९३६ अह तं घेत्तूण णराहिवेण ससिसोहणिम्मलं हारं ।
भणिओ विजआणंदो एअं चिअ पाहुडं तिस्सा ॥

९३७ वच्चसु घेत्तूण लहुं कज्जगइं जाणिऊण तं तत्थ ।
अविलंब विजआणंद पडिवहं सच्चविज्जासु ॥

९३८ एवं भणिऊण णराहिवेण उब्बिंबबालहरिणच्छि ।
विजआणंदो लीलावईए संपेसिओ पास ॥

९३९ अह ववगअम्मि कुवलअदलच्छि सो सालवाहणणरिंदो ।
विजआणंदम्मि दिणं णिसं च अप्पा वि विम्हरिओ ॥३०८॥

९४० अकअसुकव्वविणोओ अवहत्थिअरज्जकज्जवावारो ।
अणिसामिअसुहिवअणो अपसाहिअविग्गहावअवो ॥३०९॥

९४१ णिद्दासुहपरिहरिओ असमीहिअमज्जणो अणिव्वाणो ।
असुअसुईउवएसो अदिट्ठसुविलासिणीविसओ ॥३१०॥

230

before Pottisa returns. You said that someone had 932
heard and explained what that disembodied voice had
said the day of Lilavai's birth. He should be consulted 933
once again about how to bring these couples together.
How is Lilavai to be mine, and how is the *siddha* king
to be Mahanumai's?"

While the king was taking counsel with Vijaananda, my 933a
love with lily-petal eyes, Pottisa returned.

Then Vijaananda brought before his lord everything 934
Pottisa had acquired on his military campaign—
elephant herds, jewels, and gold. In that great treasure 935
store the king set his eyes on an invaluable necklace,
thick and pure, that would be a suitable gift for Lilavai.
The king took the necklace, white as the light of the 936
moon, and said to Vijaananda: "This will be my gift
to her. Bring it to her quickly, and once you know the 937
course of affairs, Vijaananda, see to it that you come
back here without delay."

With this, my fawn-eyed love, the king sent Vijaananda 938
to Lilavai. Once Vijaananda had departed, my love 939
with lily-petal eyes, King Salahana was hardly aware
of himself, day or night. He took no pleasure from 940
fine poetry, left aside the affairs of state, and stopped
listening to his friends' words and adorning his body.
He was robbed of the pleasure of sleep. He had no 941
desire for bathing. He was inconsolable. He did not
listen to instruction from the Vedas. He did not look

९४२ पोट्टिसमीसेहिँ समं णिच्चं लीलावईकहासत्तो ।
विजआणंदागमणं झाअंतो अच्छइ दिणम्मि ॥

९४३ अण्णम्मि वासरे वित्तिएण सहस त्ति विअसिअमुहेण ।
विजआणंदो दारे विण्णत्तं पुहइणाहस्स ॥

९४४ अह तेण सहरिसं कुवलअच्छि हक्कारिऊण आइट्ठं ।
विजआणंदस्स णराहिवेण कणआसणं पुरओ ॥

९४५ तो तत्थ कअपसाओ आसीणो पुच्छिओ णरिंदेण ।
कुसलं तुह विजआणंद अइचिरं चेअ आगमणं ॥३११

९४६ अविसट्टं ते वअणं विच्छाअं विग्गहं किसा वाणी ।
कीस कएण णिरोज्जाइँ तुम्ह णअणाइँ एत्ताहे ॥३१२

९४७ भणिअं च तेण णरवइ किं कीरइ विम्मुहेण हअविहिणा ।
अण्णाहुत्तं कीरइ अण्णइ परिचिंतिअं कज्जं ॥

at beautiful women. He was absorbed in talking   942
about Lilavai with Pottisa, and spent the whole day
anxiously awaiting Vijaananda's return.

Suddenly one day, the chamberlain, his face blossoming,   943
informed the lord of earth that Vijaananda was at
the gate. The king had Vijaananda admitted with   944
delight, my lily-eyed love, and pointed to the golden
seat in front of him. As he was shown the favor of   945
being offered a seat, the king asked him: "Is all well
with you, Vijaananda? You certainly took your time
returning. You're not smiling, your body looks sickly   946
pale, and your voice is thin. Why? What's the reason
your eyes are no longer shining bright?"

"Your Majesty," he said, "what is to be done? Accursed   947
fate is making things turn out very differently from
the way we had thought."

९४८ तं तह एक्केणं चिअ तुरअसहस्सेण देव सुजवेण ।
संपत्तो हं लीलावईए पासम्मि संतुट्ठो ॥३१३

९४९ दिट्ठा सा तत्थ मए मद्दंसणहरिसपप्फुअच्छिजुआ ।
लीलावई णराहिव पमुइअपरिवारपरिअरिआ ॥३१४

९५० तो से कअसंमाणो अह्लीणो तीए पाअमूलम्मि ।
सव्वाअरोवणीआसणम्मि समुअं समासीणो ॥३१५

९५१ अह सो मए णराहिव तुह जसधवलो समप्पिओ हारो ।
तीए वि तक्खणं चिअ पओहरोवरि परिट्ठविओ ॥

९५२ अह तत्थ मए भणिआ विचित्तलेहा वि तुम्ह वअणेण ।
सुअणु णिसामह सीसइ जं तुम्हप्पाहिअं पहुणा ॥३१६

९५३ अण्णेसिआइं बहुसो लद्धाइं ण ताइं मज्झ हिअएण ।
अप्पाहणक्खराइं इह तुम्हं जाइं सीसंति ॥३१७

९५४ भणिअं च तीए भाउअ एवं एअं भणंति ते जं म्ह ।
सव्वाण वि साणुभवं णेहणिबद्धाण सुअणाण ॥३१८

९५५ दिज्जंति जाइं पिअमाणुसम्मि अविहत्तहिअअभावम्मि ।
दुलहाइं ताइं णिक्कइअवाइं अप्पाहणवआइं ॥

९५६ एवम्ह सप्पसाअस्स संपअं केण सुहविणोएण ।
वच्चंति तुम्ह पहुणो दिअहा तद्दिअहरमणीआ ॥

९५७ भणिअं च मए सुंदरि इमाए तुम्हंचिआइ चिंताए ।
अविहाविअणिसिदिअहं पेच्छइ जोइ व्व झाणगओ ॥३१९

VIJAANANDA:
THE SECOND MISSION

Let me explain. I was pleased to have reached Lilavai 948
very quickly, my lord, with a thousand horse. When 949
I saw her, Your Majesty, Lilavai's eyes opened wide
with delight upon seeing me, and all the attendants
around her were overjoyed as well. Then, honored by 950
her, I happily took my seat at her feet in a chair that
had been offered with utmost courtesy. Then, Your 951
Majesty, I delivered to her that necklace, white as
your fame, and she, in turn, at once placed it on her
chest.[188] I then passed on your words to Vichittaleha: 952
"Lovely girl, my lord has a message for you. Please
listen: 'For a long time I sought the words of a message 953
to send you, but in the end, my heart could not find
them.'"

"Brother," she said, "this is just what they say all good 954
people feel when love has bound them together: It is 955
truly difficult to find words, free of all dissimulation,
to send as a message to one's beloved, with whom
one shares a single heart. Your lord has done us this 956
favor. Now tell us, in what pleasant diversions does he
spend his days, lovely with the thought of the day to
come?"[189]

"Lovely girl," I said, "he is staring off, lost in thought 957
about you and you alone, like a yogi engrossed in
meditation, unaware of whether it is day or night.

LILAVAI

९५८ णो संभरइ पलत्तं पेच्छइ ण समीवसंठिअं पि जणं ।
ण अ मज्जणं पवज्जइ ण त्थाणं देइ णिविसं पि ॥

९५९ चिंतेइ पुहइदाणेण होज्ज जइ पिअअम त्ति ता सुलहा ।
खग्गेण व होज्ज तहा वि णेअ दूरंतरं किं पि ॥

९६० इअ चिंतोअहिपडिओ परिसेसिअरज्जकज्जवावारो ।
किंकाअव्वविमूढो अप्पा वि हु णेअ लक्खेइ ॥३२०

९६१ तं तह सोऊण चिरं देवीए देव मज्झ वअणाओ ।
आमुक्को जिंभालसमिसेण हिअआहि णीसासो ॥

९६२ भणिअं च अलं पिअसहि केत्तिअमेत्तेण चित्तखेएण ।
दे ण्हावह ताव इमो दीहरपहलंघणुच्चाओ ॥

९६३ जेणम्हेहिं समं चिअ सज्जणमुहअंददंसणेच्छाण ।
जक्खमहेसिसुआणं वच्चइ पासं अणत्थमिए ॥३२१

९६४ अह तक्खणेण णरवइ णिव्वत्तासेसमज्जणाहारो ।
बहुसंमाणपहिट्ठो देवीए समं समुच्चलिओ ॥३२२

९६५ पुरओ च्चिअ संपत्तो ताणं च तवोवणं सुअम्माण ।
परपरिओसपहिट्ठो अल्लीणो ताण पासम्मि ॥३२३

९६६ तो दूरकअपणामो उवविट्ठो विमलमणिसिलावट्टे ।
देवी वि ताहिं समअं अविरिक्कसुहासणासीणा ॥

236

 He can't remember what he has just said, and he 958
takes no notice even of someone standing right next
to him. He doesn't bathe and can't stay still for even
a moment. He thinks it would be easy to gain his 959
beloved if all he had to do were to give away the entire
earth, and it would be no trouble whatever if all he had
to do were to use his sword. Thus, cast into an ocean of 960
concern, he neglects the management of state affairs,
and in utter confusion about what is to be done, he is
hardly aware of himself."

When your queen-to-be, my lord, had listened for a long 961
time to what I had to say, she let out a heartfelt sigh,
which she concealed as a yawn. "Vichittaleha, my 962
friend," she said, "this is quite enough heartsickness
for now. Look, he is tired from his long journey. Take
him straightaway to his bath, so that he can go with us 963
before sunset to the daughters of the *yakṣa* and sage,
who will surely wish to set eyes upon the radiant face
of this good man."

Then, Your Majesty, as soon as I had finished my bath and 964
my meal, I set out with your queen-to-be, delighted
by the great honor shown to me. Soon I saw before me 965
the ashram of those virtuous girls. I approached them
with delight equal to theirs. I then bowed to them at 966
a distance and sat down on a slab inlaid with brilliant
jewels. Your queen-to-be, for her part, sat down on the
same seat as the two girls.

९६७ भणिअं च ताहिँ कुसलं तुह विजआणंद सामिणो तत्थ ।
किं पडिवज्जइ सो अम्ह दंसणं जह तए सिट्ठं ॥

९६८ भणिअं च मए भअवइ सुव्वउ जं तेहिँ तुम्ह विण्णत्तं ।
थोअक्खरबहुअत्थं सब्भावसमप्पिअं वअणं ॥३२४

९६९ कइआ सो सुहिदिअहो चिंतावसणिणिणमेससुढिआइं ।
अच्छीणि तुम्ह दंसणणिव्वाणसुहं गमिस्संति ॥

९७० भणिअं च ताहिँ भाउअ जिअउ चिरं होउ तस्स सो दिअहो ।
लीलावईए करकमलसिरिसमागमसुहं जत्थ ॥३२५

९७१ पिअअमसंपेसिअणिअसरीरवत्तापसाअलंभेण ।
वड्ढाविज्जसि पिअसहि भणिआ लीलावई ताहिं ॥

९७२ एक्केक्कमेक्कपरिओसपमुइआणंदणिब्भरमणाहिं ।
सच्चविओ सो लीलावईए कंठट्ठिओ हारो ॥

९७३ तो झत्ति पअंपिअहिअअवेअणावसविसण्णवअणाहिं ।
भणिअं सहि लीलावइ रेहइ थणएसु ते हारो ॥३२६

९७४ सिट्ठं देवीए इमो विजआणंदेण उवणिओ एत्थ ।
इअ सोऊण पलत्तं मह वअणणिवेसिअच्छीहिं ॥

238

"Vijaananda," they said, "is your master back home well? 967
    Has he agreed to come and see us, as you said he
    would?"

"Your Holinesses," I said, "please hear the message he 968
    has for you. Its words are few, but its meaning great,
    delivered with complete sincerity: 'When will that 969
    blessed day come when my eyes, weary from ceaseless
    concern, attain the felicity of seeing you?'"

"Brother," they said, "long may he live, and may that day 970
    soon come when he can rejoice united with Lilavai's
    beautiful lotus hand."

They said to Lilavai: "What great fortune you have, dear 971
    friend, to be favored with the report your beloved has
    sent about his condition."

With their hearts full of joy, and delighted by their 972
    mutual satisfaction, they then turned their gaze at the
    necklace adorning Lilavai's neck. Suddenly they spoke 973
    in somber words, gripped by the anguish of their
    pounding hearts: "Lilavai, friend, that is a beautiful
    necklace on your breast."

"Yes," said the queen, "Vijaananda brought it to me." 974

१७५ एसो तुह विजआणंद सामिणा कत्थ पाविओ हारो ।
केच्चिरआलं च इमो कोसे हालस्स परिवसिओ ॥

१७६ सिट्ठं च मए तिस्सा णराहिवो वीरवाहणो णाम ।
सो मलअसेलणाहो गहिओ अम्हेहिं दिव्विजए ॥३२७

१७७ तस्स महाभंडारे उवणिज्जंते णराहिवेण सअं ।
संपेसिओ णिएऊण साअरं एस वरहारो ॥

१७८ तं वज्जवडणसविसेसदूसहं णिसुणिऊण दोहिं पि ।
तह रुण्णं जह लीलावई वि मोहं च संपत्ता ॥३२८

१७९ हा किं अविवण्णे तम्मि जाइ एवंविहं गइं हारो ।
जो तेण दुसहवम्महपज्जलिए विणिहिओ हिअए ॥

१८० हा कीस मए एवं एच्चिरआलं दुरासणडिआए ।
परिरक्खिअं हआसाए जीविअं पावकम्माए ॥३२९

१८१ एसो किर अविसारो हिअए परिभाविऊण तस्स मए ।
माहविलआए हत्थम्मि उप्पिओ कह णु विच्छुडिओ ॥३३०

१८२ हा वज्जकढिणहियवय हारस्सेयस्स दंसणे अज्ज ।
तुडिया कुमारसंगमयासा रे फुडसु एत्ताहे ॥३३१

१८३ तक्कालं जं ण मआ एअं तं कुवलआवलि फलं म्ह ।
संपत्तं सविसेसं लीलावइवसणसंजुत्तं ॥

१८४ दे वच्चसु भइणि तुमं दुसहं सहिअं इमं म्ह दोसेण ।
एअं चिअ अवसाणं अम्हं पि इह त्थिअव्वस्स ॥३३२

At that, the girls fixed their gaze upon my face and said: "Vijaananda, where did your master Hala get this necklace? And how long has it been kept in his treasury?" 975

"There is a king," I said, "named Viravahana, who is the lord of Mount Malaya. I captured him in a military campaign. When his treasuries came under our control, the king himself saw this beautiful necklace and sent it, with all honor, to Lilavai."[190] 976 977

On hearing these words, more unbearable than a lightning bolt, the two girls started weeping in a way that left Lilavai completely confused. 978

"Oh, could this necklace really have gone on such a journey if he were still alive? He surely must have placed it on his heart, burning with irresistible desire![191] Oh! Why is it that for so long I was deluded by this false hope, and now that it has been dashed, I still survive, wretch that I am? This is the necklace I put into Mahavilaa's hands, thinking it would strengthen Mahavanila's heart. How could he possibly have lost it? Oh heart, harder than diamond! Why not just break, now that, at the sight of this necklace today, all hope of union with the prince is destroyed? The fact that I did not die at the time, Kuvalaavali, has only served to bring Lilavai more distress. So go, sister Lilavai! It is my fault you have had to suffer this insufferable course of events. As for me, this really will 979 980 981 982 983 984

९८५ विजआणंदेण पुरस्सरेण तुह सहइ बालहरिणच्छि ।
गमणं अणुराअरसूसुअस्स पासं महीवइणो ॥

९८६ तं कुलिसघाअसविसेसदूसहं णिसुणिऊण णरणाह ।
लीलावई विमुज्झंतसासपसरा चिरं जाआ ॥

९८७ परिचिंतिअंम्मि हिअए हंहो हअदेव्व तुज्झ किं जुत्तं ।
सव्वाण वि समअं चिअ संहारे आअरं काउं ॥३३३

९८८ ता भणिअं जक्खकुमारिआए तुह जेण पेसिओ हारो ।
तस्सेसो पडिपाहुडकएण पेसेमि अंगुलिओ ॥३३४

९८९ जं तेण मज्झ तं तह हत्थाहत्थं समप्पिओ तइआ ।
तस्सेस च्चेअ गई संपइ अंगुलिअरअणस्स ॥

९९० एवं भणिऊण सअं एसो णरणाह जक्खवतणआए ।
पडिपाहुडं पअत्तेण पेसिओ तुम्ह अंगुलिओ ॥

९९१ भणिअं च कण्णमूलम्मि मज्झ विणिवेसिऊण मुहकमलं ।
अइरा पेसेज्जसु सालवाहणं मह सआसम्मि ॥

९९२ चित्तं चित्तगएणावि जेण तिस्सा णिरग्गलं हरिअं ।
सा कह णु तस्स पच्चक्खदंसणे मरणमहिलसइ ॥३३५

९९३ ताहं तस्स सहत्थेण एत्थ लीलावई समप्पेउं ।
पच्छा हिअअसमीहिअकज्जुच्छाहं अणुट्ठिस्सं ॥

be the end. Fawn-eyed girl, it would be good were you 985
to follow Vijaananda here to the lord of earth, who
must surely be eagerly awaiting you with love."

On hearing these words, Your Majesty, more unbearable 986
than a lightning bolt, Lilavai's breath caught in her
throat and remained there a long time.

"My god," I thought to myself, "is it really your intention, 987
wretched fate, to send everyone to their doom, all at
once?"

Then the *yakṣa* princess spoke. "I will send a gift of a ring 988
in return to the one who sent you this necklace. Here 989
is the ring he once gave me, my hand in his. Now this
must be where this jewel of a ring goes."[192]

With this, Your Majesty, the *yakṣa's* daughter herself 990
took care to send you this ring as a return gift. With 991
her lotus mouth right next to my ear she said, "Please
send this for me as quickly as you can to Salavahana,
who, though only in a painting, still managed to 992
completely steal Lilavai's heart. How indeed could she
still long for death if she were to see him right before
her eyes? Then I will give Lilavai over to him with my 993
very own hand, and afterward devote all my energy to
accomplishing what my heart desires."[193]

९९४ एवं भणिऊण तहिं सहसा संपेसिओ अहं तीए ।
लीलावईए पच्छा उल्लविअं सुअणु णिसुणेसु ॥

९९५ णिअसामिणो भणिज्जसु तुह चलणंबुरुहदंसणसुहाण ।
एवं अभाअणाहं अण्णम्मि वि होज्ज मा जम्मे ॥

९९६ एवं सव्वाणं चिअ कअप्पणामो विसाअपरिगहिओ ।
संपत्तो तुह चलणारविंदमूलम्मि एत्ताहे ॥

९९७ इअ जं जुज्जइ एवंविहम्मि कज्जम्मि तुम्ह णरणाह ।
तं अविलंबं कीरउ कज्जं अप्पाहणाणुगअं ॥३३६

244

With this she was ready to send me off at once.—Listen,   994
    my beloved, to what Lilavai said next.[194]

"Please tell your master this for me: God forbid that I   995
    should not be able to enjoy the pleasure of seeing your
    lotus feet in the next birth, just as in this one."

At this, I respectfully took my leave of everyone, and   996
    overcome with despondency, I have now come back
    to your lotus feet. Hence, Your Majesty, you must   997
    not hesitate to do what is needful in such a matter as
    this, in a way appropriate to the message you have just
    received.

९९८ तं तह सोऊण चिरं सो राआ कुवलअच्छि तव्वेलं ।
झाणट्ठिओ व्व मइमोहिओ व्व छलिओ व्व संजाओ ॥३३७

९९९ णिप्फंदगअणिरालोअलोअणो णट्ठचेट्ठणित्थामो ।
भणिओ विजआणंदेण देव अलमिह विलंबेण ॥३३८

१००० जं तुम्ह महाणुमईए पिसुणिअं तं करेह चित्तत्थं ।
को जाणइ कज्जगई एमविहा कह वि परिणमइ ॥३३९

१००१ चित्तं चित्तगएणावि देव कुसुमालिअं तए जिस्सा ।
सा कह णु तुज्झ दंसणसुहवडिआ मरणमहिलसइ ॥

१००२ भणिअं च तओ पुहईसरेण मा एरिसं समुल्लवसु ।
ण हु सामण्णजणाणं सरिस्सचित्ता पिआ अम्ह ॥३४०

१००३ एवंविहाण पत्तिअ परिहासपअंपिअं पि णिव्वहइ ।
जं पुण सब्भावगअं तं भणिअं णण्णहा होइ ॥

१००४ स च्चेअ मं ण मण्णइ अहं पि णेच्छामि अज्ज तं जाअं ।
मरणेण महाणुमईए मरणमम्हं पि रमणीअं ॥३४१

१००५ तत्थ वि गआण मरणं ताहिं समं ता वरं इह च्चेअ ।
जाणिज्जइ तेणं चिअ णिक्कइअवणेहपरिणामं ॥

१००६ अहिमुहजीहाजुअचंचलेण जइ जीविएण जिअलोए ।
लब्भइ मरणावसरो ता को अणो मरंताण ॥

१००७ जं तं केण वि असरीरिआए वाआए से समाइट्ठं ।
तं इह लोए अलिअं करेमि सच्चं च परलोए ॥३४२

THE POET:
HALA'S RESPONSE

After listening to these words, the king for a long while   998
    seemed lost in meditation, or stupefied, or enchanted.
    There was a blank look in his motionless eyes. All   999
    movement had ceased in his body, now powerless.
    Vijaananda said to him: "All right, let us not waste
    any more time. You should do what Mahanumai has   1000
    suggested, and what your heart, too, wants to do.
    Who knows? The course of affairs, such as it is, may
    well end up changing. Though only in a painting, my   1001
    lord, you managed to steal Lilavai's heart. How indeed
    could she still long for death if she were to have the
    pleasure of seeing you in person?"

"Do not speak like that," said the lord of earth. "My   1002
    beloved's heart is in no way like that of common
    people. You must understand that people like her will   1003
    fulfill even a promise made in jest—how much more
    so a promise made in all sincerity? Right now, she does   1004
    not regard me as her husband, nor do I regard her as
    my wife. If Mahanumai were to die, death would be
    preferable for the two of us, too. I will go there and die   1005
    with them. On second thought, better to do it right
    here, so that the complete sincerity of my love will be
    known to all.[195] If one gets the chance to die in this   1006
    world of living beings, unsteady as a serpent's forked
    tongue, then what would be so wrong with taking it,
    and dying? What the divine being had foretold in that   1007

१००८ इअ सो तिलोअसुंदरिसमागमासाविओअविसमत्थो ।
णाअज्जुणगुरुणा जाणिऊण पुहईसरो भणिओ ॥

१००९ हंहो सिरिसालाहण कीस तुमं एरिसं समुल्लवसि ।
पाअअपुरिसो व्व महाणुहावगुणवज्जिअं वअणं ॥

१०१० जे धम्माअ ण कामाअ णेअ मोक्खाअ एत्थ संसारे ।
ताणुप्पत्तिविणासो होइ तणाणं व पुरिसाण ॥

१०११ जम्मं मरणस्स कए मरणं जम्मस्स केवलं चेअ ।
णण्णं कुमईण फलं संसारे संसरंताण ॥

१०१२ सुमईण पुणो णरवइ अण्णाओ अणोवमाओ सिद्धीओ ।
लब्भंति अणुज्झिअजीविएहिँ इह जीवलोअम्मि ॥

१०१३ किं ण अणसि संसारे पंचत्तं जो गओ गओ च्चेअ ।
पत्तिअ सुवल्लहेहिँ मि समअं मेलावअं कत्तो ॥

१०१४ ता किं पाअअपुरिसाणुसारिणा णिप्फलेण मरणेण ।
जइ णेच्छसि इह रज्जं ता एहि विसम्ह पाआलं ॥

१०१५ तत्थट्ठुणो भोओ सग्गाहिंतो णराण धीराण ।
वाससहस्साइँ अलक्खिआइँ जरवाहिरहिआइं ॥

disembodied voice may prove to be false in this world,
but I will ensure it comes true in the next."

THE POET:
THE JOURNEY TO THE UNDERWORLD

Thus his hopes of reuniting with the most beautiful   1008
woman in the three worlds were dashed, and the lord
of earth was utterly distraught. His *guru* Naajjuna
found out and said to him:[196]

"Now there, Your Majesty. How can you talk like this?   1009
Are you a commoner, that your words should be so
ignoble? People in this world who do not live for the   1010
pursuit of what is right, pleasure, or liberation spring
up and die off like grass.[197] They are born only to die,   1011
and die only to be born again. For the small-minded,
that is all there is to worldly existence. But the wise,   1012
my lord, can obtain incomparable powers here in this
world, without having to give up their own lives. Do   1013
you not understand what death means? Once you go,
you are gone. Think about it. How would you ever see
your loved ones again? Why should you die a useless   1014
death like a common man? If you really do not want
your kingdom here, fine. Then let us go to Patala.
The enjoyments that realm offers to wise men eclipse   1015
eightfold those of heaven. There, a thousand years
pass unnoticed, without old age or disease."[198]

१०१६ एवं सुणिऊण णराहिवेण उब्बिंबबालहरिणच्छि ।
परिचिंतिऊण सुइरं पडिवण्णं भिक्खुणो वअणं ॥

१०१७ अह अण्णम्मि पहाए सुअम्मि संकामिऊण णिअरज्जं ।
संचलिओ लीलावइसंलंभणिरालसो राआ ॥

१०१८ बहु मण्णंतो तं चिअ मरणमसंतोसदिण्णणिअहिअओ ।
णाअज्जुणोवरोहेण णिग्गओ णिअपुराहिंतो ॥

१०१९ सामंतामच्चसुभिच्चबंधुसुहिजणवआण दुव्विसहं ।
दुक्खं उप्पाअंतो गोलासरिकच्छमल्लीणो ॥

१०२० णिअडोलग्गाण सएहिं दोहिं दोहिं मि णरेंदउत्ताण ।
राआ एक्केण कईसएण समअं समुच्चलिओ ॥

१०२१ णाअज्जुणभिक्खुपुरस्सरेण णइतीरसंठिओ राआ ।
विजआणंदेण समं विवराहुत्तं परिक्कंतो ॥

१०२२ अह सो पसअच्छि सुवल्लहेहिं समअं सुधीरपुरिसेहिं ।
संपत्तो विवरमुहं मइंदपडिरक्खिअदुवारं ॥

१०२३ तो तं विअडविडिंचिअवअणविमुक्काहिरावबीहच्छं ।
अवगणिऊण सव्वे वि संपइट्ठा महासीहं ॥३४३

१०२४ ता अद्धोअणमेत्ते सच्छविअं पिहुसिलासमोत्थइअं ।
हेरंबगणसणाहं बीअं दारंतरुद्देसं ॥

१०२५ तं पि तिदोसावगमे कअपुरचलणस्स मोक्कलं जाअं ।
तत्तोहिंतो अद्धोअणेण दिट्ठं भवाअअणं ॥

250

On hearing this, my fawn-eyed love, the king considered   1016
the monk's proposal for a long while, and finally
agreed.

Next morning, the king transferred his kingdom to his son   1017
and set out, impatient to win back Lilavai. His heart   1018
was given over to despair, and he was still considering
death, but Naajjuna persuaded him to leave the city.
His arrival at the banks of the Godavari River brought   1019
unbearable grief to his officers, advisers, servants,
relatives, friends, and subjects. The king had set out   1020
with two hundred personal servants, two hundred
princes, and a hundred poets. The monk Naajjuna led   1021
them to the riverbank, where the king halted before
clambering toward a cave with Vijaananda.

Then, my long-eyed love, the king and his brave   1022
companions reached the cave's mouth, where a
lion guarded the opening.[199] The beast opened its   1023
terrifying jaws wide and let out a terrible roar. But the
brave men walked straight past it and into the cave.

Then, after a few miles, they caught sight of another gate.   1024
This one was blocked with a large stone slab, and the
hosts of Heramba stood guard.[200] They uttered spells   1025
before it, and by daybreak it flew open. A few miles
from that place, they saw a temple to Shiva.

१०२६ अइउंतासोअविसालसालपीआलतालसंछण्णं ।
बउलेलावणपरिमलपरिवासिअपाअवणिउंजं ॥

१०२७ पुंणाअणाअकेसरकेअइकंकेल्लिकुरवअसणाहं ।
कुंदकुरुंटअकुज्जअकंचणकणवीरसंपुण्णं ॥

१०२८ णवचूअचारुचंपअचंदणवणदेवदारुदुमगहणं ।
मंदारमुद्धमालइमिलंतणवमल्लिआमोअं ॥

१०२९ सिअसिंदुवारपाडलपिअंगुणोमालिआसुअंधवहं ।
विअसिअसिअकमलदलोवआरचिंचइअधरणिअलं ॥३४४

१०३० महुमत्तमहुअरावलिझंकारुग्गीअपाअवणिउंजं ।
कलअंठिकलअलारावमुहलिआसेसपेरंतं ॥३४५

१०३१ अस्सत्थवरवडुंबरफणसफलुद्दामरिद्धिरमणीअं ।
सुहमाहुलिंगणालेरिकेलिदक्खाहिरामअरं ॥३४६

१०३२ इअ एरिसं कुरंगच्छि देवदेवस्स मंदिरुज्जाणं ।
जं पेच्छिऊण पावंति णरवरेंदा महासिद्धिं ॥

१०३३ तो तं भवाणिदइअं भवभूअभआवहं थुणेऊण ।
थोअंतरं कुरंगच्छि जाव पुरओ वसप्पंति ॥

१०३४ ताव तइअं दुवारं कणअकवाडग्गलादुरुग्घाडं ।
सच्छविअं भीमभुअंगणिवहणिव्विच्चुसंचारं ॥

१०३५ तत्थेक्को वरपुरिसो सच्छविओ राइणा कुरंगच्छि ।
संजमिओ भीमभुअंगपासणिवहेण णित्थामो ॥

Atimukta and *aśoka* trees, tall *sāl, piyāl,* and palm trees   1026
    offered their shade; bullet wood and cardamom
    suffused the bowers with their fragrance; jasmine,   1027
    amaranth, *kubjaka, kañcana,* and *karavīra* flowers
    mixed with patches of *puṃnāga, nāgakesara, ketakī,*
    kaṃkellī, and *kurabaka;* mango and champak grew   1028
    amid dense sandal groves and stands of pine; the scent
    of coral trees and young *mālatī* blended with fresh
    jasmine; the smells of white *sinduvāra,* pink *priyaṅgu,*   1029
    and acacia flowers coursed through it; the ground
    was scattered with offerings of white lotus petals;
    the bowers resonated with the buzz of bees drunk   1030
    on spring's abundance; the whole sky echoed with
    the drone of cuckoos; a wealth of jackfruit, peepul   1031
    and gular figs enhanced the stunning beauty of so
    many citrons, coconuts, bananas, and grapes: such,   1032
    my doe-eyed love, were the grounds of the temple
    of Shiva. At the mere sight of it, kings acquire the
    magical powers they seek.

Then they praised the husband of Bhavani, who allays the   1033
    fear of all the world's creatures, and they proceeded a
    little farther until they reached a third gate. This one   1034
    was fastened with a golden bolt, and it was crawling
    with a thick tangle of terrifying serpents. There the   1035
    king saw a man caught up in the snakes' noose-like
    grip, unable to escape. He said:

१०३६ भणिअं च अहो पेच्छह पाआलपवेसकंखिरो एसो ।
संजमिओ दुट्ठभुअंगमेहिँ अच्छइ महापुरिसो ॥३४७

१०३७ एवं भणिरस्स नराहिवस्स ते सुअणु विसहरा सव्वे ।
मोत्तूण तं जुआणं पलाइआ दसदिसाहुत्तं ॥

१०३८ तो तेण वरजुआणेण पभणिअं साहु साहु णरणाह ।
को इह तुम्हाहिंतो परवसणविणासणो अण्णो ॥

१०३९ ण तुमाहि जए धीरो परोववआरी तुमाओ ण अ को वि ।
णेअ तइंतो दीसइ णिक्कारणवच्छलो एत्थ ॥

१०४० ता किं भणामि एवंविहाण अम्हाण मुक्कवसणाण ।
जं अत्थि जं च होही तमसेसं तुम्ह साहीणं ॥

१०४१ भणिअं च राइणा सुकअकम्म कं तं ण जं तुमाहिंतो ।
संपज्जइ ता साहेह अम्ह किं अत्थ तुम्हे वि ॥

१०४२ भणिअं च तेण णरवइ उव्विसह सुवित्थरं पि साहेमि ।
कस्स व अण्णस्स मए अप्पाणप्पं कहेअव्वं ॥

१०४३ अत्थि बहुविहविहंगउलरावसंगीअमणहरणिअंबो ।
लवलिलवंगेलावणपरिमलपरिवासिअदिअंतो ॥३४८

१०४४ सुरवहुचलणालत्तअचिंचिल्लिअमणिसिलाअलुच्छंगो ।
मलओ णामेण महामहीहरो सिद्धसुहवासो ॥

१०४५ तत्थ मलआणिलो णाम वसइ सिद्धाहिवो सुविक्खाओ ।
तस्स सुओ हं पहु माहवाणिलो णाम जीअसमो ॥

"Look! This great man must have been trying to enter 1036
    Patala when these wicked serpents imprisoned him."

As the king spoke, my lovely girl, those deadly serpents 1037
    slithered off in all directions, releasing the young man.
    Then he began to speak: "Oh lord of men, thank you! 1038
    Not a soul has come to these parts—certainly no one
    who could free me from that torture, no one so wise 1039
    and beneficent, no one so selflessly devoted to others.
    What more is there to say? Now that I am freed from 1040
    my plight, all that I have and ever will have is yours."

"You seem to be a good man," said the king. "Have you 1041
    met with some failure? For what reason did you come
    here? Please tell me."

"Your Majesty," he said, "please take a seat and I will 1042
    tell you in full detail. I myself feel the need to tell
    someone.

"There is a large mountain whose enchanting slopes 1043
    echo with the call of many kinds of birds, where the
    fragrance of *lavalī*, clove, and cardamom groves fills
    the air, where the red rocks of its vales are painted 1044
    with lac from the feet of celestial women. Its name is
    Malaya, and it is the realm of the *siddhas*. There lives 1045
    Malaanila, the far-famed king of the *siddhas*. I am his
    son Mahavanila, my lord, dearer to him than life."

१०४६ अह तं सोऊण णराहिवेण उब्बिंबबालहरिणच्छि ।
अप्पाणं तिहुअणसिरिपसंगसुहिअं व परितुलिअं ॥

१०४७ भणिअं च इमो सो अंगुलिअओ जस्स दंसणेण तुमं ।
मुक्को वरवीर इमाओ झत्ति अहिबंधणाहिंतो ॥

१०४८ तो तं णिअअंगुलिअं सहसा दट्टूण सिद्धकुमरेण ।
हरिसविसाअविमुज्झंतहिअअभावं समुल्लविअं ॥

१०४९ कत्थ इमो पुहईसर लद्धो तुम्हेहिँ इअ वरंगुलिओ ।
साहेह महच्छरिअं म्ह कत्थ एसो इहं पत्तो ॥

१०५० सिट्टं च तस्स पुहईसरेण कुवलअदलच्छि णीसेसं ।
सव्वं पि महाणुमईए वइअरं साअरं तेण ॥

१०५१ तो तेण णमाइअहिअअपहरिसुप्फुल्ललोअणमुहेण ।
भणिअं तहा वि अज्ज वि कीस तुमं इह विलंबेसि ॥

१०५२ जं एच्चिरं पि कालं पुव्वविरुद्धेहिँ हअभुअंगेहिँ ।
बद्धो हं इह वसिओ तं चेअ महागुणे पडिअं ॥

१०५३ अह सो वि हु वइरासंकिएहिँ णाएहिँ मह सआसाओ ।
दूरणिहित्तो हारो सो वि गुणाणं धुरे जाओ ॥

१०५४ दे वच्चह एत्ताहे अहं पि मलआअलाओ तुह पासं ।
विसमत्थं संठविऊण गुरुअणं संगलिस्सामो ॥३४९

१०५५ एवं भणिऊण मिअच्छि राइणो मलअमहिहराहुत्तं ।
परमाणंदपहिट्ठो सिद्धकुमारो गओ सहसा ॥

Now on hearing this, my fawn-eyed love, the king 1046
considered himself as good as reunited with the most
beautiful woman in the three worlds. "Brave man," 1047
he said, "here is your signet ring, at the mere sight of
which you were instantly freed from that serpentine
prison." The moment he saw his ring, exhilaration and 1048
despair overwhelmed the *siddha* prince's heart. He
could barely get out the words: "Lord of earth, where 1049
did you get this wonderful ring? Please tell me. I'm
astonished. Where did you find it?"

My lily-eyed love, the lord of earth carefully related, in 1050
every last detail, what had happened to Mahanumai.

At that point, his heart could not contain its joy, and his 1051
eyes grew wide. "After all that," he said, "why should
you still be wasting your time here? To think that 1052
those hateful serpents kept me tied up here for so
long, and it actually turned out for the best. And best 1053
of all is that the charm that they took from me and
tossed away has fallen into your hands.Please leave 1054
here at once. I will come from Mount Malaya to meet
you: my parents must be beside themselves with
worry, so I will meet them first."

With these words to the king, my doe-eyed love, the 1055
siddha prince, completely overjoyed, left straightaway
for Mount Malaya.

१०५६ अह तं कणअकवाडं उग्घाडेऊण चंदवअणाओ ।
अल्लीणाओ किसोअरि पहुपुरओ दो पुरंधीओ ॥

१०५७ ताहिँ भणिअं णराहिव एअं रअणप्पहाए वरभवणं ।
विसह विसूरइ सा अम्ह सामिणी तुम्ह दोसेण ॥

१०५८ तं तह सोऊण णराहिवेण णाअज्जुणस्स णिअवअणं ।
वअणम्मि समप्पेऊण साअरं ताण उल्लविअं ॥

१०५९ एवं एअं जं भणह तुम्हि रअणप्पहाए वरभवणं ।
दुल्लहलंभं किं पुण एक्कं भणिअव्वअं अत्थि ॥

१०६० एसो म्ह सुमित्तो माहवाणिलो जा ण होइ सुविसत्थो ।
ताव म्हं पि ण जुज्जइ एमविहं अच्छिउं एत्थ ॥

१०६१ एवं भणिऊण विसज्जिआओ ताओ दुवे वि दूईओ ।
णमिऊण भवं णाअज्जुणेण समअं गओ राआ ॥

१०६२ संपत्तो णिअअपुरं सव्वेहिँ मि पणइएहिँ परिअरिओ ।
गोलाणइसलिलकआवगाहणो भवणमल्लीणो ॥

१०६३ जाअं वद्धावणअं सव्वाण वि घरहरं णरेंदाण ।
दिट्ठम्मि पुहइणाहे जहिच्छिअत्थे समावडिए ॥

१०६४ अह सव्वत्थाणपरिट्ठिएण सहस त्ति कडअवालस्स ।
गोसपआणअणिअमो दिण्णो पहुणा सतोसेण ॥

१०६५ ता झत्ति पओससमुच्छलंतपडिरावपूरिअदिअंतो ।
परिअट्टिओ पवड्ढंतपहरिसो कडअहलबोलो ॥३५०

At that moment, my slender love, the gate's golden bolt 1056
    flew open, and two women stepped out in front of the
    king.

"Your Majesty," they said, "this is the splendid palace of 1057
    Raanappaha. Please enter: our mistress cannot bear
    your absence a moment longer."[201]

The king heard these words, and put his careful response 1058
    to them into Naajjuna's mouth:

"As difficult as it was to reach this palace—Raanappaha's 1059
    palace, as you say—there is one thing we need to tell
    you. Until all is right with our good friend Mahavanila, 1060
    we cannot possibly stay here like this."

With this, the king sent the two messengers back, paid 1061
    reverence to Bhava, and departed with Naajjuna.

On reaching his city he was thronged by his adoring 1062
    subjects, and after bathing in the waters of the
    Godavari, he entered his palace. The princes' houses 1063
    all erupted into celebration, for their earnest desire to
    see their king again was fulfilled.

The king, firmly established in the supports of kingship, 1064
    wasted no time in giving his general the order to
    advance at dawn.[202] Immediately a clamor arose from 1065
    the camp, steadily increasing in volume, filling the sky
    with echoes as evening's darkness spread.

१०६६ सज्जेह पडउडीओ सीवह गोणीओ करह मलवाओ।
ण्णीसल्लह पल्लाणाहँ मंदुराइं तुरंगाण ॥

१०६७ णिद्धाडिज्जंतु करेणुआण पक्खाण पंच व सआइं।
अच्छंतु के वि इह समअवारणा के वि वच्चंतु ॥

१०६८ अग्गिमवाणे रट्ठउडसाहणं पच्छिमे सुलंकीण।
तलवग्गो सह पहुणा वच्चेज्जउ मज्झहारीए ॥

१०६९ जो जस्स णिबद्धो हअगओ अ सो तस्स पेसह पहाए।
करहाण सह सुसारीहिँ अत्थरा णिम्मविज्जासु ॥

"Pack up your tents, tie up your gunnysacks, and take   1066
along your bedding! Clean out the stables, and
prepare them for the horses! Bring out five hundred   1067
good elephants—let some stay behind, and let raging
bulls take the lead. The Rashtrakuta forces will take   1068
the lead, the Solankis will bring up the rear, and our
lord will lead the infantry's advance in the middle of
the column![203] Whoever has horses or elephants tied   1069
up should drive them at dawn, and get the camels into
formation!"

१०७० इअ जा पसरइ पअडो हलबोलो ताव अत्थसेलम्मि ।
अवरदिसावहुबद्धाणुराअतुरिअं गओ सूरो ॥

१०७१ दीवसिहोहा रेहंति णअरभवणोअरेसु दिप्पंता ।
मुक्का रविणा किरण व्व तिमिरपरिमाणमवगंतुं ।

१०७२ तो उअअसेलचूडामणि व्व तमणिवहवारणमइंदो ।
आसावहुवअणविसेसओ व्व दूरुग्गओ चंदो ॥

१०७३ तो चिरजग्गरसुढिओ णीसेसणिओइदिण्णगमणिअमो ।
कामिअणो वासहराइँ णिअअणिअआइँ अल्लीणो ॥

१०७४ मण्णुविलक्खो अल्लिअइ को वि माणंसिणीए संकंतो ।
पासट्ठिअचित्तण्णुअसहिभुमआसंणिओ दइओ ॥

१०७५ सोहइ विअलिअमाणं विअसंतुव्वत्तघोलिरच्छिजुअं ।
संरुद्धहासमासलपसण्णगंडत्थलं वअणं ॥

१०७६ उज्जल्लालिंगणलालसाए दइए णिरावराहे वि ।
अवलंबिज्जइ कीए वि पेम्मगओ दुद्दमो माणो ॥३५१

THE POET:
THE NIGHT BEFORE THE EXPEDITION

This noise carried through the sky while the sun, hastened   1070
    by his love for the woman of the western horizon,
    sped toward the mountain of his setting. Within the   1071
    city's houses burned the flames of so many lamps that
    it looked like the sun had released its rays to measure
    out the darkness. Then, like a crest jewel on the   1072
    eastern mountain, or a lion raging at the encroaching
    darkness, or a henna drawing on the cheeks of a
    woman of the directions, the moon rose high in the
    sky.[204]

Then, exhausted from long waking hours, couples gave   1073
    leave to all of their servants, and they all repaired to
    their own bedchambers.[205]

She was brooding, and he was at a loss. But next to her   1074
    stood her friend, who knew what she was thinking.
    By a raised eyebrow he gained admittance.

Her eyes opened slightly at first, then wide, then darted   1075
    back and forth; her cheeks, overtaken by a smile,
    became full and welcoming: as her anger melted away,
    the beauty returned to her face.

He did nothing wrong, but she drew out her anger, that   1076
    untameable elephant of love—for she secretly wanted
    him to take her by force.

१०७७ अविरअरइकेलिपसंगसोक्खपब्भारईसिकुंठइअं ।
माणणिसाणअणिसिअं होइ पुणो अहिणवं पेम्मं ॥

१०७८ णिअमट्ठिओ वि कीए वि को वि बलालिंगिऊण हसिरीए ।
हुंकारवारणोणअमुहो वि परिउंबिओ दइओ ॥

१०७९ अण्णहिअओ वि कीए वि को वि समुल्हसिअगंडवासाए ।
वोच्चत्थरअसमत्थो हीरइ विवरीअसुरएण ॥

१०८० अण्णेक्करअसअण्हा णेच्छंती णाअरं पिआ का वि ।
अद्धट्ठिअं पि दइअं धरइ बलालिंगणमिसेण ॥३५२
अवि अ ।

१०८१ तक्कालसमुइआलाववइअराबद्धवम्महरसाइं ।
एक्केक्कमंगपरिमाससोक्खपसरंतपुलआइं ॥

१०८२ णिमिसेक्कविमुक्काहरपुलइअवअणारविंदसोहाइं ।
पम्हंतरपरिघोलिरणअणिसम्मंतवअणाइं ॥

१०८३ अण्णोण्णणहमुहुल्लिहणमुक्कसिक्कारमणहरिल्लाइं ।
सेअजलोल्लिअबहलंगराअतण्णाअतलिणाइं ॥

१०८४ इअ णिअमइमेत्तमुणिज्जमाणणिरुवमसुहाणुबंधाइं ।
वड्ढिअरसाइँ मिहुणाण मोहणाइं समप्पंति ॥३५३

१०८५ तो णिद्दअरअरहसावसाणपरिसुढिअअंगमंगेहिं ।
सुप्पइ णिसावसेसं विअलिअमाणेहिँ मिहुणेहिं ॥

Love can get worn down by the constant joy of spending 1077
time together, in flirting and in lovemaking—like a
spear, it needs to be sharpened on the whetstone of
anger to grow new again.

With a smile, she embraced her submissive lover by force, 1078
kissing him as he twisted his face to suppress cries of
pain.

His heart was elsewhere, and her cheeks were shimmering. 1079
When she took him in the woman-on-top position, it
turned out he was capable of lovemaking after all.[206]
She wanted to go again, but nothing so complicated 1080
this time. So she pretended to embrace him by force,
and climbed on him just as he sat up.

What's more, the words they exchanged in the moment 1081
served to heighten their sexual desire, and the
pleasure of their caresses brought on waves of
thrills.[207] How beautiful did these thrills make their 1082
faces: their lips could not help falling open from time
to time as their mouths gasped and their eyes rolled
behind half-closed lids. They gasped as they marked 1083
each other's bodies with their teeth and nails, and they
soaked their beds with everything they had painted on
their bodies, now washed off by their sweat. Only the 1084
couples would ever know the incomparable pleasures
their encounters produced as they culminated in
overflowing *rasa*. Then, after the violent conclusion to 1085
their merciless lovemaking, their bodies went slack,

१०८६ णिब्भरणिद्दासंमिल्लपम्हजुअलाइँ होंति मिहुणाण ।
अंतोसुहपरिरक्खणघडिअकवाडाइँ अच्छीणि ॥

१०८७ अह बंदिअणुच्चरिओ पाहाउअगीअपिसुणिओ पत्तो ।
चिरकंखिअगमणपइण्णपहरिसो राइणो गोसो ॥

१०८८ ईसीसिपुव्वभाउग्गमंतथोवारुणप्पहालिद्धं ।
जाअं पारावअपक्खपंडुरं णहअलाहोअं ॥

१०८९ णिअणीडुड्डीणविहंगणिवहकोलाहलाउलिल्लाइं ।
दिणसिरिमुहदंसणलालसाइँ उट्टंति व वणाइं ॥

१०९० पसरिअपच्चूससमीरविलुलिओ गअणपाअवाहिंतो ।
अवसाअजललवोहो व्व गलइ तणुतारआणिवहो ॥

१०९१ पच्चूसगअवरुम्मूलिआए उड्डीणससिविहंगाए ।
धवलाइं गलंति णिसालआए णक्खत्तकुसुमाइं ॥३५४

१०९२ पाउं जुण्हामइरं जामिणिविलआए फलिहचसओ व्व ।
मुक्को णहाहि णिवडइ णिलीणमअमहुअरो चंदो ॥

their anger vanished, and they slept the rest of the
night. Their eyelids closed in deep sleep, the doors of   1086
their eyes closed tight to protect the pleasure inside.

Then dawn arrived, announced by the morning songs   1087
    of the king's heralds, and with it the joy of his long-
    awaited expedition. Little by little, the rosy dawn   1088
    stretched across the eastern sky, turning it the pale
    color of a dove's wing. Amid the commotion of flocks   1089
    of birds flying up out of their nests, the forests seemed
    to be rising up to catch a glimpse of the face of day's
    beauty.

The multitudes of tiny stars descended, like snowflakes   1090
    falling from the boughs of the tree that is the sky,
    shaken by the wind that is the encroaching daylight.

When the elephant that is the dawn pulls out the root that   1091
    is the night and the bird that is the moon flies off, the
    white lilies that are the constellations fall away.[208]

The moon falls from the sky, as if the woman who is Night   1092
    drank the wine that is moonlight from a clear glass
    and lets it fall from her hand—because a bee that is the
    moon's spot has landed on it.

१०९३ संमिल्हंति सुहासाअजणिअपरिओसदुव्विअड्ढाइं ।
इंतखरदिणअराअवसंकाए व कुमुअगहणाइं ॥३५५

१०९४ पिअअमवोच्छिण्णविणिंतरमणिणीसासपवणपहुओ व्व ।
उवभुत्तणेहतणुओ विज्झाअइ दीवअणिहाओ ॥

१०९५ चउजामालिंगणसुहपसुत्तपच्चुट्ठिआण मिहुणाण ।
णिद्दाविरमालसमंथराइँ अग्घंति दिट्ठाइं ॥

१०९६ णिद्दाणिहसालसविवलिअंगमासलविमुक्कसासाहिं ।
सअणाइँ कामिणीहिं पिअ व्व सुइरेण मुच्चंति ॥

१०९७ का वि करकलिअपसढिलकडिल्लदरदाविओरुलाअण्णा ।
सिचअंचले धरिज्जइ पिएण सअणं विमुंचंती ॥

१०९८ सोहंति कामिणीणं णिद्दालससोसिअंतणअणाण ।
उवआरकमलपक्खलिअगमणमसिणा पअक्खेवा ॥

१०९९ सोहइ जह मलिअपसाहणालअं कामिणीण गोसम्मि ।
वअणं सव्वाअरविरइअं पि ण तहा णिसारंभे ॥

११०० गोसग्गे गुरुणिद्दालसेण अद्धच्छिपेच्छिअव्वेण ।
तुण्हिक्केण वि वअणेण डहइ अज्झा सवत्तिअणं ॥

११०१ छउअंगि विमुक्काहरणणीसहं विलुलिआलअविसेसं ।
हरिआहरराअं परिसवंति वअणं सवत्तीओ ॥

Beds of night lotuses now closed, as if to savor the 1093
satisfaction of the previous night's pleasure and in
anticipation of the harsh heat of the coming sun.[209]
Rows of lamps, already weakened from burning 1094
all night, went dark, as if blown out by the sighs of
women who were finally leaving their lovers' sides.

The eyes of couples looked dreary and tired, for they were 1095
just now rising after having fallen soundly asleep in
each other's arms. Lazily rubbing the sleep from their 1096
eyes, or tossing their arms and legs, or letting out deep
sighs: the women were as reluctant to leave their beds
as they were to leave their lovers.

As one woman was leaving her bed her lover grabbed her 1097
by the edge of her skirt, and while she scrambled to
hold it up, her ravishing thigh peeked through.

The women's eyes were dry and heavy with sleep, but their 1098
footsteps were soft, shuffling over the lotus petals laid
out for them the previous night.

How beautiful is a woman's carefully prepared hair and 1099
makeup when the night is young? But how much more
beautiful is it, ruffled and disheveled, at night's end?

In the morning, the new wife can ignite the jealousy of 1100
her co-wives without saying a word: all she has to do
is look at them through half-closed eyes, heavy from
a deep sleep. Her jewelry is gone, her hair and *tilaka* 1101
disheveled, the rouge has wiped off her lips—when
her co-wives see her like that, my dear, they curse her.

११०२ अह एरिसे पहाए पहआए पआणअस्स ढक्काए ।
विण्णत्तो जोइसिएहिँ देव सुहअं इमं लग्गं ॥३५६

११०३ तो दिअवरवेअणिहोसदिण्णपुण्णाहमंगलो राआ ।
णीसरिओ बंदिणसअसमूहकअजअजआसद्दो ॥

११०४ तूरसअसंखकाहलढक्कारवभरिअदसदिसाअक्को ।
करितुरअरहरउग्घाअपिहिअणहमंडलाहोओ ॥

११०५ सुरसुंदरिकरकमलग्गकुसुमसंदोहसित्तसिरकमलो ।
णिअणअरसमासण्णे सुअणु समावासिओ राआ ॥३५७

११०६ अण्णम्मि दिणे णीसेसबलणिबज्झंतहारिणिवहेण ।
संचलिओ णिण्णुण्णअसमेण सरिसं चिअ पहेण ॥३५८

११०७ जणणिवहकलअलारावतासिओ ता ण संठिओ गोंठो ।
जा विअलिअणीविवरिल्हविंभला पाडिआ वेसा ॥

११०८ मअवारणभअभभज्जंतणवबइल्लेण बल्लिकरहस्स ।
विरसरसिरस्स सह खोणिआए उल्लूरिअं णक्कं ॥

270

THE POET:
THE MILITARY EXPEDITION

When dawn broke after such a night and the war drums   1102
    started ringing out, the king was informed by
    his astrologers that the auspicious moment had
    come. Then, once the sound of Vedic chanting by   1103
    excellent Brahmans had assured the king it would
    be an auspicious day, and once "Victory!" had been
    proclaimed by hundreds upon hundreds of bards, he
    set out.

As the noise of hundreds of tabors, conches, and war   1104
    drums filled the air in all directions, and as the dust
    kicked up from elephants, horses, and chariots
    blanketed the expanse of the sky, and as the women of   1105
    heaven festooned his head with heaps of flowers from
    their lotus hands, the king camped in the vicinity of
    his city.[210] The next day, he went on the march by a   1106
    route that passed through low ground as well as high,
    so that his entire army might evade parties of thieves.

The loud din of so many people frightened a mule so badly   1107
    that he threw off the courtesan riding him, and she, in
    turn, had to scramble to keep on her clothing as it fell
    from her body.[211]

The rutting elephants had so terrified a young bull that it   1108
    ripped the nose, with a chunk of cartilage, right off a
    strong camel, who was left howling.

११०९ अण्णाए को वि भणइ मा णोल्लसु किं ण पेच्छसि बइलं ।
पाडिहिसि कोहलं पिव लअडाहि इमं म्ह लिंकरुअं ॥३५९

१११० भिणणम्मि करंबअडेरअम्मि कं सवसि एत्थ हारीए ।
ण णिअसि संदणसंचूरिआइँ घअभंडअसआइं ॥३६०

१११९ एक्केक्कमकअहत्थावलंबणं जाइ को वि वंठजुआ ।
खोरेण समं सोहग्गवाअविहवेण भज्जंतो ॥

१११२ रे णिअच्छाआगव्विर मा धुणसु मुहा भुअंग जरफलअं ।
ण णिअसि दुप्पल्लाणो एसो णववेसरो अम्ह ॥३६१

१११३ अण्णाए उद्धकररोविरीए विणिअत्तिऊण पोक्करिअं ।
सुअमरणेण व ओणक्किरीए ओणक्किराण पुरो ॥

१११४ पेच्छह बप्पो वण्णवसिएण सुणएण सोणहीएण ।
विरसरसिरो हआसेण खाविओ अम्ह कुक्कुडओ ॥३६२

१११५ अण्णेण को वि भणइ कीस मुहा णीसवेसि वरतुरअं ।
एसो मह सेल्लपहारविंभलो वच्चइ वराहो ॥३६३

१११६ एवं अण्णोण्णालाववावडो कह वि वासरद्धंते ।
संपत्तो खंधारो सेलणिअंबेक्कभूभाए ॥३६४

A woman shouted at someone: "Hey, don't drive at the
    bull! Don't you see? You're going to make this baby of
    ours fall off, like a little gourd falls off its vine! Who in
    this caravan are you going to blame when your pot of
    curd rice breaks? Don't you see? These chariots are
    making dust out of pots of ghee by the hundreds!"[212]

          1109
          1110

A servant boy was traveling hand-in-hand with a crippled
    man and started talking to him as if they were a
    happily married couple: "Oh, you are so proud of
    your looks, aren't you? Stop shaking the seat, will you,
    love? Can't you see it's old and this little mule we've
    got doesn't like to be saddled?"

          1111
          1112

One of the ox-driver's wives started rushing back, crying
    with her hands in the air, and screamed in front of the
    other ox-drivers as if her son had died: "Look! My
    god! That awful noise you hear is our chicken, which
    that dog-breeder from the forest gave his stupid dog
    to eat!"

          1113
          1114

Someone else called out to someone: "There's no point in
    trying to get this horse to go any faster. He's moving as
    fast as he can with an arrow wound, poor thing."

          1115

The caravan was buzzing with exchanges like these when,
    after about half a day, it finally reached a clearing near
    the foothills of a mountain.

          1116

१११७ ताव अ खिण्णतुरंगममसिणवलिज्जंतसंदणणिहाअं ।
आसण्णघासलुण्णाणुबंधधावंतकम्मअरं ॥

१११८ आवासझंभणारंभमुक्कणीसेसभिच्चपहुणिवहं ।
करिकलुसणभअपूरिज्जमाणजलदोणिसंघाअं ॥

१११९ भारोआरणविणिविट्टुविरसविरसंतकरहसद्दालं ।
बहुविहकच्छंतरणिव्वडंतवसुहाहिवणिवेसं ॥

११२० दीहरपहपरिखेइअसुहणिअलिज्जंतमत्तमाअंगं ।
आवासिउमाढत्तं सेलणिअंबम्मि तं कडअं ॥३६५

११२१ आवासिअबलसिज्जंतरेणुपअडा समोसरंति व्व ।
आवाससमूहोवासदाणकज्जे दिसाहोआ ॥३६६

११२२ फणिणो मअकरिसंचरणमग्गभअतरलिआ वलग्गंति ।
णीसेसबलालोअणकज्जेण व तुंगसिहराइं ॥३६७

११२३ मुच्चंति रहा रहिएहिँ दीहपहणिहसमडहिअरहंगा ।
उम्मग्गगमणिणिद्दलिअसल्लसिढिलक्खसंधाणा ॥

११२४ तुरआ दरहिअपल्लाणचंचला कह वि संठविज्जंति ।
सखलिणमुहकड्डिअथोरघासवलिआ णिओईहिँ ॥

११२५ आआसपेल्लणुग्गअसेअजलालग्गरेणुपुंजाइं ।
हिअपल्लाणा वि हआ वहंति गरुआइँ अंगाइं ॥३६८

Then the formations of chariots slowed their pace 1117
somewhat, as the horses pulling them became tired,
and their attendants ran off to collect fodder in the
area, while the servants of many lords were dispatched 1118
to start putting up tents, and people rushed to fill
their water reservoirs before the elephants muddied
the water, while the camels, bleating hideously, knelt 1119
down to be unloaded, and the kings went into their
various residences, each into his own, and the rutting 1120
elephants, exhausted from their long journey, were
tied up comfortably.[213] In this way the army began to
set up its camp at the base of the mountain.

The dust stirred up by the encamped army had so 1121
completely filled the sky that it seemed to be
retreating in order to make space for even more
encampments. The trampling of the rutting elephants 1122
so terrified the snakes that they slithered to the
mountain tops as if to catch a glimpse of the army
in its entirety. When the charioteers dismounted, 1123
the wheels of the chariots were found to be worn
down with friction from the long journey, their axle-
frames loose and their pins broken, from running off
the roads. The horses became excited as soon as the 1124
saddles started to come off and began pulling out and
eating grass while the bits were still in their mouths,
before their grooms finally calmed them down. Their 1125
withers were still heavy even when the saddles were
removed, covered as they were with clods of dirt
stuck to the sweat produced from being driven to

११२६ कवलेंति मत्तकरिणो चिरेण कलिअं पि पल्लवुप्पीलं ।
कररंखोलणपसरंतपवणपरिमाससत्तण्हा ॥

११२७ संठाणं कह वि लहंति तालविंटाणिलेण छिप्पंता ।
उव्वत्तपरत्तणगलिअसेअपसरा पहू सअणे ॥

११२८ गमणाअससमुग्गअसेअदरुप्फुसिअविसमतिलआइं ।
अग्घंति कामिणीणं मउलिअणअणाइँ वअणाइं ॥

११२९ एत्थंतरम्मि पारद्विएहिँ सिरिसालवाहणणरिंदो ।
विण्णत्तो परिगहिअंतं देव सुसावअं रण्णं ॥३६९

११३० बहुविहतरुतुंगसमाससंकुला सेलकडअपडिलग्गा ।
पुव्वदिसा पडिरुद्धा णिव्विड्डं वारणसएहिं ॥३७०

११३१ इअरा वि गिरिसरीअडसमीवविडवोलिवेणुसंकिण्णा ।
सहस त्ति उत्तरासा परिगहिआ धम्मवालेहिं ॥३७१

११३२ पच्छिमदिसाए सुहसंचराए वरतुरअसाहणं दिण्णं ।
दाहिणदिसाए णिमिअं लहुक्कं कविलसंघाअं ॥३७२

११३३ एवं चिअ सीसंते संपत्तो णरवई तमुद्देसं ।
संचालिआइँ आहेडिएहिँ सावअसमूहाइं ॥३७३

such exertion. The rutting elephants chomped down 1126
on the bunches of shoots they held in their trunks,
thirsty from the lashing wind generated by their own
flailing trunks. At last the kings found rest on their 1127
beds, fanned by the breeze of palm-leaf fans that dried
the sweat that had beaded up and rolled over their
bodies. Very beautiful indeed were the faces of the 1128
courtesans, with their eyes starting to close and their
tilakas smudged by the slight touch of sweat from the
exertions of the journey.

In the meantime, Salavahana's huntsmen informed him: 1129
"This forest, Your Majesty, is rich in beasts of prey.
We have blocked off its edges for you. Hundreds 1130
of elephants have completely sealed off its eastern
side, which is right next to the ridge of the mountain
and densely packed with all kinds of tall trees. And 1131
just now archers have blocked off another side, the
northern one, which is overgrown with shrubs and
bamboo along the banks of mountain streams. There 1132
is ample room to move in the western part, but a
detachment of horses has been put there, while fierce
packs of hounds have been stationed in the southern
part."

When this was communicated to him, the king proceeded 1133
to that region, while his huntsmen started to give
chase to the many wild beasts there.

११३४ ताव अ हअहेसारवसंखोहिअरण्णसावउप्पेच्छा ।
पहरेण विणा वि मआ मअमरणासंकिरी हरिणी ॥३७४

११३५ ओसप्पइ पुल्ही रोहिएण तह सो वि अच्छहल्लेण ।
सो वि कुरंगेण ण होइ कस्स मरणम्मि मइमोहो ॥३७५

११३६ ण चलइ णवसूअसिलिंबणेहसंदाणणिअलिआ हरिणी ।
हरिणो वि पिअअमाए समअं तत्तो च्चिअ विसण्णो ॥

११३७ तिक्खखुरुप्पालुप्पंतजीविअं सहअरिं मुअंतेण ।
णिअणामसरिच्छं चित्तलेण कम्मं समाअरिअं ॥

११३८ दूरंडुीणो वि सिही परिलंघिअकरितुरंगणरणिवहो ।
पडिओ सुणआण मुहे मरणं पि सुहं ण देव्वाहिं ॥

११३९ कोंक्कंतासत्तमुहो वि मंडलो धाइ भल्लुआहिमुहं ।
दोकंखिरस्स समअं एक्कं पि ण से समावडिअं ॥३७६

११४० वावलुल्लूरिअकंधरस्स पढमं मअस्स हरिणीए ।
फुडिअहिअआए जीअं कआवराहं व पम्मुक्कं ॥

278

At that moment a doe, frightened by the forest beasts 1134
that rushed past wildly at the neighing of the horses,
thought that her mate must have died, and so fell dead
without being struck.

A fox sought protection with a tiger, a bear with the fox, 1135
and an antelope with the bear. Whose mind is not
gripped with confusion when death is imminent?

Remaining still throughout the commotion was a doe, 1136
bound fast by the shackles of love for her newborn
fawn. And for the same reason her beloved, the buck,
stayed with her.

In leaving his mate, her life cut off by a sharp arrow, the 1137
cheetah behaved in a manner befitting his name.[214]

A peacock flew a great distance, evading hordes of 1138
elephants, horses, and men, only to fly right into the
mouth of a dog. Fate would have it that even death
should not be easy.

A dog, its snout buried in the intestines of a wolf, started 1139
running after a jackal. He wanted both of them at
the same time, but in the end he was unable to have
either.[215]

When her mate's neck was crushed by a spiked mace, the 1140
doe's heart burst and she died, as if from the offense
she gave him.[216]

११४१ पहरेण मओ विरहेण तह मई घरिणिणयणसंभरिओ ।
वाहो वियलियबाहो तिण्णि वि समयं चिय मयाइं ॥३७७

११४२ केसरिगुंजारवविहडमाणगिरि विवरणीहरंताइं ।
घेप्पंति वराहउलाइँ दरियसोरटुसुणएहिं ॥३७८

११४३ ताव अ णिअकुलपच्चक्खपरिहवामरिसतंबिरच्छिजुओ ।
विणिवाइअणरतुरओ अल्लीणो राइणो कोलो ॥३७९

११४४ तो तेण दरिअकोलेण दच्छपरिहच्छवलणसीलेण ।
पहओ तुरओ पुहईसरस्स तेणावि सो कोलो ॥३८०

११४५ एवमसावअमिविहंगमं च रण्णं खणेण काऊण ।
दिवसावसाणसमए राआ कडअम्मि संपत्तो ॥

११४६ भणिओ विजआणंदेण देव इह मा मुहा विलंबेह ।
को जाणइ केरिसिआ कज्जगई होइ एत्ताहे ॥

Three died at once: the deer from the blow, the doe from   1141
    separation from her beloved, and the hunter, with
    tears streaming down, reminded of his wife's eyes.[217]

At the roar of lions, packs of boars panicked and streamed   1142
    out of mountain caves, when they were rounded up
    by fierce hounds from Gujarat. Just then, one of the   1143
    boars, eyes tinted red with rage from seeing his family
    destroyed right in front of him, was chased by horses
    and men until he came right before the king. Then,   1144
    writhing in frenzied anger, the fierce boar killed the
    horse the lord of earth was riding, and he, in turn,
    killed the boar.

In this way the king had, in short order, emptied the entire   1145
    forest of birds and beasts, and returned to his camp at
    day's end.

"Your Majesty," Vijaananda reproved him, "please do not   1146
    waste your time like this. Who knows how the course
    of affairs will turn out?"

११४७ एवं भणिओ सो तेण णरवई अगणिएहिँ दिअहेहिं ।
संपत्तो कमलदलच्छि सत्तगोआवरीभीमं ॥

११४८ तत्थावासिअणीसेसकडअणिव्वत्तमज्जणाहारो ।
परिवड्ढिअपरिओसो विजआणंदेण विण्णत्तो ॥

११४९ सो देव इह महेसी णिक्कारणणिद्धबंधवो अम्ह ।
परिवसइ महाणुमईतवोवणं जेण णे णीआ ॥३८१

११५० वअपरिणअं तवस्सिं विज्जाविहवोवलक्खिवअसुजम्मं ।
परलोअपहपवण्णं दट्ठुं तुम्हं पि तं होइ ॥३८२

११५१ भणिअं च राइणा पिअवअंस जं भणह एहि वच्चम्ह ।
किं अम्ह ण तेण कअं एत्तिअमेत्तं कुणंतेण ॥३८३

११५२ एवं भणिऊण नराहिवेण उव्विंबबालहरिणच्छि ।
विजआणंदो पढमं मुणिणो संपेसिओ पास ॥३८४

११५३ तो दूरकअपणामो सच्चविओ साअरं मुणिंदेण ।
आसण्णसमासीणो बहुसो संपुच्छिओ कुसलं ॥

११५४ भणिअं च तेण कुसलं राआ सिरिसालवाहणो एत्थ ।
तुह दंसणसुहसंपत्तिलालसो एइ अणुमग्गं ॥

THE POET:
THE BATTLE WITH BHISANANANA

Paying heed to Vijaananda, the king moved on to   1147
    Sattagodavari Bhima, my love with lotus-petal eyes,
    in a few short days. There, he set up camp, bathed,   1148
    and took a meal, and when all his needs had been met,
    Vijaananda made the following request of him:

"My lord, here dwells the great sage who became a close   1149
    friend of mine without any prompting. It is he who
    brought me to the ashram where Mahanumai was
    staying. The ascetic, full of years, has found the path   1150
    to the next world. And on seeing him, this birth of
    yours will be graced by knowledge and power."

"My dear friend," said the king, "come then, let us go to   1151
    the place you speak of. If this is all we do, will there be
    anything left undone?"

With this, my fawn-eyed love, he sent Vijaananda ahead to   1152
    meet the sage in advance. The great sage caught sight   1153
    of him and greeted him respectfully at a distance.
    They took their seats side by side, and the sage
    questioned him at length about how everything was
    proceeding.

"Everything is fine," he replied. "The king, his majesty   1154
    Salavahana, is on his way here, and he is eager to have
    the pleasure of seeing you."

११५५ तो तेण समुल्लविअं एसो सो सालवाहणणरिंदो ।
सुरसुंदरीहिँ गिज्जइ जस्स जसो दसदिअंतेहिँ ॥

११५६ ता एअस्स ण दीसइ पडिवक्खो को वि एत्थ पुहवीए ।
कवणेण व इह कज्जेण आगओ णिअपुराहिंतो ॥३८५

११५७ सिट्ठं च तेण सव्वं तं तह सोऊण सो वि परिउट्ठो ।
भणइ महेसी वद्धावणं म्ह एअं तए सिट्ठं ॥

११५८ जं कह वि महाणुमईए अज्ज हिअइच्छिअं समावडिअं ।
लीलावई वि णिव्वूढणिअमसुहभाअणा जाआ ॥

११५९ इअ एरिसे समुल्लाववइअरे णरवई वि संपत्तो ।
तत्थेसिणो सआसं परिमिअपरिवारपरिअरिओ ॥३८६

११६० तो तेण महामुणिणा सो राआ अग्घवत्तसलिलेण ।
अहिसिंचिऊण भणिओ उवविसह सुहासणुच्छंगे ॥३८७

११६१ अह सो सिंहासणकअपरिग्गहो मुणिवरेण संलत्तो ।
अज्ज म्हेहिं कअत्था णरणाह तुमम्मि सच्चविए ॥३८८

११६२ एच्चिरआलं एवंविहे वि अम्हेहि इह भवाअअणे ।
असहाआ परिवसिआ ससहाआ कुणह एत्ताहे ॥

११६३ एत्थ दिवसम्मि देवा कुणंति संगीअअं उमावइणो ।
तेहिं गएहिं णराहिव रमंति रअणीसु रअणिअरा ॥३८९

११६४ ताण वि पमुहो एक्को रअणिअरो भीसणाणणो णाम ।
तस्स भएण ण णिवसइ दिवसं एक्कं पि मुणिलिओओ ॥

The sage replied, "That king, Salavahana, the one whose   1155
     glory the women of heaven extol in all ten directions?
     His like is not to be found on earth. What business has   1156
     taken him from his city to this place?"

He explained, and the great sage was delighted when he   1157
     heard the story. "What you have told me," he said,
     "is equal, for me, to the birth of a son: Today, what   1158
     Mahanumai has long desired has somehow come to
     pass, and Lilavai, too, will enjoy happiness beyond all
     limits."

As this exchange was taking place, the king came into the   1159
     sage's presence, surrounded by a few select members
     of his retinue. The sage welcomed him by sprinkling   1160
     him with water reserved for guests, and invited him to
     sit and make himself comfortable.

Taking his own seat on the lion throne, the sage began.   1161
     "Today I have everything I could desire, now that
     I have laid eyes on you, lord of men. For so long   1162
     I have lived completely alone in this temple of Shiva,
     such as you see it now, but today you have kindly
     given me company. Here, by day, the gods perform   1163
     hymns for the Lord of Uma.* But at night, king,
     they leave, and demons come stalking. The one   1164
     who is their leader is named Bhisananana. The sages
     fear him too much to spend even one night here.

---

* Shiva, husband of Parvati (Uma).

११६५ तो तेण समं जुज्झं अज्जं चिअ होइ तुह णिसासमए ।
इअ जाणिऊण घिप्पउ एसो मंतो ममाहिंतो ॥

११६६ माआछण्णसरीरं पि रक्खसं जेण पेच्छसि णिसासु ।
तुह दंसणवहपडिओ पंचत्तं पावउ अहम्मो ॥

११६७ एवं भणिएण णराहिवेण हसिऊण से समुल्लविअं ।
भअवं अपच्छिमो अज्ज तस्स एसो णिसासमओ ॥३९०

११६८ एवं भणिऊण णराहिवेण विअसंतलोअणमुहेण ।
गहिओ मंतो आसंघिअं च तं णिसिअराणीअं ॥

११६९ अह सो तेण किसोअरि बहुसो पडिवज्जिऊण वरमुणिणा ।
संपेसिओ दिणंते णिअआवासं गओ राआ ॥३९१

ताव अ ।

११७० विमुक्ककरबंधणं गअणपाअवाहिं तओ
सरेसु रहवाहिणीविरहकाअरालोइअं ।
पडेइ लवणोअहे घुसिणबिंदुमाअंबअं
फलं व परिपक्कअं घणतमारिणो बिंबअं ॥३९२

Hence be aware that tonight, once darkness falls, you 1165
will have to contend with him, and so take this mantra
from me to be able to see that demon at night, even if 1166
he makes himself invisible with magic. The moment
he crosses your sight, that vile creature will reach his
end."

When the sage had spoken to him in this way, the king 1167
smiled and replied, "This coming night, Your
Holiness, will be his very last." With this the king 1168
received the mantra, his mouth and eyes opening
wide, and he turned his attention to the army of
demons. Then, my beauty, the great sage reassured 1169
him at length and sent the king on his way, and by
evening he had returned to camp.

In the meantime, 1170
    apprehensive about their coming separation,
the *cakravāka* birds in the ponds glared
at the disc of the sun, the rival of dense darkness,
red as a saffron dot, which,
    now shorn of its supporting rays,
fell from the sky into the salt sea
    like ripe fruit from a tree.[218]

तओ ।

११७१ जइ अत्थमिअमिअंके तमणिअरोरुद्धदसदिसाअक्खे ।
सुहसुत्ते जणणिवहे अल्लीणे अद्धरत्तम्मि ॥३९३

११७२ तेण णिसाअरवइणा णिअबलगव्वुब्भडं वहंतेण ।
संपेसिआ णरेंदस्स दोण्णि दोसाअरा दूआ ॥

११७३ तेहिँ भणिअं णराहिव दूआ णे पेसिआ णिसामेह ।
कज्जं सवित्थरत्थं जं तेण प्पाहिअं तुम्ह ॥

११७४ जह एए दो जामा पच्छिमरअणीए मज्झ उवभोगा ।
जं वसइ एत्थ भूअं आहारं होइ तं मज्झ ॥३९४

११७५ ता देसु सएण णराहिवाण समएण कुंजरसएण ।
णरतुरअपसुसहस्सेण मह बलिं जइ सुहं महसि ॥३९५

११७६ तं सोऊण सरोसं भणिआ पुहईसरेण ते दूआ ।
जह वच्चह तुम्हे च्चिअ पडिदूआ तस्स णिअपहुणो ॥

११७७ भणणइ रे रक्खस एहि जेण सुणआण बुक्कणाणं च ।
णिअकडअणिवासीणं देमि बलिं तुज्झ पिसिएण ॥३९६

Later, in the dead of night, when most people were fast   1171
    asleep and the moon's setting had plunged the world
    into total darkness as far as the eye could see, the lord   1172
    of the night-stalkers arrived with his army, swollen
    with pride in their own strength. He sent two demons
    as envoys to the king.

"Lord of men," they said, "we have been sent here as   1173
    envoys. Listen to the message he has sent you, which
    explains in precise detail what you must do:

"'Since the last two watches of the night are when I take   1174
    my meal, I shall eat any being who stays here. So if you   1175
    wish to be safe, give me a food offering of a thousand
    men, horses, and cattle, with a hundred princes, and a
    hundred rutting elephants.'"

When he heard this, the lord of earth angrily replied to   1176
    those envoys: "You two are going to return to your
    master, this time as my envoys. Tell him this: 'Hear   1177
    me, monster. You had better come here yourself, so
    that I can make a food offering of your flesh to the
    dogs and crows who infest my camp.'"

११७८ एवमवरं पि बहुसो णिब्भच्छेऊण पुहइणाहेण ।
पडिपेसिआ सरोसेण दो वि दोसाअरा दूआ ॥

११७९ तो तेहिँ गएहिँ णिसाअरेहिँ राएण कडअवालस्स ।
आइट्ठं अपहाए मा को वि चलिज्ज कडआहिं ॥३९७

११८० एक्केण सहस्सेणम्ह सरइ णरवइसुआण वीराण ।
दससाहस्सं सुव्वइ ताण बलं णिसिअराणं पि ॥३९८

११८१ एवं भणिऊण तहिं वीरसहस्सेण परिगओ राआ ।
दूरंतरं सकडआओ णिग्गओ णिसिअराहुत्तं ॥

११८२ ताव अ विअडविडिंचिअवअणविणिंतग्गिजालदुप्पेच्छं ।
लल्हक्कक्कत्तिआणलफुलिंगपिंगलिअगअणअलं ॥

११८३ पम्मुक्कफारफेक्काररावपडिसद्दपूरिअदिअंतं ।
णअणहुआससमोसरिअतिमिरपाडिअणिअरूवं ॥३९९

११८४ सरसंतमआइणिबद्धथोरखरकविलकेसपब्भारं ।
णरसिरमालामंडलिअविअडविणिअंसणणिअंबं ॥

११८५ अलिगवलसजलजलहरतमालकलअंठिकज्जलच्छाअं ।
ओत्थरिअं रअणिअराण तं बलं णरवराहुत्तं ॥

With many threats like these, the lord of earth flew into   1178
    a rage and sent back the two envoys of the night-
    stalkers. Once those demons had gone, the king   1179
    gave an order to the camp guard: "No one is to
    leave the camp until the break of dawn. Our forces   1180
    will march with a thousand men, all of them brave
    princes. The forces of those demons, however, are said
    to be ten thousand strong."

With this, the king, in the company of a thousand   1181
    warriors, set out from his camp toward the demons
    and quickly covered a great distance.

Meanwhile, the forces of the night-stalkers swarmed   1182
    toward the king—awful to look upon, with wisps of
    flame that shot out from their hideous and fearsome
    mouths, turning the sky crimson with sparks shooting   1183
    out of their ghastly hooked knives, filling the whole
    sky with thunderous echoes of their bellowing and
    howling, their bodies visible only because the fire   1184
    in their eyes dispelled the darkness in which they
    were shrouded, their masses of hair, reddish, wiry,
    and thick, tied up with entrails still oozing, wearing   1185
    around their hips horrible loincloths held in place
    by a belt of human heads, the color of bees, buffalos,
    water-heavy clouds, *tamāla* trees, cuckoos, and
    lampblack.[219]

११८६ ललक्कहक्कफेक्कारमुक्कणीसंककोक्किअभडोहं ।
संलग्गं णरवररक्खसाण णिसि दारुणं जुज्झं ॥

११८७ केणावि को वि कुविएण णरवरो णिसिअरेण तह पहओ ।
जह दोहाइअदेहो वि णिवडिओ पडिअपडिवक्खो ॥

११८८ फरुसासिपहारुक्खुडिअकंधरो को वि अमरिसवसेण ।
आभामइअणलक्खं पि मंडलग्गं महासुहडो ॥

११८९ मुच्छाविरामसंभरिअसामिसंभावणापरिग्गहिओ ।
अविणिज्जिअवेरिबलो हीरइ लज्जाए को वि भडो ॥

११९० पहरवडिअस्स कस्स वि रअणिअरो रोसहुअवहपलित्तं ।
बप्फाअंतं फुक्कारअं व उरसोणिअं पिअइ ॥

११९१ दूरेण परिहरिज्जइ दढमुट्ठिणिवीडिआसिबीहच्छो ।
रअणीअरेण सुहडो वि मुक्कजीओ वि सभएण ॥४००

292

The men and the demons engaged each other in fierce
    battle through the night. Battalions of warriors let
    out frenzied cries and howls and fell upon each other
    fearlessly.   1186

One demon struck a man down in anger, but the man,
    though his body was rent in half, still managed to
    bring down his foe.   1187

Another's head was severed by the harsh blow of a sword,
    yet out of sheer wrath he continued to wave around
    his weapon without aim, great warrior that he was.   1188

One warrior, at the moment of recovering consciousness,
    called to mind his master's good name, to which
    he was duty bound, and felt shame for not having
    completely vanquished the enemy forces.   1189

A night-stalker felled a soldier with blows, and as he
    hissed, drinking the steaming blood from his chest,
    brought to a boil by the fire of rage, he seemed to be
    blowing on it.   1190

One warrior cut such a gruesome figure, with sword still
    firmly clasped in his fist, that though he was quite
    dead, a frightened night-stalker still went far out of his
    way to avoid him.   1191

११९२ माआछण्णसरीरेहिँ तेहिँ दोसाअरेहिँ हम्मंतं ।
दट्ठूण बलं पुहईसरेण सो सुमरिओ मंतो ॥

११९३ जो जत्तो च्चिअ दिट्ठो तत्तो च्चिअ सो सिआसिपहरेण ।
दोहाइओ णरिंदेण णिसिअरो झत्ति कुविएण ॥

११९४ तो सो अतुलिअथामो वि तेण भीमाणणो णरिंदेण ।
वज्जधरेण व सेलो णिप्पंक्खो तक्खणेण कओ ॥

११९५ णिल्हूणवलणकरटंकखंडरुंजिअपिसाअसंघाए ।
सज्जुण्हसोणिअप्पवहपंकखुप्पंतवेआले ॥४०१

११९६ अल्हीणडाइणीसअसमूहपरिवेसरसिअसिवणिवहे ।
पडिउद्धग्गिद्धमंडलिमिलंतविलसंतगोमाए ॥४०२

११९७ इअ एरिसम्मि सुंदरि णीसेसे सुद्धसुहडसंघाए ।
मअउव्वरिअपलाअंतकाअरे रक्खसाणीए ॥४०३

११९८ णिअबलविणासदंसणजाआमरिसेण तेण वाहित्तो ।
णरणाहो रअणिअरेण णिसिअकरवालहत्थेण ॥४०४

११९९ णरणाह इमो सो तुज्झ अज्ज सुरवहुसुहागममुहुत्तो ।
आसण्णमच्चुसंकेअवासरो पहर एत्ताहे ॥४०५

When the lord of earth saw how those night-stalking   1192
    demons, having concealed their bodies with magic,
    were slaughtering his forces, he called to mind the
    mantra. The raging king sliced every demon his   1193
    gaze fell upon clean in half with his white sword,
    right where it stood. Before long the king had left   1194
    Bhisananana, his forces once unmatched, without an
    army, as Indra, wielder of the thunderbolt, once left
    the mountains without wings.[220]

The hordes of ghouls lying in pieces, amid severed feet,   1195
    arms, and legs; the undead flailing around in the
    mud formed by streams of warm, fresh blood; packs   1196
    of jackals howling amid the *ḍākinīs* that arrived by
    the hundreds; the ground shimmering with frogs
    who joined in with flocks of vultures that were called
    to the scene.[221] Such, my beauty, was the state of   1197
    the demons' camp, cleansed of all of its warriors,
    either dead and bloated, or running in flight, when   1198
    that night-stalker, infuriated to see the complete
    destruction of his forces, clasped his sharpened sword
    in his hand and called out to the lord of men:

"Lord of men, the moment has now come when you will   1199
    enjoy the company of heaven's women. The day
    appointed for your death has arrived. You may strike
    first!"

१२०० भणिअं च राइणा णिसिअरेस पहरेहि पोरिसासंघो ।
णिव्वडइ समासण्णेक्कमेक्ककरवालधाराए ॥

१२०१ ता भरसु को वि जइ अत्थि तुज्झ एवंविहे समावडिए ।
रक्खइ मुहुत्तमेत्तं पि जीविअं सुरवराणं पि ॥४०६

१२०२ एवं भणिरस्स नराहिवस्स भीमाणणेण पहरसमं ।
दोहाइअं सरोसेण चम्मरअणं कुरंगच्छि ॥४०७

१२०३ राएण वि सो फरुसासिपहरणिल्लूणकंधराबंधो ।
अइविरसं विरसंतो धरणिअले पाडिओ सहसा ॥

१२०४ तो तक्खणसंपुण्णेंदुबिंबसविसेसपसरिअपहोहो ।
जाओ अणण्णरूवो पुरिसो पज्जुण्णसारिच्छो ॥४०८

१२०५ तो तेण सो णरिंदो साहुक्कारक्खरेहिँ पुणरुत्तं ।
अहिणंदिऊण भणिओ ण तुमाओ पिअंकरो अम्ह ॥

१२०६ ता केत्तिअं च भण्णइ एसो हं तुह नरेंद साहीणो ।
जं महसि किंचि दुलहं पि देमि जं अम्ह साहीणं ॥४०९

१२०७ तं सोऊण सविब्भमहिअअणमाअंतकोउहल्लेण ।
राएण समुल्लविअं किं च ण लब्भइ तुमाहिंतो ॥४१०

१२०८ ता साहिप्पउ के तुम्हि एत्थ एवंविहावि एआण ।
पावमईणं हअरक्खसाण मज्झम्मि संवसिआ ॥४११

"Lord of demons," said the king, "you strike! The blows of   1200
our swords in close one-on-one combat will soon make
it clear who is the hero. The time has come. If there is   1201
anyone, even among the gods, who might save your
life for even a moment, you would do well to call upon
them now."

Just as the king was saying this, my doe-eyed love,   1202
Bhisananana flew into a rage and split in half King
Hala's impervious leather shield. The king, for his   1203
part, instantly severed the demon's head from his
neck with a blow of his sharp sword, and sent it falling
to the ground, screaming awfully along the way.

At that moment beams of light came streaming from him,   1204
even more than from the full moon, and he took the
form of a man, like the love god himself, Pradyumna,
in his singular beauty. He congratulated the king   1205
again and again with words of approval, and said to
him: "Nobody has been so kind to me as you. What   1206
more can I say? Here I am, at your service. If there
is anything that you desire, no matter how hard to
obtain, I will give it to you, if it is in my power."

The king's heart, struck by these words, could hardly   1207
contain his curiosity. "What, get something from
you?" he exclaimed. "First of all tell me who you are,   1208
and why someone like yourself was living here amid
these evil-minded demons."

१२०९ भणिअं च तेण णरवइ एअं खलु वित्थरेण कहिअव्वं ।
तुम्हेहि मि परिसुढिआ रक्खसवहदुप्पसंगेण ॥

१२१० तह वि णिसामह सीसइ गंधव्वसुओ हमेत्थ पुहईए ।
अवअरिओ सुरसरिमज्जणेक्कहिअओ दिवाहिंतो ॥

१२११ ता तत्थ मए हिमगिरिणिअंबतरुमणहरे वणुद्देसे ।
सच्छविआ तेलोक्केक्कसुंदरी कुसुमवोच्चिणिआ ॥

१२१२ अह सा मए सकोऊहलेण उवसप्पिऊण पासम्मि ।
सहस त्ति साहिलासेण पुच्छिआ सुअणु का तं सि ॥

१२१३ तो तं सोऊण ममाहि तीए णरणाह णेहलं वअणं ।
भणिअं अहमेत्थ च्चिअ वणवासिमहेसिणो धूआ ॥

१२१४ भणिअं च मए सुंदरि अविरुद्धं दंसणं म्ह ता इणिहं ।
गंधव्वेसाण कुले अहं पि विउले समुप्पण्णो ॥४१२

१२१५ चित्तंगआभिहाणो तुह दंसणकोहलेण अवअरिओ ।
जइ होसि सप्पसाआ ता जुत्तं वम्महेण कअं ॥४१३

१२१६ एवं भणिऊण मए सा णरवइ तत्थ णिज्जणे रण्णे ।
परिणीआ णिअविहिणा अच्चुग्गमहेसिणो धूआ ॥

१२१७ तो तं तिहुअणरज्जाहिसेअसरिसं सुहं विहावंतो ।
ताव ट्ठिओ णराहिव जा सो वि रिसी तहिं पत्तो ॥४१४

"Your Majesty," he said, "it would take quite a long time   1209
      to tell this story, and you must be exhausted from
      slaying all these demons. Still, listen and I will tell   1210
      you. I am the son of a *gandharva,* and the only reason I
      descended here to earth from the sky was to bathe
      in the River of the Gods.* But once I got there, in   1211
      a grove with charming trees on the slopes of the
      Himalaya I saw the most beautiful girl in the three
      worlds picking flowers. I eagerly approached her and   1212
      asked her, with longing in my voice: 'Who are you,
      beautiful girl?'

"When she heard these affectionate words come from my   1213
      mouth, Your Majesty, she said: 'I am the daughter of a
      great sage who lives in this very forest.'

"'Well then, beautiful girl, there is nothing to stop us from   1214
      looking upon each other, is there? I too was born into
      a spotless family, that of the *gandharvas.* My name is   1215
      Chittangaa. I came down to earth eager to have a look
      at you. If you would oblige me, then the god of love
      will have done the right thing.'

"With these words, Your Majesty, I married the daughter   1216
      of the formidable sage in a deserted patch of forest
      according to our own rite.[222] That must be what it   1217
      feels like, I kept thinking, to be crowned as king of the
      three worlds. And that very moment, the sage arrived.

———

* The Ganga.

१२१८ भणिअं च तेण कुसुमाल सहइ तुह अम्ह परिहवं काउं ।
एत्तिअमेत्तेणं चिअ विहवुम्माएण मत्तो सि ॥४१५॥

१२१९ ता पावेक्कमईणं मज्झे रअणीअराण रअणिअरो ।
बारह वरिसाइँ अणज्ज होसि पिसिआसणो तं सि ॥४१६॥

१२२० एवं बारहवरिसावहीए पुण्णाए नरवराहिंतो ।
पाविहिसि सिरच्छेअं तइआ मुञ्चिहिसि सावेण ॥

१२२१ ता एसो सो समओ संपइ दिट्ठुम्मि जं तए होइ ।
तं संपडिअं दे भणह किं पि जं अम्ह काअव्वं ॥

१२२२ तं तह सोऊण नराहिवेण सहस त्ति विअसिअमुहेण ।
भणिअमहो दूररं णीआ णे सुकइपरिणइए ॥

१२२३ णण्णं इमाउ अहिअं भणिअव्वं अत्थि जं भणामि अहं ।
दीसउ सा संपइ कुवलआवली विरहकिसिअंगी ॥४१७॥

१२२४ भणिअं च तेण सहसा सव्वंगुव्वूढबहलपुलएण ।
परिहाससमुल्लविअं पि जणइ नरवइ परं हरिसं ॥

१२२५ कत्तो पुण्णेहिँ विणा कस्स वि एवंविहं समावडइ ।
तह वि हु पुच्छामि फुडं सब्भावं कहसु एत्ताहे ॥

१२२६ अह तस्स तेण कुवलअदलच्छि गंधव्वराअतणअस्स ।
णीसेसं वज्जरिअं नरवइणा सहरिसासेण ॥४१८॥

१२२७ तो तेण णमाइअहिअअपहरिसुप्फुल्ललोअणमुहेण ।
भणिअं ता किं अच्छइ अज्ज वि मलआणिलस्स सुओ ॥

"'Did you think it was a good idea,' he said, 'to take 1218
advantage like this and disgrace us? Has your
arrogance driven you completely out of your mind?
Now, you scoundrel, you will spend twelve years 1219
among night-stalking demons as a flesh-eating
monster. At the end of those twelve years, when you 1220
are beheaded by a great man, you will be freed from
the curse.'"

"Now that I behold you, the moment he spoke of has 1221
arrived. Come, tell me if there is anything I might do
for you."

At this, the king suddenly smiled and said: "See how far 1222
the ripening of our good karma has taken us! There is 1223
nothing left to say but what I say right now: go and see
Kuvalaavali, who has wasted away in your absence."

An intense thrill suddenly coursed through his body. 1224
"I know you must be joking," he said, "but still,
Your Majesty, these words have given me the greatest
pleasure. How could such a thing happen to anyone 1225
without good karma? All the same, I ask you to tell me
clearly and right away what is going on."

Then, my lily-eyed love, the king told the whole story, his 1226
face beaming with delight, to the son of the *gandharva*
king.

His heart could hardly contain his delight, his mouth 1227
and eyes opened wide, and he said: "So the son of
Malaanila is still alive?"

१२२८ एत्थावसरे कुवलअदलच्छि परिओसपूरिअसरीरो ।
विजआणंदो लीलावईए तुरिअं गओ पासं ॥४१९

१२२९ अह सो वि चिंतिओ ज्झिअ संपत्तो माहवाणिलो तत्थ ।
सिद्धंगणासहस्सेण आगओ मलअसेलाहि ॥४२०

१२३० सच्चविओ सो गंधव्वणंदणो सिद्धराअतणएण ।
अमअवरिसो व्व हिअए पवरिसिओ एक्कमेक्काण ॥

१२३१ समइच्छिऊण भणिअं तेहिँ मि अण्णोण्णहरिसिअंगेहिँ ।
अहिणंदिऊण देव्वं चिरं च बहु मण्णिओ अप्पा ॥

१२३२ एरिसए पत्थावे विजआणंदो वि विअसिअच्छिमुहो ।
वद्धाविऊण कुमरीओ तक्खणं आगओ सहसा ॥

१२३३ तो दूरकअपणामो तिण्हं पि हु ताण हालपमुहाण ।
सव्वाअरोवणीआसणम्मि पुरओ समासीणो ॥

१२३४ भणिअं च राइणा पिअवअंस दिट्ठा तए महाणुमई ।
वद्धाविआ फुडं कुवलआवली विरहकिसिअंगी ॥४२१

302

THE POET:
THE MARRIAGE OF MAHANUMAI
AND MAHAVANILA

In the meantime, my love with lily-petal eyes, Vijaananda   1228
     had rushed to Lilavai, filled with relief. Mahavanila,   1229
     too, arrived on the scene at the very moment that
     the *gandharva* called him to mind, having come from
     Mount Malaya with a thousand *siddha* women. The   1230
     siddha prince beheld the son of the *gandharva,* each
     of them showering a rain of nectar, it seemed, on the
     other's heart. They embraced and spoke, each thrilled   1231
     to see the other, and, paying their respects to fate,
     they considered themselves fortunate.

While this was going on, Vijaananda, too, arrived from   1232
     congratulating the princesses, his eyes and mouth
     wide with wonder. He bowed at a distance, and then   1233
     sat down before Hala and the other two on a seat that
     was courteously brought out for him.

"My dear friend," said the king, "you have clearly   1234
     seen Mahanumai and congratulated Kuvalaavali,
     emaciated from her long separation from her
     beloved."

१२३५ भणिअं च तेण णरवइ एक्कासणसंठिआओ दिट्ठाओ ।
तिहुअणसिरीउ णज्जइ णज्जइ अह तिण्णि संझाओ ॥४२२

१२३६ वद्धाविऊण सिट्ठं चित्तंगअमाहवाणिलेण समं ।
संपत्तो णरणाहो जाअं हिअइच्छिअं तुम्ह ॥

१२३७ चिराअलसंचिओवड्ढिआइँ एआइँ ताइँ तवतरुणो ।
भुंजइ फलाइँ भअवइ संपइ जिअलोअसाराइं ॥४२३

१२३८ तो ताहिँ तं सुणेऊण झत्ति रोमंचकंचुइल्लीहिँ ।
एक्केक्कमवअणपुलोइरीहिँ बहु मण्णिओ देव्वो ॥४२४

१२३९ परिसिट्ठं पि ण सद्दहइ ताण हिअएच्छिए समावडिए ।
सव्वाण वि मेलावे गंधव्वणरिंदसिद्धाण ॥

१२४० पुणरुत्तपेच्छिरीणं अण्णाण वि परिसराण जा सिट्ठं ।
ता झत्ति धाविआओ अलआहिमुहं वअंसीओ ॥

१२४१ मग्गो च्चिअ ण पहुत्तो अलआहिमुहं पअत्तचित्ताण ।
वद्धाविआण णलकूवरस्स परिउट्टवअणाण ॥

१२४२ तो सो दइआए समं समअं विज्जाहरेंदहंसेण ।
णलकूवरो तहिं चिअ संपत्तो समुअपरिवारो ॥४२५

१२४३ तो तेहिँ मज्झ विज्जाहरिंदजक्खाहिवेहिँ दोहिँ पि ।
वद्धाविएहिँ णरवइ एक्कोक्खअणिहिवरो दिण्णो ॥

"Your Majesty," he said, "I saw them sharing a single seat.   1235
It looked like the beauty of the three worlds, or the
three *sandhyās*.[223] I congratulated them and said: 1236
'What all three of you desire in your hearts has come
to pass. The king has arrived with Chittangaa and
Mahavanila. Now, Your Holinesses, you can enjoy the   1237
fruit of the tree of your penance. It has taken a long
time to ripen, but it now excels anything the world has
to offer.'

"No sooner did they hear this than their hair stood on end   1238
and, looking into each other's eyes, they gave their
highest regards to fate. Though they were told their   1239
heart's desire—meeting with the *gandharva*, the king,
and the *siddha*—had come to pass, they could hardly
believe it.

"As they shared the news with those around them who   1240
were always preoccupied with their plight, some
friends of theirs hurried off to Alaka.[224] The journey   1241
was nothing to them, as their hearts had set out for
Alaka long before them. There they congratulated
Nalakubara, delight blossoming upon their faces.

"Nalakubara then arrived there* with rejoicing retainers,   1242
along with his wife and the *vidyādhara* king Hamsa.
When I congratulated them, Your Majesty, the   1243
vidyādhara and *yakṣa* kings both gave me the gift of

—————

* The ashram of Mahanumai and Kuvalaavali.

१२४४ भणिअं च वज्जरेज्जसु एअं सालाहणस्स पुणरुत्तं ।
भण्णइ ण तुमाहिंतो अण्णो पिअबंधवो अम्ह ॥

१२४५ ता पेसिज्जउ चित्तंगएण सह माहवाणिलो अज्ज ।
अविलंबं वीवाहो भणिओ देवेहिँ जक्खाण ॥४२६

१२४६ जेणण्णम्मि सुदिअहे वीवाहो णरवराण जह भणिओ ।
लीलावईए तह उण तुम्हं पत्ते सिलामेहे ॥४२७

१२४७ तं तह सोऊण णराहिवेण उब्बिंबबालहरिणच्छि ।
विजआणंदाहिंतो सिद्धाहिवणंदणो भणिओ ॥४२८

१२४८ णिसुअं भो जं णलकूवरेण अप्पाहिअं म्ह सदएण ।
दे वच्चह सह चित्तंगएण हिअइच्छिअं ठाणं ॥४२९

१२४९ तो ते छउअंगिमहारवेहिँ मंगलणिहोसमुहलेहिँ ।
तूरेहिँ संखकाहलमुइंगघोसेहिँ संचलिआ ॥४३०

१२५० विजआणंदेण पुरस्सरेण रमणीअणोवगिज्जंता ।
तद्देसणिवेसिअसहरिसच्छिजुअला समल्लीणा ॥४३१

१२५१ समुहागअस्स णलकूवरस्स कअचलणवंदणा दो वि ।
उवसप्पिआ पिआमुहपच्चुग्गअदंसणुक्कंठा ॥४३२

१२५२ दिट्ठा ते ताहिं पिआ तेहिं वि णिअपिअअमाओ दोहिं पि ।
एक्केक्कमवअणणिवेसिअच्छिजुअलेहिँ पुणरुत्तं ॥

१२५३ तो हिअअद्धवहविलंबिएहिँ अप्पत्तसुहपसंगेहिँ ।
अणुणअवएहिँ णिअपिअअमाओ किं जं ण भणिआओ ॥

an inexhaustible treasure and said: 'Please tell Hala,   1244
and repeat it to him, that no kinsman of ours is dearer
to us than he. Send Mahavanila and Chittangaa to us   1245
today. The gods have declared that the marriage of the
yakṣa girl should take place without delay, so that your   1246
marriage to Lilavai, as is prescribed for human beings,
should happen on some other auspicious day with
Silameha in attendance.'"[225]

On hearing this from Vijaananda, my fawn-eyed love, the   1247
king said to the son of the *siddha* king, "I received   1248
a message, good sir, from kind Nalakubara. He
wants you to proceed to the place your heart desires,
together with Chittangaa."

Then, my love, they set out with the thunderous noise   1249
of all kinds of auspicious sounds: the clanging of
metal, the blowing of conches, and the beating of
two-sided drums. With Vijaananda leading the way,   1250
and beautiful women singing their praises, the two
girls made their way, their eyes joyfully fixed on
their destination. Nalakubara came out to meet   1251
them, and the two of them bowed down to his feet
before proceeding to their beloveds, who were
coming forth to meet them as well, eager to see them
face to face. They looked upon their lovers, and both   1252
of them, in turn, upon their beloveds. Their eyes
were fixed immovably on each other's face. The   1253
men's hearts had stopped them halfway to feeling
the joy of their touch, and they offered endless
apologies to their beloveds.

१२५४ दे पसिअह कं तं जं भणम्ह गरुआवराहपंकम्मि ।
विच्छूढा हअदिव्वेण एच्छिरं तेण तविआओ ॥४३३

१२५५ अह एवं उवलक्खाविऊण सा माहवाणिलेण तहिं ।
गहिआ जक्खेससुआ हत्थाहत्थेण हरिणच्छि ॥४३४

१२५६ तो सा सव्वेविरंगुलिणहमुहसिप्पंतसेअसलिलेण ।
अग्घं व देइ पिअसंगमस्स हत्थुल्लएण पिआ ॥४३५

१२५७ तो पिअअमाकरग्गहफंसुग्गअपुलअपूरिअसरीरो ।
सप्परिओसो सो माहवाणिलो वेइमारूढो ॥

१२५८ अच्छीहिं चिअ सा तेण पिअअमा णेहणिब्भरमणेण ।
आलिंगिअ व्व परिउंबिअ व्व रमिअ व्व पीअ व्व ॥४३६

१२५९ चित्तंगओ वि पुरओ रअणावलिविरइअम्मि पलंके ।
आसीणो पिअजाआमुहकमलणिवेसिअच्छिजुओ ॥

१२६० एत्थावसरे कुवलअदलच्छि सुजवेण जाणवत्तेण ।
लीलावईए णिअकुलहरम्मि संपेसिओ दूओ ॥४३७

१२६१ तो उग्गए मिअंके णिव्वत्तविवाहमंगलमुहुत्ते ।
सज्जीकआओ जक्खंगणाहिं आवाणभूमीओ ॥

१२६२ अमअरसभेअतण्णाअपल्लवोत्थइअविअडपेरंता ।
णिम्मविआ वरकुसुमोवआररअपिंजरा वसुहा ॥४३८

१२६३ तो णिअअपिआपिअपणइपरिगआ पत्तपरमपरिओसा ।
छिण्णच्छिण्णासु मणोहरासु भूमीसु आसीणा ॥४३९

१२६४ विविहाइँ विविहवण्णुज्जलाइँ सहआरसुरहिवासाइं ।
णीलुप्पलपरिमलवासिआइँ दिज्जंति पाणाइं ॥४४०

"Please forgive us! What can we say? It was our   1254
    accursed fate that mired us in the mud of our grave
    transgressions, and that is why you have suffered for
    so long." Mahavanila then looked at the daughter of   1255
    the *yakṣa* king, my doe-eyed love, and held her hands
    in his. With her hand dripping sweat from the tips   1256
    of her trembling fingers she seemed to be granting a
    welcome offering to her reunion with her beloved.[226]

Then, as he shivered all over at the touch of his beloved's   1257
    hand, Mahavanila ascended the platform with great
    delight. It was as if he were, with his eyes, embracing   1258
    his beloved, kissing her, making love to her, and
    enjoying her, his heart overflowing with love.[227]
    In front sat Chittangaa on a palanquin adorned with
    strings of jewels, his eyes fixed on his dear wife's lotus
    face. At this moment, my love with lily-petal eyes,   1260
    Lilavai dispatched a messenger on a swift ship to her
    family home.

When the moon had risen, and the sacred hour of the   1261
    wedding had passed, the *yakṣa* women prepared
    the drinking hall. They encircled a patch of ground   1262
    with a wide border, strewn with sprouts soaked in
    varieties of nectar, and reddened it with the pollen of
    beautiful flowers. Then, with unparalleled delight,   1263
    people started to arrive in the company of their lovers
    and friends, and each group took their seats in a
    different charming area. They were served drinks of   1264
    various kinds and colors, fragrant with mangos, and

१२६५ दिट्ठेहिं चिअ मइरापरिमलमिलिआलिमुहलिअमुहेहिं ।
चसएहिं विलासवईण होइ मअणालसा दिट्ठी ॥

१२६६ पढमं चिअ जुण्णसुरापसंगपरिवड्ढिआणुभावेण ।
चसएण करवलग्गेण वलइअं वम्महेण धणुं ॥४९१

१२६७ जह जह पिज्जइ मइरा तह तह सणिअं मओ समल्लिअइ ।
जह जह अल्लिअइ मओ तह तह सोहा समारुहइ ॥४९२

१२६८ चिरजंपिअं भरिज्जइ तक्खणभणिअं पि झत्ति पम्हुसइ ।
असमंजसं पि भणिअं छज्जइ महुमअविआरेण ॥४९३

१२६९ महुमअवसपम्हुट्ठावराहपरिउंबिआ वि दइएण ।
अणुणिज्जइ पच्छा भरिअमण्णुवलिआणणा का वि ॥४९४

१२७० कीए वि महुमआरुणकवोलविणिओअवज्जिअं दट्ठुं ।
अवणिज्जइ सवणासोअपल्लवं पिअअमेण तहिं ॥४९५

१२७१ अवराहसमुप्फुसणं माणतरुम्मूलणं पिआ पिअइ ।
पिअअमकरग्गहुत्ताणवअणिविणवेसिअं मइरं ॥

१२७२ अण्णोण्णाहररसपाणसुहपसुत्तेहि सिद्धमिहुणेहिं ।
घिप्पइ चिरेण चसअं विलक्खभावागअमुहेहिं ॥४९६

१२७३ पिअमुहपीओव्वरिअं थोवं थोवं चिरेण का वि पिआ ।
अमअं व पिअइ सरअं सरोसपडिवक्खसच्छविअं ॥

१२७४ गेअं सहत्थतालं मुहमद्दलणच्छिअं पहसिअं च ।
सहइ विलासवईणं सुपसण्णपसाहिअं वअणं ॥४९७

redolent of the blue lotus flowers that garnished them.
Simply on seeing the glasses, their rims buzzing with   1265
bees drawn by the liquor's aroma, the women's eyes
became listless with intoxication. No sooner did   1266
the glass touch their hands, its splendor magnified
by the presence of aged liquor within, than the
love god bent his bow. The more they drank, the   1267
tipsier they became, and the tipsier they became,
the more lovely they seemed. They would talk at   1268
length, then at once forget what they had just been
talking about. The liquor's effects gave their speech,
senseless as it was, a certain charm. One minute the   1269
liquor made a woman forget her lover's offenses, and
she accepted his kisses. The next, she remembered
her anger, turned her face away, and accepted his
apologies. Seeing that the *aśoka* frond tucked behind   1270
her ear no longer had a role to play—the wine had
already reddened her cheeks—her lover removed
it. From her lover's cupped hands held before her   1271
mouth a woman drank it in: liquor, obliterator of his
offenses, eradicator of her anger. It took a while for   1272
the *siddha* couples to lift their glasses, and then too
with embarrassment on their faces, since they
had nearly passed out already from drinking from
each other's lips.[228] One woman kept drinking the   1273
tiniest dregs of sugarcane spirits her lover had left her,
as if they were nectar, to the angry glares of her rivals.
It was all beautiful: the girls' singing and clapping,   1274
their dancing to the drums, their laughter, and their
faces, joyful and skillfully made up.[229]

१२७५ दरविहडंतकडिल्लं विअलिअरसणं पडंतपावरणं ।
दरलुलिआलअतिलअं दरमत्तं सहइ रमणिअणं ॥४४८

१२७६ इअ महुमअमुइआसेससिद्धगंधव्वजक्खजणिवहे ।
संपत्तो तइअदिणावसाणसमए सिलामेहो ॥

१२७७ तो सो पिआए समअं सव्वाण वि एक्कदेसमिलिआण ।
विज्जाहरेंदपमुहाण झत्ति पुरओ समासीणो ॥४४९

१२७८ समइच्छिऊण सुंदरि सव्वेहि मि तेहिँ सो सिलामेहो ।
भणिओ पिअतणआए दंसणसुहमणुहवेत्ताहे ॥४५०

१२७९ ता सरअसिरीए समं संपत्तो पिअसुआए वरभवणं ।
सच्छविआ सा कुवलअदलच्छि लीलावई तेण ॥४५१

१२८० अग्घाइऊण सीसे पणामपच्छुट्ठिआ समासत्ता ।
सासीसं ससणेहं गहिआ जणणीए उच्छंगे ॥४५२

१२८१ ताव अ विज्जाहरसिद्धजक्खगंधव्वमाणुसाणं च ।
वअणाइँ णिअच्छंती मुक्का सावेण सरअसिरी ॥

१२८२ तक्कालं बंधुसमागमेण परितोसिआए संभरिओ ।
एसो वि सावसमओ जो सो भणिओ गणेसेण ॥४५३

१२८३ अह सा कमसो गुरुबंधवेहिँ परिआणिऊण ओसत्ता ।
सविसेसं पडिवण्णं वद्धावणअं असेसेहिँ ॥

१२८४ तावाणंदपरंपरपरितुट्टुग्घुट्ठमंगलरवाइं ।
पहआइँ पणच्चिअपरिआणाइँ परिओसतूराइं ॥

The beautiful women were most lovely when they 1275
were slightly drunk: their skirts slightly undone, their
belts slipping, their shawls falling, their lac *tilakas*
slightly smudged.

In this way the *siddhas, gandharvas,* and *yakṣas* were all 1276
happily in their cups when, during the third watch,
toward the end of the day, Silameha arrived. He and 1277
his wife took a seat at once before the *vidyādhara*
king and all the rest, gathered in one place. They all 1278
embraced him, my love, and said, "Now you will have
the joy of seeing your dear daughter." With Saraasiri 1279
to guide him, my love with lily-petal eyes, he came
to the house where his daughter was staying, and he
beheld Lilavai. As soon as she rose to bow to them, 1280
her mother embraced her, sniffing at her head, and
held her tight to her bosom.[230]

When Saraasiri looked upon the faces of the *vidyādharas,* 1281
siddhas, yakṣas, gandharvas, and men, she was freed
from her curse. At that time, when she was delighted 1282
by the assembly of her relatives, it occurred to her that
this was the moment Ganesha said the curse would
end. When they realized this, her elders and relatives 1283
embraced her one by one, and all congratulated her
heartily. Then the drums of happiness were beaten, 1284
while attendants danced and those who took delight in
such a joyful turn of events made auspicious noises.

१२८५ अण्णम्मि दिणे णीसेसबलपहाणम्मि वासरारंभे ।
चेत्तूण ण्हवणअं कुवलआवली राइणो पत्ता ॥

१२८६ तो सो सिरिमंडवमज्झदेसविरइअचउक्किचिंचइए ।
चउपासणिवेसिअकणअकलसकअचारुपरिवेसे ॥४५४

१२८७ णवहडणपाउआरअणकंतिविच्छुरिअविअडपेरंते ।
वज्जेंदणीलमरगअमणिचच्छिअपिहुलवित्थारे ॥४५५

१२८८ पज्जालिअकणअपईवपअडपरिवड्ढमाणसिरिविहवे ।
आसीणो णरणाहो समुअं सुहमज्जणावीढे ॥४५६

१२८९ थुव्वंतो गंधव्वच्छराहिँ सिद्धंगणाहिँ गिज्जंतो ।
विज्जाहरजक्खविलासिणीहिँ णिम्मज्जिओ पढमं ॥

१२९० ताव अ तूरेहिँ महारवेहिँ विविहेहिँ मंगलीएहिँ ।
ण्हविओ परिहासुल्लाविरीए रंभुब्भवाए तहिं ॥४५७

१२९१ तो सो सिअवारणपट्टिसंठिओ सेअवाससिअकुसुमो ।
सेओहंसविलित्तो सिआअवत्तो समुच्चलिओ ॥

१२९२ समुहागएहिँ विज्जाहरिंदणलकूवराइपमुहेहिँ ।
दिट्ठो अद्धपहे च्चिअ सव्वेहि मि सप्पणामसिरो ॥४५८

१२९३ तो तेहिं चेअ पुरस्सरेहिँ उब्बिंबबालहरिणच्छि ।
संपत्तो णरणाहो आवासं सिंघलेसस्स ॥

314

THE POET:
THE MARRIAGE OF HALA AND LILAVAI

On the day when the astrological signs were most   1285
favorable, Kuvalaavali visited King Hala at dawn with
materials for bathing.[231]

The king happily lowered himself into a pleasant bath—   1286
enclosed by a four-walled curtain set up in the
middle of his private apartment, with a beautiful halo
produced by golden ewers placed on all four sides, its   1287
ample ledge sparkling with light from the jewels of
newly made sandals, covered along its wide diameter
with diamonds, sapphires, and emeralds, with the   1288
firelight of golden lamps distinctly augmenting its
royal elegance—and he was bathed the first time by   1289
beautiful *vidyādhara* and *yakṣa* girls, while being
praised by *gandharvas* and *apsarases* and serenaded
by *siddha* women, and then, to the accompaniment   1290
of loud drums and auspicious noise of all kinds, by
Rambha's daughter, making jokes all the while.

Then, seated on the back of a white elephant, dressed   1291
in white clothes and decked with white flowers,
besmeared with white sandal paste, and with a white
parasol, the king set forth. Well before he arrived,   1292
he was spotted by the *vidyādhara* king Hamsa,
Nalakubara, and others who had come out to meet
him, and he bowed his head to them. They then led   1293
the king, my fawn-eyed love, to the residence of the
lord of Sinhala.

१२९४ जं तं रंगावलिरइअविविहसअवत्तसत्थिअसणाहं ।
रमणिअणाहरणमऊहजालबज्झंतसुरचावं ॥४५९

१२९५ बहुविहविचित्तकुसुमोवआरचिंचइअचारुधरणिअलं ।
देवंगुलोअपलंबमाणमोत्ताहलत्थवअं ॥४६०

१२९६ पडुपडहसंखकाहलमुअंगसंवलिअमंगलणिहोसं ।
जुवईअणकअपरिहासमणहरं मंडवद्दारं ॥

१२९७ खित्तो से दहिअक्खवओमीसो अविहवाहिँ मंगलिओ ।
बलिभाअणो णरेंदस्स कणअतलिआपरिट्ठविओ ॥

१२९८ तावच्छिऊण दारं दइआकोऊहलेण णरणाहो ।
सुइरेण संपइट्टो आसीणो पट्टतूलीए ॥४६१

१२९९ दिट्ठा विरलसिअंसुअसंपाउअवअणकमललावण्णा ।
लीलावई णरिंदेण साअरं सहरिसंगेण ॥४६२

१३०० सप्परिहासं जुवईअणेण संतोसतोसविज्जंतो ।
तत्थच्छिऊण सुइरं णरणाहो वेइमारूढो ॥

१३०१ तो जाअवेअकअचउपआहिणो पत्तपरमपरिओसो ।
गुरुविप्पकअपणामो पुणो वि तत्तो समासीणो ॥४६३

१३०२ अह वेइसमुत्तिण्णस्स राइणो सिंघलंगणा एक्का ।
आरत्तिअतलिआसत्तकरअला उवगआ पुरओ ॥

१३०३ ताव अ विज्जाहरबंदिणेण सहस त्ति विअसिअमुहेण ।
सालंकारं सुमणोहरं च गाहाउलं पढिअं ॥

When the king reached the courtyard gate—where all   1294
    manners of lotuses and swastikas were drawn as
    raṅgolīs on the ground outside, and the light from
    the jewelry of beautiful women coalesced to form a
    rainbow, where wonderful flowers were scattered   1295
    on the ground, and clusters of pearls hung from
    a beautiful canopy, where piercing kettledrums,   1296
    conches, gongs, and tabors mixed with other
    auspicious sounds, all the more charming for the
    playful talk of beautiful women—the married women   1297
    placed before the king a golden plate full of cooked
    rice and curd as a wedding offering.[232]

After the king had waited some time at the gate, eager to   1298
    see his beloved, he entered and took his seat upon a
    cushion. Raptly he gazed upon Lilavai, the loveliness   1299
    of her lotus face hidden behind a gossamer white
    veil, and a thrill coursed through his body. The king   1300
    lingered there a while, enjoying the company of the
    young women and their lighthearted jokes, then
    ascended the marriage platform. With the greatest   1301
    delight he encircled the fire four times, bowing to the
    elders and the Brahmans, then once again sat down.

When the king descended from the platform, a Sinhala   1302
    woman approached him with an *ārātrika* tray in
    her delicate hands.[233] At that moment the face of a   1303
    vidyādhara bard suddenly lit up, and he recited these
    charming, richly figured verses.[234]

317

देव णिअच्छसु।

१३०४ अण्णोण्णसमीवणिवेसणिच्चलं समिअसद्दसंलावं।
णेउरकलहंसजुअं सुअइ व पअपंकअणिसण्णं ॥४६४

१३०५ थोरोरुजुअब्भंतरसंदाणिअसिचअपअडिअपहोहो।
रसणादलसंकंतो रमणे रमइ व्व जोइक्खो ॥४६५

१३०६ तंसोणअविसमविसंघडंततिवलीतरंगपरितणुए।
धुअसंचआ वि अहिअं रेहइ रोमावली उअरे ॥४६६

१३०७ कमपसरिअभुअजुअलुच्छलंतलावण्णजणिअपरिवेसो।
पसरइ अलद्धथामो दूरअरं दीवउज्जोओ ॥

१३०८ वेल्हलहलभुवोवग्गणविसमसमुल्हसणसंगलिज्जंतो।
परिभमइ णाहिमंडलविओअविरहाउरो हारो ॥

१३०८क भुअभामिअतलिअपईवपअडिओ थणहरे सहइ हारो।
मेरुअसिंगजुए णं चलंतगंगापवाहो व्व ॥४६७

१३०९ णिम्मज्जिअविउलकवोलकंतिमासलिअपम्हवित्थारो।
तलिआए समं परिभमइ तरुणमअवाउरा दिट्ठी ॥

१३१० इअ तुह इमीए णरवर वाससहस्सं अलक्खिवअजराए।
भामिज्जउ कअकोऊहलाए आरत्तिअपईवो ॥

१३११ अह सो तत्थ णरेंदो रइतणहुत्तावलो णिसारंभे।
अल्लीणो वासहरं णरणाहो पिअअमाए समं ॥४६८

१३१२ एत्ताहे तुह कुवलअदलच्छि किं जंपिएण बहुएण।
सा राई तस्स णराहिवस्स उज्जग्गिरस्स गआ ॥

"Look, my lord! Sitting still next to each other, their   1304
    chiming at an end, her anklets are like two geese
    asleep at the lotuses that are her feet. The lamp,   1305
    reflected in the plates of the sash around her waist,
    casts its light onto the cloth tied between her full
    thighs, as if playing between her legs.[235] As she tilts to   1306
    the side, and her slender waist is rippled by the three
    folds joining each other at angles, her line of hair,
    though no longer straight, is all the more beautiful.
    When she raises her arms their radiant beauty forms   1307
    a halo around the lamp's light, which, unchecked,
    diffuses far and wide. Her necklace, twisting with an   1308
    uneven glimmer as her graceful arms swivel around,
    is writhing in the agony of separation from her navel.
    As her arms bring it around in a circle, the tray's lamp   1308a
    shines on the necklace lying on her breast: the white
    Ganga streaming down Mount Meru's two peaks.[236]
    With long and thick eyelashes erasing even her   1309
    cheeks' abundant beauty, her gaze—a net for catching
    the deer that are young men—moves in circles along
    with the tray. In this manner, best of men, may she   1310
    eagerly encircle you with this *ārātrika* lamp for a
    thousand years, free from old age."

As night began the king, impatient with desire, went to his   1311
    bedroom with his beloved. What more should I tell   1312
    you, my love with lily-petal eyes? The king passed the
    night without sleeping a wink.

१३१३ एव पहाए संते सव्वेहिं मि तेहिँ दिव्वपुरिसेहिं ।
बहु मण्णिऊण दिण्णाओ णिअअणिअआओ सिद्धीओ ॥

१३१४ अंतद्धाणं सिद्धाहिवेण जक्खेण अक्खअं कोसं ।
गंधव्वेण अ दिण्णं दिवम्मि गमणं महीवइणो ॥४६९

१३१५ हंसेण वि से देण्णं वअथंमरसाअणोसहं मंतं ।
पडिवण्णं जं अण्णं पि किं पि तं तुज्झ साहीणं ॥४७०

१३१६ एवं बहुसो पडिवज्जिऊण सो सुअणु णिअपुराहुत्तो ।
संपेसिओ सहरिसो राआ लीलावईए समं ॥

When dawn arrived the demigods all showed their thanks   1313
    by gifting him their special magical powers. The king   1314
    of the *siddhas* gave the king invisibility; the *yakṣa,*
    an inexhaustible treasury; and the *gandharva,* the
    ability to fly. Hamsa, too, gave him a spell and an   1315
    herbal potion to stop him from growing old, and said,
    "Whatever I possess is at your disposal." With this   1316
    offer, and many others, my love, he sent the happy
    king and Lilavai on their way.[237]

१३१९क इत्थंतरम्मि ते वि हु विज्जाहरसिद्धजक्खगंधव्वा ।
संपत्ता सहस च्चिअ साणंदा णिअअठाणेसु ॥४७१

१३२० तह सो वि सिलामेहो दोतिण्णि पआणआइँ गंतूण ।
विणिअत्तो तणआए रअणाहरणाइँ दाऊण ॥

१३२०क सिंहलदीवम्मि गओ सह सरअसिरीइ भिच्चपरिअरिओ ।
णिव्वत्तिअलीलावइविवाहसुहवड्ढिआणंदो ॥

१३२०ख अह सुअणु सो णरिंदो लीलावइलंभजणिअपरिओसो ।
णिअठाणे संपत्तो णवणववड्ढुंतकल्लाणो ॥

CONCLUSION
[MANUSCRIPT B]

In the meantime the *vidyādharas, siddhas, yakṣas,* and   1319a
gandharvas also reached their homes with joy.
Silameha, for his part, accompanied them for two or   1320
three stages of the journey, then turned back, having
given his daughter gifts of jewelry.[238] He went back   1320a
to the island of Sinhala with Saraasiri and a train of
servants, his joy amplified by the pleasure he took in
getting Lilavai married. Then, my love, King Salahana,   1320b
delighted to be bringing back Lilavai, returned home,
his good fortune ever increasing.

१३१७ इह तुह इमीए णरवर वाससहस्सं अलक्खिवअजराए ।
लीलावईए समअं वच्चंतु अलक्खिआ दिअहा ॥४७२

१३१८ इअ विविहपआरं जक्खगणा आसीसिऊण णरणाहं ।
णिअणिअवासाहुत्तं सव्वे ते उवगआ झत्ति ॥

१३१९ पूअं काऊण तिलोअणस्स भत्तीए णग्गपासुवअं ।
णमिऊण सलीलं कुवलअच्छि सालाहणो चलिओ ॥

१३२० तह सो वि सिलामेहो दोतिण्णि पआणआइँ गंतूण ।
विणिअत्तो तणआए रअणाहरणाइँ दाऊण ॥

१३२१ पुहईसरो सतोसं लोलावइवअणपेसिअच्छिजुओ ।
विजआणंदेणाणंदिओ परं वट्टइ सलीलं ॥

१३२२ सामंतमहंतासण्णदिण्णभअभीमभेसिअदिअंतो ।
सिग्घअरं संपत्तो सभुत्तिविसए पइट्ठाणं ॥

१३२३ जं तं तोरणतुंगअरगुड्डिआहट्टसोहसोहिल्लं ।
सोहिल्लदेउलारामसंकुलं तुंगपाआरं ॥

१३२४ पाआरदारथिररअणविब्भमारामरंजिआवअवं ।
अवअवविच्छुरिआसण्णदीहिआपडिमसंकंतं ॥४७३

१३२५ संकंतसुंदरीरुंदमंदसंमद्दसोहणाउण्णं ।
उण्णअघणचक्कलथणहरेसु भेसविअपहिअअणं ॥

CONCLUSION
[MANUSCRIPTS P AND J]

"May you and Lilavai, free from old age, be so happy   1317
   that you do not even notice the days passing for
   a thousand years." Thus did the crowds of *yakṣas*   1318
   bless the king, in many ways, before they all set out
   for home. Hala payed devoted worship to Shiva,   1319
   the three-eyed god, bowed to the naked Pashupata
   ascetic, and then, my love with lily-petal eyes, set
   out at leisure. Silameha, for his part, accompanied   1320
   them for two or three stages of the journey, then
   turned back, having given his daughter gifts of
   jewelry.

The king proceeded at leisure, felicitated by Vijaananda,   1321
   and delightedly fixing his gaze on Lilavai's face. In no   1322
   time he reached Pratishthana, in his own territory,
   inspiring awe as far as the horizons and striking fear
   into the hearts of nearby vassals.[239]

With its arches, tall guard stations, and markets, its beauty   1323
   was resplendent; resplendent were the temples and
   gardens that crowded it, and tall its ramparts.[240]
   Its ramparts' gates were studded with jewels, and   1324
   breathtaking gardens adorned its neighborhoods.
   Its neighborhoods had inlaid pools that reflected the
   city's beauty. The city's beauties jostled with each   1325
   other in streets that were always full. Full, firm,
   and round, their breasts inspired awe in visitors.

१३२६ पहिअअणकलअलाराववाहरिअमगगभग्गदिट्ठिवहं ।
दिट्ठिवहणिहिअसुविहिअविचित्तअम्मे सुजणणिवहं ॥४७४

१३२७ एअस्स मज्झआरे सुवण्णकअथंमरअणचिंचइए ।
संपत्तो राआ तक्खणम्मि देवीमहाभवणं ॥

१३२८ सा वंदिअ चिट्ठाइअचलणा हअसअलकलिमलुप्पंका ।
रंगावलीए सक्खं णिअआवासं गओ राआ ॥४७५

१३२९ एत्थ समप्पइ एअं संखेवुप्फालिअं कहावत्थुं ।
अइवित्थरेण कहिअं मअच्छि को भाविउं तरइ ॥

१३३० भणिअं च पिअअमाए रइअं मरहट्टदेसिभासाए ।
अंगाइँ इमीए कहाए सज्जणासंगजोग्गाइं ॥

१३३१ एअं जं अम्हं पिअअमाए हिअएण किं पि पडिवण्णं ।
तं ण तहा जहसंतं सुअणा गेण्हह पअत्तेण ॥

१३३२ सुअणखलेहि अलं चिअ गुणदोसे जे णिअंति किं तेहिं ।
गुणदोसरआ जाणंति मज्झिमा कव्वपरमत्थं ॥

१३३३ अट्ठारहसअसंखा अणुदुसंखाए विरइअपमाणा ।
एस समप्पइ एण्हिं कह त्ति लीलावई णाम ॥

१३३३क दीहच्छि कहा एसा अणुदियहं जे पढंति णिसुणंति ।
ताण पियविरहदुक्खं ण होइ कइया वि तणुअंगि ॥४७६

॥ इअ लीलावई णाम कहा समत्ता ॥

326

Visitors' chatter filled the busy streets, blocking
    all lines of sight. Lines of sight fell on the various
    occupations people in the crowd were pursuing.   1326

At that moment the king reached a great temple of the   1327
    goddess in the midst of this city, adorned with jewels
    and golden pillars. The king worshiped the goddess   1328
    who had been installed there to remove all the
    defilements of the dark age, and went to his residence,
    marked with *rangolīs*.[241]

Here ends this story, told to you in brief compass. If I   1329
    were to tell it at length, my doe-eyed love, who could
    appreciate it?

Then my beloved said: "You have composed it in the   1330
    local language of Maharashtra. Good people would
    surely embrace the story in each of its parts."[242] Will   1331
    good people not make an effort to accept, just as it
    is, everything that I have told my beloved and that
    she approved of in her heart? Away with good people   1332
    and bad as well, away with all who probe, whether
    for virtues or faults. The average person, who enjoys
    its faults as well as its virtues, understands a poem's
    real meaning. This story, called *Līlāvaī*, ends here,   1333
    composed in the equivalent of eighteen hundred
    anuṣṭubh verses.[243]

Those who recite and listen to this story every day, my   1333a
    love, will never experience separation from their loved
    ones.

ABBREVIATIONS

ed   The readings of Upadhye's 1966 edition of *Līlāvaī*. When letters in parentheses follow "ed," they refer to the witnesses on which Upadhye's text is based.

P   A transcript, prepared by Jinavijaya Muni, of a Devanagari palm-leaf manuscript from the Saṅghavī Pāḍā Bhaṇḍāra in Pattan (No. 316 in Dalal's 1937 catalogue), 131 folios, not later than 1300 C.E. Variants from P recorded by Jinavijaya Muni from a Devanagari palm-leaf manuscript at the Jinabhadra Sūri Bhaṇḍāra in Jaisalmer (No. 237 in Dalal's 1923 catalogue), 142 folios, 1208 C.E.

B   A transcript of a Devanagari manuscript from the Anupa Sanskrit Library in Bikaner (No. 3281), 89 folios (the folios numbered 51 to 70 are lost).

N   Images from microfilm reel A39/10 of the Nepal-German Manuscript Preservation Project of a palm-leaf manuscript of *Līlāvaī*, 83 folios, probably not later than 1300 C.E.

K   The readings reported from an unknown manuscript in Ramakrishna Kavi 1926.

Upadhye's edition is the source for all readings reported from P, J, B, and K.

NOTES TO THE TEXT

१   पईवा] J; पईआ N, मऊहा ed.

२   Not found in any manuscript, but reconstructed from the commentary in B.

३   Verse 12 is not found in N.

४   Verse 14 is not found in N.

५   In N, the verses printed here (and in Upadhye's edition) as 15 and 16 appear in the reverse order.

६   Verse 16a is found only in J.

७   सुरसं] ed; सरसं B.

८   विंभल] conj. Csaba Dezső; विम्वल ed.

९   रंभा] PN; रुंभा J, भंभा B ed.

१० N skips from the middle of the second line of this verse to the following prose section.

११ B writes this verse twice, with पसरंमि for णिअरम्मि and सारिया वि for सारिसाहिं in the second.

१२ Hemachandra at *Deśīnāmamālā* 7.19 reads लंपिक्खो.

१३ अला] N; लया P, कला ed.

१४ Verse 62a, very similar to 62, is only found in B.

१५ लोअ॰] K; लोया॰ ed (unmetrical).

१६ पणइआण] JBN; ॰ईण ed.

१७ This verse is found only in J, no doubt suggested by the previous verse. It is identical to *Vajjālagga* 635. The word पत्तलाहत्थो is obscure (*Pāiasaddamahaṇṇavo* defines पत्तली as a kind of tax); Jain and Jain 1990 are probably not far off in interpreting it as a decree (घोषणापत्र).

१८ विअसिअमुहीहिं] NBP; वियसियासाहिं ed (J).

१९ वासभवणं] PB; भुयणवासं ed (J). B and N present an alternative for the first line: beginning with the prose sentence अइ चंदलेहे ण णिअसि, B reads the line मलयसमीरसमागमवसपसरियकुसुमरेणुपडिहत्थं. The reading of N is almost identical, with a few errors.

२० In B and N, the position of 98 and 99 is reversed (the original order must have been as printed here, as the description moves from head to toe).

२१ Verse 106a is found only in B.

२२ Verse 106b is found only in B.

२३ मअण] ed; णअर NB (incorrectly written as वयर).

२४ पिहु] em. Upadhye; पिवि PJB.

२५ तद्देसआलिएहिं] ed; तद्देयसालिएहिं J, तदिअसालिएहि N (likely an error for J's reading).

२६ B omits the first line of verse 131, and combines the second line with the following half-verse: ताव पइट्ठो सविसायहरिसिओ सुयणु परिहारो "at that time, my dear, the chamberlain entered, looking visibly upset." N omits the second line, and reads a rather corrupt version of B's additional half-verse (तात पिअट्ठो सविसाऽपहरिसो सुअणु पडिहारो).

२७ The first vowel of केणवि must exceptionally be read as short (or corrected to किणवि).

२८ Before verse 136 N reads णीमुहप्पे से अत्थिणा पुहइह णाहेण.

२९ Verse 136a is only found in P. I have retained its orthography, but I follow Upadhye in correcting एरस to एरिस in the second line.

३० कुमारेण] conj. Upadhye; कुमारिलेण N, ed.

३१ होही] N; होहि ed.

३२ Verse 172 is not in N.

३३ °ल्हसिओ] PBN; °ललिओ ed (J).

३४ उव्वूढ] conj.; व्वढ P, थूढ J, उच्छूढ B (whence Upadhye's छूढ), उवूढ N.

३५ पडिअ] P; घडिअ ed.

३६ Upadhye prints एत्थम्हे हि (also elsewhere in the text), but we should read एत्थम्हेहि, as the poet often uses the instrumental form अम्हेहि for the nominative.

३७ उवरुज्झह] B; अवरुज्झह ed.

३८ Verse 222 is also found at *Vajjālagga* 65, which reads नवरि "only" instead of णेह "love."

३९ Verse 227 is missing in B and N.

४० Verses 243 to 249 (and their Sanskrit commentary) are missing in B.

४१ जणिअ] ed (JBP); मेत्त N.

४२ Upadhye conjectured कमला उण जए for कमलाओ णज्जइ, probably before writing about the use of णज्जइ (a word that expresses a simile) in his endnotes.

४३ Verse 255 is missing in N.

४४ भणामि अम्हाण भणिअव्वं] JN; विणयोणयउत्तिमंगाओ ed.

४५ भणिउं] N; भणियं ed.

४६ तो तं] NB; एवं ed. सिप्पंत] PBN; सिद्धंत ed (see Turner 1922–1966, no. 13388, *siktá*).

४७ Verse 271 is missing in manuscript N.

४८ Verse 271a is found only in B. It is probably an interpolation on the basis of the preceding verse.

४९ Verse 272 is missing in NJ, and read by PB. It is also likely an interpolation (B gives the same number for this and the next verse).

५० मारुअ] NB; माहव ed.

५१ मउइअपहम्मि] ed, N; मुइअहिअआहिं implied by the commentary in B.

५२ तत्थ अ विजा] conj.; तत्थ विजा N, तत्थ विज्जा ed. Upadhye noted (ed p. 351) this verse as transmitted is metrically incorrect.

५३ करण] presupposed by the commentary in B; किरण in the manuscripts.

५४ The manuscripts give different onomatopoetic sounds in this verse (सुं PJ, डं N, फुं B).

५५ भअवअं गणाहिवइं] N, ed; पिच्छिऊण गणणाहं B. उवहसिउं] conj. Upadhye; उवहसिअं N, ed.

५६ B reads उव सहि इमाइ पिच्छह विरूवसोहाइ at the beginning of this verse.

५७ चित्त] ed (BJ); वित्त PN.

५८ N adds अह before verse 316.

५९ चिंताभरं समुव्वहइ] ed; चिंताभारं उव्वहइ N and (probably) B. N copies this verse twice, the first time inattentively and reading काणं वरलभो गअवटिअठि [gap] चिंतिअं ताव पि अप्पिअए after सोक्खवस.

६० परिआलिओ] N; पुरिबालियाओ J, परिवारिओ ed.

६१ वट्टिअ] PBN; वड्ढिअ ed (J).

६२ ते] ed (P); दे B, ए JN.

६३ हिअअ] ed; सहिअ N.

६४ B begins verse 345 with जत्थ य; N inserts जहिं into the second line.

६५ दिणहरो॰] N; दिणयरो॰ ed.

६६ N lacks verse divisions from 348 to 351.

६७ After सुहिअ in verse 350, N skips to the beginning of verse 351.

६८ B only reads up to णिअंब verse 352.

६९ विसट्टंत] ed; परिद्धिअ N.

७० Verse 354 is missing in N.

७१ सुहासीणा] BN; समासीणा ed.

७२ अब्भुट्ठाणम्] PN; सब्भुट्ठाणम् ed (JB).

७३ सुसराउ] ed; सरसाउ B, सुरसाओ N.

७४ वत्तणावट्ट] ed; पट्टियावंध B, वंतिआविद्ध N.

७५ कमला] ed; पउमा B, पउआ N.

७६ विणिम्मिअं] NB; च णिम्मियं ed (P).

७७ ०मेक्कंपंसूपकीलिआ] ed (P); ०मेक्कपसूहिं कीलिआ N, ०मेक्कंपंसूए कीलिया J, ०मिक्कमिक्कंमि कीलिया B.

७८ B reads के तुम्हाणे जीवियफलदाणदाढाउ in the second half of verse 376.

७९ णअणवअणाए] BN; वयणणयणाए ed.

८० Verse 381 is missing in N.

८१ समअं] BN; समुयं ed.

८२ ०उण्णइ] BN; ०उण्णय PJ (with orthographic variants).

८३ वलिआ] ed; किडिआ N.

८४ After दोण्हि पि in verse 404, N skips to verse 405 (which begins with these words).

८५ For the second line of verse 412, B reads दूरे अलया नयरी कुमार णे संसरिज्जासु.

८६ Instead of reading the second half of verse 420, N skips ahead to the second half of verse 421.

८७ तह जह] BN; जह तह ed.

८८ अमअ] PB (अमय); अण्ण ed (J).

८९ साअरेहिं] PN; साअरेण ed (JB).

९० अम्हेहिं] ed (P), printed as अम्हे हिं; अम्हे वि NB.

९१ वि] BN; अ ed.

९२ पूइअरुइ] ed (PJ); पूआरइअ BN.

९३ ओहुत्तगरुअ] ed (J); उवहुत्तगरुअ B, उहुत्तगरुअ N, अत्थयरिहुंत P.

९४ विअडरविकणअ] ed; मेरुतवणिज्ज N (!).

९५ वणराइतरुगहणं] N; रण्णं व वणगहणं ed (J), रत्नं व भुवणयलं B (favored by Upadhye), रत्तं व गयणयलं P.

९६ उम्मुहफुरंतं] ed; पसरिअकिरंतं N. सहइ] ed; सरइ JN.

९७ N skips ahead from the first line of 458 to the second line of 459.

९८ According to Upadhye, B reads verse 467 in place of verse 464.

९९ एवं] ed; एअं NB.

१०० भूमीओ] P and presumably N (skipping the first भूमी); भूमीउ B, भूमीए ed (J).

१०१ After the end of 466, N skips ahead to the end of 467 (वणमहं etc.).

१०२ After मऊह in verse 468, N skips ahead to the same word in verse 469.

१०३ व] N; य ed.

१०४ सिणिद्धुअं भावअंतीए] from B (सिणिद्धुयं भावयंती); सिणिद्धुया भावयंतीए ed (J) (सिणिद्धसा भावसंतीए N), सिणिद्धभावं समोइण्णा P. The verse is not numbered in P.

१०५ Upadhye was tempted, as am I, to read भवणमारूढा with B instead of किर समारूढा (ed and N).

१०६ णडिआण] NB; तवियाण ed. अंगाण] NB; अम्हाण ed.

१०७ अण्णं तं] N, confirming Upadhye's conjecture; अन्नन्नं P, अण्णनूं J, अन्ने ते B.

१०८ All manuscripts read सरिसेहिं, but the sense of सरसेहिं is better (suggested by Upadhye, ed p. 360).

१०९ Ms. B has a gap of about 20 folios starting from this verse and going up to verse 806.

११० लोअवअणाण] N, confirming Upadhye's conjecture; लोवयणाण PJ. N reads पिहिह after तुम्हाण and then skips to the beginning verse 514.

१११ N skips verse 513.

११२ संकहासत्तमाणसो] ed; संकहाकित्तणेण सो N.

११३ तामस] N; तह सं ed.

११४ दुद्ध] conj. Upadhye; दुट्ठु PJN.

११५ गुहाहरुत्थाइं] ed (J); गुहाहरत्थाइं PN.

११६ सुणिसण्णो] conj. Upadhye, confirmed by N; सुविसण्णो ed.

११७ णिज्जइ] ed; णज्जइ N, and presumed by gloss in P.

११८ दुसहो] ed; दुल्हहो N.

११९ तं सि] ed; तं पि conj. Upadhye (तं N).

१२० मणअंपि] PJ; मणयम्मि conj. Upadhye, भणम्मि N.

१२१ विण्णाणराअ] conj. Upadhye; विण्णाणुराय ed, चित्ताणुआअ (for चित्ताणुराअ) N. संवाओ] NJ; सब्भावो ed (P).

१२२ तओ] ed; तए N. P has a note to अवंम्ह (sic), निसुयं च तुह मए वयणं, which is probably copied from another manuscript.

१२३ तत्तो] ed (P); तो तं J, ता तं N.

१२४ हिअं मह मअणहुअवहपलित्तं] ed; मह हिअअविअंभिोमअणो N.

१२५ समागमुद्दूमिआण] ed (P); समागमे दूमिआण JN. डज्झउ] ed (PJ); उज्झउ N.

१२६ जाणसु] ed (PJ); सवाण N.

१२७ झूरसु] conj. Upadhye; रूरसु P, तुझ्झ J, सरसु N.

१२८ परिअणो] ed (PJ); परिसरो N. जह तहअ] N, ed (P); जेण J. कीरउ] ed (PJ); कीरइ N.

१२९ अम्हारिसिआ] N; तुम्हारिसिया ed (PJ).

१३० असावण्णं] ed (J); असामण्णं PN.

१३१ ०आरिवक्खो] N, ed (J), with minor variants; रिउचक्को P. णाम] N, ed (J); जाओ P.

१३२ खग्गमग्गे] ed (J); खग्गमग्गं P, सुवणुखगे (= सुअणुखगे) N.

१३३ तरु] N, ed (J); बहु P.

१३४ Verses 585a, 585b, and 585c are only found in manuscript J.

१३५ मअण] ed (PJ); काम N.

१३६ Verse 588 is missing from N.

१३७ पोत्तजीविआहरणा] ed (PJ); जीवमुत्तआहरणा (unmetrical) N.

१३८ कंद] ed (PJ); पत्त N. तरु ed (PJ); वर N.

१३९ विडव] ed (PJ), but we must understand विडवि (so Upadhye); विविह N.

१४० रविकिरणा] N; तरणिकरणिअरं] ed (PJ), unmetrical.

१४१ N skips from पहा in verse 602 to पेच्छंतो in verse 603.

१४२ इमे दिट्ठे] ed (PJ); तुमे दिट्ठे N.

१४३ महुर] conj. Upadhye, confirmed by N; मुहर ed (PJ).

१४४ णव] ed (PJ); वण N. विणोअअं] ed; विणासअं (!) N. N breaks this verse into two.

१४५ The scribe of N has skipped from दंसण in verse 610 to दंसण in the next verse.

१४६ जह] ed (PJ); जइ N.

१४७ हिअअ PN; हिअइ ed (J).

१४८ रसाअलं म्ह] ed (conj. Upadhye); रसायलम्ह PJ, रसाअणं च N. P reports a variant reading आलावरसोवलं च पंफदियं, which partially agrees with the reading of N (एमणरसाअणं च पफुंदिअं).

१४९ विअ] ed (PJ); चिअ conj. Upadhye, अ N. ॰संभरंतीए] N, ed (J); ॰संभवंतीए P.

१५० ॰साआस] PN; ॰सूसास ed (J). मुह] N, ed (J); सुह P.

१५१ पोरत्थिएहिं] ed (PJ); पोरच्छिएहि N. The latter is closer to Hemachandra's पोरच्छ in *Deśīnāmamālā* 6.62, although त्थ and च्छ are very easily confused.

१५२ संबज्झइ] ed (PJ); संकज्जइ N. दीसइ] ed (PJ); ईसइ N.

१५३ N omits verse 622.

१५४ सिलिंब] ed (J), and *Deśīnāmamālā;* सिलंब NP. सहस्साइं] ed (PJ); सआइं N.

१५५ णिव्वत्तिओ] N, ed (conj. Upadhye); णिज्जत्तिओ PJ. णडिआए] ed (PJ); मूढाए N.

१५६ N omits verse 627.

१५७ णिव्विन्न] ed (PJ); णिव्विंत N.

१५८ पिअअम] ed (PJ); पिअसहि N. देव्वो] N; देवो ed (PJ).

१५९ कह विपरिणमइ] ed (PJ); कत्थ परिणामो N.

१६० विगअरोसो] ed (PJ); गअसिणिणहेवो (?) N.

१६१ N skips from आहवगिआण in verse 633 to (roughly) सुइरण्णेसण of verse 634.

१६२ These four verses (numbered as 635a, 635b, 635c, and 635d) are found only in P. Upadhye notes that the copyist of P reported that these verses are added on a separate folio from another manuscript. The orthography of P has been retained.

१६३ गंधव्वेण वि कयावराहेण is Upadhye's conjecture for P's गंधव्वेणावि कयवराहेण.

१६४ सिरिसि हओ is Upadhye's conjecture for P's सिहआ (the copyist has left blanks indicated by dashes).

१६५ हरिओ णवरि पिओ कत्थ वि पएसे is Upadhye's conjectural restoration of P's हरिऊणत्थ वि पएस्स.

१६६ वडण] N, ed (J); विहण P, पडण J.

१६७ विआणाओ] ed (P); विमाणाओ JN.

१६८ The verb विमालेमि, securely attested by the manuscripts, is obscure; the translation is *ad sensum* (taking it as roughly equivalent to पालेमि).

१६९ मोह] ed (PJ); आल N.

१७० अवङ्झे] ed (PJ); अहत्थे N. कलुणासआ मुणिणो] N, ed (P); कलुणा महामुणिणो J.

१७१ पवज्जिस्सं] conj. Upadhye (confirmed by पवज्जिम्मं N); पविज्जिस्स PJ.

१७२ The transmitted reading is विओयअणाहा "without a protector because of separation" (PJ, for which N reads विओअणाहा), which requires the *o* to be short. In the text I follow Upadhye's conjecture वि उअ अणाहा.

१७३ विलविऊण] ed (PJ); पलविऊण N.

१७४ दुक्खावगमोवाओ] ed (J); दुक्खावसमोवाओ NP.

१७५ वरिल्हं] N, ed (P); विरल्हं. जमहरवत्तणि] ed (J); जमहरवोत्तणि P, जमवहसत्तणि N.

१७६ पुव्वं] ed (PJ); पठमं N.

१७७ अइ ed (PJ); इअ N. रसेण] N, ed (P); सरेण J. होहि] N, confirming Upadhye's conjecture; होह ed (PJ). After this I follow N's reading, which is slightly more satisfactory than PJ's (खणं अहं खु जणणी य तुह पत्ता).

१७८ Verse 654a is only found in P, where it is given the same number (54) as the following verse.

१७९ N does not read the second line of verse 655, but skips ahead to वासो म्ह of verse 656.

१८० अंबाए] ed (PJ); माआए N.

१८१ तेणेत्तिअं is a conjecture of Upadhye's for the transmitted तेणत्तिअं.

१८२ णिवारेमि] ed (PJ); विचारेमि N.

१८३ Verse 662a is only found in P.

१८४ सिट्ठो] N; दिट्ठो ed (P), देट्ठो J.

१८५ पसरंतं] ed (PJ); पेरंत N. Upadhye has read with P in verse 669 (हरिन्-क्खुक्क्त्तिअदिग्गइंद etc.). I have read with J, which is corroborated both by N and a variant reading reported in manuscript P.

१८६ संठिअं] ed (PJ); वडिअं N.

१८७ Verse 671 is missing in N. दुव्विसट्टाइं] ed (P); दुव्विय‌ट्ठाइं J.

१८८ विअ] conj. Upadhye (probably confirmed by विवअं N); च्चिय ed. After विअ in the second line, N reads भअवं दूरुग्गओ सूरो.

१८९ कसण] N, ed (J); करुण P. णहाहि तमणिवहो] ed (P); णहाहिवमणिवहो JN.

१९० विउडिंतो] ed (PJ); विउडेउं N.

१९१ णिवडइ] N; णिबिडइ ed (PJ). मिलंतेसु चक्कवाएसु] ed (PJ); मिलंताण चक्कवाआण N.

१९२ ओलुंपिअस्स] ed (J); ओलुंख्विअस्स NP. The former, but not the latter, appears in Prakrit dictionaries.

१९३ Verse 678 is missing in N.

१९४ सुजवेण] N, P; सुजणेण ed (J). संपत्ता] N (metrically necessary); पत्ता ed (PJ), Upadhye had conjectures पत्ता मे.

१९५ अणिमज्जिअ] N, ed (J); अणुसज्जिय P. There is a metrical problem in the first half, noticed by Upadhye (ed p. 368), that I have not been able to correct.

१९६ अदिहिवत्तं] ed (J); अदिसिवत्तं P, अविहिवंतं N, which agrees with the variant reading (अविहवंतं) reported in P.

१९७ Verse 684 is not found in N (it must simply have been omitted, since it completes the sentence begun by the previous two verses). Upadhye conjectures हु for दु PJ.

१९८ तामं] ed (J); ताव N, नाम P.

१९९ णअरीए] ed (PJ); वसईए N.

२०० दीसिहिसि] conj. for N दीसीहिसि; दीसहसि ed. सुमईहिं] N, ed (J); सुगईहिं P.

२०१ गमण] N, confirming Upadhye's conjecture; गहण PJ.

२०२ तहिं] N, ed (J); वहिं P.

२०३ मरणाण] conj. Upadhye; मरणेण mss. (the letters ण and णे are almost identical in the early Devanagari script). मणे] ed (PJ); अहं N. मरणे] ed (J); मरणेण PN.

२०४ दुव्वोझं] J (supported by N's दुवोवं); दुव्वोज्जं ed (P). कढिण ed (J); यडिय P, सार N.

२०५ संवाआ] NJ; संवापा P, संवाया ed.

२०६ हा अणंतगुणभूमि हा दइअ] ed; हा सुहासअ अणंतगुणभूमि N.

२०७ एण्हिं] based on इण्हिं ed (PJ) and एण्ही N. किं] ed; किर J, कर N, उण किं P.

२०८ Upadhye: "This gāthā, No. 716*1, is not given by J. It is found in P only; but the copyist observes that this gāthā is written

above [the line, or on the margin] from some other work. P puts
No. 16 for this as well as the next gāthā." The verse is also missing
in N.

२०९ This verse is found in all three manuscripts that transmit this
part of the text (PJN), but according to Upadhye, the copyist of P
notes that it was added from an additional manuscript source, and
gives it the same number (19) as the following verse. All
manuscripts share the solecism आराहसु भवाणी (more correct would
be भवाणिं).

२१० इह इमीए] ed (PJ); भाउअ N.

२११ पुव्वज्जिअअसुहं] NP; असुहज्जियपुव्व ed (J).

२१२ जं इमाओ इह जाअं] ed (PJ); भट्ट ज (= जं) इमाओ वि N.

२१३ एत्थेक्कं] ed (J), supported by एच्छेक N; एक्केक्क P. दिवस] ed (PJ); देश N.

२१४ एत्थं] ed (PJ); सो वि N.

२१५ The transmitted reading मज्जाणावलिमज्जण (PJ) or मज्जाणअरिज्जण (N)
is unsatisfactory, so I follow Upadhye's emendation to मज्झणावेल्ह-
मज्जण.

२१६ रमणि] ed (J), कमिणि N, करणि P. णहअलोरुद्ध] conj. Upadhye, confirmed
by णहअलोरुरुद्ध N; णहयलारुद्ध ed (PJ).

२१७ गआ] ed (PJ); सरा N.

२१८ समोअरंत] PN; समोसरंत ed (J).

२१९ गुण] ed (PJ); खल N. क्वलिआ] N, ed (P); क्वणीय J.

२२० णिक्केव] ed (णिक्कव P, णेक्केव J); विक्केव N. विमूढ] ed, mss.; वगूढ conj.

२२१ ॰ड्डिअ] ed (J); ॰ट्टिय P, ॰ठिअ N.

२२२ विढत्त] ed (PJ); विहुत्त N. बंधुज्जिअ] conj.; वंधुज्जितिय P, वंधुज्जिझ्झाय J, वंधुकुअ
N, बंधुज्झिय conj. Upadhye. भमर] ed (PJ); रुमेअ N.

२२३ समाणिअ] NP; समाणवि ed (J). कुसुम] ed (PJ); सुअणु N.

२२४ णिव्वविआरत्तभावरच्छीण] ed (PJ); णिव्वविआपंथपहसिरच्छीणाण N.

२२५ मज्जणा] ed (PJ); जोव्वणा N.

२२६ N only gives the first half of verse 757, and subsequently its
verse-separating marks are offset by one half verse, until the
scribe recognized his mistake at verse 771.

२२७ भसलेण] ed (PJ); भमरेण N.

२२८ तो से] ed (PJ); घेत्तूं N.

२२९ परिवालिआ] ed (PJ); परिआलिआ N.

२३० भीअं व] ed (J); भीयं च P (N has भीरं अंविवि).

२३१ होंत] cf. होत N; होंति ed (PJ) [marked as problematic by Upadhye].
णव] ed (PJ); वर N.

२३२ सुविसिट्ठ] N; सुविसुद्ध ed (PJ).

२३३ परिवेसो] ed (PJ); संकंतो N.

२३४ सहइ भुमआवलीजअलं] ed (PJ); मणहरं व सणवासंसो N.

२३५ सिरीए] ed; सिरि JN, मिसगं (?) P.

२३६ भंगुरो] ed (PJ); मणहरो N.

२३७ Verse 777 is missing in N. P is also missing the last three words of the first line due to a lacuna.

२३८ Verse 780 is missing in N.

२३९ किं एसा णाअवहू णु होज्ज] ed (PJ); ता किं एसाणेण अंगणाण N.

२४० जो] ed (PJ); तो N. अब्बीअं] ed (Upadhye, based on अव्वीयं J); अव्वीयं P, अट्ठीअं N.

२४१ णिसामेसु] ed (PJ); णिसामेह N.

२४२ विडवाउलं] ed (PJ); मिहिराउलं N.

२४३ पिंग] conj. Upadhye's edition reads पिञ्झ (a misprint for पिञ्च, for which Upadhye conjectured पोञ्झ); N reads पिक्क.

२४४ राइणो] N, confirming Upadhye's conjecture; राइणा ed (PJ).

२४५ पवेस] ed (PJ); पएस N.

२४६ केण कज्जेण] ed (PJ); सहरिसा एत्थ N.

२४७ णिसंको] ed (PJ); सअण्हो N.

२४८ अमुणिअ] ed (PJ); अपुणीअ N. परिणिज्जसि] N; परिणीयसि ed (P), परिणिहिसि J.

२४९ कुलहरं जम्ह एत्ताहे] ed (PJ); वित्थरत्थ कहेअव्वं N.

२५० N copies 802 twice. मणोहरा रम्मा] ed (PJ); मणोहरारामा N.

२५१ तत्थ अ विजा] conj. (cf. v. 282); तत्थ विज्जा ed, तत्थ विजा N. Upadhye noted the metrical problem (ed p. 371).

२५२ गुरुअणेण] ed (PJ); पिरिअणेण N (a curiosity, since *piri* means 'big' in Kannada).

२५३ Manuscript B resumes with the commentary to this verse, after a large gap that began with verse 501. N also skips the second half of this verse and the first half of the following verse.

२५४ चिरपरिचअविम्हआए सामि तहिं] ed (PJ); लब्ब्ोणयनयणदावि[य]मुहीए B.

२५५ णिरासंको एवविहं तुम्ह] ed (PJ), N; मा णराहिव उहयाणासि उहयलोयसुहं B.

२५६ परिलिओ] ed (P); परिविओ conj. Upadhye, परिमिओ BN. बंदिणजअ] N, ed (J); बंदिणजण P, वंदीयण B.

२५७ N skips the second half of verse 815 and the first half of 816.

२५८ राइणा तत्थ] N, ed (P); रायराएण B.

२५९ हट्टेहिं] ed (PJ), N; हट्टेसु B. वडाओ अ लोएण] conj.; वडाओ य लोएहिं ed, वडायाउ लोएण B, वजओ अ लोएण N.

२६० णिवहो] ed; सत्थो N. दिण्णाइं विप्पबंदिण बहुविहआइं च दाणाइं] ed; B and N give some version of दिण्णाइ कणअदाणाइ वंदिण विप्पाण वहुआइं (much corrupted in the case of B).

२६१ हे उज्झाअसीसहा] ed (P); उवज्झाआ पेच्छिं NB. लिहेऊण] ed; णिएऊण N.

२६२ दाविआ] N, ed; दंसिया B.

२६३ गेअं पि गिज्जंतं] ed; रासो वि गिज्जंतो N.

२६४ अविअण्हं] ed; अविसण्णं NB. णिमिसं] ed (BP); णिविसं NJ.

२६५ पव्वअं] N, ed (PB); पह्लवं J.

२६६ णिसामेसु] ed (J), B (णिसामहिं); ण साहेसि NP.

२६७ N skips back to the end of verse 832 after संकप्पालिहिअं and begins to recopy verse 833 up to दिअसं.

२६८ परिअणं] ed; सहिअणं NB.

२६९ ण कहेमि] ed (ण कहेसि N); साहेमि B.

२७० सिद्दाण ed (J), N; सिद्धाण PB.

२७१ पसाहिआवअवो] ed; पसाहियसरीरो B (ओसहिअंससिरो N).

२७२ कंधराबंधो] ed; कंठसंबंधो (for सवधो) N. विअडोर] ed, N; विपुलोर B.

२७३ उइओइअ] ed (J); उहओइय P, उइउहरि B, उइओहअ N. N's reading would mean "descended from a noble family on both sides."

२७४ मण] ed; मह N.

२७५ अवंगेहु॰] ed (J); अवंगहु॰ P (Upadhye notes that the हु looks like कु), अवग्गेक॰ N. B reads अवक्कंतमत्तभूमयंचलहिं.

२७६ धणिअं] N, ed; सणिअं B.

२७७ खलसिविणअं] N (P खलंसिविणयं); खलु सिविणयं ed (B खलु सविणयं).

२७८ पाअवुब्भंत] PN (J ब्भंत); पावयज्झंत B, पायवब्भंत ed.

२७९ ण घरे] N, ed (B); णयरे JP.

२८० उद्देसिअं] ed; उद्देसिं N.

२८१ मरणे वि] ed (J); मरणा वि P, मरणं पि BN.

२८२ हिअइच्छिअं] N, ed; the gloss in P suggests जहिच्छिअं.

२८३ N skips from पिअसहि in verse 866 to सलज्जा[ण] in verse 867.

२८४ सहरिसाए] suggested by Upadhye (he has not given the source of the reading) and corroborated by सहरिसाआ N; सरिसाए ed.

२८५ तीए] ed; तइया B, तेण N.

२८६ दंसण] ed; मंगल N.

२८७ समुल्लवसु] ed; समुल्लवह B (॰हव N).

२८८ इअं] ed; इह BN.

२८९ मा भणसु एत्ताहे] ed; मा मह भणिज्जासु B (मा मं भणेजासु N).

२९० कह वि कह वि] ed, N; कह वि नेय B. N skips the second line of verse 886 and the first line of verse 887.

२९१ मज्झा] ed; अम्ह N.

२९२ आणवेसि एत्ताहे] ed; अवसतं करणीअं (?) N.

२९३ पत्ता अ] ed; अन्नेय B, अणेअ N.

२९४ णिव्विड्ड्ं] ed; दुपेत्थं (= दुपेच्छं) N.

२९५ णिहोसं] ed; रवेहिं N.

२९६ कुवलअमालाए] ed; कुवलआवलीए N. Evidently a metrical alternative.

२९७ N skips the second line of verse 908.

२९८ थामाहिं] ed; वामाहिं B, लागाहिं N. हक्खुविउं] ed (P); हस्सवियं B, दक्खविअं N.

२९९ सीलाओ] ed; सीलाण BN.

३०० कमेण] ed (कम्मेण N); पुणो वि B.

३०१ ववगआ] ed; पडिगआ N (crossed out).

३०२ कुडुंबं म्ह] ed (कुडुंवम्ह PN); कुडुंवस्स J, B has a lacuna.

३०३ ण अ पोरिसेण] ed; णअणेरिसेण N.

३०४ मणोरहाणं] ed (PB), मणोहराणं NJ.

३०५ सो ड्डिअ] N, ed (P); सो वि हु B.

३०६ Verse 933a is found in manuscripts B and N, and not P and J,
but Upadhye notes that P numbers the preceding verse 932, and
the following verse 934. ता कुवलअदलच्छि] conj. (कुवलअदलच्छि N); ता
कुवलयच्छि B; तावय कुवलयच्छि conj. Upadhye.

३०७ महाकोसे] ed (JB), N; कहाकोसे P.

३०८ अप्पा वि] ed (J), N; अप्पे वि P, अप्पम्हि B.

३०९ सुकव्व] ed; सकम्म B; N's गअमह is corrupt.

३१० परिहरिओ] ed; परिअरिओ N. अणिव्वाणो] ed; अलद्धसुहो N.

३११ पसाओ] ed, N; पणामो B.

३१२ कीस] ed; कस्स BN.

३१३ पासम्मि संतुट्टो] ed; पासं सुसंतुट्टो BN.

३१४ पप्फुअच्छि] ed; फुल्लियच्छि B (पप्फुल्लिअच्छि N).

३१५ संमाणो] ed; जअसद्दो N. तीए] ed; तस्स N.

३१६ Verse 952 is missing in N.

३१७ हिअएण] ed; वअणेण N.

३१८ ते जं म्ह] ed (ते जम्ह P); अण्णे वि BN.

३१९ पेच्छइ] ed; अच्छइ BN.

३२० रज्जकज्ज] ed, N; सकलरज्ज B.

३२१ सुआण] ed (JB); धुआणं NP.

३२२ पहिट्ठो] PBN; पइट्ठो ed (J).

३२३ पुरओ ड्डिअ] ed; तुरिअअरं N. परपरिओस] ed, N; परिअरिओ स B. N jumps
from पहिट्ठो here to (स)विमलमणिसिलावट्टे of the next verse.

३२४ विणत्तं] ed, N; संदिठुं B.

३२५ कमलसिरिसमागमसुहं] ed; कमलसंगसुहणिव्वुओ B (कमलसंगसुहतच्छइं N).

३२६ पअंपिअ] N, ed (JB); वियम्हिय P. N skips from लीलावई (sic) in the second
line of verse 973 to कत्थ तए पाविओ हारो, found in 975, and then reads
verse 974, then skips 975 and reads 976. P reports the following

342

variant reading for the last half of the second line of 973: केण तुहं एस अप्पिओ हारो.

३२७ तिस्सा] ed (PJ); भअवइ NB.

३२८ च संपत्ता] ed; समल्लीणा NB.

३२९ एवं] ed; पिअसहि N.

३३० अविसारो] ed (अवसरो N); सो हारो B.

३३१ Verse 982 is only found in PJ, and not in NB.

३३२ इह] NB; इय ed.

३३३ सव्वाण वि समअं चिअ] ed; सव्वाण किं संज्जुत्तं N.

३३४ अंगुलिओ] ed (J); अंगुलिअं N, अंगुलिउं P, अंगुलियोः B.

३३५ हरिअं] ed; गहिअं N. तस्स] ed; दइअ NB.

३३६ कज्जम्मि] ed; कालम्मि NB.

३३७ चिरं] ed; परं N.

३३८ गअणिरालोअ N, ed (JB); निच्चलालोय P.

३३९ चित्तत्थं] ed; विणत्तं N.

३४० सरिससचित्ता पिआ अम्ह] ed; सरिसा सा पिअमा अम्ह N, सरिसा चिंता वियाणम्ह B.

३४१ अज्ज] ed, N; नेय B.

३४२ से समाइट्टुं] ed, N; तेण आइट्टुं B.

३४३ राव] conj.; र्‍वा ed (a misprint?).

३४४ विअसिअसिअ] conj. Upadhye (otherwise the verse is two *mātrās* too short); विअसिअ mss.

३४५ The first half of verse 1030 is identical to that of 594.

३४६ B and N read the second line of verse 1031 differently, which I reconstruct as follows: रमणीअमणिसिलाअलफुरंतवणराइसोहिल्लं. "an arcade of trees shimmered over the stone ground, dazzling with jewels."

३४७ Verse 1036 is not in N.

३४८ N jumps from परिवासिअ in verse 1043 to verse 1047, skipping 1044, 1045, and 1046.

३४९ संगलिस्सामो] PN, संमिलिस्सामो B, संगमिस्सामो conj. Upadhye.

३५० परिअट्ठिओ] N, परिवड्डिओ ed.

३५१ अवलंबिज्जइ] N, confirming Upadhye's conjecture; अविलंबिज्जइ ed. गओ] conj.; गअं N (P गयं), गइं J, गइ B. The commentator takes it in the meaning of "elephant."

३५२ अण्णेक्क] conj., आणेक्क ed. The commentator understands आणिक्य to be a term of art for sideways lovemaking.

३५३ After verse 1084, N skips to the second line of 1086.

३५४ Verse 1091 is not found in B or N.

३५५ संकाए व] N; संकाए य ed.

३५६ विण्णत्तो जोइसिएहिं] ed; विण्णत्तं जोइसिएण BN.

३५७ सुर] ed; पुर BN.

३५८ णिबज्झंत] ed; निवज्झंत P, णिवज्झंत J, विमुंज्झंत B, णिवहुत्त N.

३५९ णोल्हसु] ed (P); पिल्हसु B, मेल्हसु N. इमं म्ह लिंकरुअं] ed (J); इमम्ह डिंभरुयं P, इमम्ह डिम्हत्तअं N, वम्ह डिक्करुयं B.

३६० भिण्णम्मि] ed (PJ); भग्गमि N, भज्ज्ंमि B. करंबअडेरअम्मि] ed (PJ, with some variants); करंवयदोहणंमि B, करम्वअभण्डअम्मि N. कं] ed (J), N; किं PB.

३६१ गव्विर] ed; वज्जिर N. धुणसु] ed (BP); धणसु J, विहण N. मुहा] ed (J); दुमा P, तुमं, मुहअ N.

३६२ पेच्छह बप्पो वण्णविसिएण सुणएण] ed (P); वणिविसिएण पिच्छह अव्वो सुणएण B, अरीअवणं पच्छह वप्पो वण्णविसिएण सुण्णहिअेण N. सोणहीएण] ed (B); सोणभीएण P, सिण्णहीएण J, om. N.

३६३ वराहो] ed, N; the meaning of वराओ seems more suitable here.

३६४ एवं अण्णोण्णालाव] ed (P); इअ अण्णोण्णालाव N, इय एवंणोण्णालाव B.

३६५ सुहणिअलिज्झंत] ed, N; सुढिलनिलिज्झंत B.

३६६ Verse 1121 is missing in B.

३६७ Verses 1122 to 1127 are missing in N. मग्गभअ] ed; सग्गभग्ग P, मग्गेभय J, माजभय N.

३६८ रेणु] P; फेण ed (JB).

३६९ Upadhye's edition reads परिगहियं तं, but I have followed his note (ed p. 380) to read परिगहिअंतं as a single word.

३७० समास] ed (P), N; तमाल B.

३७१ गिरिसरीअड] ed (J); गिरिसिरीयड P, गिरिसरीतड B, सिरीसंराअड N. विडवोलि] ed (J); वडवोरि P, विडवालि B, वडल्लि N. परिगहिअ] ed; संगहिया B (संगआ N).

३७२ वरतुरअसाहणं] ed; करितुरअसहस्सं N. कविल] ed; सुणह N.

३७३ एवं चिअ सीसंते] ed (J); एवं सिट्ठे संते PB, एवंविद्धेसे N.

३७४ हेसारव] conj. Upadhye; हिंसारव mss. B omits a portion of verse 1134.

३७५ ओसप्पइ] ed; उअसिप्पइ N, उयसप्पइ B. N reads up to the syllable त of तह and then skips to the beginning of verse 1136.

३७६ धाइ] ed; धरइ N. कंखिरस्स] ed; कंखिराहि N.

३७७ Verse 1141 is not in B and N.

३७८ गिरि] B; करि ed (J), कर P. Verse 1142 is not in N.

३७९ N only gives the second half of verse 1143 (it also skips the preceding two verses).

३८० Verse 1144 is missing in N.

३८१ णे] ed (B); ण PN.

३८२ पवण्णं] ed; निसण्णं B, विण्णं N. तुम्हं पि तं होइ] ed; तुम्हं पि जा माइ N, जुज्जं च तुम्हं पि B.

३८३ एहि] ed; एवं N. किं अम्ह ण तेण] ed (P); किं म्ह ण तेण J, कं जम्ह न तेण B, कज्जम्ह
तेण ण N.

३८४ भणिऊण] ed; सुणिऊण N.

३८५ कवणेण व इह कज्जेण] ed, N; केण व कज्जेण इहं B.

३८६ परिमिअपरिवारपरिअरिओ] ed; च सुअपरिवारपरिअरिअं N.

३८७ महामुणिणा] ed (B), N; मुणिणो P. सो राआ] N, ed (JP omit सो); नरनाह
B.

३८८ सो सिंहासण ed, N; तत्थ सुहासण B.

३८९ रअणीसु] ed; रअणीए N, B.

३९० Verse 1167 is missing in B. It is read by PJN.

३९१ तेण किसोअरि] ed, N; तिलोयसुंदरि B.

३९२ सरेसु रहवाहिणी] ed (J); सरोसरहवाहिणी P, सरोसरणं ह कामिणी B, सरावसलवारिणी
N.

३९३ जइ अत्थमिअ ed (J); उदयत्थंमि P, उयअत्थमिय B, तुउअत्थ (?) N.

३९४ मज्झा] ed; अम्ह N. जं वसइ] ed (J); जं वसइ P, संचरइ B, ज चरइ N. मज्झा] ed;
अम्ह NB.

३९५ पसु] N, ed; दस B.

३९६ भणणइ] ed; भणयं (भणियं) B, साहसु N. णिवासीणं] conj. Upadhye, N (reads
दासीण afterward); नवसीणं PB, समासीणं J.

३९७ चलिज्ज ed; वलेज्ज N.

३९८ वीराण] ed, N; धीराणां B.

३९९ पाअडिअ] ed; णअट्टिअ N.

४०० दढ] ed; दिट्टु N.

४०१ णिल्लूणवलण] JN; णिल्लूणचलण ed, निल्लरचरण B, निल्लूणवकण P. रुंजिय] ed;
खंडिय B, भंडिअ N. Before this verse, N reads तावो (= तओ?), and B
reads तओ.

४०२ रसिअ] ed (JB); रमिअ NP.

४०३ उव्वरिअ] ed (J); उव्बरिय P, उच्छरिअ N, उद्दरिय B.

४०४ जाआमरिसेण] ed; पज्जलिअरोसाणलेण N.

४०५ सुहागम] ed; समागम BN.

४०६ समावडिए] ed; णिसासमए NB.

४०७ सरोसेण] ed, N; नरिंदस्स B.

४०८ अणण्ण] ed, N; अणंत B.

४०९ पि देमि जं अम्ह साहीणं] ed; तं देमि तुहज्ज दे भणेसु B; पि देमि तुझज देव भणं N.

४१० सविब्भम] ed; सविम्हअ N.

४११ साहिप्पउ] P, N; साहिज्जउ ed (B).

४१२ ता इणिहं] ed; किं एत्थ N. विउले] ed; विमले N (in agreement with verse
610 above).

४१३ अवअरिओ] ed; अवसरिओ N.

४१४ विहावंतो] ed; च भुंजंतो B, विहावेअन्तो N.

४१५ सहइ तुह अम्ह] ed; ण सहए अम्ह N, सहइ एअम्ह B.

४१६ अणज्ज होसि] ed; अंते जाहा N.

४१७ दीसउ] ed, N; दीसइ B.

४१८ ०सासेण] conj. Upadhye, N (०सासेणं J, ०सासेणे P); संगेण B.

४१९ तुरिअं गओ] ed; संपेसिओ N.

४२० चिंतिओ] ed, N; विम्हिओ B. आगओ] ed; परिगओ BN.

४२१ तए] ed (B), N; मए P. Verse 1234 is missing from J. It is read in PBN.

४२२ एक्कासणसंठिआओ] ed; एक्कपएसट्ठिआसु NB.

४२३ संचिओवड्ढिआइँ] ed; संपडिओवट्टिआइ N, कंखिओवच्छियाइ B.

४२४ देव्वो] P (N देवो, B दिव्वो); अप्पा ed (J).

४२५ N skips from समअं in the first line of verse 1242 to विज्ञा० (विज्ञा०) in the first line of verse 1243.

४२६ देवेहिँ] ed (JB); देव्वेहिं P, देव्वेण N.

४२७ सुदिअहे] N, ed; सुहलग्गो B. जह भणिओ] ed; सुहे लग्गे N.

४२८ भणिओ] ed, N; पत्तो B.

४२९ सद्दएण] NPB; सद्देण ed (J).

४३० संखकाहलमुइंगघोसेहिँ संचलिआ] ed; संखकहलनिहोसहोसेहिं संचालिया B, पढमे तेहिं वंदिदिअअरसमूहेहिं N.

४३१ समल्हीणा] ed, N; समासीणा B.

४३२ Verse 1251 is missing in B, although a Sanskrit translation is given in the manuscript.

४३३ कं तं जं भणम्ह] N, ed (P); कं तं जण्ण भहह J, कहं तं जंपणम्ह B.

४३४ हरिणच्छि] NB; पसयच्छि ed. I have chosen the reading for the alliteration.

४३५ णहमुहसिप्पंत] ed (J); णहमुहच्छिवप्पंत N, नहमुहच्छिप्पंत B, नहसेप्पंत P.

४३६ णिब्भर] N, ed; विब्भम B. In manuscripts B and N, verse 1259 is read before verse 1258.

४३७ सुजवेण जाणवत्तेण] ed; सुजावेण सुहविमाणेण N.

४३८ रसभेअतण्णाअ] ed (P); रसायपइण्ण J, रसइवसपवण B, रसोसेवण्णेवण्ण N. पल्लववोत्थइअविअड] N, ed; पल्लवछन्नविडव B. वर] ed; सुर N.

४३९ णिअअपिआपिअ] N; णिअणिअया पिय ed. आसीणा] ed, N; आरूढा B.

४४० सुरहिवासाइं] ed (B); लग्गवेढाइं N.

४४१ वलइअं] N, ed; सज्जियं B.

४४२ After सणिअं N skips to the पि in the first line of the following verse.

४४३ पि झत्ति पम्हुसइ] ed; फुसिज्जइ फुडत्थं B (N apparently पिअम्हसिज्जइ फुडंभूं). छज्जइ] ed, N; रेहइ B.

४४४ परिउंबिआ] ed; परिओविआ N.

४४५ विणिओअवज्जिअं] ed (J); विणिओअवज्जिआ NB; कंतीए निज्जियं P. सवणासोअ] NJ; सयणासोय ed (P); सयणासोग B.

४४६ पसुत्तेहि] ed; पसत्तेहिं B, पअंतेहिं N.

४४७ गेअं] ed (गीअं N); गिज्जइ B. पहसिअं] ed; दुहसिअं N, च हसियं B.

४४८ पावरणं] ed; पंगुरणं BN.

४४९ समासीणो] ed; समह्लीणो NB.

• ४५० B reads the second line ता भणियो पियतणयामुहदंसणसुहमणुभवेहि; N as भणिओ तं पिअअतणामुहदंसणसुहमणुभवह एत्ताहे.

४५१ तेण] ed; तेहिं B, ताहिं N.

४५२ पच्चुट्ठिआ] ed; पवट्टिआ N. समासत्ता] ed, N; समासत्था P, समासत्तो J, समोसत्ता B.

४५३ वि साव (विसाव?)] ed (J), N (विसाय P); समाव B.

४५४ पास] ed, N; दार B.

४५५ विअड] ed; पअड N. चच्चिअ] ed (P, वज्झिय J); संचिय N (संचय B).

४५६ समुअं सुह] ed (J); ससुयं सुह P, सुसुअं व N, सुअसत्थे B. मज्जणावीढे] conj. (मज्जाणावीढे in ed is probably a misprint); मज्जणावेढी N.

४५७ ॰विरिए] ed (J); ॰विरीहिं PN (॰विरीहिइ B).

४५८ N skips from पमुहेहिं to पुरस्सरेहिं in verse 1293, and combines these words into पमुस्सरेहिं.

४५९ रंगावलिरइअविविहसअवत्तसत्थिअ] ed; रंगावलिविइंनसुपसत्थसत्थिय B, वराणाव-लिविच्छुण्णं पसुअसट्टिअ N.

४६० चिंचइअ] ed; देवइअ N.

४६१ For the first line of verse 1298, B reads कोउहरे संपत्तो वट्टियकोलाहलो नरवरिंदो. PJN give the reading in the text.

४६२ संपाउअ] ed; संत्थाइय B, पाडिअ N. साअरं सहरिसंगेण] N, ed (PJ); साहिलासत्थिविच्छोहा B.

४६३ पुणो वि तत्तो समासीणो] N, ed (JB); तत्तो वेइं समुत्तिन्नो P.

४६४ ॰संलावं, ॰जुअं, ॰णिसण्णं] ed; ॰संलावो, ॰जुओ, ॰णिसण्णो NB.

४६५ पअडिअपहोहो] ed; पडिआवअवा NB. N appears to have ended around verse 1305. No further folios are available, and the writing is cramped in the last line of the final folio, which preserves verse 1305 (although in an unusually corrupt form, reading the second line रसणविलिअरहइमइव्व).

४६६ तंसोणअ] ed; तो सोन्नरव B.

४६७ Verse 1308a is not found in any manuscript. Upadhye reconstructed it from the Sanskrit commentary in B.

४६८ B reads the first line as: अह सो सहसालिंगणरसिओ सालाहणो निसासमए.

४६९ B reads the second line as: खेगमणं तह गंधाहिवेण दिणो महीवइणो.

४७० B reads the second line as: पडिवन्नं अन्नं पि हु ज अम्हं तुम्ह साहीणं.

४७१ Verse 1319a, 1320a, and 1320b are only found in B. The final verse in B is 1320b, which ends with the auspicious word कल्लाणो, "good fortune."

४७२ Verses 1317–1319, and 1321–1333, are found in PJ, but not B.

४७३ Upadhye reads ॰वयवं at the end of the first line of 1324, and अवगय (following J; P reads मरग) at the beginning of the second line.

४७४ णिहिअ] conj.; णिहित्त ed (unmetrical). अम्मे सुजण] ed; अम्मसुजण suggested by the gloss in P.

४७५ ॰प्पंका] J; ॰प्पंको ed (P).

४७६ Upadhye says of verse 1333a: "This *gāthā* is found only in P, but not in JB. It may be noted that it is written on the lower margin of the palmleaf ms. and in a handwriting different from that of the text." I have not normalized the orthography of this verse.

NOTES TO THE TRANSLATION

1   Although Shiva and Parvati are the principal deities in the story itself, the author begins by praising Vishnu, in various avatars, for seven verses. The avatar praised in the first verse is the Man-lion (Narasimha), who deprived Vishnu's discus, named Sudarshana, of the opportunity of killing the demon Hiranyakashipu. Vishnu is subsequently praised as the Dwarf (Vamana, v. 2) and Krishna (vv. 3–4, 6–7), and in his cosmic submarine form (vv. 5–5a). Praises of Shiva and Parvati come later (vv. 8–11).

2   In his Dwarf (Vamana) avatar, Vishnu took three steps, measuring out the netherworld, earth, and, with his last step, empty space. The last of these is identified with Vishnu (his "unembodied self").

3   Krishna's brother, Balarama, once laughed at him for being unable to cross the threshold of a door, despite being a form of the supreme god Vishnu.

4   Vishnu, in his Krishna avatar, killed the demon Arishta, who took the form of a bull. Arishta, like Keshin mentioned later, was sent by Krishna's uncle Kamsa to kill him. The weapon that Death (Kala) wields is a noose.

5   Shesha is the many-headed serpent who lives in the ocean and on whose coils Vishnu and Lakshmi, his consort, sleep; Vishnu wears the luminous *kaustubha* gem on his chest.

6   These actions of Krishna are construed in sequence (*yathāsaṃkhya*) with their objects. The two *arjuna* trees that Krishna uprooted were actually two *yakṣas,* or demigods, who had been cursed.

7   The divine river Ganga and the crescent moon are both found in the hair of Shiva, here called Rudra.

8   This verse, in the *vaṃśastha* meter, uses a figure wherein each of the adjectives can be read in two senses, one relating to the standard of the comparison (suns), and the other to the target (good people).

9   The commentator suggests that good people avoid mistakes because they are afraid of the censure of bad people, and hence bad people, too, are not really bad. The poet seems to reject this idea with the following verse. Upadhye offers a different interpretation: even if there is not ultimately a difference between good people

and bad people, poets nevertheless act as if there is one, and hence the poet is following convention.

10 This verse contains an "apparent contradiction" (*virodhābhāsa*), one of the poet's favorite figures, in which a seeming contradiction is resolved by reading one of the words in a different meaning. In this case the word *saloṇa*, meaning "salty," would contradict the sweetness of the woman's lips, and hence it is read in the alternate meaning of "lovely."

11 *The three holy Vedas:* the *Ṛgveda*, the *Yajurveda*, and *Sāmaveda*. *The three sacred fires:* the domestic (*gārhapatya*), eastern (*āhavanīya*), and southern (*dakṣiṇa*), which are set up for Vedic sacrifices. *Three goals of life:* doing what is right (*dharma*), power (*artha*), and pleasure (*kāma*).

12 The word *koūhaleṇa* may be used adverbially to mean "with eagerness" or "with curiosity," but it is much more likely in this context that the author is providing his name as Kouhala, given that his father and grandfather have also been named.

13 The figure in this verse is identification. *Pearl-strewn:* Hardened secretions from the cheeks of rutting elephants are called "pearls." The poet's wife, according to the Sanskrit commentary, is Savitri; the poet never addresses her by name, however.

14 This verse, in the *śārdūlavikrīḍita* meter, is quoted in Vāgbhaṭa 1915: 21, and Trivikrama 1954, under 1.1.22 (only the first three words).

15 This verse is quoted by Bhoja as an example of a figure called *mālādīpaka*, or "garland-lamp," in Bhoja 1934: 529 and Bhoja 2007: vol. 1, 605. It is quoted as an example of *śṛṅkhalā*, or "chain," in Śobhākaramitra 1943: 166 and Ruyyaka 1934: 1060.

16 Geese are said to eat the stalks of fresh lotuses, whose astringent quality is said to give their calls a more clear and resonant quality than they would otherwise have.

17 *The women of the ten directions:* the ten directions (the four cardinal directions, the four intermediate directions, and the zenith and nadir) are often figured as young women. Here the swaying of trees is compared to the designs painted on their faces (*viśeṣika*). See *Subhāṣitaratnakośa* v. 196 for a similar image.

18 By poetic convention, pairs of *cakravāka* birds (ruddy shelducks) are separated during the night and reunited during the day. Here the moonlight deceives them into thinking that it is day.

19   Literally "taste," *rasa* refers to aesthetic emotions in Indian poet-
      ics, which can be "savored" by the listener. See Pollock 2016.

20   *My love with lily-petal eyes:* the author addresses his wife through-
      out the story with epithets such as this.

21   This classification is given in Ānandavardhana 1940: 330. Probably
      earlier than *Līlāvaī* is the *Story of Samaraiccha* (Haribhadra 1935),
      which also relates this classification at its very beginning. Kouhala
      signals the fact that he does not have firsthand experience of these
      texts with the "hearsay" particle *kira* (translated as "apparently").

22   Verse 41 explains what type of story *Līlāvaī* is. "Regional" (*desī*)
      words are those that do not have a clear Sanskrit equivalent, and are
      usually one of the most difficult aspects of understanding Prakrit
      texts.

23   *All the right elements:* literally, its composition has good junctures
      (*sandhi*), which probably refers to the progression of the plot.

24   *Ashmaka:* the region near the Godavari River in what is now
      western Maharashtra. *The Boar:* when the earth was dragged to
      the bottom of the ocean by a demon, Vishnu in his Boar avatar
      slew the demon and raised the earth back up. There is a pun on
      garuabhāvāe, which means "importance" in the case of her contact
      with the god Vishnu, and "weight" in the case of the gems she
      acquired while at the bottom of the ocean.

25   *Dance to Prakrit songs:* the *carcarī,* a song in Prakrit accompanied
      by a dance, associated with springtime festivals. See Bhayani
      1993b.

26   *Golden age:* the *kṛta-yuga* is the first of four mythical ages (the
      others are the *treta-, dvāpāra-,* and *kali-yuga*), which are character-
      ized by successive moral decay. *The creator's template: sikkhaṭṭhāṇa,*
      "place of instruction." The idea is that Ashmaka was the template
      from which the creator (Prajapati) copied as he learned how to
      create the rest of the world.

27   After this verse, which the text breaks into rhythmic prose
      (Upadhye, with the help of H. D. Velankar, tried to identify the
      verse forms, see ed pp. 335–336).

28   *Social orders:* the division of society into four distinct *varṇas,* or
      orders, namely Brahmans, Kshatriyas, Vaishyas, and Shudras.

29   *Dark age:* the *kaliyuga,* the present age and the most morally
      degraded of the four (see note to v. 47).

30   The three adjectives in this verse each have two meanings, one that

applies to the rivers and another that applies to the women. The figure is "condensed expression" (*samāsokti*).

31 *Moonstones:* the *candrakānta* or *candramaṇi*, a stone said to liquefy when the moon's rays touch it. *Smoke-blackened sky:* according to poetic convention, peacocks dance at the onset of the monsoon season; the peacocks mistake the smoke rising from sacrificial fires for monsoon clouds.

32 *Women with midnight trysts:* the *abhisārikā*, a woman who goes out at night to meet a lover, requires the anonymity of darkness, but the houses in Pratishthana were lit with jeweled lamps (for *gharamaṇi* in the sense of "lamp," see *Setubandha* 10.52 and Rāmadāsa's commentary thereon in Pravarasena 1895). The commentator imagines that the light pours into the streets because the walls of the houses are made of crystal, as noted in verse 62a below.

33 Women washing turmeric off of their bodies is a motif of Prakrit literature: see *Seven Centuries* 58 (Hāla 1881), which the present verse echoes (*ajjea haliddāpimjarāi golāi tūhāiṃ*).

34 Kouhala now shifts to a series of verses that involve the figure of "praise in the guise of criticism" (*vyājastuti*). Verse 62 is quoted in Bhoja 2007: 1384. The idea here seems to be that the scent of jasmine itself resolves any quarrels between lovers; no apologies are necessary.

35 This story refers to the king as Salavahana, Salahana (both Prakrit versions of the Sanskrit name *Sātavāhana*), and Hala. They are considered synonyms by most authors, including Hemachandra, who includes them in several of his lexicons. "Satavahana" was the name of a dynasty, and "Hala" was the name (perhaps the pen name) of an individual king in that dynasty, who is credited with editing the anthology of Prakrit poetry called *Seven Centuries* (*Sattasaī*).

36 The figure in this and the following two verses is "apparent contradiction" (*virodhābhāsa*), where the contradiction is resolved by reading one of the words in a different sense, which is indicated in the text. See note to verse 16a.

37 The two adjectives in this verse can be read differently to apply to both the moon and the king (another example of "condensed expression," or *samāsokti*).

38 According to a poetic convention, the plants (*osahi*) that grow in mountain caves give off a reddish light at night.

39 This verse probably refers to Hala's reputation as a patron of literature. See the introduction.

40 This verse is also found in Jayavallabha's *Vajjālagga,* v. 635.

41 The god of love (*Kāmadeva*) is represented with a bow and arrow made out of flowers.

42 The word *tilaa* refers to a forehead mark (around which the yellow flowers of the *karnikāra* are described as an additional decoration), but it may also refer to sesame.

43 This verse echoes a well-known Prakrit song in the first act of Harsha's seventh-century play *Ratnāvalī* (*paḍhamaṃ mahumāso jaṇassa hiaaï kaṇaï midulāi paccā viddhaï kāmo laddhappasarehi kusumabāṇehiṁ:* "first spring softens hearts, and then the love god's flower-arrows, finding an easy way in, pierce them"), as noted by Upadhye (ed p. 337).

44 Quoted in Bhoja 2007: vol. 2, 1422.

45 Quoted by Jayaratha in Ruyyaka and Jayaratha 1939: 75. The commentary suggests that a girl would be beckoned, or called, by her girlfriends upon the arrival of her lover.

46 The leaves of *palāśa* trees (the Flame of the Forest) are red. Upadhye notes that the custom of wearing red garments on a wedding day is mentioned also by Haribhadra in his *Story of Samaraiccha* (see also Chandra 1973).

47 Here the wind is figured as an unfaithful male lover (*parimala* can refer to both fragrance and sexual union).

48 Mount Meru was thought to occupy the center of the universe. *Women of the directions:* see note to verse 28.

49 Chandaleha is the name of one of Hala's queens in several other stories. See Rājaśekhara 1932, p. 147.

50 *Bedroom:* the idea is that the sky is suffused with pollen in the same way that a bedroom is suffused with incense or perfumes.

51 The following verses (94–100) describe the designs painted on a courtesan's body. Possibly what is intended is that the reed used to apply the paint is a "kinsman" of the plants that the god of love uses as arrows.

52 The alliteration in the original text, *pattattaṃ pattaṃ pattalacchi pattaṃ,* involves a figure called *yamaka,* or "twinning," which requires each instance of *patta* to have a different meaning. For that reason, I prefer the interpretation "petal-eyed" as the primary meaning of *pattalacchi* (involving the *deśī* word *pattala,* which

Hemachandra actually derives from a hypothetical Sanskrit word *pattrala*, "leaflike"), rather than "girl who has obtained beauty," which is certainly present as a secondary meaning).

53 Milk is harmful to snakes. Upadhye interprets this verse to mean that "to paint an already attractive girl so charmingly is to make her fatally tempting: this is as dangerous as serving milk to a serpent" (ed p. 338).

54 *Realist style: viddha* refers to a realistic mode of representation in painting (ed p. 338, citing Raghavan 1933; see also Kansara 1972).

55 *Salons:* the *goṭṭhī* is a meeting of poets and scholars at a royal court and involves public recitation of poetry (and on-the-spot composition of poems), critical evaluation, and so on.

56 *Yakṣas* are demigods, dwarfish in stature, who are often represented as guards or protective deities, and associated with wealth. The commentary explains that spies are called *yakṣas* because (like *yakṣas*) they know how to disguise themselves. Upadhye suggests that this remark has a double meaning: *ṇaresa* could mean "snake charmer" in addition to "king," and *kaḍaa* could mean (a snake charmer's) "ring" in addition to "court."

57 These two verses (106a and 106b) interrupt the speech of the minister's son in verses 105–106 and 107–109.

58 Pottisa is listed as one of the authors in *Seven Centuries* (*Sattasaī*), the anthology of Prakrit poems said to have been compiled by Hala/Salahana, in a number of commentaries on that anthology. Vijaananda seems to be fictional.

59 *Dance:* A *carcarī;* see note to verse 46.

60 *Officers: bhoa* refers to a particular type of feudal lord, attested in Satavahana-era inscriptions.

61 *Gossiped:* the commentary understands by *saṇṇā* in-group codes such as *mūladevī* and *karapallavī,* which operate by a transposition of sounds, much like "pig Latin." The word could simply mean "hand signals."

62 Upadhye suggests (ed p. 341) that the elderly doorkeeper is trying to improve his vision by holding his hand over his eyes.

63 *Bhatta Kumarila:* Kumarila is, like Pottisa, listed by the commentators on *Seven Centuries* as one of the poets whose work was included in that Prakrit anthology (see Hāla 1942 and Hāla 1980).

64 *Bhatta Kumarila's feet:* the commentary explains that Vijaananda,

in his current state, is unfit to look upon the king himself. *Embraced:* the word is defined by Prakrit lexicons as "to go," but in its various occurrences in this text, the meaning "embrace," provided by the commentator, is more appropriate.

65   *Full of wishes that remain unfulfilled:* literally, "a source of good desires." The implication is that the various relationships described in Vijaananda's story await their fulfillment. Note that the word *koūhaleṇa* occurs in this verse, where it must be taken as an adverb ("eagerly"), as Upadhye notes (ed p. 320). Still, in V. Raghavan's review (printed in ed p. 389), he says that "the spirit of gāthā 146 would support the taking of Kautūhala as the author's name." Probably Raghavan meant that the word *koūhaleṇa,* despite its adverbial construction in the context of Vijaananda's story, would remind the reader that Kouhala was the story's author.

66   The previous verse (146) begins Vijaananda's speech, which continues to verse 920 and takes up well over half of *Līlāvaī.* "Malaya" is the western coast of southern India, roughly equivalent to the modern state of Kerala. The "Pandya king" probably refers to the king of the Tamil country, the modern state of Tamil Nadu. Vijaananda's conquest of Malaya will turn out to be important to the plot of the story (see vv. 976–977).

67   *Texts on statecraft: attha-satthehiṃ,* an example of which is the eponymous *Arthaśāstra* ascribed to Kauṭilya. The previous verse lists the four "strategies" (*upāyas*) that are listed in Kauṭilya's work as alternatives to war.

68   *Ancestral home of Lakshmi:* Lakshmi is said to have been one of the products of the primeval churning of the ocean. *Abode of Vishnu:* Vishnu is said to live in the ocean (specifically the ocean of milk, where he sleeps on the serpent Shesha). *Women who are the directions:* see notes on verses 28 and 91.

69   The phrase *paricintiaṃmhi hiaeṇa* ("I thought to myself") is used often in *Līlāvaī:* it literally means "my heart considered," and it always introduces an internal monologue.

70   The figure here is "apparent contradiction" (see note to v. 16a). The basis for the contradiction in all three cases is the conceit that the *apsarases* (semidivine women of great beauty, similar to nymphs), the cosmic poison (*kālakūṭa*), and the elephant Airavata and the horse Ucchaihshravas—which two subsequently belonged to Indra—were all produced by the churning of the ocean.

To understand the first phrase, we must know that Rama crossed the ocean on his way to Lanka, and to understand the last, we must know that the ocean gave shelter to the mountain Mainaka when Indra was cutting off the wings of the other mountains.

71 Again the figure is apparent contradiction, although the contradictions are chained in this verse. Liquor (*surā*) was another product of the churning of the ocean. (The commentator suggests that *asuro*, "without liquor," has an additional meaning, namely that the god Vishnu resides there; this seems unlikely to me.) The ocean may be "drunk" in the sense that its waves are always swelling and swaying. Whereas a drunk is expected to transgress boundaries of propriety, the ocean is commonly said to stay within its limits. The word *savāṇia* means both "engaging in trade," which forms a contradiction with staying within boundaries (since traders travel), as well as "full of water," which forms an obvious contradiction with having no water. (Alternatively, *virasa* could refer to the absence of taste, which would also form a contradiction, since water is either sweet—that is, fresh—or salty.) Compare Pravarasena's *Setubandha* 2.18 (translation in Handique 1976): "Even though restless, it remained steadfast by respecting its limits. It abounded in riches, even though its treasures had been taken out by the gods (during the churning). It was unscathed, even though churned; and oozed nectar, even though its waters had a briny taste" (*caḍulaṃ pi thiīa thiraṃ tiasukkhitta-raaṇaṃ pi sārabbhahiaṃ | mahiaṃ pi aṇoluggaṃ asāu-salilaṃ pi amaa-rasa-ṇīsaṃdaṃ ‖*).

72 The "causeway" is the rock formation (called "Rama's Bridge" or "Adam's Bridge") that stretches between India and Sri Lanka. According to Ramayana tradition, the bridge was built by monkeys, at the direction of their king Sugriva, in order to reach Lanka and defeat Ravana.

73 Lakshmi sleeps by Vishnu's side in the ocean, hence it is her "bedroom."

74 As noted above (v. 170), liquor was one of the products of the primeval churning of the ocean. The idea here is that *kesara* flowers smell like wine (hence the flowers are likely to be *Mimusops elengi*, as Nimkar notes).

75 The flowers of the *saptaparṇa* tree are often said to smell like temporin, the liquid produced by the temporal glands of an

elephant during rut.

76   In this story, the *siddhas* (literally "perfected ones") are human-like beings with magical powers who inhabit the southern mountains. Sandalwood, clove, and cardamom are all associated with the southernmost parts of the subcontinent.

77   *Rameshvara:* an image of Rama in a shrine, now the site of a twelfth-century temple, at the place in South India where Rama is believed to have crossed the ocean to Lanka on the causeway that was mentioned previously.

78   Here again the figure is apparent contradiction (*virodhābhāsa;* see note to v. 16a). Once we know that these adjectives qualify the word "ship" in the next verse, we must reread them all to yield a suitable meaning. I agree with Nimkar, rather than the commentator, in reading *suamme* as "well-born" rather than "of good deeds."

79   *Dark age:* the Kali age, the last and present of the four ages, or *yugas,* associated with moral impurity and the decay of the social order (see note to v. 47). Sattagodavari Bhima is, in this text at least, the name of the forested region near the mouth of the Godavari River. Upadhye identified it with Draksharama (or Daksharama).

80   *The body of the love god:* Shiva incinerated the love god, Kama, who was thenceforth known as "the incorporeal" (*ananga*). Tripura (the triple city), Andhaka, and the elephant demon are all enemies previously vanquished by Shiva.

81   *Three cosmic qualities: sattva, tamas,* and *rajas. Triad: trayī* usually means the three Vedas, but it must mean something else here (the commentary in B says the past, present, and future; the gloss in P says accomplished, fully accomplished, and still to be accomplished); possibly it is the triad of the three previously mentioned triads.

82   The Pashupatas are a group of ascetics who are devoted to Pashupati ("lord of the beasts"), one of the forms of Shiva.

83   Devotees of Shiva wear strings of *rudrākṣa* beads (dried red seeds) like rosaries.

84   Presumably this refers to the ascetic's desire to have Vijaananda stay with him, expressed in v. 217.

85   A common sculptural motif in Indian temple architecture, a *śālabhañjikā* depicts a woman standing next to a tree and attempting to break its branches.

86   *Bull-pavilion:* the part of the temple that housed an image of

Shiva's mount, the bull.

87 *Balconies:* I follow Nimkar's guess in taking *tavaṃga* in this sense; it is not listed in lexicons.

88 *Welcome offering: aggho,* an offering presented to a guest upon arrival, usually consisting of water with flower petals in it.

89 *At some distance from them:* I take *dūrāsaṇṇa* literally; the Sanskrit commentary of B, and Nimkar, take it as *adūrāsanna* ("at not much of a distance").

90 *Thousand eyes:* Indra is said to have gotten a thousand eyes when cursed by Gautama after Indra attempted to seduce the sage's wife, Ahalya. Compare *Taraṅgalolā* 975 (Bhayani 1993a).

91 *Bark garments:* ascetics usually wear clothes made out of tree bark (*valkala*). *Fame and Prosperity:* Fame (*kittī*) and Prosperity (or Lakshmi, here called *kamalā*) are both personified as women, and both are traditionally white. The idea is that Mahanumai and Kuvalaavali's bark garments make them look as white as Fame and Prosperity personified.

92 *At the time of its churning:* as noted above, Lakshmi is said to have emerged from the ocean when it was churned by the gods in order to produce the nectar of immortality. H. C. Bhayani compared this verse to *Taraṅgalolā* 39 (Bhayani 1993a).

93 The commentary explains "pure" (*suī*) as "of pure descent on both his mother's and father's sides."

94 The sense of *sa ccia bhūmī suhehiṃ saccaviā* is not clear; the idea is that the two girls agree to host Vijaananda because he is a guest of the sage.

95 Following the sage's introduction, Mahanumai addresses Vijaananda—as do others in the story—as *bhaṭṭaütta,* literally "son of a Brahman."

96 Verse 271 begins Kuvalaavali's story, which continues until 887 (with a two-verse interruption from Vijaananda at 727–728).

97 *Family Mountains:* the *kula-parvatas* are the seven principal mountain ranges in traditional Indian cosmology, although according to many sources, Meru is not included in this list: chapter seventeen of Rajashekhara's *Kāvyamīmāṃsā,* for example, lists Mahendra, Malaya, Sahya, Pariyatra, Shuktiman, Vindhya, and Riksha. These verses (273–280) present a description of Mount Meru that forms a single syntactic unit in Prakrit (a *kulaka*); it bears close comparison with the famous *kulaka* that describes Mount

Himalaya in the beginning of Kālidāsa's *Kumārasaṃbhava* (1.1–17).

98 *Elephants of the directions:* the cardinal directions are often figured as elephants.

99 *Kinnaras:* another kind of semidivine being, usually depicted with a human body and a horse's face. The reading adopted here, *mārua,* refers to a type of deer (the *vātapramī,* according to the commentator); Upadhye's reading refers to the Kinnaras drinking liquor (*māhava*).

100 *Tumbura:* a mythical musician (*gandharva*). *Brahma's goose:* Brahma's mount is the goose.

101 The *pārijāta* tree is a mythical tree said to exist in Indra's heaven. *Along roads that are sticky with:* the reading implied by the commentary is *muia-hiaāhi,* "with hearts gladdened by."

102 *Vidyādharas:* another kind of semidivine being, endowed with magical powers (*vidyās*).

103 Verses 286 to 290 present a syntactically unified description of Ganesha's dance. This recalls the first verse (*nāndī*) of the play *Mālatīmādhava* (Bhavabhūti 2007).

104 *Risqué jokes:* a traditional component of Indian weddings, told by the bride's female relations.

105 Verse 323 is quoted in Bhoja 2007: vol. 2, 893.

106 As Upadhye notes (p. 354), the phrase *kiṃ bhaṇaha* ("what is that you say?") serves to introduce a question or statement from an interlocutor, in this case from Vijaananda. *Her position:* as a princess.

107 The words in this verse carry a secondary meaning—"redness" can mean "desire," and "play" can refer to sexual enjoyment—that anticipates the coming scene.

108 For the image see verse 172.

109 *Submarine fire:* in Indian cosmology, a fire (called Vadava) was thought to burn in the depths of the ocean.

110 *Snakes:* poetic convention holds sandal trees to be inhabited by poisonous snakes. The implication is that the sandal trees are close to the sun because of Mount Malaya's elevation.

111 *Dried up:* because the grass and the ground are the same green color, the grass is only conspicuous when it dries up and turns yellow-brown. The figure in this verse is "exaggeration" (*atiśayokti*).

112 The following three verses (353–355) are linked by a device in which the last word of each line is repeated in the beginning of

the next line (called *śṛṅkhala,* or "chain"; see Balbir 1995).

113 An image of the god of love was sometimes installed at the base of an *aśoka* tree and worshiped during certain festivals (see the first act of Harṣa's *Ratnāvalī*).

114 *Kerala:* in this story Kerala is a city, rather than a region. The surrounding region of Mount Malaya probably stands in for the Western Ghats in the modern state of Kerala.

115 Literally "playing in the same dirt"(*ekkapaṃsukīlia*).

116 *The god of love:* for this interpretation of *chaṇa-vammaha,* see Upadhye's note (ed p. 356). The erotic undertones (or overtones) of these verses are even more manifest in Prakrit, in which the word "play" (*ram-*) commonly refers to sexual enjoyment.

117 The ground, which is red, is figured as having received its red color from the soles of Kuvalaavali's feet, which are painted with lac.

118 *Melted:* because Mahanumai started to sweat profusely. This verse is quoted in Bhoja 2007: vol. 2, 891 and 1090. Upadhye notes (ed p. 358) that Hemachandra cites the word *vārīmaī* at 8.1.4 in his Prakrit grammar (Hemacandra 1877), possibly from this verse.

119 *Give me your attention: saccavijjāsu* would normally mean "look," but the verb might originally have the meaning of "fix one's attention on" (Tieken 1992).

120 My interpretation of this exchange between Mahavilaa and Mahanumai differs somewhat from Upadhye's and Nimkar's. Mahanumai is afraid that she will never see Mahavanila again, and says this to Mahavilaa frankly. Mahavilaa, in response, puts her at ease by saying that they will see each other often in the future.

121 The figure of "corroboration" (*arthāntaranyāsa*) is enhanced by the condensed expression (*samāsokti*) in the words "position" (both physical and social) and "obscurity" (both darkness and loss of face). Upadhye (ed p. 358) takes *laṃghio* as "traversed," i.e., looked upon, and suggests a different meaning: at evening, as opposed to noon, the sun is weak enough to be looked upon—and thus insulted—by men.

122 As in the previous verse, we have "condensed expression," this time involving the words *sūro* (sun and hero) and *pacchimāe* (western and final). The idea is that a dying hero is carried by his comrades.

123 On *cakravāka* birds: see note to verse 29.

124 Upadhye draws our attention to a similar simile in the *Slaying of the Gauḍa King* (*Gaüḍavaho*), verse 1115.

125 As *vasuāa* typically means "dried" (cf. v. 484), I understand the reference to be a crocus, typically deep blue, that has become pale upon drying out. Upadhye offers (ed p. 359) the alternative that *vasuāa* means "dew" (cf. Sanskrit *avaśyāya*) and hence the simile compares the night's face to a crocus covered in dew.

126 According to poetic convention, sandalwood trees are inhabited by snakes. The herbs referred to in this verse are probably those that counteract snakes, but because they are compared to the sun, they might be the herbs that, according to poetic convention, are said to give off light.

127 *Submarine fire:* see note on verse 344.

128 On B's reading, the flag is flying ahead of the moon's house rather than his chariot.

129 *Displaced:* following Nimkar's suggestion.

130 The Vindhya mountains are dark (because of their *khadira* trees) but have light streaks because of their waterfalls.

131 *Women with midnight trysts:* see note to verse 56.

132 Mahanumai's chest could be red *as* lotus pollen (the redness happening because of her fever), or red *from* lotus pollen (which is applied, like sandalwood paste, as a cooling remedy).

133 Quoted in Bhoja 2007: vol. 2, 893.

134 Quoted in Bhoja 2007: vol. 2, 906.

135 There are textual problems with this verse; I follow Upadhye's suggestion (ed p. 360).

136 Quoted in Bhoja 2007: vol. 2, 1229.

137 *Toward the south:* presumably toward Mount Malaya, although it may be significant that the south is associated with Yama, god of death.

138 Following Upadhye's suggestion (ed p. 361) that it is Mahanumai who read the letter.

139 *Necklace:* given by Mahanumai to Mahavilaa earlier (v. 430), and now in Mahavanila's possession.

140 *The lady of the west: vāruṇī,* the western direction personified as a woman. Note that this description of sunset by Mahavilaa (516–528) seems to describe exactly the same sunset that Kuvalaavali had described earlier (436–457).

141 *Paritaliṇa* should mean "very thin," but Upadhye tentatively understands it as "gathered at the bottom" as does Nimkar following him.

142 There are double meanings in verse 519, with *āsāmuha* referring to the "faces" of the directions, which are indistinguishable at night, as well as containing the word for "hope," and *loa* referring to "light" and "people."

143 *Mount Mandara:* used as the rod during the mythical churning of the ocean of milk.

144 The adjectives in 528 all have a double meaning, referring to qualities of the moon and to an ideal lover.

145 *Recount them:* a pun on the word *guṇa*, "good quality," which also has the sense of multiplication.

146 *The seventh rasa:* after the six physical "tastes" (in contradistinction to the eight or nine aesthetic emotions, which are also called *rasas,* see the note on v. 33). This verse is quoted in *Subhāsiyagāhāsaṃgaho,* verse 117 (Jineśvarasūri 1975).

147 This verse, like the last, is quoted in *Subhāsiyagāhāsaṃgaho,* verse 118 (Jineśvarasūri 1975).

148 Quoted in Bhoja 2007: vol. 2, 895 and 1347.

149 Upadhye notes (ed p. 363) that a verse nearly identical to 569 occurs in the *Agaḍadatta* story in Devendra's commentary (1123) to a canonical Jain text, the *Uttarādhyayana Sūtra.* This verse, or its source, is quoted in Bhoja 2007: vol. 2, 1228.

150 *Impossible: duppariālla* is so defined by Prakrit lexicons; *duḥparipālya,* the gloss in manuscript P, followed by Upadhye in his Sanskrit rendering and Nimkar in his translation, would be "difficult to maintain."

151 This verse is quoted in *Subhāsiyagāhāsaṃgaho,* verse 121 (Jineśvarasūri 1975).

152 *That goes against your birth:* translating J's *asāvaṇṇaṃ (a-sāvarṇya)* "contrary to the principle of marrying within one's caste"; the reading of P and N, *asāmaṇṇaṃ,* simply means "strange."

153 *Apsaras:* see note to verse 169.

154 This verse is in an as-yet unidentified meter; see ed p. 365.

155 *Drew a line on the ground:* a sign of bashfulness.

156 The last sentence is not clear: Upadhye suggests (ed p. 365) that "she means to say that any girl would very much like the idea of being lovingly looked at by him."

157 I take *avasārio* from *avasāritaḥ* and not, as Upadhye would have it (following the gloss in manuscript P), from *aprasāritaḥ.*

158 A *svayaṃvara* is an event at which the woman selects her own

husband, usually on the basis of some feat of strength.

159 We learn later (vv. 1209–1220) that Viulasaa has cursed Chittangaa, and the copyist of manuscript P has included the following verses (635a–d) that anticipate these details from a different manuscript source. In fact, from verse 642, it appears that Kuvalaavali did not know of the curse.

160 This verse is in the *śārdūlavikrīḍita* meter. *Darkness...shadow:* these are the same words in Prakrit (*chāya*); the figure is a simile that employs double meaning (*śleṣa-upamā*).

161 I translate the reading of NJ (and the variant in P), which compares the sky to the mythical elephant-demon (*gajāsura*) slain by Shiva. In P, the sky is compared to a sky elephant (*diggaja*) that has been flayed by a lion, elephants being associated with the eight directions in the sky (see v. 275).

162 The image is based on the conventional equivalence between the opening and closing motions of eyes and of flowers.

163 The word for "rays" and "hands" is the same.

164 The idea is that the ponds are already so red due to pollen and *cakravāka* birds that the influx of red light from the dawn has no effect.

165 I follow Upadhye's Sanskrit gloss in taking *dihivatta* as *dhṛtipātra-*, a caretaker.

166 *Brahma-rākṣasas:* Brahmans reincarnated as demons as punishment, loosely equivalent to ghosts.

167 *Three goals:* see note to verse 18.

168 *Hundreds of years:* I follow Upadhye in interpreting a *jua-* in this context as five years. Evidently the life span of *siddhas* was longer than that of human beings.

169 I understand "heart's desires" (from v. 721) as the subject of this verse.

170 *Guards:* many of the words in this section are rare, but for *aṇuggīṇa* in the meaning of "guard" I rely on the gloss in P.

171 The syntax of verse 735 is difficult, and the translation provisional.

172 All of the details in verses 738–739 (a syntactically connected unit or *juala*) point to the high royal status of the woman, even before she is identified as a princess.

173 *Thighs:* the word *ūruveḍha* suggests the meaning "a covering around the thighs," but it is used further on (v. 747) in a context that suggests the meaning "thighs." I cannot make sense of the

reading *vimūḍha* in this context. Perhaps we should read *vagūḍha* ("embracing").

174 The *bandhujīva* flower's petals are the color of red lips.

175 *Milk ocean:* the goddess Lakshmi, as well as several divine women called *apsarases,* are said to have been produced when the mythical ocean of milk was churned. See note to verse 169.

176 The idea of this verse is found elsewhere in Sanskrit and Prakrit literature, for example, *Seven Centuries* (Hāla 1881) verses 234 and 271, and *Tarangalolā* 48. The preceding passage is a "toe-to-head description" (*nakha-śikhā-varṇanā*) found in many classical works.

177 Upadhye (ed p. 370) points out that these two verses are based on the same idea as Kalidasa's *Vikramorvaśīya,* act I, verse 8.

178 Most of the items mentioned here, as Upadhye notes, were produced at the churning of the milk ocean, including the *kaustubha* gem (subsequently worn on Vishnu's chest, see v. 5), the goddess Lakshmi (v. 166), the *pārijāta* tree (which once adorned Indra's heaven), and wine (v. 170).

179 All of the beings named in this verse are demigods. *Asuras* are a kind of demon, and *nāgas* the serpentine creatures said to inhabit the subterranean world of Patala.

180 Taking *guḍiā* in the meaning of Marathi *guḍhī,* a pole erected outside of a door on certain occasions (Upadhye, ed p. 372, refers to Marathi *guḍīteraṇ*). The figure here is a kind of *dīpaka.* I also take *devaṅga* in the sense of *devaṅgaṇa.*

181 *Consolation:* taking Upadhye's suggestion that *rajjaṃ* should mean *rañjaṇa,* "consolation" ("entertainment" in Nimkar's translation), or *aṅgarāya,* "bodily adornment," rather than a "kingdom" (as B's gloss takes it).

182 Verses 838–841 form a "head-to-toe description" (*śikhā-nakha-varṇanā*); compare the corresponding toe-to-head description of Lilavai (vv. 764–775). *Marks,* etc.: these bodily marks are supposed to be the signs of a born emperor.

183 V. Raghavan, on the basis of *Yājñavalkyasmṛti* 1.13.313, glossed the word *uioia* (*uditodita*) as "'possessed of virtues enumerated in texts,' 'well-established,' 'learned' or 'cultured.'" The word is used of families (*vaṃśa* or *anvaya*) in inscriptions where the meaning that I have given it is near at hand.

184 Suddhasahava ("pure-natured") was the name of an early Prakrit

poet (see Bhoja 2007: vol. 2, 678).

185 *Both:* implied by the plural form *tumhāṇa.* Kuvalaavali's reunion with Chittangaa is thus introduced as an essential part of the conclusion.

186 Here it is implied that Kuvalaavali is older than Mahanumai, who in turn is older than Lilavai. Their weddings will be celebrated in this order.

187 See the introduction regarding legends about Hala.

188 *White as your fame:* fame is conventionally represented as white.

189 *Taddiaharamaṇīā* is "somewhat cryptic," as Upadhye notes (ed p. 376). Nimkar plausibly interprets it to mean the day on which Salahana and Lilavai will meet. In this passage Vijaananda speaks to Lilavai through her friend Vichittaleha.

190 As we will learn later (vv. 981, 1053), the necklace belonged to Mahavanila, and was given to him by Mahanumai. He had dropped it when he was abducted by serpents. How the necklace had come into the possession of this Viravahana, who is never mentioned again, is not specified.

191 The speaker of verses 979–985 is Mahanumai. Recall that Mahanumai had given the necklace to Mahavanila through Mahavilaa (v. 430).

192 *He once gave me:* see verses 420–422.

193 *What my heart desires:* Mahanumai's reunion with Mahavanila.

194 Verse 994 involves an unusual change of speaker: the first line is spoken by Vijaananda, and the second line, as indicated by the term of address, by the poet Kouhala.

195 The phrase *ṇehapariṇāma* (literally "full development of love") recalls a similar phrase in *Uttararāmacarita* act 1, verse 35 (Bhavabhūti 1932).

196 The Buddhist monk Nagarjuna, a key figure in the development of Mahayana Buddhism, lived in the time of the Satavahana dynasty, probably in the late second century C.E. Here, the memory of that Nagarjuna, who is also reputed to have visited the world of the *nāgas,* is conflated with the memory of a powerful alchemist (*siddha*) who entered the historical record several centuries later.

197 *What is right, pleasure, or liberation: dharma, kāma,* and *mokṣa;* three of the four commonly accepted goals of human life (see note to v. 18; the last is *artha,* wealth or power).

198 *Enjoyments:* Patala, the subterranean realm of the *nāgas,* is

associated with the enjoyment of sensual pleasure.

199 *My long-eyed love:* the word *pasaa* has sometimes been taken to refer to a deer (see Hemacandra 1938, 6.4), probably because of this expression, but it likely derives from *prasṛta*, "long, extended."

200 *A few miles:* literally, half a *yojana* (a measure of distance roughly equivalent to six miles).

201 Of this Raanappaha ("Jewel Light") the story has nothing more to say.

202 *The supports of kingship* (*sthāna*): army, treasury, city, territory.

203 This verse refers to two dynasties that held power in central and western India in the later first millennium, and that were probably contemporary with the author (since neither dynasty was contemporary with the Satavahanas). The Solankis (here, *sulaṃkī*) are known in Sanskrit sources as Chalukyas.

204 *Woman of the directions:* see note to verse 28.

205 This section (1073–1101) forms a set piece about the love affairs of anonymous men and women. This *topos* dates to at least the fifth century, when Pravarasena included such an episode in his *Setubandha,* but it is thematically connected to the erotic poetry of the earlier *Seven Centuries* (*Sattasaī*).

206 Cheeks smeared with red ghee indicate that a woman is having her period.

207 Nearly all of the words in verses 1081–1084 (which constitute a syntactic unit) are complex adjectives describing the sexual encounters (*mohaṇa*) of the couples, that is, their affairs. The verses are connected by the repetition of a single word (*pulaïa* in 1081–1082, *vaaṇa* in 1082, *mukka* in 1082–1083); for this device see Schubring 1955.

208 Verse 1091, not found in B or N, is almost certainly interpolated. It circulated widely: the verse is ascribed to the otherwise-unknown poet Vamautta in Svayamabhū 1962: 103. Hemachandra also cites it, almost certainly from Svayambhu, in Hemacandra 1961: 5. It is also found in Dhaneśvara 2004: 3.245, and it is partially quoted in Bhoja 1934: 121.

209 *Saṃ-mil,* "to shut," here refers to both flowers and eyes (see note to v. 671).

210 *Women of heaven:* according to the reading of B and N, "women of the city."

211 In this section (1107–1115) a few scenes from the commotion of the

army are presented, often with very colloquial (and hence rather obscure) bits of dialogue.

212 Probably the speaker of 1110 is the same as the woman identified in 1109.

213 *Kings:* Hala is the commander in chief of the expedition, but as noted above (v. 1068) there are a number of other kings present in his service.

214 The identity of the *cittala-* is uncertain, but the verse indicates it was connected with *citta,* meaning either "heart" or "strange." The similarity between the English words "cheetah" and "cheater" evokes the connection, whatever it was meant to be.

215 The identity of the animals in this verse is not clear. *Bhallua-* is probably the jackal, as the commentator takes it (*bhālū* in Marathi, as Upadhye says in ed p. 380).

216 The doe's offense was continuing to live for a moment after her mate had died, as the commentator explains.

217 A woman's eyes are often compared to the eyes of a frightened doe, as Kouhala's frequent epithets for his wife attest (see vv. 42, 938, etc.).

218 Verse 1170 is in the *pṛthvī* meter.

219 *Hooked knives:* the *kartikā* is a small hooked knife used for cutting flesh from bones, and is commonly associated with demons; here they are represented as shooting out sparks.

220 The word "without an army" (*ṇippakkho*) also means "without wings," referring to the mythical story of Indra cutting off the wings of the mountains.

221 *Ḍākinīs* are female spirits who haunt places associated with death. Upadhye (ed p. 382) and Nimkar following him take *vilasanta-* as *virasanta-,* "howling," and hence understand the word *gomāu-* (literally "sounding like a cow") to mean "jackal." I take it in the meaning of "frog."

222 *According to our own rite:* The "*gandharva* marriage" is the term for a marriage that involves neither rituals nor the consent of the bride's parents, but only the consent of the bride and groom.

223 The three *sandhyās* are sunrise, midday, and sunset.

224 Understanding *puṇaruttapecchiriṇaṃ* as *punarukta-apekṣiṇīnām,* on Upadhye's suggestion (ed p. 383).

225 *So that your marriage to Lilavai:* recall that Lilavai had vowed (v.

880) not to be married until Mahanumai and Kuvalaavali were reunited with their beloveds, so Mahanumai's marriage is a precondition for Lilavai's.

226 *Welcome offering:* see note on verse 249. A modified version of this verse appears in Bhoja 2007: vol. 2, 1593.

227 Quoted in Bhoja 2007: vol. 2, 1106.

228 B's reading would give us "indulging in" rather than "passed out from."

229 *Dancing to the drums:* I understand *muhamaddala-* to refer to a particular type of drum (with two "faces"). Nimkar takes the compound as an identification ("drums [that are] their mouths").

230 *Sniffing:* Sniffing at the head was a common way for parents to display affection in India; see Hopkins 1907: 130.

231 *When the astrological signs were most favorable:* we expect (following v. 1246) Hala's wedding to occur on an astrologically significant day, and hence I follow Upadhye's suggestion (ed p. 384) of interpreting the difficult phrase *ṇīsesabalapahāṇammi* in terms of planetary objects.

232 *Married women:* literally "non-widowed" (*avihavā*). *Raṅgolīs:* designs painted on the ground outside of a residence.

233 The *ārātrika* (Hindi *āratī*) ceremony involves moving a tray containing candles or a lamp in circles in front of a person or an image.

234 The following verses (1304–1310) are the bard's description of the Sinhala woman as she waves the candle before King Hala.

235 We must imagine that the sash around the Sinhala girl's waist is made up of small interlinked plates of shining metal.

236 Upadhye notes (ed p. 385) that this verse, reconstructed from the Sanskrit commentary in B, is very similar to a verse found in the *Vajjālagga* (Jayavallabha 1969: v. 306).

237 As explained in the note to the text, the manuscripts transmit different versions of the ending. I present these endings serially, maintaining Upadhye's numbering, beginning with the conclusion according to manuscript B, then according to manuscripts P and J. (N does not transmit the conclusion.)

238 *Gifts of jewelry:* the commentator specifies that the jewelry will be a gift to Lilavai's in-laws. This verse is found in both versions of the conclusion.

239 *Striking fear:* presumably because, after Hala's marriage to Lilavai,

he will rule the world (v. 158).

240   Verses 1323 to 1326 repeat the last words of each line in the first words of the following line. See note to verse 352. *Guard stations:* my guess for *guḍḍiā,* based on one meaning of the root *guḍ,* "to guard." Nimkar translates as "flagpole." See also note to verse 818.

241   On *rāṅgolīs,* see note to verse 1297.

242   *Local language of Maharashtra:* In fact in the literary language, Prakrit (see v. 41), long associated with Maharashtra and the Western Deccan. See Ollett 2017: 120, 131. *Embrace:* because the word for "parts" also means "body," the sense is that good people would physically embrace the story if they could.

243   An *anuṣṭubh* verse contains 32 syllables, so the text should be 57,600 syllables. Upadhye reasons (ed p. 18) that his edition, as printed, contains about 57,858 syllables, or 1,808 *anuṣṭubh* verses. Thus the equivalent of 8 *anuṣṭubh* verses will have to be removed. Which ones? Upadhye notes that 1319a, 1320a, and 1320b do not belong with the version of the text that contains this statement about its length, and likewise 1333a is a later addition.

GLOSSARY

Sanskrit names are followed by only their Sanskrit forms; Prakrit names are followed by their Sanskrit and Prakrit forms.

AIRAVATA (*airāvata*) the mythical elephant of Indra, produced by churning the ocean of milk

ALAKA (*alakā*) a city on Mount Himalaya, ruled by the *yakṣa* king Kubera

apsaras a female demigod who lives in Indra's heaven and is occasionally sent to earth to tempt sages; in this story Rambha is an *apsaras*

BHAVANI (*bhavānī*, wife of Bhava, that is, Shiva) a name of Parvati

BHISANANANA (Sanskrit *bhīṣaṇānana*, Prakrit *bhīsaṇāṇaṇa*, terrifying face) a demon (*rākṣasa*) who haunts the grounds around Sattagodavari Bhima

CHANDALEHA (Sanskrit *candralekhā*, Prakrit *candalehā*, sliver of the moon) a courtesan of King Salahana's court in Pratishthana

CHITTANGAA (Sanskrit *citrāṅgada*, Prakrit *cittaṅgaa*) a *gandharva* prince who marries Kuvalaavali

gandharva a kind of demigod associated with music and said to have lustful tendencies; in this story Chittangaa is a *gandharva*

GANESHA (*gaṇeśa*, lord of hosts) the elephant-faced son of Shiva who supervises Shiva's hosts (*gaṇas*)

GARUDA (Sanskrit *garuḍa*, Prakrit *garula*) Vishnu's mount, an eagle who is the sworn enemy of snakes

GAURI (*gaurī*, white) a name of Parvati

HALA (Sanskrit and Prakrit *hāla*) see SALAHANA

HAMSA (Sanskrit and Prakrit *haṃsa*) the king of the *vidyādharas*, father of Vasantasiri and Saraasiri; he reigns from the city of Sulasa

HARA (*hara*) a name of Shiva

HARI (*hari*) a name of Vishnu

HERAMBA (*herāmba*) a name of Ganesha

KERALA (*keralā*) a city on Mount Malaya, ruled by the *siddha* king Malaanila

KOUHALA (Sanskrit *kautūhala*, Prakrit *koūhala*) the author of *Līlāvaī*

KRISHNA (*kṛṣṇa*) one of Vishnu's incarnations, known for his childhood exploits in Vraj, and later his guidance of the Pandava brothers during the Mahabharata war

KUBERA (*kubera*) a *yakṣa* who

rules as king in Alaka; known as the lord of wealth

KUMARILA (Sanskrit and Prakrit *kumārila*) an adviser of King Salahana

KUVALAAVALI (Sanskrit *kuvalayāvalī*, Prakrit *kuvalaāvalī*, stand of water lilies) the daughter of the human sage Viulasaa and the *apsaras* Rambha; she is sent by her mother to live as the adopted daughter of Nalakubara and Vasantasiri in Alaka, and befriends their daughter Mahanumai

LAKSHMI (*lakṣmī*) goddess of wealth and prosperity, wife of Vishnu

LILAVAI (Sanskrit *līlāvatī*, Prakrit *līlāvaī*, graceful) a princess of Sinhala, the daughter of King Silameha and the *vidyādhara* Saraasiri; she falls in love with King Salahana after seeing his portrait

MAHANUMAI (Sanskrit *mahānumatī*, Prakrit *mahāṇumaī*, great approval) the daughter of the *yakṣa* Nalakubara and the *vidyādhara* Vasantasiri, who falls in love with Mahavanila; her adopted sister is Kuvalaavali

MAHAVANILA (Sanskrit *mādhavānila*, Prakrit *māhavāṇila*, springtime breeze) a *siddha* prince, son of Malaanila and Kamala, who falls

in love with Mahanumai

MAHAVILAA (Sanskrit *mādhavīlatā*, Prakrit *mahavīlaā*, *mādhavī* vine) a friend of the *siddha* prince Mahavanila and the keeper of his garden

MALAANILA (Sanskrit *malayānila*, Prakrit *malaāṇila*, breeze of Malaya) the king of the *siddhas*, who reigns from the city of Kerala, and the father of Mahavanila

MALAYA (*malaya*) a mountain in the far south of the subcontinent, where Kerala, the city of the *siddhas*, is located

MERU (*meru*) the golden mountain at the center of the earth

NAAJJUNA (Sanskrit *nāgārjuna*, Prakrit *nāajjuṇa*) a monk who advises Salahana and takes him to the underworld; there was a historical Buddhist monk by this name whom legend associates with journeys to the underworld

nāga a serpentine creature, said to inhabit the subterranean realm of Patala as well as Mount Malaya

NAGARI (Sanskrit *nāgāri*, Prakrit *nāāri*, enemy of serpents) name of the serpent-repelling ring given by Mahavanila to Mahanumai

NALAKUBARA (Sanskrit and Prakrit *nalakūbara*) the son of Kubera, king of the *yakṣas*, who reigns from the city of Alaka; he is the father of Mahanumai

PARVATI (*pārvatī*, daughter of the mountain) the daughter of Mount Himalaya, and Shiva's wife

PASHUPATA (*pāśupata*) a member of a religious movement devoted to *paśupati* (Shiva)

PATALA (*pātāla*) a realm below the surface of the earth, inhabited by serpents

POTTISA (Sanskrit and Prakrit *poṭṭisa*) one of the generals and advisers of King Salahana

PRATISHTHANA (*pratiṣṭhāṇa*) the capital city of King Salahana, modern Paithan in Maharashtra

RAMBHA (Sanskrit and Prakrit *rambhā*) an *apsara* sent by Indra, king of the gods, to tempt the sage Viulasaa; she is the mother of Kuvalaavali

SALAHANA (Sanskrit *sātavāhana*, Prakrit *sālāhaṇa*) also called Hala or Salavahana, a king who rules from Pratishthana; Satavahana was the name of a historical dynasty of kings, and besides appearing in several legends, a king by this name is said to have been the author of a Prakrit anthology called *Seven Centuries* (*Sattasaī*)

SALAVAHANA (Sanskrit *sātavāhana*, Prakrit *sālavāhaṇa*) see SALAHANA

SARAASIRI (Sanskrit *śaracchrī*, Prakrit *saraāsirī*, autumn beauty) a *vidyādhara* princess, daughter of Hamsa and Pauma, who was cursed by Ganesha to live in the world of human beings, and then married King Silameha of Sinhala; she is the mother of Lilavai

SATTAGODAVARI BHIMA (Sanskrit *saptagodāvarībhīma*, Prakrit *sattagodāvarībhīma*) a holy place where the seven streams of the Godavari River empty into the Bay of Bengal; it is the site of a Shiva temple and a monastery; nearby is the ashram of Mahanumai and Kuvalaavali

SHESHA (*śeṣa*) the cosmic serpent on whose coils Vishnu and Lakshmi sleep

SHIVA (*śiva*, the auspicious one) the god associated with the final destruction of the universe

siddha a kind of demigod, endowed with magical powers; in this story Mahavanila and his parents, Malaanila and Kamala, are *siddhas*

SILAMEHA (Sanskrit *śilāmegha*, Prakrit *silāmeha*) the king of Sinhala and father of Lilavai

SINHALA (*siṃhala*) the island of Sri Lanka

SULASA (*sulasā*) a city on the southern slopes of Mount Meru, ruled by the *vidyādhara* king Hamsa

VASANTASIRI (Sanskrit *vasantaśrī*, Prakrit *vasantasirī*, spring beauty) a *vidyādhara* princess, daughter of Hamsa and Padma, who married

Nalakubara; she is the mother of Mahanumai and the adoptive mother of Kuvalaavali

VICHITTALEHA (Sanskrit *vicitralekhā*, Prakrit *vicittalehā*, striking drawing) a friend and attendant of Lilavai

vidyādhara a kind of demigod, endowed with magical powers; in this story Vasantasiri and Saraasiri, and their parents Hamsa and Pauma, are *vidyādharas*

VIJAANANDA (Sanskrit *vijayānanda*, Prakrit *vijaāṇanda*, delight in victory) an adviser to King Salahana

VISHNU (*viṣṇu*) a major god known in a number of avatars, including Krishna

VIULASAA (Sanskrit *vipulāśaya*, Prakrit *viulāsaa*, large-hearted) a king who had become a sage and was then tempted by the *apsaras* Rambha; he is the father of Kuvalaavali

yakṣa a kind of demigod, often represented as a guard or protective deity; in this story Nalakubara is a *yakṣa*

BIBLIOGRAPHY

Editions and Translations

Upadhye. A. N. 1966 [1949]. *Līlāvaī: A Romantic Kāvya in Māhārāṣṭrī Prākrit of Koūhala, with the Sanskrit Vṛtti of a Jaina Author.* Singhi Jain Series 31. Revised 2nd edition. Bombay [Mumbai]: Bharatiya Vidya Bhavan.

Nimkar, S. T. 1988. *Koūhala's Līlāvaī-Kahā.* Ahmedabad: Prakrit Vidya Mandal.

Jain, Rajaram, and Vidyavati Jain. 1990. *Mahākavi Koūhal viracit 9vīṃ sadī kā deśya-mahārāṣṭrī prākṛt meṃ likhit premākhyān Līlāvaī-kahā.* Ara, Bihar: Prācya Bhāratī Prakāśan.

Other Sources

Ānandavardhana. 1940. *The Dhvanyāloka of Śrī Ānandavardhanā-chārya with the Lochana and Bālapriyā Commentaries by Śrī Abhinavagupta and Panditrāja Sahṛdayatilaka Śrī Rāmaśāraka.* Edited by Pattābhirāma Śāstri. Kashi Sanskrit Series 135. Benares [Varanasi]: Chowkhāmbā Sanskrit Series Office.

Balbir, Nalini. 1995. "Formes et usages de la concaténation en prakrit." In *Sauhṛdya-maṅgalaṃ, Studies in Honour of Siegfried Lienhard on his 70th Birthday,* ed. M. Juntunen, W. L. Smith, and C. Sunesonin, 5–25. Stockholm: Association of Oriental Studies.

Bāṇa. 1909. *Bâṇabhaṭṭa's Biography of King Harshavardhana of Sthânîśvara, with Śaṅkara's Commentary, Saṅketa.* Edited by A. A. Führer. Bombay [Mumbai]: Government Press.

Bhāmaha. 1909. Appendix VIII in *The Pratâparudrayaśobhûshaṇa of Vidyânâtha.* Edited by Kamalâśaṅkara Prâṇaśaṅkara Trivedî. Bombay: Government Central Press.

Bharata. 2001. *The Nāṭyaśāstra of Bharatamuni, with the commentary Abhinavabhāratī by Abhinavaguptācārya: Vol. II (Chapters 8–18).* Revised edition by V. M. Kulkarni and T. Nandi. Baroda [Vadodara]: Oriental Institute.

Bhavabhūti. 1932. *Uttararâmacharita.* Edited by C. Sankara Rama Sastri. Madras [Chennai]: Sri Balamanorama Press.

———. 2007. *Rāma's Last Act by Bhavabhūti*. Translated by Sheldon Pollock. New York: New York University Press.

Bhayani, H. C. 1993a. "Some Prakrit Verses of Pādalipta and the Authenticity of the *Taraṁgalolā*." In *Indological Studies: Literary and Performing Arts: Prakrit and Apabhraṁśa Studies*, 129–138. Ahmedabad: Parshva Prakashan.

———. 1993b. "Some Specimens of the *Carcarī* Song." In *Indological Studies: Literary and Performing Arts, Prakrit and Apabhraṁśa Studies*, 34–53. Ahmedabad: Parshva Prakashan.

Bhoja. 1934. *The Saraswatī Kaṇṭhābharaṇa by Dhāreshvara Bhojadeva*. Edited by Kedārnāth Śarmā and Wāsudev Laxmaṇ Śāstrī Paṇśīkar. Bombay [Mumbai]: Nirṇaya-Sāgara Press.

———. 2007. *Śṛṅgāraprakāśa [Sāhityaprakāśa] of Bhojadeva*. Edited by Rewāprasāda Dwivedī. 2 vols. New Delhi: Indira Gandhi National Centre for the Arts.

Chandra, Moti. 1973. *Costumes, Textiles, Cosmetics and Coiffure in Ancient and Mediaeval India*. Delhi: Oriental Publishers.

Chojnacki, Christine. 2008. *Kuvalayamālā: Roman jaina de 779 composé par Uddyotanasūri*. Volume 1: *Étude*. Marburg: Indica et Tibetica Verlag.

———. 2016. "Charming Bouquet or Wedding Garland? The Structures of the Jain Heroine 'Novel' in Prakrit from *Kuvalayamālā* (779) to *Maṇoramā* (1082)." *Asiatische Studien/Études asiatiques* 70, no. 2: 365–398.

Daṇḍin. 1957. *Kavyalakṣaṇa* [sic] *of Daṇḍin (also known as Kāvyādarśa), with Commentary Called Ratnaśrī of Ratnaśrījñāna*. Edited by Anantalal Thakur and Upendra Jha. Darbhanga: Mithila Institute of Post-Graduate Studies and Research in Sanskrit Learning.

Daśavaikālika Sūtra: Āgama Suttāṇi (Saṭīkaṁ) Bhāga 27: Daśavaikālika-mūlasūtraṁ. 2000. Edited by Muni Dīparatnasāgara. Ahmedabad: Āgama Śruta Prakāśana.

Dhaneśvara. 2004. *Siridhanesaramuṇīsaraviraiyaṁ Surasuṁdarīcariyaṁ*. Edited by Mahāyaśā Śrījī. Surat: Śrī Oṁkārasūri Jñānamandira.

Ferstl, Christian. 2020. *Transgressive śivaitische Praktiken in frühren Darstellungen der Sanskrit- und Prakrit-Dichtung. Eine literarisch-kognitivistische Studie*. Ph.D. dissertation, University of Vienna.

Gerow, Edwin. 1979–1980. "Plot Structure and the Development of Rasa in the Śakuntalā." *Journal of the American Oriental Society* 99, no. 4: 559–572 and 100, no. 3: 267–282.

Hāla. 1881. *Das Saptaçatakam des Hâla*. Edited by Albrech Weber. Leipzig: Brockhaus.

———. 1942. *Hāritāmrapītāmbara's Gāthāsaptaśatīprakāśikā: A Hitherto Unpublished Commentary on Hāla's Gāthāsaptaśatī*. Edited by Jagdish Lal Shastri. Lahore: Jagdish Lal Shastri.

———. 1980. *Hāla's Gāhākosa (Gāthāsaptaśatī) with the Sanskrit Commentary of Bhuvanapāla: Part I*. Edited by M. V. Patwardhan. Ahmedabad: Prakrit Text Society.

Handique, Krishna Kanta. 1976. *Pravarasena's Setubandha*. Ahmedabad: Prakrit Text Society.

Haribhadra. 1935. *Samarāicca-kahā* [First Two Chapters] *of Haribhadra-Sūri*. Edited by M. C. Modi. Ahmedabad: Gurjar Granth Ratna Karyalaya.

Hemacandra. 1877. *Hemacandra's Grammatik der Prâkritsprachen (Siddhahemacandram Adhyâya VIII)*. Edited by Richard Pischel. Halle: Waisenhaus.

———. 1938. *The Deśīnāmamālā of Hemachandra*. Edited by R. Pischel and introduced by P. V. Ramanujaswami. Bombay [Mumbai]: Department of Public Instruction.

———. 1961. *Chando'nuśāsana of Hemacandra Sūri*. Edited by H. D. Velankar. Bombay [Mumbai]: Bharatiya Vidya Bhavan.

Hopkins, E. Washburn. 1907. "The Sniff-Kiss in Ancient India." *Journal of the American Oriental Society* 28: 120–134.

Ingalls, Daniel H. H., Jeffrey Mousaieff Masson, and M. V. Patwardhan, trans. 1990. *The Dhvanyāloka of Ānandavardhana with the Locana of Abhinavagupta*. Cambridge, Mass.: Harvard University Press.

Jacobi, Herman. 1876. "Ueber das Vîracaritram." *Indische Studien* 14: 97–160.

Jayavallabha. 1969. *Jayavallabha's Vajjālaggaṃ*. Edited by M. V. Patwardhan. Ahmedabad: Prakrit Text Society.

Jineśvarasūri. 1975. *Jineśvarasūri's Gāhārayaṇakosa*. Edited by Amritlal M. Bhojak and Nagin J. Shah. L. D. Series 52. Ahmedabad: L. D. Institute of Indology.

Kane, Margaret Lynn. 1983. *The Theory of Plot Structure in Sanskrit Drama and Its Application to the "Uttararāmacarita."* Ph.D. dissertation, Harvard University.

Kansara, N. M. 1972. "Art Notes on Design-Drawing, Painting and Picture-Galleries in the *Tilakamañjarī*." *Sambodhi* 1, no. 2: 43–52.

———. 1975. "The Treatment of Suspense (*Kathā-rasa*) as a Conscious

Narrative Skill in Dhanapāla's *Tilakamañjarī.*" *Sambodhi* 4, no. 1: 35–54.

Ollett, Andrew. 2013. "The *Gaṇacchandas* in the Indian Metrical Tradition." In *Puṣpikā: Tracing Ancient India, Through Texts and Traditions*, ed. Nina Mirnig, Péter-Dániel Szántó, and Michael Williams. Vol. I, 331–364. Oxford: Oxbow.

———. 2018. "The Taraṅgavatī and the History of Prakrit Literature." In *Jaina Studies: Select Papers Presented in the "Jaina Studies" Section at the 16th World Sanskrit Conference, Bangkok, Thailand, and the 14th World Sanskrit Conference, Kyoto, Japan*, ed. Nalini Balbir and Peter Flügel, 129–164. Delhi: D. K. Publishers Distributors.

———. 2017. *Language of the Snakes: Prakrit, Sanskrit, and the Language Order of Premodern India.* Oakland: University of California Press.

Pollock, Sheldon. 2016. *A Rasa Reader: Classical Indian Aesthetics.* New York: Columbia University Press.

Pravarasena. 1895. *Setubandha of Pravarasena.* Edited by Paṇḍit Śivadatta and Kâshînâth Pâṇḍurang Parab. Bombay [Mumbai]: Nirnaya-Sagara Press.

Raghavan, V. 1933. "Sanskrit Texts on Painting." *Indian Historical Quarterly* 9, no. 4: 898–911.

———. 1963. *Bhoja's Śṛṅgāraprakāśa.* Madras [Chennai]: The Theosophical Society.

Rājaśekhara. 1932. *Caturviṃśati-Prabandha or Prabandhakośa by Rājaśekharasūri.* Edited by Hiralal Rasikdas Kapadia. Forbes Gujarati Sabhā Series 12. Bombay [Mumbai]: Forbes Gujarati Sabhā.

———. 1934. *Kāvyamīmāṃsā of Rājaśekhara.* Edited by C. M. Dalal and Pandit R. A. Sastry. Baroda: Oriental Institute.

Ramakrishna Kavi, M. 1926. "Līlāvatīkatha." *Bhārati* 3, no.3: 4–13.

Rudraṭa. 1928. *Kāvyālaṅkāraḥ.* Edited by Durgāprasād Dvivedī and Wāsudev Laxmaṇ Śāstrī Paṇśīkar. Bombay [Mumbai]: Nirṇaya-Sāgara Press.

Ruyyaka. 1934. *Sāhityamīmāṃsā.* Edited by Sāmbaśiva Śāstrī. Trivandrum Sanskrit Series 114. Trivandrum [Tiruvananthapuram]: Government Press.

Ruyyaka and Jayaratha. 1939. *The Alaṅkārasarvasva* [sic] *of Rājānaka Ruyyaka, with the Commentary of Jayaratha.* Revised edition by Girijāprasād Dvivedī. 2nd edition. Bombay [Mumbai]: Nirṇaya-Sāgar Press.

Schubring, Walther. 1955. "Jinasena, Mallinātha, Kālidāsa." *Zeitschrift der Deutschen Morgenländischen Gesellschaft* 105: 331–337.

Seth, Hargovind Das T. 1986 [1928]. *Pāia-sadda-mahaṇṇavo: A Comprehensive Prakrit–Hindi Dictionary.* Delhi: Motilal Banarsidass.

Śobhākaramitra. 1943. *Alaṁkāraratnākara of Śobhākaramitra.* Edited by C. R. Devadhar. Poona [Pune]: Oriental Book Agency.

Sohoni, S. V. 1999. "Hāla and Nāgārjuna." In *The Age of the Sātavāhanas,* ed. Ajay Mitra Shastri, 205–208. New Delhi: Aryan Books International.

Svayambhū. 1962. *Mahākavi Svayambhū kṛta Svayambhūcchanda.* Edited by H. D. Velankar. Jodhpur: Rajasthan Oriental Research Institute.

Taraṅgalolā. 1979. *Saṃkhitta-Taraṃgavaī-Kahā: An Early Abridgement of Pādalipta's Taraṃgavaī with Gujarati Translation.* Edited and translated into Gujarati by H. C. Bhayani. L. D. Series 75. Ahmedabad: L. D. Institute.

Tieken, Herman. 1992. "Hāla's *Sattasaī* as a Source of Pseudo-Deśī Words." *Bulletin d'études indiennes* 10: 221–267.

Trivikrama. 1954. *Prakrit Grammar of Trivikrama with His Own Commentary.* Edited by P. L. Vaidya. Sholapur: Jaina Saṃskṛti Saṃrakṣaka Saṅgha.

Tsuchida, R. 2002. "Über die direkte Quelle für die kaschmirischen Versionen der *Bṛhatkathā.*" *Indologica Taurinensia* 28: 211–250.

Turner, R. L. 1922–1966. *A Comparative Dictionary of Indo-Aryan Languages.* London: Oxford University Press.

Vāgbhaṭa. 1915. *Kâvyânuśâsana of Vâgbhatta, with His Own Gloss.* Edited by Pandit Śivadatta and Kâśînâth Pandurang Parab. Bombay [Mumbai]: Nirṇaya-Sâgar Press.

Vākpatirāja. 1975. *Gaüḍavaho by Vākpatirāja.* Edited by N. G. Suru. Prakrit Text Society Series 18. Ahmedabad: Prakrit Text Society.

Warder, Anthony Kennedy. 1983. *Indian Kāvya Literature.* Volume 4: *The Ways of Originality (Bāṇa to Dāmodaragupta).* Delhi: Motilal Banarsidass.

Weber, Albrecht. 1883. "Ueber Bhuvanapâla's Commentar zu Hâla's Saptaçatakam." *Indische Studien* 16: 1–204.

INDEX

Abhinavagupta, xxvn2
Ahalya, 358n90
Airavata, 49, 51, 77, 133, 355n70
Alaka, xii, xiii, xv, 89, 109, 305
Anandavardhana, vii, xxvn2,
    xxvin14, 351n21
Andhaka, 57, 357n80
Andhra Pradesh, viii, xxvn4
Apabhramsha, xxiv, xxvin9
Arishta, 3, 5, 349n4
Arthaśāstra, 355n67
Ashmaka, 17, 351n24, 351n26
Avadhi, xxiv

Bahulaiccha, 9
Balarama, 3, 349n3
Bhadrabahu, xxvn7
Bhamaha, xxvn6
Bhavabhuti, 359n103
Bhavani, xviii, 197, 253; favor of, xx,
    183, 185, 219; temple of, xxii, 65;
    Gauri, 5, 187, 201; Parvati, 57,
    65n, 79, 285n, 349n1
Bhisananana, xiii, xiv–xv, 61, 283,
    285, 295, 297. *See also* Chittangaa
Bhoja: on *Līlāvaī* as story, x, xxiii,
    xxviinn31; verses partially
    quoted by, xxviin32, 366n208;
    verses quoted by, xxiii, xxviin32,
    350n15, 352n34, 353n44,
    359n105, 360n118, 361nn133–
    134, 361n136, 362nn148–149,
    368nn226–227
Bhuaṇasundarī, xxiv, xxvin9
Bhusanabhatta, 9

Bhuvanapala, xxvin17
Brahma, 9, 77, 359n100
Brahmans, vii, 63, 317, 351n28,
    363n166; chanting by, 271;
    dharma taught by, 169; gifts to,
    35, 39, 205; Vijaananda as son of,
    71, 358n95
Buddhists, 365n196

Chalukyas, viii, xxvn4, 366n203;
    Solankis, viii, 261, 366n203
Chandaleha, 31, 33, 353n49
Chandi, 5
Chittangaa: cursed, xv, 301,
    363n159; meets Kuvalaavali,
    xii, 155, 299; reunion with
    Kuvalaavali, xiii, xv, 305,
    307, 309, 365n185. *See also*
    Bhisananana

Daksharama (Draksharama), viii,
    xxvn4, 357n79
Dandin, xxvn6, xxviin31
Daśavaikālika Sūtra, xxvn7
Deccan, viii, xv, 369n242
Devendra, 362n149
Dhaneshvara, xxiv, xxvin9,
    366n208
Dhvanyāloka, vii
Draksharama. *See* Daksharama

Ganesha, 81, 83, 85, 87, 201, 203,
    313, 359n103; Heramba, 79, 251
Ganga, 149, 193n, 299n, 319, 349n7
Garuda, 77, 107, 125, 173

ABOUT THE BOOK

Murty Classical Library of India volumes are designed by Rathna Ramanathan and Guglielmo Rossi. Informed by the history of the Indic book and drawing inspiration from polyphonic classical music, the series design is based on the idea of "unity in diversity," celebrating the individuality of each language while bringing them together within a cohesive visual identity.

The Prakrit text of this book is set in the Murty Sanskrit typeface, commissioned by Harvard University Press and designed by John Hudson and Fiona Ross. The proportions and styling of the characters are in keeping with the typographic tradition established by the renowned Nirnaya Sagar Press, with a deliberate reduction of the typically high degree of stroke modulation. The result is a robust, modern typeface that includes Sanskrit-specific type forms and conjuncts.

The English text is set in Antwerp, designed by Henrik Kubel from A2-TYPE and chosen for its versatility and balance with the Indic typography. The design is a free-spirited amalgamation and interpretation of the archives of type at the Museum Plantin-Moretus in Antwerp.

All the fonts commissioned for the Murty Classical Library of India will be made available, free of charge, for non-commercial use. For more information about the typography and design of the series, please visit *http://www.hup.harvard.edu/mcli*.

Printed on acid-free paper by Maple Press, York, Pennsylvania.